Acclaim for *The Master's Wall*

"It's a grand thing to find an intriguing story told by a talented storyteller, and that's just what we have in *The Master's Wall* by Sandi Rog. This story has it all: ancient Rome, authentically depicted; a hero worth rooting for; and a feisty, charming heroine—all flowing through a rousting tale beautifully spun. Rog—and every reader—has a winner with this one."

Robert Liparulo
Bestselling Author of *Comes a Horseman,*
Germ, and the *Dreamhouse Kings series*

"Powerful, faith-challenging, epic in nature, *The Master's Wall* beckons readers to ancient Rome where Sandi Rog delivers a captivating story that transforms lives—and not only those of her characters. Highly recommended!"

Tamera Alexander
Bestselling Author of *Within My Heart*
and *The Inheritance*

"...If you love gladiator scenes—you'll love this book. If you enjoy coming-of-age stories, you'll enjoy Alethea's journey from girlhood to adult. If you thrive on romances, the sweet love story will grasp your heart. A must read for all the right reasons."

Darlene Franklin
Author of *The Prodigal Patriot*

"What a compelling novel! I was pulled into David's world from the beginning of the book and couldn't wait to get back to it every evening. Rog's writing is very clean, but not only that, it's vivid, colorful and emotional. She weaves a strong faith message in without being preachy, and the analogy to Jesus' sacrifice for us through what happens to David is so touching. I cannot wait to see what comes next from the pen of Sandi Rog."

Golden Keyes Parson
Author of *In the Shadow of the Sun King*
2009 ACFW Book of the Year Finalist

"*The Master's Wall* is a meticulously researched story that grips you tighter and tighter with every page you turn. Sandi Rog has a knack for engaging, nail-biting narrative—I'm glad to see this is the first in a series, because I definitely want to read more from her."

Alison Strobel
Author of *The Weight of Shadows* and *Reinventing Rachel*

"…a sweeping tale of pain and healing, forgiveness and redemption, and, most importantly, love. With every word, every phrase, Rog weaves a tale so compelling that readers will not be able to put it down. When they do so, it will be with tears borne of appreciation for a truly inspirational read."

Jane Choate
Author of *Bride Price*

"Filled with fascinating details of life in first century Rome, *The Master's Wall* is a story that will linger in readers' memories."

Amanda Cabot
Author of *Scattered Petals*

"Sandi skillfully transported me back to the harsh world of Roman rule with this engaging story about David and Alethea that moves at breakneck speed. I also learned a great deal about the courage of the 'early adopters' of Christianity."

Mike Yorkey
Co-author of *The Swiss Courier*
and the Every Man's Battle series

SANDI ROG

THE MASTER'S WALL

Iron and the Stone
Book 1

DeWARD
PUBLISHING COMPANY

The Master's Wall
DeWard Publishing Company, Ltd.
P.O. Box 6259, Chillicothe, Ohio 45601
800.300.9778
www.deward.com

The Master's Wall is a work of fiction. Names, characters, places, and incidents are either a product of the author's imagination or are used fictitiously. Any resemblance to actual persons, living or dead, events, or locales is entirely coincidental.

Printed in the United States of America.

ISBN: 978-1-936341-02-3

For You, my Master, my Love.

I hope and pray You are pleased.

To My Children,

May the Lord be Master of your hearts and the Love of your lives.

Do not think that I came to bring peace on earth;
I did not come to bring peace, but a sword.

For I came to set a man against his father,
and a daughter against her mother,
and a daughter-in-law against her mother-in-law;

And a man's enemies will be
the members of his household.

—Jesus Christ—

THE MASTER'S WALL

one

Rome, AD 76

David tried not to cry, tried not to breathe or make a sound as he crept along the dark street. Careful not to trip on the flat stones, he recalled how that morning he'd taken this same path, chasing friends between the alleys, pretending they were gladiators fighting at the Circus Maximus. Now again he followed the enemy. Only this enemy was real. There were three of them. And they had taken his parents.

Mamma. Abba.

He wanted to shout out their names, to cry out to them.

He could still feel Mamma's hand in his. Could feel her letting go as the soldiers pulled her away. Could feel her *stola* ripping as he clutched it. All he had left was the shredded fabric from her dress still in his hand.

How empty his hand felt now that she was gone.

He made a fist. All he had in the world. Snatched away. And now their lives might depend on him. On what he would do at this moment. But he was just a child, a boy. What could he do? He'd follow them, see where they were taken. Then he could get help. Manius would know what to do.

Voices carried off the mud-brick apartments. David pinned his back against a wall. A shadow moved and he glanced down. A rat scurried across the large stones through the empty street. He released his breath, only then realizing he'd been holding it.

Slowly, he peered around the wall. His fingers quivered as he gripped the brick. Three soldiers towered over his parents in the small street. They looked like giants. Giants with horsehair crests on their heads. Half human, half animal.

One burly monster hurled Mamma forward. She stumbled, but caught herself against Abba's back and clung to his tunic. Abba helped her up and held her against him, but another soldier jerked them apart. These soldiers treated his parents like slaves, like common criminals. They weren't any of those things.

The soldier brandished chains in front of Mamma's face, laughing. Her eyes widened, and David knew she was scared. He'd seen Mamma scared before when he'd come home late one day. She had that same look in her eyes. She'd knelt in front of him and pulled him into her trembling arms. "David. How could you do this to me?" David's stomach had hurt because he'd frightened her. And now, he felt the same way. But what could he do?

The soldier chuckled as he knelt to bind her ankles, while another soldier held her from behind.

Abba would do something. He had to save Mamma. But now Abba's arms were bound behind his back.

The man's large hands locked the shackles into place on Mamma's ankles. He then ran his fingers up Mamma's leg, pulling her stola up to reveal her thigh. "Nice." He ended the word on a long hiss.

"Let her go!" Abba pushed away from a soldier with his shoulder and lunged forward.

The third soldier rushed over, grabbed Abba, and held him back. He motioned toward the man touching Mamma. "Aulus, shouldn't convicts pay the full penalty for their crimes?"

"Oh, yes." Aulus smiled and continued to touch Mamma, to touch her in places David had never seen Abba touch her. The man's big hands on her body made her look small, helpless.

Stop. David clenched his teeth. *Stop it right now.*

The burly soldier's hands ran all over her, frightening her.

Someone had to stop him. But no one else was around to help.

No one but David.

"Get away from her!" David ran straight for the soldier.

"No!" Mamma shouted.

Aulus bent and caught David by his arm and leg, lifting him off the ground. The man swung him as if it were a game.

"Leave him!" Abba shouted from the spinning street.

David pried on the man's hand, noticing a missing finger. But the force of the spin pulled on his limbs, pulled on his body, until suddenly, he found himself hurtling through the air.

"Look at him fly!" Aulus's laugh echoed off the apartments.

David's fingers clawed the air and his limbs flailed. He slammed into a wall. A burst of pain cracked audibly through his chest and searing light behind his eyes dazed him. He slumped to the ground. He struggled for breath, but no air came in. His lungs were like rock.

Air. He needed air.

Panicked, he grasped the wall for support, giving his chest room to expand. But he still couldn't breathe. His lungs wouldn't move. He gulped in air and gulped again, until finally he dragged in a breath. Knife-like pain stabbed his chest as it swelled.

He could breathe. At last, he could breathe.

Short, rapid breaths gave him strength. He kept them shallow, not too deep or it hurt. He focused on the ground, concentrating on each intake of breath.

The soldiers' torches reflected off the watery filth between the smooth stones at his feet. He looked up and a blurred image of Mamma came into view. Abba held her, just like he used to. He'd make her smile. She'd laugh and dance around him. Abba would turn and follow her. Then she'd sing, her voice carrying over them as if they were the only ones that existed in the world. David loved to hear her sing. Her voice made him warm, like holding his face up to the sun. But as he watched Abba hold Mamma, the haze cleared, and he saw chains dangling from her ankles, muck gathering along the hem of her stola. And instead of Abba, Aulus held her, touched her.

She shrieked.

It made David's gums tingle.

Aulus shoved Mamma toward a cart. She stumbled and landed on her knees.

White-hot anger surged through David. The wall and street shuddered. He scrambled to his feet and slammed, shoulder first, into the soldier's midriff, crushing himself against the iron giant. Pain ripped through David's body as he reeled back, the stench of the man's sweat clinging to him.

Laughing, Aulus grabbed David's tunic and jerked him to a stop. "Can you believe this whelp? Can't be more than ten but keeps coming back for more."

Alcohol on the man's breath fouled the air, and a wicked scar raged from his right eye down to his mouth. David wanted to rip into it. "Don't touch her!" Just past the man's elbow, he caught sight of Abba's tall frame buckling from the blows of another soldier. "Stop!" David swung his fists, batting air as hatred flamed through his mind.

Aulus flung him to the ground.

David's arms slapped against the stones. The stabbing sensation gripped him, and he froze, stunned by the impact. He groaned and curled against the wrenching in his chest.

"Want to see your son die?" Aulus drew his sword.

"God, save him!" Abba's words pierced David's heart.

Aulus raised his sword.

Moonlight reflected off the blade. David froze. Fear clutched his throat. He would actually die.

"Aulus, enough!" A new soldier grabbed Aulus's wrist. "Leave the boy."

Aulus stepped back. He scowled at the man and jerked his wrist free. He lowered his sword, revealing another large scar on his bulging arm.

"Let's go." The man spoke with an air of authority the other three soldiers lacked. "We've got what we came for." The superior looked around with disapproval in his eyes then turned to the cart. He motioned to Abba who lay on the ground, hands tied behind his back. "Put him in the wagon."

David pushed against the stones in an attempt to rise, but pain dragged him back down. "No." He tried to shout, but his voice was a ragged breath. He had to get up. He had to follow them.

"Get up, David," Abba would say when he'd fall. He'd give him a hand and help him to his feet. "It hurts now, but not forever. Just get up. Never stay down." David pushed again, but his strength left him, and all he could manage was a roll.

As the soldiers walked by, Aulus nonchalantly swung his sword at his side, slicing David's face.

David squealed, grasping his cheek. Warm blood streamed onto his hand and down his neck. Anger scorched away his fear and he jumped up to go after the soldier, but the knife inside his body seared through his chest. He dropped to his knees. The ground moved in waves like water, and shadows clouded his vision.

"Daaviiid, Daaviiid!" Mamma's cries carried through the streets and through his foggy mind. The clatter of the cart's wheels grew distant and faded into the darkness.

He collapsed on the ground. It pulsated beneath him, beating against his body. Beating against his arms and menacingly against his chest. A rushing wind filled his ears and blackness enveloped him.

Ω

A sour odor filled David's nostrils. His stomach contracted and his slicing ribs cut off his breath. His eyes flew open.

He glimpsed a scraggly beard. He blinked and tried to focus. A man hovered over him. Part of his wrinkled face lit up in the moonlight, casting a shadow over one eye.

"The gods of fortune be praised." The man's smile revealed missing teeth. "You're still alive."

Where was he? Stones ground beneath David's fingers and back. Why wasn't he in his bed? Where was Mamma? Abba? Then he remembered soldiers.

He touched his cheek, accidentally scraping away part of the crusted surface. Blood trickled onto his fingers. He trembled. This was no dream.

The man pulled on David's arm, struggling to pick him up.

Pain ripped through David's chest, and he wailed, choking on each breath as his feet left the ground.

"Nice build and strong." The man poked and prodded him. "Solid, with meat on your bones. Not like those spindly street urchins. Your value will be great." The man bound his hands, then dropped him into a small cart, racking David's ribcage.

Again, darkness claimed him, but the stench of urine and vomit roused his senses. The peddler threw a scratchy cover over him, then hacked and spit. "A nice profit."

"*Elohim*, don't let my parents . . . ." Tears blurred David's vision and burned the wound on his cheek, each intake of breath stopped short by the pain in his chest.

"You're an orphan now, boy. You belong to me. They will die under the hands of Caesar."

David's thoughts shifted to his little sister, hiding under her blankets and crouched in her nook, her wide eyes peering up at him. "No." Realization of what he'd done slammed into him as the cart wrenched with a start, yanking him into a black haze. "*Eloi*—" Hot and cold waves rocked over him. His tongue felt thick. "Sarah . . . please save—"

The peddler chuckled, and the cart jerked, tormenting David's body as it lumbered down the road.

"The Roman Empire has iron feet, boy. It'll stomp on you anytime it wants."

Ω

The morning sun cast lances of light over the blue and purple valleys. A breeze carried the scent of flaxen crops and manure to the early risers.

Titus strode along the pasture in front of his caravan. He took pride in the way his white tunic contrasted with his dark Ethiopian skin. Despite the fact that his gold earring revealed his status as a slave, it hung attractively below his headscarf, and the gold band just above his elbow shimmered in the sun. Even as a slave, he was more valuable than most free men. And his fine appearance would serve him well in the marketplace.

Gasparus, one of the inferior slaves, led a mule piled with Titus's belongings. Gravel crunched under the mule's hooves in the quiet air and the load swayed. The rest of the slaves walked behind, carrying their few possessions on their heads and hips.

They passed a small cottage perched away from the lane. A boy circled from behind the house, guiding sheep across the small road. He yelled a greeting to the caravan. The herd quickened their pace and a dull clanging from their bells hung on the air.

Titus gazed into the cloudless sky. "It's good we left before sunrise. It's going to be a hot day."

Gasparus murmured agreement.

Thank Fortuna, Titus wore his *keffiyeh* to protect his head from the rising sun's rays. The daughters of the night would certainly take notice of the ruby brooch clasped in its center. A jewel of great value. Egyptian blood also ran through his veins. He was a handsome man, and he knew it. Indeed, these were not traveling clothes, but he had no fear of robbers and thieves. He was a man of large stature, and a fighter. Every thief in the past who had tried to rob him repented of his ways. Assuming death caused repentance. The jewel-hilted sword hanging at his side, the final touch to his attire, stated that he was a man of wealth and strength and not one with whom to make trouble.

The caravan trudged along the gravel road leading to the Via Labicana, passing green fields on their left. To their right, delicate flowers glowed blue in the early morning light. The sounds of sheep and goats bleating grew faint as they neared the city.

They came to the Porta Esquilina. The square gate loomed over Titus and his men, and the arched passageway swallowed them as they walked beneath the gate's portals to the bustling streets on the other side. Shoppers carried cloth bags and baskets, weaving their way to various shops. The sweet aroma of baking bread enticed him.

The caravan took a shortcut through the Subura Valley, a neighborhood where broken shutters hung from apartments. Titus eased his followers through the narrow streets, just wide enough for the mule's load. Women collected water from outdoor fountains or shook out dirty rugs that had little hope of getting clean. A baby wailed for its mother. Chickens squawked, beating their wings, and artfully dodged the passersby.

Near the Forum, the streets widened and were paved with stones. Titus and his followers crossed from one raised sidewalk to the other, avoiding the deposited filth.

Thank the gods he didn't live in this crowded city. Life at the villa was peaceful and quiet, but more importantly, clean.

Just outside the Forum, he stopped. "The rest of you take the belongings to the house." He motioned toward Gasparus and the stronger slaves closest to him. "You four come with me." He watched as the rest of the caravan made its way toward the Palatine Hill. They would pass near the construction of Vespasian's new amphitheater. He'd heard that it would be the largest coliseum Rome had ever built. He looked forward to seeing its progress later that day.

As he dismounted the steps to the Forum Romanum, the aroma of baked bread and pastries again wafted over him. His mouth watered. He would purchase some bread as soon as he finished business.

He went through the Forum where vendors had set up stalls of various sizes for the week's market. The clanging of iron rang in his ears. Two men hovered over a pole, pounding it into shape. Slaves carried their masters in litters. The colorful upholstered stretchers glided by, while other men and women walked. Voices and laughter echoed off the white columns of the Basilica Julia as it came into view from across the plaza, a court of justice and also a center of business.

He came upon the Tullianum. Many famous prisoners had resided in this state jail, including traitors of Rome from the new sect of the Jewish religion.

Martyrs intrigued him. He admired anyone willing to die for his convictions, even if it was for a god that defied Caesar. Titus prided himself on his open mind; he worshipped all the gods. Engraved images of the new Christian god, along with Jupiter, Saturn, Pax, and several others were enshrined in his chamber back home.

Today, a platform was set up in front of the Tullianum where slaves stood on display for prospective buyers.

Ω

"Stand up straight so he can look at you." The dealer struck a ragged man on his legs with his stick.

Titus stood on the platform with his hands behind his back, scrutinizing the man before him. How this brought back memories. There was a time when he himself had been sold and bought. Barbarians had murdered his father, raped and killed his sweet mother, and brought him all the way to Rome, selling him the same way these men were being sold. He had been a young man then, practically a boy.

He frowned. "This one has lice. Shave him." He moved with disgust to another slave. Had he changed so much? Had he managed to become like those barbarians? True, he wasn't raping women and pillaging other men's property, but his heart was cold and empty. His lonely bones cried out for something. For what, he wasn't certain. He examined the next man, was satisfied, and made his purchase.

He stepped off the platform, preparing to go to the docks where he would find more slaves.

"One slave boy. One boy for sale!" a rickety voice called out. An old peddler pushed a cart between the shoppers.

Titus motioned with his chin to the lump in the cart. "Let me see."

The old man pulled back a tattered cloth. The boy's hands were tied and his mouth gagged. Tears streamed down cheeks caked with dried blood and dirt.

Titus saw his younger self. The thought struck an emotional chord, one he hadn't felt in years. Not since he was with his family. He shook it off and straightened. "What are you trying to sell me, old man?"

The boy tried to sit up, then slumped back into the cart.

"He's a great buy, really." The man's shaggy beard wagged up and down as he spoke. "He just needs a good bathing. Once he's cleaned up, I'm sure he'll make a fine worker."

Titus examined the boy. He looked strong and would make a good fighter. His teeth, biting over the gag, were clean, and he had a good build, not scrawny. He'd been well cared for, too well. Might he be a Roman citizen? If so, Roman law prohibited his sale.

"Where did you find him?"

"In the street. He was half dead, but I brought him back to life." The peddler smiled, revealing black gums and rotting teeth.

Titus looked into the child's eyes. They flashed with fear and anger. Every time the boy squirmed, he winced as though in pain.

Titus had a suspicion the boy was indeed a Roman citizen. Would he know his rights?

"Remove the gag."

The old man did as he was told. The boy shook his head free from the old man's grasp.

"What's your name, boy?" Titus asked.

The child didn't answer but glared at him through narrowed eyes.

Yes, Titus saw himself. "Your name," he said, his tone more forceful.

"David," the boy said, giving in, his glare not quite as fierce but still present.

A Hebrew. Nothing to worry about. Titus smiled with satisfaction and leaned close to him. "Listen to me, and listen well. You are hurt. I have a doctor, a fine Greek doctor, that can make you well, but you must cooperate." Titus's eyes locked onto the boy's. The stench of vomit and urine stung his nostrils.

Exhaustion reflected from the boy's face and he nodded.

Titus gave orders to his slaves. "Find an open litter." He could make the boy walk, but a hired litter would keep him from becoming more damaged. He pulled the old man aside and haggled with him.

After the deal was made, the litter arrived and Titus unbound the boy, picked him up, and laid him on the stretcher. "Take him to the house and have the doctor look at him. I'll come when my work is done."

Two slaves hoisted the litter over their shoulders and carried the child to the house on the elite Palatine Hill.

two

David sensed someone in the chamber. He opened his eyes. A dark face smiled down on him. The man who'd rescued him from the peddler.

"I'm Titus." He broke a golden-brown loaf of bread and offered David a piece.

David hesitated, but the aroma found an empty feeling in his stomach, so he greedily accepted it. He bit into the hard crust, savoring the flavor.

"The doctor told me your ribs are broken." Titus's deep voice filled the small room. He held David's face. "Let me look at that."

David stopped chewing while Titus examined his cheek. The sweet unfamiliar smell of the man's cologne made him realize all over again that he wasn't home, that he didn't belong here.

"I see he closed your face up quite nicely. Good thing the cut struck your cheekbone."

David became conscious of the ants' teeth holding his skin together and shuddered at the thought.

Titus nodded as though satisfied. He let go, and David resumed chewing, anxious to fill the hole in his belly. "The doctor says it won't be long before you'll be well again." Titus spoke slowly and with precision. His deep voice soothed David's battered body, as if stroking him with his words. "I'm glad to hear that, because if the master learns I've spent his hard-earned money on a useless slave, he'll feed me to the dogs."

David stopped short of taking another bite and tried to take in the man's last words. Wasn't the man going to find his mamma and abba? Didn't he rescue him to help him?

Titus sat on the bed, resting an elbow on his knee. "I don't know what happened to you last night, but life as you knew it is over. You are now owned by Vibian Cornelius Aloysius."

Owned? The only people that owned David were his parents, not some stranger.

Titus flicked his earring. "I'm a slave too. Master of Slaves." He grinned, showing off white teeth. "Life under Aloysius can be good. He's a wealthy man who owns many slaves."

David slowly gasped for air between the pains in his chest. Titus's words made him feel like he was drowning. And the more he said, the deeper David sank.

"As long as you work hard and do a good job—prove yourself worthy—the master will like you," Titus said. "He liked me so much, he offered me freedom. But I chose to stay. If I had left, my life wouldn't be as good as it is now." He chuckled. "I have every luxury life can offer, there's no good reason for me to leave." Titus ran the length of the bread under his nose, taking in its scent.

David watched and listened, unable to take another bite of his own bread, and barely able to swallow the bits left over in his mouth.

"After I'm finished here in Rome, we'll go back to his estate outside the city."

The clean bedding and the food in David's hand did little to remove the invisible chains binding him to this room, to this bed. The bandages supporting his chest clenched like restraints.

A slave. *A slave?*

David had known slaves. But never had he imagined what it might mean to be one. To be bound to a master, to obey and do his every will.

Titus ran a large hand over his shaved head. "Few people would have bought a slave in your condition. I likely saved your life." He took a bite of his bread, chewing it slowly, deliberately. "If I bring you to the master's villa and you run away, I'll be the one to suffer. Yes, you'll suffer too. When they find you, they'll kill you, or flog you and sell you to someone else." The man's gaze swept over him. "Someone far crueler."

David's ribs and cheek throbbed. He didn't know what to say. He wanted Abba to walk through the door and take him away from this place, take him away from this man.

Titus pointed his bread at him. "I pulled you out of trouble. If you do anything foolish, it'll be on my head. I've served under Aloysius for many years, but all it takes is one foolish act on your part and I'll be lunch for the wild beasts. And if I'm lunch, then you're lunch." He took another bite, tearing it with his teeth.

David imagined his body being torn like the bread, being eaten alive by wild animals like the bodies of criminals in the Circus Maximus. Sometimes, unknown to Abba, he and his friends would sneak in and catch a glimpse of the games. He never considered what it might be like to be a part of the entertainment. He shuddered. He wanted to cry, to find his mamma, to shout for Abba. But a dark dread washed over him. They would never come. David would never see his parents again. Abba, who'd spent hours teaching him. David would never again look into his mother's smiling face.

"You'll have a good home if you do as you're told." Titus smiled.

David stared at the stranger sitting on the bed. Titus had saved him, but he'd also stolen something from him.

His freedom.

Yet, if this man hadn't bought him, he'd most likely be dying in that foul-smelling cart. He fisted the soft blankets in his hand, the only form of comfort he had, the only sense of warmth. He wanted to curl up in them and go to sleep forever. If he could hold his breath long enough, maybe he would die.

When he was younger he'd hold his breath for as long as he could and wait to see what would happen, to see if he would die.

Not because he didn't want to live, he was just curious. But an irresistible urge to breathe always overwhelmed him and he'd gasp in air. Besides, he couldn't die. If he were gone, who would take care of—

Sarah.

His head ached. He couldn't be a slave. He had to find her. At the same time, he could be dead. Or, *she* could be dead. He shook the thought from his mind. If he kept thinking of that he'd never survive.

He focused his gaze on the dark man. "Why did you save me?"

Titus picked lint off his tunic. "We need a boy. Besides, you have what it takes to be a good worker. You're a fighter. I see it in your eyes." Titus lifted David's chin and gazed at him, neither smiling nor frowning. Studying him as one would study an item purchased at the market. "Now, get some rest." He stood to leave.

David's parents had owned slaves and treated them well. He recalled Abba saying that a slave should obey his master and that it was a sin to escape. Now he realized that was easy to say when you weren't the one enslaved.

David didn't know what Abba would do in this situation, but he did know one thing: He'd escape and find Sarah.

Ω

David leaned over the *latrina*. He found himself here every morning. As soon as he awoke and remembered his parents were gone and he was a slave, he rushed to the kitchen, dropped to his bruised knees, and vomited. His ribs exploded in pain with each retch. Again, his stomach turned. He gripped the seat and heaved.

For the last two weeks, he had watched for his chance to escape. But just when he'd found an opportunity and slipped out of the house, Titus had caught him and flung him back inside. The fall had winded David, and the pain was as great as when Aulus had tossed him on the ground. After that, his courage left him. As Titus had said, his situation could be much worse. He knew enough about slavery to realize that he was well off. He had a nice bed and good food. These luxuries were better here than at home.

Home.

Mamma and Abba were gone.

Sarah. Gone.

He kept hoping that maybe they'd escaped the soldiers. That they'd find him and come for him. But as each long day of waiting, each long day of hoping turned into another day of nothing, his stomach hurt even more. The thought that they would never come kept jumping out at him like wicked shadows in his mind.

Again, his stomach retched and pain stabbed his chest. Clutching the latrina's seat, he gasped in short breaths to keep from hurting.

The day Titus had caught him trying to escape, David had begged him to search for Sarah. Finally, Titus had gone himself, after making David promise that if he were to go, David would never again try to leave. For Sarah, David made the deal readily, recalling Abba's words, "Let your yes be yes and your no be no." In honor of his abba, David would keep his word. When Titus returned, with no news of Sarah, David begged him to let him go find her, but Titus refused. "There is nothing for you there!" Titus stood over David, as if he were an ant about to be stepped on. "You belong here now." His words were so fierce that chills shuddered up and down David's spine.

Now he was bound. Bound by his word.

The walls closed in around him, and he couldn't breathe, despite the wrenching in his gut. Titus stuffed him into a cage. A cage that was too small. He wanted to break out, break free of its bars. He didn't belong in this new world. This closed-in world Titus created for him.

There was a time when he was free. A time he felt safe. Despite the secrets, despite having to hide, he still felt protected. To think this could actually happen to him, to his family, seemed impossible. Unreal.

But it was possible. And real.

He was alone, completely alone.

If Elohim really loved him and cared about his family, how could He let this happen? David had seen others suffer. And most of them seemed to have amazing strength. Why didn't he feel strong? Why did he feel so weak, so empty?

He squeezed the latrina's seat until his knuckles turned white. A wail tore from his throat. *"Eloi* where are You?" he shouted.

It no longer mattered that he leaned on the filthy seat. He slumped down on the floor, but because of the pains in his chest, it brought no comfort.

He cried.

His voice carried off the walls in the empty kitchen, and he knew other slaves could hear him, but he didn't care. Mamma and Abba weren't coming back. Hope was gone. What would he do without them? Sobs choked him and his ribs punished him for it. He groaned and laid his head against the seat, only to bump his sore ear. With trembling fingers, he felt for the new slave earring and turned it back and forth, the way Titus taught him.

When he could cry no more, relief filled his stomach, though a painful knot in its center never went away. He stood on wobbly legs and took the ceramic bucket from the shelf that divided the latrina from the stove. With quivering arms, he poured the kitchen waste-water into the hole, flushing it. His weak movements reminded him of Old Man Tychicus. David was only ten years old, but this must be what it felt like to be old.

That same day, they left the Palatine Hill and David trudged with the other new slaves to their new home.

Home.

He'd never been this far away from home. He'd felt lost when he was still in the busy city, but at least then he was closer to where his parents had been, closer to familiarity. But the more distance he traveled, the more that ache in his stomach grew, and the smaller the cage became. He struggled to keep up with the other slaves, all men who were older than David. They were bound together by a rope on their left ankle, and for each step the slave in front of him took, David had to take one large step to keep up. It didn't help his aching ribs, and the coarse rope around his ankle rubbed him so raw, it made the pain from the small rocks in his sandals unimportant.

"Up ahead," Titus said with a wave of his hand, "is the Vibian Hill. There lies the family estate of Vibian Cornelius Aloysius, your new home."

To the left of the grand villa, a gradual incline of the Vibian Hill stretched out about a mile. Grapevines lined each green row. It was as though Elohim had come down and woven even rows of greenery from the top of the hill to its base. The tapestry spread out against the blue sky. David imagined flying, soaring high above the luscious hill. The familiar sensation of flight, the sensation he'd experienced when the soldier threw him, washed over his limbs. Sparks of anger ignited. He didn't know how, but one day he'd make that soldier pay. Pay for taking his family away, for hurting Abba, and most of all, for hurting Mamma.

Titus waved an arm toward the breathtaking view. "That's the vineyard. Aloysius grows his grapes on this side of the hill. Caesar depends on him for native wine, but most people want foreign wines."

David's mouth grew dry and his heart pounded as they neared a wall fortifying a magnificent villa. Small watchtowers bordered the vineyard along the barrier. What would he find behind this high wall? Protection? Death? Endless days of abuse?

"The villa has two main entrances," Titus said. "Each entrance has armed slaves guarding the doors. Many slaves live on the far side of the hill, and that's where most of you will go today. You'll labor in the vineyard outside of the wall's protection. The household slaves will work here in the villa." Titus eyed David.

David took that to mean he'd be a household slave. How protected would he be locked up behind this stone wall? Would he find a way to escape? How many homes did this man, Aloysius own? He had so many questions. Would he be reprimanded for speaking without having been spoken to first? What were the rules for their slaves?

"Whose house was that in Rome?" David's curiosity won over his fear.

Titus dropped back to the end of the line where David took his long steps to keep up. "It belongs to your master, Aloysius. Hired servants keep it up while we're away."

Titus walked on ahead and led the slaves to the front entrance on the south side of the estate. He didn't seem to be angry about David's question, but he didn't smile either. David thought it might be better to keep quiet next time. He could find answers to his questions by asking other slaves at the villa.

Other slaves. He was actually one of them. Would he ever be free again? "Work hard and do a good job—prove yourself worthy—and the master will like you," Titus had said. "He liked me so much, he offered me freedom." Maybe David could earn his freedom like Titus had? He'd do everything in his power to gain back his freedom.

Freedom was all he wanted, all he cared about. Perhaps there was hope. Hope of escaping the cage Titus had locked him in.

On this side of the estate, double wooden doors opened up on the great wall to a wide vestibule where a large mosaic stretched out across the floor. The doors slammed behind him, trapping him inside the entry hall. David wanted to run to the doors, bang on them, and shout for someone to let him out.

"Unbind the rope," Titus said.

A slave rushed to obey.

Cool relief swept over David's ankle as the rope slid off. He kicked his toes on the floor behind him to remove the pebbles. His soles reveled in the newfound smoothness of his sandals.

Now he could run. He imagined running, working to open the door, but unable to unlock the latch. Whether he got through or not, Titus would catch him, and like he'd done before, toss him on the ground. Just the thought made his ribs hurt. Or worse, he would end David's life with his jeweled sword.

A large Medusa stared at him from the center of the mosaic as if it read David's thoughts. He fought the urge to shake his fist at it.

He knew it was supposed to ward off evil spirits. Several Romans had them in their homes, including their close friend, Manius, who had a similar mosaic removed once he became a follower of Yahshua. Some said the gods would curse him for it and make him suffer within the week, but nothing happened.

Instead, it seemed like the curse fell on David's family. Forced to live in the poorest neighborhood in Rome. The Subura Valley. They hadn't been there long before his parents were taken away.

Titus motioned the new slaves through the vestibule, opening and closing doors on one side, revealing a large vegetable garden. Dark-blue and white tiles dotted the cemented floor, surrounding the mosaic. The walls were shaped into columns at every corner and bowed upward, meeting in the center of the ceiling, where a single column came down to the floor. The walls displayed life-size mosaics of battle scenes between well-known gladiators, depicting their triumphs and their defeats. David ran his quivering fingers along the graphic details of each intimidating picture.

Gladiators. The worst of sinners. They murdered people and called it a game. Despite the wickedness, something intrigued him about the sport.

A door to the left of the vestibule opened to a grand courtyard where trees, neatly trimmed bushes, flowers, and statues lined well-groomed paths—a perfect place to run away and hide. On the other side was the entrance to the house. Instead of going in, they walked to the left along a portico. David slowed as the courtyard disappeared and reappeared behind the arched pillars running along the porch. They finally entered the house to the right through a small door and proceeded down a narrow corridor.

"Hmm, it smells good in here." Titus peered into the kitchen to his left, with David close behind him.

A round woman stood over a masonry stove as pots steamed in front of her. Bronze pans, ladles, and other kitchen utensils hung on the wall.

"And you're not getting any." She smiled and waved a spoon at Titus, her face red from the heat.

Smoke from a lamb roasting on the gridiron found its way through the window above the stove. David breathed in the savory aroma. It put an ache in his heart. A vivid reminder of the succulent meat the church and his mother on occasion served to him and his father. His mouth watered; he could almost taste the meat.

He also noticed a latrina next to the stove, located in the same place as in the house on the Palatine. He wondered if he would be vomiting there in the morning.

The woman winked at him before he turned to follow Titus.

"Oh, I'll get some," Titus said. "You can be sure of that. Don't worry, boy, you'll get some too." Titus chuckled, the low rumble carrying off the walls.

David's stomach growled, despite the knot in its center that wouldn't go away.

They entered the *atrium*. The immense, rectangular-shaped room with its vaulted ceiling made him feel small. Blue diamond-shaped tiles sprinkled over the white floor and columns towered to the ceiling at every corner.

Titus ordered the new slaves to stand in the center of the atrium next to the *impluvium*. David ran his hand along the smooth edge of the large marble fountain that collected rainwater from an opening in the roof. He'd heard of people living in villas, but to actually see this massive house made him miss his dingy but cozy little home.

His gaze darted around the room. Intricate designs of red, blue, and gold adorned the walls and ceiling. Artwork wound over the chamber doors on the north and south sides of the atrium. Murals of opened windows bordered the pillars, depicting rich landscapes, much like the vineyards he had just seen.

A man with blond hair combed fashionably forward and meeting the wrinkles near his eyes entered the atrium with an authoritative air.

Titus ordered the slaves to stand in a row.

Evidently, this was Aloysius. David's eyes never left his new master. So, this was the man who owned two homes and the magnificent vineyards. He stood at an average height, and for an old man, hadn't yet lost his healthy physique.

David was conscious of his bandaged chest, and the cut on his cheek itched. It took all he had to keep from scratching. He swallowed hard and stood tall. It was important to make a good impression. Earning his freedom was his new goal—or escaping. Whichever came first.

Aloysius looked David up and down and circled him. "What did you buy this one for?" His master's clean-shaven face emphasized his straight nose, and he reeked of cologne.

"We need a boy of his stature. He will be a sparring partner for Marcus and Lucius," Titus said.

"There weren't any in better condition?"

David's heart pounded, and his hands grew clammy.

"No, Master," Titus said.

Aloysius rubbed his chin, looking David over again. "If he grows into those hands and feet, he's sure to be tall." He studied his face. "Nice. Well proportioned." He nodded and pursed his lips. "The boy has potential." He waved his hand, showing off his elegant rings. "Give him to Cornelia for now. He can do light work for her until he's strong." Aloysius's toga fell in crisp folds as he continued down the line of slaves, observing, scrutinizing, and making comments.

David exhaled, realizing he had been holding his breath. He didn't want to be a slave, but he also didn't want to know what would happen if Aloysius had rejected him.

The tension eased from his jaw, and he looked straight ahead.

A little girl with a slightly upturned nose peeked out from behind a nearby column, bringing to mind the way Sarah would peer out from behind Mamma's skirt. Only, instead of blonde hair, dark curls bounced around rosy cheeks and fell freely over her shoulders. She clasped the ends of a sheer linen sash that draped around the waist of her white stola. Her huge, brown eyes peered at him from under thick lashes.

He didn't dare blink, fearing she might disappear.

three

Alethea stared at the rugged-looking boy. His windblown hair fell in wisps over his brow. A gold earring emphasized his square jaw, and a gold armband clasped above his left elbow marked him as one of Grandfather's slaves. A fresh scar traveled under his eye along his cheekbone, and his chest was wrapped in bandages above the beige tunic looped at his waist. Her gaze wandered back to his captivating face. Ice-blue eyes met hers. She gasped and ducked behind the column.

After the slaves were led away, and she was safe from being seen by Grandfather, she crept into the *tablinum*. She slipped through the heavy crimson curtain and into the small room between the atrium and the indoor courtyard.

She held her breath when she saw Grandmother and Aunt Fabia kneeling before the shrine. Usually they prayed in the morning.

"What are you doing here?" The mounds of white curly hair perched on top of Grandmother's head reminded Alethea of the sliced boiled eggs she'd refused to eat the night before. "You should be in your lessons."

"Decimus told me to leave." Alethea looked down. She left out the "because I wasn't paying attention" part. Before Grandmother could respond, she slipped through the curtain on the other side of the tablinum and entered the *peristyle*.

Flowers filled the indoor courtyard with a sweet fragrance. Alethea especially liked the jasmine and breathed in its scent. She wandered between the plants and marble statues, following the patterns of flowers in the colorful mosaic on the floor. Uncle Servius leaned against one of the high tables. She stopped in mid-stride and her legs couldn't move.

Slowly he turned as he set down his drink, his red nose standing out more than ever. Why was his nose always so red, almost matching the red tint of his hair? He let out a playful growl. Relieved, she scurried away, but he caught her around the waist.

"What are you doing here, *Aucella?* Shouldn't you be in your lessons?" He tickled her before she could answer.

Laughter and giggles exploded from her even though she didn't want to be happy, but the tickling made not laughing impossible.

He finally set her down, wobbling to one side and giving her one last poke.

Just to please him, she forced a grin, all the while trying to swallow the lump that filled her throat. Her *mpampas*, her precious daddy, used to tickle her like this. To her dismay, tears welled in her eyes. She quickly swiped them away.

Uncle Servius knelt down. He touched the tip of her nose and grinned.

Thankfully, he wouldn't scold her.

He cocked his head, and a broad smile formed on his thin face. He yanked his red hair so that it stood on end. His hazel eyes bulged like those of a wild beast and he hopped on all fours, making funny noises and faces until the corners of her mouth tugged into a smile.

"Cheer up! Cheer up!" he said, between hops. His lanky arms and legs made his gestures silly. He chased her around the courtyard until she burst out laughing. He made funny faces as he leaped over small statues and greenery. After another leap, he banged into a column, and quickly hugged his arms and legs around it.

She froze. "Are you hurt?" Her feet found movement and she ran to him.

He faced her with crossed eyes and crooked lips.

Relief poured over her and she laughed.

He remained in his silly position, making different faces all the while.

Laughter and giggles took over until her stomach hurt.

The schoolmaster, Decimus, came out of the lesson chamber, catching Uncle Servius in his loony pose. His eyes fell on Alethea, then again on Uncle Servius, clearly annoyed to see she wasn't being punished for being dismissed from her lessons. He gave her a look that told her he'd take care of her punishment himself for her lack of discipline.

Alethea stepped back, wishing she could hide behind a plant, but they were too far away.

Uncle Servius spotted Decimus. He jumped to his feet and stood erect, straightening his tunic. His hair, still sticking up, made his long form look even taller. He put on an air of elegance for the teacher.

Alethea covered her mouth, stifling another giggle.

Decimus politely nodded to Uncle Servius. "Would you please keep down the noise? The other children are studying." He looked pointedly again at Alethea, then turned and left the room.

Alethea ran into her uncle's arms. "You are so silly!" She kissed his cheek. He was the only one who had shown her any care or concern these last four weeks.

He smiled down at her, his hazel eyes shining.

He was a fun uncle, but in the back of her mind, she wondered if he would ever hurt her if she displeased him. Her misery came flooding back.

"I miss my old schoolmaster." Really, she missed anything that was from home, but most of all she missed her mpampas. She wrapped her arms around her uncle's neck and rested her head on his bony shoulder. "I want to go home."

He held her close and caressed her head. "I know, Aucella." He then held her away and smiled. "I have an idea. Why don't you see if the cook has something yummy for you?" He set her down and took her by the hand. "Come, we'll go together."

She bit her lower lip, thinking of what Grandmother or Mamma would expect. "Shouldn't I go alone or send one of the slaves to bring something to me?"

"Aaahhh, yes, that would be the proper thing to do, wouldn't it?" Uncle Servius lifted his nose and pinky in the air. "But I wish to care for Aucella myself. Without the right kind of care, we may never hear our little bird sing again." He winked.

She forced a smile. She doubted anybody or anything could ever make her sing again.

When she looked up at him, he squeezed her hand and crossed his eyes.

She giggled.

With hair still standing on end, he gallantly escorted her to the most inferior side of the house, the kitchen.

Later, Alethea wandered outside, carrying a bowl of grapes. She found the boy she'd seen in the atrium, standing alone on the east porch. He held his head high and stood with a confident air. She walked up to him, staring at his bandages and scar. Dare she speak to him? Of course, she could speak to him. He was just a slave after all. But something about him made her unsure. Unsure of her superiority as his mistress. He was different from the other slaves. Still, her curiosity was greater than her fear.

"What happened to you?" she dared ask.

The boy leaned against one of the pillars with his arms crossed, gazing toward the south side of the estate.

She turned to see what he might be looking at. From this distance, she could see over the wall to the golden fields and the road that led to Rome. Seeing nothing of interest, she turned back to him. "How did you get that cut on your face?"

He glanced down at her from the corner of his eye, shifted his stance, but didn't answer.

"What are those bandages for?" She examined his chest and

smirked at the sight of his belly button below the tight strips of cloth. Smiling, she looked up at his face.

He frowned.

Determined to make him happy, she held the bowl of grapes up to him.

He shook his head and looked away.

Shrugging, she took a grape and bit into its top. She sucked on its juice until the entire grape imploded into her mouth. "Are you going to be my mamma's slave?" she asked, still chewing.

The boy dropped his hands. "Do you always ask so many questions?"

Swallowing the grape, pip and all, she shivered and hugged the bowl to her chest.

He crossed his arms again and leaned back against the pillar.

She thought to remind him that he was a slave and had no right to snap at her like that, but she had the distinct feeling she'd better not put him in his place.

While biting into another grape, she noticed him glancing down at her. He no longer appeared irritated. She even thought he might smile, but his lips never moved. She took courage and with a sideways glance, surveyed him from his feet to the top of his head. A red mark circled his left ankle, and his legs were long. Taking in his height, she became caught up in his face and his blue eyes as they traced the road that led to Rome.

Under normal circumstances, she would have been too frightened to talk to an older boy, even if he was a slave. But his eyes were like Mpampas's eyes, and her mpampas was a nice man, so this boy must be nice too.

She wondered about his family. Obviously, her grandfather hadn't purchased his parents. "Where are your mommy and daddy?"

A frown came over his face. He shifted and slumped against the column, staring at the ground.

Her heart sank. From his reaction, she could only assume the worst. "Are they . . . dead?"

He kicked a pebble. Closing his eyes, he nodded. He sat heavily on the porch and ran his hands through his hair.

She stared into her bowl. She knew how painful it was to lose a parent. But to lose both of them, that had to be much worse. She wanted to make him feel better, but knew she couldn't, so she said the only words that came to mind. "That's sad."

After a moment of silence, she held the grapes out to him again. This time he took one, and she sat down next to him.

He spit a pip into the small courtyard next to the porch.

"My daddy is dead too," she said. "They killed him because he followed a man named Jesus."

His gaze snapped to hers. "Your daddy was a Christian?"

She nodded.

"I'm a Christian." His eyes widened.

She nearly choked on her grape. "You better not tell anyone, or they'll kill you too." She glanced around them, looking for any listeners. Thankfully, they were alone.

"I'm not afraid of anyone." His eyes flashed. "Let them do what they want." He flung another pip. He winced and put his hand against his chest, massaging it.

She shuddered at his anger, even though it wasn't directed toward her.

After a long pause, he spoke. "Who killed him?" This time his tone was gentle.

She gazed down at the plump grapes, losing her appetite as she thought about that day. "My grandfather did it. They tied Mpampas to his horse and dragged him away. I saw it happen." Her eyes watered and her nose burned as she tried not to cry. Thinking of it made her stomach hurt. She pulled a thin leather band from her hair. "I found this." She held it up for him to see. "It was my mpampas's."

She wound the thin band around her fingers and held it to her nose, taking in Mpampas's scent. "I found it in the dirt where the horse dragged him away. He wore it around his head." She stared at the ground. Tears slipped down her cheeks and splattered onto the porch. "My poor mpampas." She wiped away her tears. It was very naughty to cry for Mpampas, but she couldn't help it. "Poor . . . Mpampas."

The boy sat with his shoulders slumped and a frown on his face. He took the bowl and handed her a grape. "What's your name?"

"Alethea." She sniffed and wiped her nose.

"How old are you?"

"Seven."

"I'm David."

"Please don't tell anyone that you're a Christian. I don't want you to die too."

He didn't answer. Instead, he handed her another grape and ate one himself.

She sat on the porch for a long time, eating grapes with David. She liked the way his jaw moved when he chewed. It was a strong jaw, the kind that suited a boy like him, definitely not a girl's jaw. She became lost in his clear eyes. So much like Mpampas. Mpampas would look down on her and his eyes would light up with a smile. She wondered if the same would happen with David.

He glanced at her.

Her heart quickened and she looked away.

He didn't seem to mind her staring, and he even did the same. Every time she looked up, there he sat, gazing at her. His eyes seemed to be smiling. Just like Mpampas.

A grin tugged at her lips as she slowly lifted her gaze back to his.

He looked away and spat out a pip.

She ate another grape and watched birds fly overhead. It was as though her loneliness flew away with them. Their singing sparked a hint of joy deep within her. She wanted to hang on to this moment for as long as she could.

She leaned in close to David. "Shall I sing a song?"

He raised a questioning brow.

"It's a song my mpampas used to sing."

From his reaction, she figured he wasn't interested. But that didn't bother her. Once he heard her voice, he would want her to sing. Just like Mpampas and the rest of the family.

He studied her with those familiar blue eyes, but he finally half smiled and nodded.

The dimples in his cheeks snagged her attention as she sprang to her feet.

Her soft voice amplified off the arches along the portico and sent a chill up her spine. The Greek words dripped off her lips like the sweet juice from a grape.

"Oh, if I had wings like a dove!

I would fly away and be at rest.

Yes, I would wander far off

And remain in the wilderness.

I would hurry to my escape

Far away from wind and storms."

She sang louder, hoping to make David smile again. She glided along the porch, the skirt of her stola waving and dancing to the rhythm. Her fingers fluttered in the air to the music, and she rocked back and forth, watching her sash float around her. The high note was coming, her favorite. Surely, he would smile now. She hit it hard, her own voice surprising her. Beautiful.

Hoping to catch a smile, she turned toward David, but he hovered over the bowl with bulging cheeks and gobbled down more grapes.

She spun around and twirled her sash in circles above his head, hoping to gain his attention, giggling between lyrics. Strands of his hair lit up like gold from the sun's rays, matching her bracelets. She wanted to touch it, but she didn't dare.

She skipped around him.

"Here, catch." Without warning, he tossed a grape.

To her surprise, she caught it. She popped it into her mouth with glee.

His face lit up with a big smile, exposing those wonderful dimples, his eyes shining.

She grasped the ends of her sash and whirled away, singing the same tune. She glanced over her shoulder at him.

He lifted his face to the sun. To her delight, he laughed. With the back of his hand, he wiped away some juice that dripped from the corner of his mouth.

"What's your name, boy?"

Alethea froze at the familiar voice.

Mamma.

David sprang to his feet, holding his chest.

From the tone of her voice, they were in trouble. For what, she didn't know.

Her mamma stood in the doorway with Paulus on her slender hip. Alethea wondered how much her little brother missed Mpampas. Paulus called for him on occasion, but he was too young to understand that he would never see Mpampas again.

Mamma's lips pinched together in an agitated frown.

"David."

"David?" Her mouth turned down as though she just tasted a sour grape. "That's not the name they gave you when you were purchased, is it?"

Alethea's eyes darted to David.

He focused his gaze on the bowl, and a long uneasy pause filled the air before he answered. "Damonus." He cleared his throat. "The name is Damonus."

Her mamma handed Paulus to a female slave who appeared in the doorway. She then turned and looked down her nose at David. "You will work for me until you're well." She wagged a slender finger at Alethea. "You may dance and sing for your grandfather and the rest of the family, but certainly not for a slave. It's improper." She glanced in David's direction.

He stared at the bowl, studying the grapes as if he'd never seen them before. His eyes shifted to the ground, not once making eye contact with Mamma.

Alethea glanced down in the same direction to see what he might be looking at, but saw nothing of interest other than the large, beige stones beneath their feet.

She glanced back up, and Mamma's eyes bore into hers. "I don't want to see this kind of behavior from you again." She put her hands on her hips and raised a brow. "Is that understood?"

Alethea didn't realize she had done anything wrong. She used to sing and dance for Mpampas and the rest of the family often, but of course, they weren't slaves. She curtseyed and with a small voice said, "Yes, Mamma."

Mamma turned toward David. "As for you, boy, you will refer to me as 'Mistress.' The men, you will refer to as 'Lord' or 'Master.' You will also show the same respect toward my daughter." She waited with folded arms for a response.

"Yes—yes, mistress."

"Good."

She knelt down and pulled Alethea to her. Her look softened. "Where is Portia? You shouldn't be out here alone with this boy."

"She probably thinks I'm still in my lessons."

Mamma raised a brow and nodded. "Yes, she probably does, of course." She brushed a curl from Alethea's face. "You are just a child, but if you want to be a proper lady, you must behave like one." She sighed and half smiled. "I must say, it's nice to have our Aucella back." She stood to leave. "I'll send Portia to you."

Mamma shot David a haughty glance. She turned with her nose in the air, went inside, and closed the door.

David's eyes flashed at Alethea. He thrust the bowl into her midriff and marched away.

What had she done? Why was he angry with her? She followed him through the small courtyard.

He kicked a small statue, making it fall over and crack. He marched through the gate, turned away from the stables, and headed into the bare field to his right where Alethea and the other children played.

Halfway through the field, he stopped, turned, and glared at her.

She stood motionless, then took a step in his direction. When he did nothing, she took another deliberate step.

He turned away, kicked hard at the dirt, and buckled over, grabbing his ribs.

She ran up to him.

"Leave me alone," he said between clenched teeth, his face wincing in pain.

Hurt, she backed away. She had lost her new friend.

He slowly straightened, staring past her as he took in a careful, long, deep breath. He then turned to go, his hands clenched in fists. The glare of the sun reflected off the golden armband just above his elbow.

Beyond the field to their left, a forest of trees spread to the wall. To the right of the trees, south of the field, David wound his way to the top of a mossy hill and gazed over Grandfather's wall.

Alethea held the bowl against her hip. Heart in her throat, she decided the trees looked more inviting than David. Staying near the boy, she picked a few of the flowers—weeds, her mamma called them—and poked several in her hair. When she spun around, David was watching her. She hesitated, then shyly smiled and waved.

He half grinned, sending her a thrill of hope. She hadn't lost her friend after all. Massaging his ribs, he turned back toward the wall.

Later as she strolled to the house, she watched David from the corner of her eye. She wasn't certain, but she thought he might be crying. He sat on top of the hill with his hands in his hair, and his shoulders trembled.

He must be crying for his mamma and mpampas. She wanted to go to him, but she sensed he wanted to be alone, so she sat down where she was. In the middle of the dirt field, with David's back to her, she hugged her knees to her chin. As she watched him cry, the wind drew her attention to the trees. Their leaves rustled and their branches bowed with sadness. A small rain cloud in the distance wept over the countryside. She looked at the flowers she had collected. Were they sad too?

Her thoughts turned to her grandfather who had caused so much grief. She used to love him, until he took away the one she loved most. Mpampas's smile and blue eyes flashed through her mind. His brown curly locks always gave him a messy appearance, but he had been a handsome man, and strong. She remembered sitting on his arm after he scooped her up from the floor. His laughter, the twinkle in his eyes, and the stories about his God turned over in her mind. He'd never hold her again. She'd never know the strength of his arms, the comfort when he wrapped her in them. She would never again be his Aucella.

A lump came to her throat and her nose burned as hot tears welled in her eyes. She burst into sobs and wept for Mpampas. Sorrow raked through her, making her body tremble, and she couldn't stop crying. Thankfully, no one else was around to see as tears flowed down her cheeks and her heart released the hurt she had been so afraid to set free. Everyone hated Mpampas and rejoiced in his death, but she would love him forever and ever. She loved him much more than she loved Grandfather. She loved Mpampas more than there were stars in the sky and more than there was sand on the ground.

She wiped her cheeks, looked down at her tear-stained hands, and recalled Mpampas's words.

"He keeps your tears in his bottle."

She wondered who cared enough to keep her tears in his bottle. Mpampas or his God?

four

Alethea's stomach roiled at the thought of seeing Grandfather. It had been a while since she had to join the other children and serve the adults, but today her mamma made a point of her helping again, so she carried a tray of food into the dining chamber.

"Out of my way, twig." Vibia shoved by her. She walked toward Grandfather's table, her lips turned up into a smug grin.

Alethea held tight to her tray and glared at her cousin. She turned back to her task and spotted David out of the corner of her eye. He fanned Mamma with a giant peacock fan while she reclined on a settee in front of a small table, waiting to be served. His eyes met hers and a smile tugged at Alethea's lips, but she forced it away. She didn't want anyone to know about their special friendship.

"That's enough, boy." Mamma waved her hand. "Leave us."

Despite the heavy tray quivering in her arms, Alethea watched David leave. Hopefully, she'd be able to talk with him again soon. The moment he disappeared through the door, an empty feeling settled in her stomach. She set one of the heavy platters of cold meat on a small table.

"Aucella." Her grandfather's voice boomed, sending a shudder down her spine. She had dreaded the day he would call her to him. He reclined on a couch at the far end of the tables with Uncle Servius, away from the women.

Grandfather smiled. A smile that said everything was back to normal. A smile that said killing her *mpampas* was of no concern. "I hear you've been singing again."

Her stomach tied into one great knot.

"Come, let me put my arms around you, and we'll sing one of our favorite Latin pieces." He motioned to the others around the tables. "Certainly it will give everyone great pleasure to have such fine entertainment as we dine."

She swallowed hard. How could she sing for him, let alone stand the feel of his arms around her? Having avoided him successfully these four weeks, she now came face to face with her grandfather-turned-monster. To think, she used to run freely into his embrace and laugh without a worry in the world. If he was powerful enough to take her father's life, he could take her life as quickly as Zeus could say his name.

Her hands trembled as she placed the last platter of vegetables on the table, nearly knocking over one of the goblets. Alethea hesitated and stepped back. She must obey. The thought of Grandfather's punishment made her heart clench.

"What's wrong with you, child?" Grandfather frowned. "Come to me."

She willed her body to move and took a step toward her grandfather. Small strands of his fake blond hair combed forward reminded her of the Medusa in the entry hall. What if his stare caused her to turn to stone? Or suppose he tied *her* to a horse?

She took another tentative step, then stopped, unable to make her feet move any farther. A cold chill shuddered through her entire body and she froze. Had she turned to stone?

Grandfather straightened. His eyes widened and he slammed his fist down on the table. Alethea jumped as did everyone who reclined on the couches, including Uncle Servius.

"Do not defy me, Aucella." He then settled back against the cushions all fluffy and pretty against his hard ugly frame. "Come to your grandfather like you always do, and let's sing," he said with a false calm she recognized.

The dread on the faces of those around the tables made Alethea's own terror grow as great as Rome itself. If Uncle Servius, Aunt Fabia, and Mamma were afraid, then certainly she had reason to be afraid. Everyone's eyes were on her, urging her to obey. Everyone but Mamma's. If only Mamma would meet her gaze and let her know everything would be well. But Mamma stared at her plate, unwilling to give Alethea any reassurance, which meant that everything was *not* well. Why wasn't Mamma looking at her? Why couldn't Alethea move? Hopelessness swallowed her, and she was certain Grandfather would put her to death for not joining him in song. She tried to force her legs to move, but they wouldn't.

She imagined snakes growing from Grandfather's head, while Mother, Grandmother, and Uncle Servius hardened into stone images. No one could help her. The silence buzzed through the room. Her breathing echoed in her ears. She stood alone against this terrible monster as his face reddened with rage.

Mpampas. Gone.

Death. All around.

Inside herself, she sank into a black abyss. Alethea threw out her hands and screamed in wild terror. Would anyone help her? She searched their shocked faces as the horror escaped her throat in a shrill cry.

Vibia stopped setting Grandfather's table and snickered. Aunt Fabia stopped in the midst of taking a dainty bite of food. Grandmother gaped, and her mamma continued to face her plate, eyes clenched shut against the high shrill of Alethea's voice. Uncle Servius stared, eyebrows raised. And Grandfather sat frozen with his mouth half open, as Alethea's scream echoed off the walls.

Out of breath, her long scream died to a hoarse whisper in the depths of her throat. No one rescued her. She gasped and bolted from the room. She ran to the tablinum and wrapped herself in the thick massive curtains, hoping nobody would find her and force her to return.

"You frightened the poor child!" Grandmother's voice carried from the dining chamber. "You can't expect her to sing if you frighten her so."

Alethea wiped her tears and nose on the curtains as she listened. The only person in the household who wasn't afraid of Grandfather was Grandmother Renata.

"She will not defy me!" Grandfather shouted. "Why did she scream at me? I am not a demon."

"She watched her father die by your hands. What do you expect?"

Alethea shuddered and huddled farther into the curtain, wrapping it around her trembling body.

"She wasn't supposed to see that." Grandfather's voice calmed. He almost sounded concerned.

"Give her time, Aloysius. She will come to you and be your little bird when she's had enough time to get Galen out of her mind."

"Do not mention that traitor's name again." Grandfather's voice was grave.

"But he is, or was, her father—"

Platters and goblets clattered to the floor. Alethea imagined her grandfather had knocked down one of the small tables of food with his fist, something she'd seen him do before.

"You will not mention that name in this house again, Renata!"

Grandmother cleared her throat. "I will do as you say, but this display of behavior is barbaric."

Grandfather's rage even affected Vibia. Her cries, a high soprano, grew to a feverish pitch.

"Oh, be quiet!" Grandfather shouted.

Except for Vibia's sniffles, silence followed. Alethea peeked around the curtain and towards the door of the dining chamber. A few slaves stood outside, their eyes wide.

"Slave!" Grandfather shouted.

The slave closest to the door jumped, and with one long stride, entered the chamber.

"Clean this up and bring us more food. Orator!"

Startled, the orator fumbled to gain control of his scrolls, but one landed on the floor. He left it and bounded into the dining chamber.

"Recite something cheerful."

When the orator began, Alethea's eyes wandered past the slaves standing outside the door. Two more slaves who held bowls with damp cloths entered the chamber. Another stood, holding his lyre. The rest of them held trembling fans, but one slave's fan did not waver.

David. And he looked right at her.

Her heart stopped. He knew where she was. Would he tell? She slowly pulled the curtain back around her face and hid behind its massive folds.

Nobody came to her after the meal, and she ignored their calls as their voices echoed off the vaulted ceilings. When familiar chatter filled the air, she peeked around the curtain and saw her cousins walking to the dining chamber after the adults had left. Marcus and Lucius wrestled as they made their way toward the door, and Vibia walked briskly with an air of confidence, her chin held high.

The slaves clanked the trays when they brought her cousins their food, but Alethea stayed behind the curtain. Cousin Vibia laughed, and Alethea imagined everyone reclined around the tables, enjoying the meat and vegetables. Remembering the lamb she'd served, the wine rolls, and even the green beans spiced with pine nuts, made her mouth water. Her stomach growled, but she didn't dare venture out.

Her body warmed the curtain, and she grew sleepy, so she nestled into her little cocoon, passing the time with a silent song Mpampas used to sing.

Cool air awoke Alethea, and she found herself in Grandmother's arms. "We've been looking everywhere for you."

Unable to cling to Grandmother, sleep and exhaustion weighed down her arms and legs.

"All the other children are asleep by now. The rest of us are outside relaxing in the garden."

Grandmother Renata hummed a lullaby while she carried Alethea to her bedchamber, changed her clothes, and laid her on the bed.

"Try not to let that burly old grandfather of yours frighten you. He loves you dearly," she whispered as she brushed the curls from Alethea's face.

Grandmother glanced over to where Vibia slept. She then leaned in closer to Alethea. "Of all the grandchildren, you are his favorite. That's why he wants you near him. You bring him great joy, Aucella. Don't be so fearful." Her grandmother sighed. "I dare say you are the only one in the household he seems to favor." She winked and smiled. "Other than me, of course."

Grandmother Renata kissed her forehead. She stood and walked toward the door. "You will apologize to your grandfather first thing in the morning."

The fact that Alethea brought Grandfather so much pleasure relieved her, but only a little bit. Right now, she could only see the hateful man who ordered his slaves to tie Mpampas to the horse. His red angry face, his arm motioning the slaves to grab her father, his sharp finger pointing. She shivered. How could she ever sing and dance for that man again?

"Grandmother?"

Her grandmother turned.

"Where is Mamma?"

"I'll send her to you." Grandmother smiled. The kind of smile that used to warm Alethea to her toes, but now it left her cold and alone.

Alethea waited into the wee hours of the night, too frightened and sleepy to leave her chamber. The night drew out like a long rope that had no end. Between the haziness of sleep and wakefulness, she finally sensed her mamma's presence.

Mamma whispered, her voice carrying over her like a small wind through her mind, weeping into her blankets. "My poor child. I'm to blame."

five

"Alethea . . . ."

A voice echoed in the darkness of her mind. A voice with a warm, motherly tone she'd heard before. But it no longer touched Alethea with the softness of a blanket she'd want to curl up in. Nothing touched her anymore.

She opened her heavy eyelids and found Portia standing over her.

"Time to wake up."

Alethea blinked the sleep from her eyes.

Portia smiled, her blonde hair pulled back to the nape of her neck. Her light blue mantle fell gracefully over her shoulders, the folds of fabric shimmering in the light from the high window. No one in the household was as light and fair skinned as her nursemaid, and in the glow of the sunlight, she looked like a goddess. She was always a pleasant sight in the morning, or at any time of the day, but ever since that last night at home, Alethea felt a certain uneasiness about her, as though she could no longer be trusted.

Portia eased the covers off and helped Alethea to her feet.

What a long night, and yet it didn't feel quite long enough. Sleep still pulled at Alethea's body. By the brightness of the chamber she could tell she'd slept longer than usual. She yawned and stretched, willing her body to come alive.

"It's late." Portia sorted through Alethea's clothing. "I let you sleep longer than I should have. Obviously you needed it." She held up a clean stola for Alethea to wear. Portia sighed and shook her head. "You poor child."

Portia took her by the hand and led her through the atrium. Alethea let her pull her along, her limbs heavy with sleepiness. Why was she so tired? Memories of the night before slammed into her and she came fully awake. She dreaded a meeting with Grandfather. Would he punish her for her naughty behavior? She'd heard rumors of his beatings, and she shivered at the thought of receiving one.

Alethea glanced around the atrium. Would Grandfather be waiting for her? She didn't see him, but it felt as if the walls had eyes and they would find a way to notify Grandfather of her presence.

They passed through the east door and came out onto the long porch where she'd met the slave boy the day before. David. She wondered where he might be. He hadn't snitched on her last night, something for which she was very grateful. She hoped to see him again that day. They walked along the porch toward the baths on the north side of the house. Would Grandfather be waiting for her in the plaza?

They turned to the left, and Alethea closed her eyes, certain she felt Grandfather's terrifying presence. She opened them just as they neared the steps, and to her relief he wasn't there.

Releasing a long breath, Alethea followed Portia through the empty plaza, which was sometimes used for fencing or disciplining slaves. Slaves would be tied to one of the large wooden stakes at the far end to be flogged. The stakes stood higher than Titus.

Alethea wondered if Grandfather would have her scourged like his slaves. She'd never seen a slave scourged. Though her older cousins, Lucius and Marcus, told her stories. Lucius always hid around the corner to watch when a slave got whipped; he was so cruel. She felt sorry for a slave if they got punished, especially if they were nice.

Two wide steps on the other side of the stakes led to a path that circled around the house. From there, stairs led up to the slaves' chambers above the south porch. Alethea looked toward the stairs, hoping to find David. He wasn't to be seen, and before she knew it, they hurried through the doors, under the arches, past the changing chambers and cold bath chamber, and went straight to the hot bath chamber.

"I had the slaves keep the ovens aflame, though it won't be quite as hot as usual." Portia lifted Alethea's night stola over her head and helped her step down into the warm water.

Alethea studied the mosaic in the pool. Usually the steam kept her from seeing the painted sea nymphs swimming along the pool's bottom, both the sons and daughters of Triton the powerful sea god. Along the edges were various types of fish and colorful coral reefs. If only she were Triton. She could escape Grandfather's wrath.

Portia lifted her own tunic to her knees, sat on the bath's edge, and scrubbed Alethea. Normally, Alethea would have used this time to ask questions. But nothing was normal anymore, especially after what she had done last night. She missed her own bath at home. It wasn't as fancy as this, but it was home. And this was not.

While Portia scrubbed her raw, Alethea imagined herself as the powerful sea god, fighting against her grandfather. She recalled how Mpampas had told her that the name Aloysius meant famous warrior. It was a name given to her great-grandfather, and now her grandfather had taken it as his own. But Alethea couldn't help thinking the only people Grandfather warred against were members of his family.

When she stepped out of the pool, the cold tiles chilled her feet. She shivered as Portia dried her off.

"Sorry, there's no time to apply any of your mother's perfume and oils." Usually Alethea would have been taken to a cold bath, then to a dressing chamber. There, she would be rubbed down with oils to keep her skin from becoming too dry and then scraped clean with a shell, but Portia, in her haste, dressed her right there.

She tried not to frown. It was always a treat to wear her mamma's perfume. It made her feel less alone, especially now with Mpampas gone.

Portia then wrapped Alethea's heavy, wet hair around the cloth and took her into the makeup chamber.

Vibia was already sitting in her wicker chair. That told her again how late she was, but perhaps she need not worry, her mamma likely wouldn't miss her. She wondered if her mamma ever missed her since they came to live with Grandfather.

A nursemaid twisted Vibia's auburn hair into braids and wound them into folds on top of her head. Alethea wished she could be as beautiful as Vibia. Her cheeks were always rosy. Or was that paint? Vibia's mamma sometimes let her wear makeup. Vibia was nice and plump, a sign to all that she came from a rich family. Alethea ate all she could but remained as thin as a hairpin, as her grandmother would say, just like Marcus and Lucius. She mourned being shaped like a boy.

Vibia glanced in Alethea's direction. "What are you staring at?"

Alethea stuck her tongue out at Vibia as she climbed onto a wicker chair.

"I'm afraid we won't be doing anything special with your hair today," Portia said. "Don't be too disappointed. You're so beautiful with those natural curls. It'll look lovely no matter what we do."

Alethea winced as Portia yanked a comb through the tangles in her long, dark hair. She stared at the cosmetics on the table and wondered if Mamma had thought of her that day. Her mamma had seemed like her old self back on the porch the day before, so why didn't she come to her bedchamber last night? Or did she come? Maybe it was a dream?

Portia handed Alethea her mamma's mirror while she worked on her hair. Her face shone clear in the polished silver, but her puffy eyes still looked and felt tired. Portia tied Alethea's hair into one long braid, letting wisps of curls fall around her face. She then wrapped the long braid into a bun and pinned it securely in place. "Good. This way you won't have water dripping down your back."

Portia put her face down next to Alethea's, and they looked into the mirror together. "There now. Don't you look lovely?"

Portia smiled down at her, a smile that seemed sincere. But could she be trusted? Alethea found it difficult to trust anyone after watching Grandfather snatch the most important person from her life.

Portia and the other nursemaid led Vibia and Alethea toward the dining chamber. Vibia didn't say a word, and Alethea would usually do all the talking while they were together, but not today. Vibia was always so prim and proper that next to her Alethea felt like a lopsided goat. They crossed the small plaza, passed the large wooden stakes, and entered the house. They walked down the narrow corridor that went right past Grandfather's office chamber. Vibia took small dainty steps, while Alethea strode along, hoping Grandfather wouldn't spot her.

"Why are you in such a hurry, Alethea?" Vibia called out too loudly. "Don't you want to greet Grandfather this morning?"

Vibia had a look of exaggerated innocence on her face, and Alethea wondered if Vibia knew she would be in trouble. Besides that, since when did they greet Grandfather when walking past his office chamber? Usually, they would be reprimanded for disturbing him.

"Aucella!"

A cold, almost painful chill prickled down Alethea's spine. Grandfather.

"I'll explain to your mother why you're not with us." Portia gave her a pat and a smile.

Alethea wondered if her mamma would even notice, let alone care. But she still hoped Mamma would care enough to come and rescue her from Grandfather.

Portia and Vibia's nursemaid escorted her to the dining chamber, and Alethea watched their backs as they left her to stand alone in the hall. She couldn't help but think they were running away by the quick pace of their steps, doing exactly what she felt like doing.

Alethea twisted her clammy hands. With a constricting throat, she did an about-face and shuffled into Grandfather's chamber.

He stood before a slave who read from a small scroll. Grandfather motioned for him to leave.

She took a deep breath, trying to remind herself of Grandmother's words about her being his favorite. She hoped it was true and that it would benefit her now.

Grandfather stood over her, his dark eyes surveying her.

She looked down, unable to bear his unrelenting gaze.

"Why did you run from me last night?"

Her eyes brimmed with tears. "I was afraid." She didn't think she would be able to talk because of the knot in her throat, but somehow the words made their way past the knot and spilled from her lips. So much for being the mighty Triton.

Grandfather sighed long and hard. "You have no reason to be afraid." He turned from her, holding his hands behind his back. "If you had done as you were told and remained in the house, you would not have seen what happened to your father." He spoke in a firm tone, stepped toward the couch, and reclined on the cushions. "Your father was a rebel. A traitor to our gods and to the empire. Only men such as he need fear my wrath, and you're not one of them. Your gods are my gods, and you'll not worship the god of your father, so you will stop being afraid." He leaned on his elbow. "Now, what do you have to say for your horrible behavior last night?"

"I'm sorry, Grandfather." Her voice sounded small, even to her own ears, and she choked back a fearful wail.

He smiled. "You're forgiven, Aucella." He held his arms out to her. "Come to me. Let me dry your tears."

Not wanting to cause more trouble for herself, she didn't hesitate.

He wrapped her in his arms and wiped her tears with his fingers. His touch sent a cold shudder down her back.

"There's no need to be afraid." He waved his hand, and she noticed the rings she used to play with when she sat on his lap. "I gave him a chance to choose between his family and his god." He pulled her close. "You were there, you heard it. I said to him, 'You may have your family returned to you this night if you simply deny this god of yours.' But he refused." Grandfather frowned. "He didn't love you, Aucella." He shook his head, and his eyes misted as he squeezed her close. "I'm so sorry." He dabbed his eyes.

"If he had just worshipped Rome's deities *and* his god, there wouldn't have been a problem." He sighed and ran his hand over her hair. "He believed in a myth and rejected the true gods of Rome."

Alethea swallowed hard, choking down the words that contradicted everything her father had taught her.

Grandfather hugged her, pressing his cheek against hers.

She wanted to pull away, but didn't dare, her body stiff against his.

"I have missed my Aucella these last weeks. When your mother told me you had been singing on the porch, I thought you would be ready to sing during the evening meal. I was surprised when you didn't come to me."

"I'll come to you now, Grandfather." She heard herself say the words, but a hollowness filled her heart; she feared he might hear it in her voice. She would never reveal her true self, not ever. She would pretend to love him, pretend to love his gods, but the secret place of her heart would never be his. It made her empty inside. Not only did she have no more Mpampas, but no more Grandfather— not the Grandfather she thought she knew anyway. Never had she felt so alone, and it amazed her that she could feel that way when surrounded by so many people, people who said they loved her.

Her grandfather, Vibian Cornelius Aloysius, a man of power, caressed her cheek. "Dance for me, little bird, and let me hear you sing."

She wanted to tell him that she hadn't yet eaten, but decided she had better do as he said. She sang a Greek song, in secret defiance, since her mpampas was Greek. She also danced and forced a smile. In the meantime, her stomach growled.

By now, she knew she would not suffer his punishment. Whatever it might have been, she didn't want to know. Relief sprang forth in her song. Still, it was all a farce, every move, and every sound, fake. She hated being this way. But if it meant staying alive, she was willing to pretend, and willing to deny the God of her father.

Filling her mind with Mpampas, she sang and danced for him.

To her relief, Grandfather was entertained by her act, and to her near pleasure, he joined her in song. She smiled more easily now, and the tears dried on her cheeks. She was Triton, the powerful sea god. And she had won the first battle with her grandfather. He was taken in by her performance, but where she triumphed in victory and in spite, was that he sang one of Mpampas's favorite songs. For the first time ever, she saw her grandfather as a fool.

six

David awoke with a start. Something rested on his chest. Was it a mouse? He opened his eyes and indeed something black sat on him. He leaped out of bed and it dropped to the floor.

Titus, standing at the door with a torch, roared with laughter.

David's face went hot with embarrassment as his ribs throbbed painfully from the movement.

"Pick it up," Titus said.

Now fully awake, David picked up the ball. The leather globe fit neatly in his palm.

"You're going to learn to juggle. Get dressed and meet me in the plaza." Titus placed the torch in the bracket just outside the door and left.

David glanced around the chamber. The torch outside gave just enough light for him to see that the three boys with whom he shared the quarters were already gone, probably working in the stables. Two of them were twins and all three of them were younger than David. Good thing they hadn't witnessed his foolishness.

He got into his tunic. How long had he been here at the villa now? A little more than a week? So far he hadn't had any problems with Aloysius, whom everyone feared. David feared him too, but after observing him these last few days, he'd figured out how to please him. Only those who showed their fear made him angry. The only people he seemed fond of were his wife, Titus, and Alethea.

Aloysius terrified Alethea, but at the same time, she was courageous. She faced her fear head on. At least she didn't run off screaming anymore. He chuckled to himself. She reminded him so much of Sarah—his little Sarah.

Regret choked him as he grabbed the ball and stepped out onto the balcony. A slight chill hung in the air, and to his left, the sun hid below the horizon. The darkness reminded him of how alone he was in the world. No Mamma or Abba, no family, no Sarah. He didn't want to go into the plaza while darkness lingered. Instead of taking the stairs, he walked along the balcony to his left, which wound its way around the house, passing other slaves' quarters. He could barely make out the dirt field to the east of the estate. The courtyard just below the balcony cast haunting shadows between the trimmed bushes and statues. The sun's first beams of light peeked over the horizon, reminding him that Titus waited.

As he went back toward the stairs, the view of the vineyards over the western wall made him stop. The green vines glowed under the early morning rays and the sky changed from purple, to silver, to gold. Shadowed workers made their way to the fields. An altar stood at the top of the hill. An altar to Mars, the Roman god of agriculture. It unnerved him to think he now belonged to people who worshiped strange gods. Just beyond the altar, the hill sloped toward the south to a small village where the vine keepers lived.

It might be easy to escape this place. The wall stood about ten feet high. He could probably get over it if he ran fast enough. With enough momentum, he could climb up it. He wondered how smooth the stones were.

Why had he given Titus his word to stay? The promise he made ate at him. Of course, he'd only given his word because he thought Sarah would be found. He'd been certain of it. Now who would find her?

Since she wasn't at the apartment, he held onto the hope that Manius had found her. Manius and Abba used to meet every morning to work on manuscripts. Surely, he had come again that morning and found her. David squeezed the ball. He shook his head in an attempt to shake away his frustration. He tossed the ball and caught it. Titus would be wondering what kept him.

After he made his way down the stairs, he came around into the plaza. Its fluted columns and large beige tiles made him feel important. He served under a wealthy family. Most fascinating were the sea nymph statues at the entrance of the baths where he waited in boredom every morning for Cornelia. He sometimes imagined what it would be like to swim with the half-fish deities far away in the deep blue sea.

On this side of the plaza, three large wooden stakes loomed over David. He'd heard stories about their use from other slaves. He imagined torturous lashes of the cat-o'-nine-tails, tearing away flesh from a slave's back. He shivered, praying he would never have to feel the pain of a whip. Thoughts of escape enticed him. But he couldn't go against his word. "Let a man's yes be yes and his no be no." His father's voice echoed through his mind, beating like a drum since the day he gave his word. He fisted the ball in his hand until his knuckles turned white.

Lucius, Alethea's bully of a cousin, fondled one of the sea nymph statues, off in his own world and unaware that anyone watched.

David stopped to see what he might do.

Marcus bounded toward the bath's entrance and caught his younger brother in a headlock.

"Let go of me!" Lucius shouted.

"Not until you say—"

"No! Let . . . go . . . *now!*"

David remained hidden behind one of the tall stakes, watching the two boys. Suppose they thought he was spying? He'd better come out of hiding.

"I heard you hit Vibia."

Lucius incessantly pestered Vibia, their younger sister, as well as Alethea.

"How do you like it, huh? Why don't you pick on someone your own size? Say you won't do it again."

Lucius didn't answer, his face red as a radish and his teeth bared.

"You know Father will do nothing if I tear you apart here and now, and I'll do it." He applied more pressure to the headlock. "Apologize now."

"Ow! Leave me. I won't do it again." By now Lucius whimpered and when Marcus released him, he stumbled away.

"Damonus." Marcus looked right at David.

He realized Marcus spoke to him. It was difficult getting used to a new name.

"Father says you can go fishing with us later. Would you like that?"

Surprised by the invitation, David wondered if slaves were allowed to go fishing with their masters. He had been bored to death serving Cornelia, and to do something fun was just what he longed for.

"Sure, I'd like that," he said, fearing he sounded too eager.

"Good." Marcus nodded. "I'll send for you when it's time." He then went into the house.

What a surprise that someone from Aloysius's family was friendly. David thought his only friends were to be his chamber-mates.

"So you're the one who broke my statue in the east courtyard."

David recognized the voice, and this person knew of his little crime. He held his breath and turned.

Ace half smiled. "Don't do it again."

"No, sir," David said, exhaling in relief. Ace was the keeper of the gardens, but according to the stable boys, before he came to the villa he was a teacher. With brown hair combed neatly forward, he kept himself as well trimmed as the gardens. "Titus says you're going to be my tutor."

"Yes. Titus and I've been breaking in the new field slaves. Things have finally slowed down, so when Cornelia is resting, meet me in the slaves' dining chamber and we'll begin your lessons."

"What about Marcus and Lucius? Will they come too?" David secretly hoped Marcus would be there.

"No, they have their own lessons with Decimus. This will be informal training and our little secret." Ace gave him a hard look.

"What about the stable boys?" David hoped for company and friends.

"No. You belong to Titus." Ace put his hands behind his back, straightening in his white tunic, and looked David over. "Have you settled in?"

David nodded. "Yes." Really, nothing exciting had happened at all. He wished something would; anything was better than the slow boredom of each long day.

"If you have any trouble, let me know."

"Yes, sir." Ace's concern surprised David. Since he spent most of his days following Cornelia around, he hadn't had much opportunity to meet or get to know Ace.

"Until later." Ace gave him a friendly squeeze on the arm and turned to go.

Titus appeared from around the corner and without warning, tossed him a ball.

David caught it with his free hand.

Titus tossed another just like it.

David caught the ball against his chest between the first two.

Titus came to him with a small net bag and tied it onto David's belt. "Keep these with you wherever you go."

One by one, David dropped the balls into the bag, but Titus prevented the last one. "Toss it into the air like this." He demonstrated by tossing the ball just above eye level and catching it in his hand.

David took the ball and did the same.

"Don't throw it too high, and practice this first with one hand and then the other. When you're not busy fanning Cornelia or running errands for her," David sensed a bit of sarcasm in his voice, "I want you to practice catching the ball, just like you saw me do."

David tossed the ball several times with his right hand. Simple. Was this a joke?

"Practice with your left hand; the right hand won't be a problem for you."

David tossed the ball with his left hand. It felt awkward.

"Practice with that hand all day. Also, learn to catch the ball this way." Titus tossed the ball, but instead of just letting it fall into his hand, he snatched it out of the air.

"Why do I have to do this?"

"You'll have to learn to juggle if you're to be a fighter," Titus said as he went up the steps. He walked off, and as he rounded the corner he called out, "All day, left hand only."

David shook his head and tossed the ball. He snatched it out of the air the way Titus had done. At least this was better than standing around all day with nothing to do. In fact, it might be fun to learn how to juggle. He recalled seeing men do similar tricks at the Forum, not to mention swallowing fire and all sorts of unusual spectacles.

"Damonus, Cornelia is ready for you," Fabia's slave called out to him. She peered out from the hall that went by Aloysius's office chamber.

David stashed the ball in his net bag and went to help Cornelia carry her garments to the baths. He had never known such laziness, yet it was normal here at the villa. There was a slave for everything. Such a boring job, doing all these meaningless tasks for Cornelia. Strange to think she was Alethea's mother.

He caught a glimpse of the silly girl several times this last week. If she didn't remind him of Sarah and have such a cute nose, he might have found her annoying.

He walked through the atrium and arrived at Cornelia's chamber door.

"You're late."

Late? David swallowed. How could he be late? Was he supposed to wait outside her door all morning? And wasn't he actually Titus's charge? Before he could say anything, she tossed her garments at him. Luckily, he didn't let any fall. It would give her another reason to snap.

"Don't let it happen again."

"Yes, mistress."

She shot him an angry look.

"I mean, no, mistress." David could never say or do the right thing with Cornelia. He knew she despised him, and he could do nothing to please her. He was not equal to her station, and she was determined not to let him forget it. He had known people who treated their slaves like family, but none, save Titus, were treated that way here. After the invitation from Marcus to go fishing, David had an inclination that he also might be treated well. He hoped one day to be as important as Titus. Then maybe he'd gain his freedom.

"Tonight, I expect you to wash my feet before the evening meal."

"He will do no such thing."

David turned to see Aloysius. He sucked in a breath and his feet became fixed to the tiles. His first personal encounter with the master since his arrival.

"If you expect decent service from the slaves you will not belittle them." Aloysius put his hands behind his back. "I've hardly seen you venture outdoors. Were you planning on walking in the dust?" His voice held a hint of sarcasm. "We already have someone to wash our feet, and you will not make him do it. This is Titus's boy." The last words were said as though he issued a command, all sarcasm vanished.

David held his breath, relieved to know his status was above such demeaning and undesirable tasks. Would Cornelia lash out?

"I didn't realize you valued this one." Eyes riveted to the floor, her face paled and her voice became quiet.

A tinge of anger shot through David. She spoke as though he were a piece of furniture. Yet he had heard much worse insults, so he should be grateful. Still, he despised being a slave. One day, he would be free.

Aloysius grunted and walked away.

Cornelia turned up her nose and walked past David. He followed her in silence to the baths entrance where a female slave awaited them and took the garments.

"Wait here until I'm finished." Cornelia's voice was still sharp, but it had lost its flair since Aloysius's rebuke.

David stood outside the door. This could take hours.

He used his time to follow Titus's instructions and tossed his ball, up and down, up and down. Grateful for the distraction, he stayed busy while he waited, and it kept his mind off more painful thoughts. The sea nymph's comfort wasn't as necessary, but eventually even tossing the ball became boring.

He threw the ball against the wall. It fell straight to the ground. He picked it up and paddled it back and forth from hand to hand. When paddling it between his hands no longer interested him, he tried the same thing with his feet. That proved more challenging, but he still grew restless, thinking about fishing with Marcus and his lessons with Ace.

He glanced above the atrium at the slaves' chambers and recalled how the slant of the roof created an opening in the center of the atrium above the fountain. The opening was out of sight, but he mentally measured the distance between him and where it should be. He glanced around the plaza. No one was there. And no one would likely be near the atrium. He squeezed the leather ball in his fist, took a step back, and pointed his left arm and forefinger toward the target. He threw the ball high, arching it towards the roof's opening.

His ribs burned, but that didn't matter. He dashed for the atrium. As he charged down the hall past Aloysius's office chamber—luckily no one was there—he heard a splash and a woman yelp.

In the atrium, a maidservant stood alone with hands on her chest and a wild look of fright on her face.

He forced back a chuckle.

"Something fell into the impluvium. I think it was a bird or an animal." She pointed a quivering finger at the fountain.

David jumped onto the edge of the pool, proud of his good aim. He wanted to shout victory, but the woman watched in stunned silence. He also had to make haste and get back to Cornelia. He jumped into the fountain, and water soaked his tunic as he fished out the ball.

He glanced around again. So far, no one but the one servant had witnessed his game. Maybe he should throw the ball back through the roof? Maybe he could get it as far as the plaza? But what if it got stuck? And how would he explain that to Titus?

Anxious to return to his post, he leaped out of the fountain, nodded to the maidservant, showing her the ball—not an animal or a bird. He hurried to leave, then skidded to a stop and turned to face her.

"Don't tell?"

The woman smiled, hands on her hips, and shook her head. "Be gone. You're dripping water all over the place, and I'm the one who has to clean it up."

He ran and slid over the tiles back to the plaza, nearly losing his balance. Thankfully, Cornelia was still in the baths. He glanced back at the roof with a sense of pride and victory. Same time tomorrow he would do it again.

The following day, Titus met David in the plaza again. This time he showed David how to juggle two balls in one hand.

"When the first ball reaches its highest point, throw the second ball up behind it, like this." Titus juggled the two balls in one hand with ease. He did the same in his other hand, then tossed the balls one by one to David.

David threw the second ball up too high. The next time, he threw it out too far. Then it wasn't high enough. Each time he tried to catch the second ball, he forgot to catch the first, or he would remember to catch the first and forget to catch the second.

Titus laughed. "Not too high, Damonus. Relax your arm, just like I showed you yesterday. Learn to do this with each hand." He smiled and turned to go. "Keep practicing."

David tossed one ball and then the other. He caught one, but the second time they both fell to the ground. As he picked them up, a giggle came from the porch near the stairs. He knew that giggle well.

Alethea stood behind one of the large wooden stakes, watching him. Slowly, she stepped away and came toward him. As usual, she danced as she walked, wearing a long stola without a belt. Her hair hung in a thick braid where loose strands went wildly astray.

"You need to comb your hair," she said.

"*My* hair? Obviously you haven't looked in the mirror."

She turned her nose in the air. "Of course not! I'm waiting for Portia to take me to the baths."

David tried not to smile at her efforts to imitate her mother's tone. She might be a little girl, but he got butterflies in his stomach whenever she came around. Maybe it was because she reminded him of Sarah? Maybe because she treated him more like a friend than a slave? Or maybe he felt close to her because they had so much in common? She was the only real friend he had right now. He'd enjoyed fishing with Marcus the day before, and his chamber-mates were friendly enough, but she was the only one he could be open with about his faith. He wondered if she had any friends she could trust. "I'll get a comb for you." She skipped into the baths and returned. "Sit down and let me do your hair." A big smile broadened her face.

He certainly didn't think she was serious. Only girls or servants combed one another's hair, not boys.

She frowned. "You have to sit down." She sounded disappointed. Facing the ground, she pouted, but her dark eyes peered up at him.

Would she cry? If so, then he'd really be in trouble. He didn't want to hurt her feelings, so he looked around to see if anyone watched. The porch above the atrium was empty; no slaves were in their chambers at this time of day. No one was in sight at any of the doors. All was quiet, so he sat on a step at the edge of the plaza where he could keep a lookout. Such a dangerous situation for something so insignificant. He could get punished if found in this position. Alethea didn't seem to have any concept of this.

She combed through his hair. "You know, you ought to comb your own hair. It's very lazy and careless of you to have someone else do it."

"Take the plank out of your own eye." He tossed one ball up and caught it.

She raised her eyebrows at him.

She must not understand. Abba used to say things like that. "Maybe I don't want to have my hair combed?" He tried not to sound frustrated and tossed the ball again. He could be trying his aim for the fountain again, but instead he was stuck being made beautiful at the risk of a beating. Was it irony that he faced the wooden stakes?

"Why do you say such strange things? You sound like Mpampas." She combed slowly from the nape of his neck to his forehead. Then she brought the comb forward behind his ears. It sent tingles down his back and arms.

He stopped playing with the ball. Though in his relaxed state, he still kept an eye open for intruders. "Why do people call you Aucella?"

"My mpampas gave me the name." She took in a long breath and smiled. "We used to dance and sing together. He called me his little bird, and ever since then the rest of the family calls me that." She frowned. "But I don't like it when Grandfather calls me Aucella." She smiled and put her face close to his.

Her nose was so close, his eyes crossed.

"You may call me little bird if you like." She started on his hair again with renewed vigor. "It's settled. My mpampas is no longer here, so for now on I will be your Aucella—not Grandfather's. He will still call me by that name though." She waved the comb in his face. "But I'll pretend he's saying Alethea."

David's cheeks warmed. Again she reminded him of Sarah. He resolved then and there, he would take care of her the way he should have taken care of Sarah. Did that mean he wouldn't try to escape? If he escaped, who would take care of Alethea? He tossed the ball again to try and distract himself from his thoughts; he missed.

Alethea giggled.

"What are you laughing at?" He hoped she wasn't laughing because he dropped the ball.

"One piece won't stay down." She spit on her hand and wiped it in his hair.

"Hey!" He jumped up.

She tried to pull him down. "I'm not finished yet."

David dropped back on the step. He hoped the spit would dry fast. How disgusting. He also hoped nobody came and saw him in this embarrassing position. Thoughts of being punished were no longer important when he realized how he must look. He didn't mind the combing so much, but if anyone came and made fun of him, he might give them a solid punch, slave or not.

He tossed his ball again and caught it. "Aucella means little bird, but what does Alethea mean? It's not a Latin name. Is it Greek?"

"It means truth. My mpampas's name was Galen Aletheos, and of course, I'm named after him."

Oh, yes, truth. He knew that. Why didn't he make the connection? He'd only read it a thousand times in his father's scrolls.

"You're not Roman." She continued her administrations on his hair. "Are you named after your mpampas?"

"I call him Abba, but his name was Aaron." It felt good to say his name; it made Abba seem alive again. His thoughts turned back to Alethea's name. "Hmmm, truth. God's word is truth. Abba would say that. What else did he say . . . ?" He tried to imagine his abba speaking. "God seeks those who worship Him in spirit and in truth." He was pleased with himself. He wanted to remember everything Abba used to teach him. "I like your name."

Just then, the door to the atrium opened and closed. Alethea quickly stepped aside and hid the comb behind her back.

David let the rest of the balls fall down the steps and bent to pick them up. His heart raced in his chest as he faced the ground. He feared the person coming might notice the heat on his cheeks.

Portia came from around the corner with Paulus on her hip. She smiled and took Alethea by the hand. "Let's get you cleaned up."

He watched Alethea go, relieved they hadn't been caught. She glanced over her shoulder and waved at him with her braid, flashing him a big smile, then skipped away with Portia.

He messed his hair and went about juggling, his face still warm. He couldn't keep the two balls in the air.

As the months went by, David became a good juggler. So good, he even learned to juggle knives. Titus also taught him how to juggle in pairs, which was quite fun. He and Titus practiced in the gymnasium where there was less distraction.

Often, Aloysius came to watch them, and David worked hard to impress his master. The hope of freedom was always on his mind.

David and Titus juggled balls, sticks, arrows, knives, and wooden swords. Real swords were too dangerous.

In the gymnasium, Titus stood several feet away from David. "Catch this." He threw a stick in David's direction, but David jumped away from it. Titus wasn't tossing the stick up like he did when they were juggling. Instead, he threw it straight at him. Titus had another stick. "Catch it, Damonus. Pretend we're juggling together." He threw the stick.

The rules of juggling flashed through David's mind. He reached out and missed the stick. Normally the stick would be turning circles in the air and land right in his hand. But this was different. Sometimes they used techniques where they would grab the object. Perhaps if he did that he could catch it?

"Snatch it out of the air," Titus said. "Concentrate and relax." He threw another one.

David relaxed and grabbed it.

"Good. When it comes right at you, jump back and grab it." Titus threw another stick. "Catch."

David jumped back and caught it.

They did this until Titus was out of sticks. He then picked up the wooden swords that lay at his feet.

David didn't mind catching the sticks, they were light and didn't have any sharp edges. But if Titus planned on throwing the swords as hard and fast as he threw the sticks, David wasn't sure he could catch them.

Titus took one of the wooden swords by the handle and held it back over his shoulder. He then pointed at David with his free hand.

David's heart hammered. He knew what was coming.

"Now, when I throw this at you, I want you to jump to the side and catch it by its handle, like you did the sticks. Just relax, and remember the rules of juggling. Concentrate on the handle, not on the blade." Titus drew the wooden sword back farther. "Ready?"

David wanted to run. "Ready."

Titus threw the sword hard and fast, as if it were a javelin.

It came right at David. He sprang to the side and ducked.

It landed in the sand behind him.

"Focus on its handle and don't be afraid." Titus prepared to throw another.

It was only wood. Wood couldn't do that much damage. David held his breath. He focused on its handle, jumped back, reached out, and caught the sword.

He did it! Catching the sword because of its size was actually easier than catching the sticks. He wanted to do it again, and when he looked up, Titus was ready to throw another.

David dropped the sword, jumped to the side, and caught the next one.

Titus threw another, and David caught it.

After the swords were all thrown, Titus picked up the javelins. Thick wads of cloth were wrapped around their sharp heads.

"These are the most difficult to catch because they're fast. You must be alert." He took one and made ready to throw it. "The same rule applies for the javelin as for the sword. Jump to the side and focus."

David took a deep breath, beginning to feel confident. After all, he just caught several flying swords, this should be easy. Too bad Aloysius wasn't here to see this.

He shook out his hands and slightly bent his knees. "Ready."

Titus threw the javelin hard and fast.

It flew much faster than the sword. David reached out too slow and dove out of the way. He slammed his fist on the ground and crawled to his feet. It seemed impossible. Only a gladiator could catch something like this.

"Relax and focus." Titus threw another.

David reached out and took hold of the javelin. Did he actually catch it? He looked down at his hand. Yes, he'd caught it. Chills went through him as he dropped it and readied himself for the next.

When they were finished for the day, it occurred to David that he ought to be learning how to throw a javelin, not catch it. "Why aren't you teaching me how to fight?"

"A good warrior first learns how to protect himself before he learns to do harm to his opponent. When you learn how to disable your enemy, then you can attack."

"What do I need to do, wait until he runs out of javelins or is foolish enough to throw his sword?"

Titus gazed hard at David. He turned and picked up one of the wooden swords and shields. Titus handed the sword to David. "Swing at me."

David carefully swung his sword at Titus.

"No! Swing like you mean it. Put your weight into it and all your strength. I have my shield, I'm protected."

David took a deep breath and swung his sword with all his might in hopes to impress Titus with his strength.

Titus jumped back, and instead of using his shield to block the swing, he used it to push the sword farther in the direction it was going. He then grabbed the handle of the sword and yanked it out of David's hand, making him fall forward.

David landed on all fours, stunned by the smooth quick movement of Titus. He crawled to his feet, relieved that his ribs didn't hurt. In fact, they didn't even feel sore.

Titus looked down at him. "You have a lot to learn."

seven

"Hold on! Don't let go!" David shouted.

Marcus rode the sow, his head and spindly arms bobbing in the air.

The twins who shared David's chamber doubled over with laughter, and the dog raced past them, barking.

David couldn't keep from laughing.

He and Marcus had tied a rope around the sow's neck, and the children took turns riding it. The poor animal didn't know where to run. She turned in all directions and squealed madly. Marcus's thin brown hair bounced as the swine tore up and down the field. He lost his grip, slid off, and dragged a few feet.

"Let go of the rope!" David shouted, running after them.

The rest of the children shrieked with laughter and took off after the pig, running and waving their sticks. They managed to corner her against the south wall next to the hill.

David and Marcus were the instigators of the day's frenzy, and they wrestled with the sow, forcing her against the wall. David steered clear of her mouth, fearing he might get bitten. If Marcus hadn't been there to help him, he never would have taken this on by himself. The angry sow let out a piercing squeal. The slave girls, along with Vibia and Alethea, covered their ears. The animal pushed back and forth, knocking him against the wall, and the rope burned his hands. By this time, he was nearly on top of the sow and thought she might try to run again. Luckily, the stable boys jumped in to help.

Lucius pushed through the girls.

"It's my turn! I want a turn!"

"You just went before me." Marcus struggled with David and the other boys to keep the animal in her place. "The others . . . want a ride too."

Lucius's eyes welled with tears and his face reddened, matching the tints in his chestnut hair. He stomped off and yelled a few things that everyone ignored.

David spotted Alethea. Dirt littered her white stola, and loose tresses fell from her thick braid, clinging to her flushed cheeks.

"You want a ride?" he asked, fighting the sow.

"No!" Alethea stepped back, her eyes widened, and she waved her hands in front of her as if to push the very idea away. "If she falls on me, I'll get squashed."

David laughed, trying not to lose his hold, his muscles now aching. He imagined Alethea flattened by the pig. There really wouldn't be much left of her if the animal fell on that twiggy, frail body.

Marcus grabbed one of the stable boys who begged for a ride and set him on top of the sow. "Hold onto the rope and squeeze with your legs, that way you won't fall off."

The boy nodded in readiness, Marcus and David released the sow, and she squealed off. The children shrieked with excitement and ran around the hill, chasing her toward the stables.

David jogged behind, watching the boy ride away. He held on fairly well. He might last longer than Marcus. David's arms were heavy from the strain of fighting with the animal. He was glad for the short break.

He was nearing the stables when Marcus came next to him, his form meeting David eye to eye. "We're going hunting this afternoon. Father says you're to join us."

David nodded. He enjoyed his adventures with Marcus. Hunting was just one of the many things they did together.

"Damonus." Titus stood in the gate of the courtyard, looking serene and polished. A stark contrast with the game taking place. "Come."

David followed him toward the gymnasium. "Your ribs are obviously healed. It's time to begin the most difficult part of your training."

Ω

David and Titus stood alone in the open-air gymnasium. The soft sand crept comfortably between David's toes. These past months had been quite good, now that he had Marcus and the stable boys as pals, and he especially enjoyed the time he and Titus had spent in the gym. He had become a good juggler, and he liked to spend his free time showing off for the children and other slaves.

The members of the family, including Aloysius, enjoyed it as well, except for Cornelia, but she never enjoyed anything. She seemed angry at the world, so over the months he learned not to take it personally. He'd also avoided getting into trouble. Until now, nobody had caught him throwing balls into the fountain, and Alethea turned out to be a perfect guard to make sure no one was looking.

"When I was born, my father lived in the far east, in Asia." Titus towered over David, and he spoke in crisp tones. "He was a silk trader and spent many years learning their ways and customs. The people there don't depend on brute strength, but on wits." Titus straightened his bracelet. "They fight with swords, much like we do, but they also fight without weapons." He picked lint off the front of his tunic. "When I was a child, they taught me their methods, and this is what I've been teaching you."

Titus circled him and walked with his hands behind his back. He seemed especially serious today. "You're a unique boy and very lucky too. The gods must favor you, because you ought to be dead."

David swallowed hard. Titus hadn't spoken to him about the gods in all the time he'd been at the villa. What would Titus do if he spoke the truth about his faith? Perhaps kill him.

David could spare his own life. He could lie about his beliefs. But the thought made him want to vomit. Was he willing to die for his God? He prayed for strength and courage. "Only one God has shown me mercy, Master. He sent you to rescue me, and for that, I'm grateful." David breathed, proud of how mature and strong he sounded.

"Hmm, you worship only one god." Titus came to stand in front of him. He looked him up and down. "The only people I know who worship one god are the Jews and the Christians. Which one are you?"

"I'm a Christian." David's world spun.

"I see. So you worship the god of the Jews." Titus looked down his nose at him. "You're just a child. A child worships the gods of his father. One day you will also worship my gods and the Roman gods."

David's heart pounded in his chest. He wondered if Titus could hear its drumming. "I worship the God above your gods and above all Roman gods." If his life ended here and now, at least he would not die in shame, having denied Elohim. He knew many Christians who stood up for their faith, even in the face of death. Now it was his turn.

He made ready to defend himself. He waited for Titus to strike. Although Titus showed no expression on his face, David thought he detected a hint of a smile in his eyes.

"What was your father's profession, Damonus?"

"He was a scribe, Master."

Titus was thoughtful and quiet; finally, he smiled. "You're a courageous young man. Your father would have been proud. You'll make a good fighter."

Aloysius appeared at the door. He crossed his arms and braced his legs apart, watching, scrutinizing.

Titus shot his hand above David and shouted, "First lesson!"

David ducked, nearly choking on his spit. He thought Titus was going to hit him.

Titus bent closer. "You will learn to fall." The whites of his eyes flashed, and his lips curled into a wry smile.

Relief washed over David. He'd survived. Then his mind reeled. What did he say? Something about falling? With the conversation about his faith still fresh in his mind, he couldn't follow Titus's line of thinking. He took in a deep breath and looked around. He thought he would finally learn to spar, but there were no swords.

"What about weapons?"

"No weapons today."

David had looked forward to the time he would learn to sword fight, and now again, he would have to wait.

Titus first showed him some important stretches. They worked on his arms and then his legs. Titus held his hands flat before him and moved them as if he were dancing. Some of his movements were swift as though slicing the air. Then he moved in slow, deliberate, even motions.

Titus told David to imitate these movements.

All the while, Aloysius watched them, so David did his best to be impressive, even though he had no idea what they were doing or why they were doing it.

David hesitated when Titus dropped into the splits. "You must learn that pain is in your mind. It's your mind that will control the level of pain. Stretch your legs, Damonus."

David eased his legs into a split position.

"Now farther."

He hesitated. He didn't think he could stretch them farther.

"Don't think about the pain. Focus your mind on what you want from your body. Focus on the things around you, the air, the feel of the sand. Don't focus on the pain. You control your body, it does not control you. Will it to obey."

Hoping to please Aloysius, David did as he was bid and stretched his legs out until they hurt. His face heated at the pulling agony of unused muscles. After several seconds, the pain began to subside.

"Do it again."

He stretched his legs even farther. It didn't matter what Titus said, pain was pain and this hurt, but he willed his body to obey and tried to focus on impressing Aloysius. Anything to get his focus off the pain. This was just the beginning. One day, he would please his master enough to earn his freedom.

After the stretching and strange hand movements, Titus stood and waited for David to climb to his feet.

"A bad fall could kill you." Titus straightened with his hands behind his back. "If you get knocked down by your opponent and hit your head on the ground or break a bone, it'll be difficult, if not impossible, to jump back up and defend yourself." Titus circled him again.

David fought the urge to turn and follow.

"You should always practice falling even when you're a great fighter. No matter how good you are, you'll do more falling than fighting." Titus stopped in front of him. "Remember how you learned to jump back from the sword? Many times you will need to dive and fall from a sword. What you're about to learn will help you do that."

Titus motioned for David to kneel. He then placed his hand on David's forehead. "I'm going to push you. Put your chin to your chest, and as you fall back, roll into it."

Titus pushed him back. David, keeping his chin firmly on his chest, rolled into the fall and came up on his knees.

"Very good. But next time, come up onto your feet."

Titus had David falling in every direction and all over the place. "Tuck and roll," he said. "Always keep your chin down."

David learned many new ways of falling. He fell only from his knees: forwards, backwards, and side to side. He also learned to fall without catching his weight with his hands.

"Use your shoulder and roll into it, chin down."

Once David mastered this, Titus made him fall from a standing position. He imagined diving into one of the swimming pools at the baths. When he hit the ground, he went into a roll.

David tucked and rolled until sweat trickled down the sides of his face and he was so dizzy he couldn't see straight.

Every now and then, his gaze went to Aloysius, curious to know what the master thought of these strange lessons. But the interest in his master's eyes told David the man was entranced. Filled with wonder, perhaps even longing.

Titus knelt on his knees. "Sit up and face me."

David sat on his knees before Titus.

"I have a lot to teach you. You'll learn to move like the beasts of the earth." Titus waved his hand in the air. "I will teach you to fly like a bird, to slither like a snake, and to be as ferocious as a tiger."

David felt foolish, like the pig squealing in the field. He definitely wasn't a tiger or a bird; a snake maybe, since he felt like lying flat on his belly from exhaustion.

Aloysius turned and left the arena. David's hopes went with him. Had his master been pleased? Impressed with his performance?

"What about swords?" he asked, impatient to learn what interested him most.

"You'll learn how to sword fight, but not from me. You'll learn with Marcus and Lucius under their instructor."

"When do they have their lessons? Why aren't they here now?"

"I won't teach them what you're learning."

David rubbed his arms and legs that quivered from the exertion. "Why are you teaching me this?"

"If I had children, they would learn these things from me. But I chose not to have children to be raised as slaves. You are to be the son I will never have."

David let his words sink in. He was grateful to Titus for saving his life. He and Titus had also grown closer over the past months, and David liked him. He had to admit that Titus was the closest he had to a father and definitely deserved his respect, but that didn't mean he would become Titus's son. The last thing David wanted was to be forced to call Titus Father. He didn't want to hurt Titus, but honesty would be best.

"I have only one father and he is dead." Saying the words out loud drove an ax through his heart. He'd only spoken openly to Alethea about his parents, but even then, he didn't say much.

"I won't take the place of your father. I'll only teach you how to survive and how to fight." Titus's gaze held David's.

David couldn't help but notice how Titus's words clashed with those of his father. Abba would never have stressed any importance on learning how to fight. David thought about fighting. It was rather fun and swords intrigued him. The things Titus taught him slowly made sense. And the desire to defeat the evil soldier, Aulus, played prominently in his mind.

He imagined facing the soldier that nearly killed him the night his parents were taken. He pictured Aulus swinging his sword the way he had when he'd cut David's cheek. But instead of lying there helpless, David pushes the sword away, causing the soldier to fall heavily to his knees. Then he leaps far above the soldier's head. He lands with power, and the ground shudders.

The soldier charges him, and David falls into the splits, grabbing his sword by its handle. He flings the warrior violently to the wall. David then springs to his feet, seeing his enemy's shocked, ugly scarred face. He towers over the once great warrior, who now cowers at his feet, and raises the sword high above his head, brandishing it with a hearty laugh. He brings it down with violent force into the wicked man's skull. David, the great fighter, more powerful than any gladiator, the great avenger, reigns victorious over his enemies!

His thoughts snapped back to Abba. He'd always taught that God was love and that David should strive to be like *Jehovah*. Those who live by the sword, die by the sword, his abba used to say. It was about being meek; you were power under control. David liked the sound of that. Power under control.

He looked up at Titus, the dark man sitting before him, once a stranger, now a friend. Still, David longed for Abba.

Ω

After David cleaned up in the baths, Titus escorted him to his chamber above the atrium.

"Wait here until I return."

David fell onto his bed, exhausted. His knuckles ached and his muscles quivered from the intense workout.

When Titus returned, he held four thick scrolls in his hands.

David straightened. He knew those scrolls.

"When I went to your home, I found these." Titus dropped them on the bed.

David held his breath as he untied the leather thong that held the spools together. He put them down on his bed and lay them apart. His hands quivered, not from the workout anymore, but because of what he was about to discover. Could these be what he thought they were?

He slowly stroked the parchment of one as he unrolled it and recognized Abba's handwriting. The memoirs of Matthew. Another, a letter of the acts of the apostles of Christ. He opened the other scrolls. The book of Daniel the prophet and John's Revelation. Abba had made him memorize every written line, as well as paragraph upon paragraph from other letters. That didn't mean he understood everything; he could simply quote them. "These . . . belonged to my father." He choked on his words.

"I'll let you have them because they belonged to your father. But take care that the master doesn't learn of your God."

"Why give them to me if it's dangerous to have them?"

A low, rumbling chuckle carried off the walls from Titus, something about it was dark, sinister. "Do you not realize you're in danger of losing your life every day? One misstep from you, one foul mood from the master, could be your death." He snorted. "Your life is already in danger, boy."

David realized then that Titus had been testing him in the gymnasium when he had questioned him about his faith. "You read them?"

Titus nodded. "I found others, but they were water-damaged."

David remembered his home, a single chamber apartment. The soldiers had ransacked the place. His father kept all his scrolls on a high table. The water his mother kept in the room from the outdoor fountain must have damaged the others. His mamma. How he missed her warm touch, her kisses, and her songs.

Titus tossed a coin on the bed.

David hesitated, then picked it up and turned it over in his hand. Just a Roman coin. On the back, an elegant woman sat on top of seven hills. *The harlot named Babylon is the city of Rome.* His father's voice echoed in his mind, reminding him of the mental picture he had of the harlot sitting on a beast with seven heads, drunk on the blood of the saints.

"The city of seven hills." Titus folded his arms and leaned against the doorpost. "Had I not read the letter of Daniel, I wouldn't have understood the revelation of that writer, John." Titus straightened. "A serious so-called 'prophesy.'" He turned toward the door. "The fall of Rome." He chuckled. "Impossible."

David looked up; he was alone. He took in the familiar scent of the parchment. He kissed the scrolls, and tears flowed freely down his cheeks. He ran his fingers up and down the painstakingly drafted words. His abba's hands once touched this parchment. He had spent long hours making copies of any letters the church received. And John's revelation was the most exciting, the most encouraging.

"Jehovah-Shammah, thank you. Thank you for giving me this small part of my father." He gazed down at the scrolls, tears blurring his vision.

"These are the words of the Lord," Abba used to say.

David touched the spool's handle. The magnitude of what was written on these sheets of parchment filled his mind, sent chills over his body, and the hairs on his forearms rose. These scrolls were an open door to the world from his past, a world that began two nights before his parents were taken away, the night he was immersed into Christ, when his heart pounded as heavily in his chest as it did now.

"You never left me." David wiped away his tears. "I'm not alone. You'll always be here."

He rolled up the scrolls then lay on the bed and gently, but firmly, held them to his chest.

A murmuring song filled his head. A soft voice whispered through his mind and danced through the room. Mamma's voice.

Mamma smiled and kissed his cheek. Her sweet scent mingled with her whispering words.

"Don't cry, my son." She brushed David's hair from his forehead, her gentle caress and the warmth of her voice touching his skin. "The Lord will work all things out for good."

She kissed him again softly, tenderly, her fingers stroking his cheek. She stood to leave and draped her cloak over her shoulders. As she opened the door, a cool breeze chilled him.

Then she was gone.

David's eyes flew open. He bolted upright in bed. The chamber door had swung open from a gust of wind and slammed against the wall. How he longed to be back in that dream. But his mother's words echoing in his mind drew his attention to those same words repeated by fellow Christians in their secret meetings.

He glanced down at the scrolls. He would devour every word Abba penned until he knew he was pleasing to Elohim. He shivered as he contemplated his situation. Though orphaned and a slave, weren't things working out well for him? Very well, indeed.

He held the scrolls to his cheek. "Mamma and Abba taught me well, Elohim. I will make You proud."

eight

For three years David hadn't set foot outside the villa's walls, which made finding an opportunity to escape impossible. So, like a dog eager to please his master, he spent every moment entertaining Aloysius in an attempt to earn his freedom.

But now, with Aloysius away from the villa, the master's wall didn't feel quite as confining, so David agreed to play with Marcus and the stable boys. Together, they carried several wooden swords and shields to the field. As they neared the hill, Alethea's screams and cries carried through the air, mingled in with Vibia's crying.

David dropped his equipment and ran toward the hill.

Lucius laughed and held a doll high over Vibia's head. She jumped up and down, trying to get the doll. He threw it over the wall.

Vibia screamed and pounded her older brother, but her blows didn't faze him, and he mimicked her. Tears covered Vibia's face. Her reddish brown hair was pulled back into a large braid. It swung around as she turned and ran, screaming and crying, toward the house.

David ran up to Alethea who stood against the wall with her face in her hands. "Did he hurt you?"

She shook her head.

He was relieved to know she wasn't hurt, but Lucius had done something to her and just as he was about to ask, Marcus ran up to Lucius and grabbed him by the arm.

"What'd you do that for?"

Lucius wrenched his arm free. "They were making trouble."

"That's not true!" Alethea's dark eyes filled with tears and her cheeks flushed. "We were playing in the woods when Lucius jumped out and scared us. He grabbed our dolls and wouldn't give them back." She clenched her fists and stomped her foot. "He even broke the arm off mine." She wiped her tears with the back of her hand and looked at David. "Mpampas made her for me, now she's gone." She wailed and ran past the boys toward the house.

David clenched his fists, trying his best to control his anger. He hated to see her cry.

"Your daddy was a rebel!" Lucius shouted after her. "Anything he made ought to be destroyed." Lucius turned toward the boys with a look of triumph.

David wanted to tear Lucius's head off and stomp on it, but he stood as still as he could, remembering his father's words about self-control.

Marcus knocked Lucius on the back of his head. "You can thank Fortuna that Grandfather and Father aren't here, or they'd whip you good."

If only they were here. David would have found secret pleasure in Lucius's punishment.

Lucius strutted away from the boys toward the swords and shields. "Holy Jupiter! Are we going to play Troy?"

"What do you think?" Marcus ambled toward him.

"Fortuna is smiling on me today." Lucius went after the swords and picked the one he wanted. When he found one, he chose his shield. "Who's going to be it?" He looked around. "I think Damonus should be it."

"I think you ought to be it," Marcus said.

"No," Lucius whined. He wielded his sword and pointed it in David's face. "He's the slave. He ought to be it."

Marcus picked up a sword and knocked Lucius's out of his hands, nearly nicking David in the face.

David stepped back. Anytime Lucius was around, there was nothing but trouble. His patience with the little nit wore thin.

"I'll be it." Marcus picked up Lucius's sword and tossed it to David.

"That was mine!"

"Not anymore," Marcus said, smirking.

David picked up a shield, wishing Marcus hadn't given him Lucius's sword. It would only cause more trouble.

Marcus drew a long line across the field with his wooden blade.

One of the twins yanked on David's tunic. "I don't understand this game."

David bent down. "The idea is for all of us to get Marcus to cross this line. Once he's crossed, he loses."

"Oh," the boy said. "That ought to be easy."

But it wasn't easy. The game was fierce and David charged after Marcus. All the things Titus had taught him flashed through his mind, including what he'd learned from Lucius and Marcus's instructor. He and Marcus clashed swords and the other boys moved in on them.

David imagined Marcus as Aulus, the evil soldier who had taken his parents. He thrust his sword hard at him, just missing him in the gut. Marcus blocked another swing with his shield and charged forward. David dove to the ground, avoiding Marcus's blade. He came to his feet and roared inside. He was a great warrior who had come to destroy the soldier and avenge his family.

He went after Marcus again. He pounded him, hitting his shield, arms, and legs, weakening him.

"Get out of my way, fool!" Lucius shoved one of the twins to the ground.

Marcus swung his sword at David and waved his shield in the other boys' direction. He ran.

David shouted a warrior's cry and charged after Marcus. The rest of the boys came upon Marcus, but he broke free from the group.

David ran with might, power, and strength. He, the mighty warrior, would avenge his family! He spotted Lucius out of the corner of his eye, swinging his sword at his legs.

With no time to react, Lucius's sword sliced David's feet out from under him, and he hit the dirt hard, sliding on his front. He laid on the ground, stunned, the fallen warrior slain by one of his own.

"He's mine!" The brunt of Lucius's shield slammed against David's back. "Did you see that?" Lucius's laughter echoed through the field.

David rolled over and glared at Lucius's big, laughing mouth. His shins throbbed, and he spit dirt out of his mouth.

"You're supposed to be on my team!" David climbed to his feet and with a lunge, he tackled Lucius to the ground. Lucius's shocked, freckled face became the object of David's fury, and he pounded it as hard as he could.

Lucius ground his hand into David's face.

David flung it away. He sprang forward, straddling Lucius. He pinned his shoulders to the ground and held his arms down with his knees. He punched him in the mouth, then in the cheek, and was about to crush his nose when Marcus grabbed him from behind, clamping down on his arms. Two more boys dragged David off.

"Damonus!" someone shouted.

David kicked and squirmed, trying to break from their grasp. He ached for one last punch to Lucius's nose, but the boys lifted David to his feet.

He fought to break free. He twisted and turned.

"Damonus, stop! Damonus!" the boys shouted.

David's world spun, and he ached to pound Lucius as he still lay on the ground, whimpering. He was nothing but a baby.

"Damonus!" Titus's voice silenced all the shouts.

David broke from the boys' grasp and found himself standing before Titus. His spinning world came to a shuddering stop. The other boys dropped back, and David stood by himself.

Titus's eyes bore into David's and his lips curved downward into a bone-chilling frown. "Go to your chamber."

David didn't waste any time. Even though his fists itched for Lucius, he marched through the boys toward the villa. He was about to kick dirt on Lucius as he walked by when Marcus yanked Lucius to his feet.

David walked backwards to watch the scene.

"Get up, you blubbering goat!" Marcus got in his face. "You deserved it, dog." Marcus pushed him. "If you ever do that again, I'll pound you, myself."

It was satisfying to see Marcus put Lucius in his place.

Lucius whimpered and ran past David to the villa. David fought the urge to chase after him and tackle him again.

Later, David sat on his bed, still too angry to regret what he had done, when Titus entered the chamber and stood over him.

"I spoke with Marcus and he told me what happened. I also spoke with Renata to question what type of punishment she deems appropriate for your behavior."

David dared to meet Titus's gaze. Would he be banished, killed, flogged? He certainly deserved punishment.

"You will be whipped."

David's hands suddenly went cold, and fear like a sudden rain shower ran from his head to his toes. His mind immediately went back to the one whipping he'd seen. Titus was an expert with the cat. Nine long leather thongs; each had bits of glass tied into their ends, and each lash tore into the man's bare flesh, leaving bloody stripes over his back, stomach, chest, legs, and upper arms. The man had passed out before all the required lashes had been delivered. But even though the man was unconscious, Titus delivered the last stroke.

Titus tossed a breechcloth onto his lap. "Put this on and make haste. Master Lucius and I will be waiting for you in the plaza."

David took off his dirty tunic and put on the cloth, exposing his bare chest and legs. His fingers trembled as he tucked the extra material into his girdle. He thought to escape, but where would he hide? Where would he run? Eventually, he would be found and tied to one of the stakes. He didn't want Lucius to see that he was afraid.

Lucius would only play on his fear, and David would never hear the end of it.

"Jehovah-Shammah, let me survive." He said the words aloud. Perhaps passing out wouldn't be such a terrible thing?

His knees weakened as he shuffled down to the plaza where Titus stood with the cat. Lucius looked smug, with his arms folded over his chest. David noticed with satisfaction that Lucius's eyes were red and swollen and his nose was packed with wads of linen.

He had smashed him in the nose after all. A ripple of victory ran up his spine, but the sight of the stake shot cold chills of fear back down.

Titus, a frown etched on his face, placed the cat under his arm, and without a word, he tied a heavy leather strap around one of David's wrists. The touch made his arms weak and his mouth went dry. Titus then wrapped his arms around the large, dreaded stake, and bound both hands together.

Splinters rubbed into David's chest and arms when he moved. He couldn't help but watch Titus as he stood next to him, wanting to see the look on his face when he administered the first blow. Titus took the cat out from under his arm and held it out to Lucius.

"Me? You want me to flog him?"

"Damonus has shamed you, therefore you must regain your honor," Titus said with a coolness in his tone that made David shiver.

David would have preferred that Titus whip him. Having Lucius do it made his blood boil.

Titus shook the whip, insisting Lucius take it.

Lucius held out a quivering hand and accepted the cat.

"Strike ten times, save one." Titus stepped away and crossed his arms.

Lucius stepped out of David's view. He heard the cat slither along the plaza's stones.

He looked for the slave who held a bowl, and the other who would hand him the stones to count the strikes. They were out of view.

David tensed when the whip sang through the air. The cat's tails wrapped around his body and he jumped. The splinters from the stake stabbed into his skin, but there was no pain from the whip.

"One!" Titus's voice boomed.

Again, the cat sang out, wrapping around his body, and its tips thrashed against the wooden stake on the other side, with only the thongs wrapped around his back.

Where was the pain?

"Two!" Titus boomed.

Every swing of the cat and feel of its tails made David shudder, and his body was wet with perspiration. At one point, the tails had wrapped around his face. Suppose it had gotten him in the eye? Again and again, the cat sang out, but there was still no pain.

"Eight!" he heard Titus call out.

Only one more to go—but where was the sting, the bite, the pain that would bring him to his knees?

The cat sang, and this time its vicious tails tore into David's flesh. Pain seared like fire across his arms and back. His knees buckled. He screamed and arched, no longer caring that the splinters dug into his chest and arms. The pain was overwhelming, and he pressed the top of his head hard against the stake. Heat pounded to every limb as his heart slammed against his ribs. He forced back the tears that threatened; he would not give Lucius the pleasure.

Lucius shouted victory.

Titus was there, calmly untying David. "That was ten, save one."

"What? But I only got him one time!" Lucius shouted.

David's hands were free. His arms and chest felt chapped and raw as his back twitched with pain. His mind returned to when the soldier had cut his cheek. Just think of it that way. It's nothing more than a cut, but it was far more painful than anything he ever remembered.

Titus frowned. "If we waited for you to hit him nine times, the goddess of peace would declare war. Speak to your instructor about your skills with the cat." He took the whip, slung it over his shoulder, and turned to a slave holding two small bowls and a cloth. "First clean his wounds, then apply the honey."

The slave nodded and scurried over to David as Titus left the plaza.

The slave cleaned the wounds on David's back and arms. It burned like fire.

Lucius glared at David and thrust his freckled nose into his face. "Next time you need a flogging, I will do it and I will do it right." Lucius spat on his face.

David straightened from the onslaught. He forced his chin up a notch, not daring to raise his fists. He refused to flinch, refused to give Lucius the satisfaction. David's gaze burned into Lucius as the spit rolled down his cheek and onto his neck.

Finally, Lucius turned and stormed off.

David wiped the spit off with the back of his hand.

The slave then applied the honey. "This will prevent infection." The ointment soothed him, although the cuts continued to burn.

With quivering fingers, David plucked out some of the splinters from his skin. Tears threatened. He'd disappointed Titus. Lucius was just a pest.

When the slave finished cleaning his wounds, David sat heavily on the step and worked out his splinters. His back and arms still hurt and burned.

"How're you doing?" Marcus came up beside him, tossing a ball in the air.

David shrugged, not trusting his voice, fearing he might cry. He appreciated Marcus's concern.

"You're lucky Grandfather's in Rome. If he'd been here, he would have had Titus thrash you." Marcus tossed the ball up and tried to hit it with his bicep the way David would when he juggled, but it flopped to the ground. "You remember hearing about the volcano erupting in Heraculum and Pompei?" He scooped up the ball. "He and Father are finding out about the destruction; they might even go there. If they go, they'll be gone for a long time." He tossed the ball with his other hand and missed. It rolled on the ground. "By the time they get back this'll all be forgotten."

Marcus, giving up on the ball, shifted his weight to one leg and stuck a thumb in his belt. "I wouldn't be surprised if Titus purposely had Lucius flog you. Everyone knows Lucius doesn't know how to use the cat. Besides, Lucius deserved what he got."

When Marcus left him, David wandered into the woods next to the field. He knew he would have to make things up to Titus. In self-loathing, he side kicked a tree, his wounds tingling with pain. How could he be so foolish and let his temper get the best of him? Just that morning he had made an appointment with Ace after supper to share his father's scrolls. Now Ace would never be interested. David was a fool to think he could start acting like a grown man and be the Christian example he ought to be. At thirteen, and almost considered a man, he had failed. He not only disappointed Titus, worst of all, he disappointed Elohim. He grabbed a pinecone and threw it.

Pondering his dilemma, he leaned back against the wall but immediately shrieked and jumped away, his back burning like fire. He ran his hands through his hair. He thought of Yahshua and how He had suffered thirty lashes save one; and those who had applied the lashes knew how to use a cat. David only had a small taste of what His suffering must have been like.

"I'm sorry, Father. I should never have pounded Lucius. The problem is if the situation was the same, I'd do it again!" He clenched his fists in frustration. How would he ever earn his freedom if he couldn't control his temper?

Sighing, he looked up at the trees.

A large pine grew right next to the top of the wall. Its branches could easily be reached. He could climb up and over the wall. Taste freedom. Escape.

Suddenly, nothing mattered. It didn't matter that he disappointed Titus. It didn't matter that he lost his temper. None of it mattered.

He headed straight for the tree.

nine

David stood on top of the wall. He shaded his eyes from the sun as he gazed across the golden fields to the road that led to Rome.

Freedom. He could snatch it out of the air just like that. That confining cage suddenly flew wide open and he could climb right out.

A slave should obey his master. His father's voice echoed in his thoughts. So easy to say the words when not a slave. He shoved the memory to the back of his mind. He knelt down, contemplating the jump. A nearby hill made it possible for him to reach the ground on the other side.

When his feet hit the ground, he looked around him, as if his being on the other side of the wall might set off trumpeted alarms. But nothing happened. The wind blew and the birds continued to sing.

He jogged next to the wall, staying close to cover for fear there might be guards in one of the towers. When he got closer to the road, he would slip away from the safety of the wall. In the meantime, he leaped over bushes and weeds that threatened to keep him captive.

You have my word. This time David's own voice carried through his mind. He remembered the deal he made with Titus, to never again attempt an escape. He let the broken promise fly away into the wind. After all, Sarah was never found. Still, as he ran, his word became worth no more than wind, worth no more than the hot air coming out of his mouth. Let them all fly away, as he himself also flew.

Nothing would hold him back this time. He'd finally escape the life that only promised future scourging and slavery. He was free. At last, he could go home. The life he knew at the villa faded behind his feet as they flew towards freedom. No cords held him back. No chains bound him.

A small doll with a missing arm caught his eye. It lay helplessly on a bush, abandoned and left to be exposed to the winds and rains. David slowed his pace. It belonged to Alethea. Her tear-streaked face flashed through his mind.

Breathless, David stopped. She, like the doll, was abandoned. Left alone to be exposed to the storms of her family. He knelt and picked it up.

He was wrong. A chain did bind him. A single cord did hold him back.

Ω

After making things right with Titus and learning that Ace was still interested in reading his father's scrolls, David searched for Alethea. Since she was nowhere to be seen in or near the house, there was only one place she could be.

He found her hanging upside down from a low tree branch in the woods. Her long dark hair hung unbound. She sang one of her Greek songs, as usual, and held a handful of flowers to her nose. Her bracelets jingled from her movements, and she had tied her stola at her ankles, apparently to keep it from falling down over her head.

He forced back a chuckle, then cleared his throat.

"Aucella, I have something for you." It was easy for him to call her Aucella. He was determined to do everything for her that he didn't do for Sarah, and the name suited her. She was very much like a little bird, always singing and dancing, not to mention hanging around in trees.

Her eyes widened. She swung from the branch, and dropped down in front of him.

"Really? What do you have?" She untied the stola from around her ankles, pulled her disheveled hair out of her face, and picked up the flowers she had set on the ground. Her brown eyes lit with excitement when she noticed he hid something behind his back. She scrambled from side to side, trying to peek behind him. "What is it?"

He jumped away from her, enjoying his game even though it stretched the wounds on his back; he tried to ignore the pain. He wore a tunic from the waist down today to keep the wounds from rubbing against his clothing.

She persisted. He took a few steps back and couldn't keep from chuckling. Finally, he held out the doll.

She stopped jumping, clasped her hands together, and gasped. A big smile brightened her face. She grabbed the doll and cuddled it to her cheek, lavishing it with kisses.

"You found her!" Her eyes brimmed with tears, then she stopped and looked at him. "What about Vibia's doll?"

"I found it and gave it to her."

Alethea examined the doll. "You fixed her arm!" She kissed it and hugged it. "Mpampas made her for me."

He couldn't help but think of Sarah as he watched Alethea. She'd hugged her doll the same way, caring for it as if it were a kitten.

She gazed up at him. "What's wrong?"

"You remind me of Sarah." His own words surprised him. It was the first time he had spoken of Sarah since he'd asked Titus to search for her.

"Who is Sarah?"

He cleared his throat, not sure he wanted to talk about her, but he had already said more than he intended. "She's my little sister."

"You had a sister?" Her eyes widened.

He nodded. "She doesn't look like you, but she had a doll too. She would hold it and kiss it, just like you're doing."

A wisp of hair fell into her face. He thought of Sarah's curls and her innocence, so much like Alethea.

"She was only six when . . . ." When what? When he'd abandoned her. He stepped away and ran his hand through his hair, fighting off the memory.

"Did she . . . die too?" Alethea whispered.

David shook his head, determined to believe Sarah was safe. If she were dead, he would never forgive himself. "No." He prayed this was the truth. She had to be safe.

Something inside drove him on. He felt the need to tell her all the bad things he had done. "I left her alone the night my parents were taken." He remembered Sarah's eyes and how fearful they had been when he'd hastily tucked the covers around her and reassured her that he would return. How could he have been so foolish to leave her alone?

"I thought I could help my parents. I told her to wait until I got back."

He couldn't believe he was sharing these things, but somehow it felt good to finally tell someone what he'd done. He recalled how his mother sang to Sarah as she lay curled on her lap. He remembered at the time his father was working on the copies of his letters to the church. All was quiet, peaceful as his mother's voice carried off the walls in their small apartment. Then the soldiers burst through the door. His mother screamed, Sarah cried. The soldiers dragged his parents out the door, accusing them of treason, of defying Caesar. His father had shouted at David, "Stay with your sister!"

David shook his head, thinking how he'd gone after the soldiers, in his haste leaving poor Sarah alone. Maybe if Alethea could forgive him, so could Sarah?

"I never returned." He barely got the last words out, the lump in his throat was so large that he clenched his teeth and forced back tears that threatened.

Alethea gazed into his eyes for a long time.

It made him uneasy, but he dared not look away. His heart pounded. Would she forgive him?

"You must hate your God for what He's done to you." She frowned.

Her words shot out like a slap. He straightened and searched her face. She didn't blame him, she blamed Elohim. How could she say something like that? She even referred to Him as *his* God.

He tried to form an answer, to shake the confusion from his head. "Why do you talk this way? Didn't your father teach you—"

"Sshhhh." She put her fingers to her lips and looked around. "My father taught me all about his God, but I won't make Him mine."

"Why not?"

"Grandmother says that no god is worth dying for."

"But He died for you."

She went silent and straightened the wool braids of her doll's hair.

Why was she acting this way? He'd assumed all these years she was a believer. What happened? She was awfully young when she'd lost her father, and it'd been three years, which was a long time. Aloysius and the rest of her family were a powerful influence. She must be speaking their words and not her own.

She looked around them, her face reflecting fear. "My gods are the Roman gods." She said the words with an air of confidence, but he could see they weren't coming from her heart.

"What do you know about Yahshua?" He knew he made her nervous, but it was for her own good. He had to find out what she remembered.

She glanced behind her and to each side. She urged him to follow deeper into the woods. Finally, when she stopped, she looked at the ground as though ashamed. "I know that Yahshua, as you call Him, was God's Son. The God who made you and me. Yahshua died to save us from . . . ." She looked up at him, her brows furrowed.

"Sin."

"Yes." Her eyes searched his face. "What is sin?"

She seemed sincere.

"Sin is when you do something wrong or not good."

"Oh." She nodded as though satisfied. Then she frowned. "But your God is dead, just like my father is dead, and one day you will be dead for serving Him."

Her words jolted him. He took a deep breath. "Yahshua is not dead. He came back to life."

She raised her brows. "Grandmother said that was a lie."

"It's not a lie." David took a step closer. "Elohim—God—can do anything. He made you and me, didn't He? So why can't He make someone come back to life?" He picked up a stone. "He could turn this rock into a person if He wanted to." He tossed it in the air and caught it.

She furrowed her brows, as though pondering his words, and suddenly her face brightened. "Where do I pray to your God?"

"You can pray to Him from anywhere."

"Where is His temple?"

"You don't have to go to a temple to pray to Him."

She put her hands on her hips. "Every god has a temple."

He couldn't resist, he bent down and tapped her upturned nose. "If you became a Christian, your body would be His temple. That's why we can pray to Him from anywhere, and we can tell Him anything. He knows all about us."

"How do I pray to your God?" She stomped her foot.

He wondered if she heard or understood anything he just said. "Like this." He took her doll and set it on the ground. They held hands, clasping the flowers between their fingers. Her hands were small in his, so much like Sarah's.

He looked up to the sky as his father used to do many times. "Dear Father in heaven, You are so good. Forgive us when we do wrong, and help us to forgive others when they hurt us." He repeated some of the words he remembered his own father saying in his prayers. Then he added, "Please, help Alethea to want You for her God." He glanced down at her as he said the words.

Her eyes were closed, and her face gave nothing away.

"You are mighty, powerful, and greater than all the gods created by man. Please make Alethea see how true and real You are. In Yahshua's name, I pray. Amen."

He watched her, waiting for a reaction.

She opened one eye and looked up at him. "Is that it?"

"You can talk to Him much longer if you'd like."

"Alethea!" A voice came from the edge of the woods.

"It's Portia." A look of fear washed over her face. "She can never know what we're talking about."

"Alethea." Portia's voice drew near.

Alethea whispered, "I will pray to your God tonight." She flashed a smile and handed him the flowers. She scooped up her doll and started towards Portia.

He grabbed her by the arm and whispered in her ear. "God is bigger than your grandfather."

Eyes wide, she stopped walking. "Bigger than Grandfather?"

He squeezed her arm and nodded.

She smiled, then quickly turned and left, working her way through the trees.

David crouched behind a thicket.

"There you are." Portia's kind voice carried in the distance. "What does a girl like you find so fascinating about these woods?"

He knew the answer to that question. The woods were the only place she could escape the watchful eyes of her family.

"Give her strength, Jehovah-Shammah," David whispered under his breath. "But more importantly, give her courage."

Ω

That night, Alethea said her first prayer to David's God.

"To the God of David, I pray. David told me about You. You are a very powerful God. You are bigger than Grandfather." A thrill of joy swept through her. "He said You could raise people from the dead. I wanted to ask if . . . if You would please raise Mpampas from the dead? And let him come take me and Paulus away." She sighed. "You are a nice God too. Thank You for hearing me when I pray, no matter where I am." She paused, trying to remember how to end. "Oh yes, I pray to You with Yahshua's name. Amen."

A sense of peace washed over her. She felt the way she did when Mpampas was alive . . . cared for, and no longer alone. Her blankets felt like arms, holding her, hugging her as she drifted off to sleep.

Ω

David had finally shown Ace his father's scrolls. He learned that Ace had knowledge of the Hebrew Scriptures and was eager to learn what his father had copied. It wasn't long after studying the scrolls that Ace gave his life to Christ. Which meant David was no longer alone. Ace was now his brother in Christ. Now together they reached out to other slaves at the villa. And Ace was able to teach what he knew about the Hebrew Scriptures to the rest of the people gathered with them.

David, with his chamber-mates and a female slave from the house, all sat in a small circle behind the stables as they listened to Ace. The moonlight reflected off Ace's smiling face, and the smell of manure and a nearby torch wafted over David.

"David often refers to God as Elohim," Ace whispered to them.

This got David's attention since Ace mentioned his name.

"The word Elohim is plural. The Hebrew Scriptures say that we are all made in the image of Elohim. What could that mean?"

David waited for the others to answer. They'd already been taught so much about what Christ did for them, that Ace told David he wanted to explain Elohim. That sounded good to David, but where he was going exactly, David didn't know.

"From what I've read in the Hebrew Scriptures and from these letters to us Christians," Ace motioned toward the parchment unrolled on the ground in front of them, "it's my understanding that Elohim is made up of three Persons: God the Father, the Son, and the Holy Spirit. What do we have in our lives that resembles that?"

Tempted to blurt out what he knew, David waited for someone to answer.

Finally, one of his chamber-mates spoke up. "Well, there's a father and a son."

David raised his eyebrows. That was obvious, but what did it have to do with people being created in God's image?

To David's surprise, a huge grin spread across Ace's face and he nodded. "Elohim wants us to understand Him by what He's created. He created people and told them to have children, thereby creating a family."

David leaned forward.

"Fathers and children have characteristics of those roles found in Elohim," Ace said. "In the same way, the wife has characteristics similar to those ascribed to the Holy Spirit." He held up his hands toward David as if warding off a rebuttal. "I'm not implying that God has a gender or that the Holy Spirit is a woman. The family is created in Elohim's image. The father, the mother, and the child are patterned after Elohim.

"Each Person fulfills an essential purpose. Without one of them, Elohim would not be complete and perfect. Elohim would not be Elohim. So it is with family. Each person is important and necessary to complete the family. They are each their own person, and yet they are one."

David leaned on his knees. He'd been made to memorize the Hebrew Scriptures, and he'd never forget the creation of mankind—though he'd forgotten a lot after that—but he'd never given much thought of what it meant to be created in Elohim's image. He thought it meant that people were intelligent beings. But Ace was saying it meant more. That the father was created after God the Father, the son after the Son, and the mother . . . the mother was created in the image of the Holy Spirit. It made perfect sense to David because the Holy Spirit was known as the Comforter, and when David thought back to his mother, that's the purpose she'd fulfilled.

Hmm. David sat back and rested, satisfied, against the wall as Ace answered questions from his chamber-mates and the woman. Elohim really was amazing.

ten

Alethea hid inside the stables and watched the boys race toward the other end of the field. When all their backs were turned, she ran as fast as she could into the trees.

Out of breath, she leaned against a tree trunk and looked back. They hadn't spotted her. It wasn't fair that the boys were allowed to play, while she and Vibia were stuck in the house. So, while Vibia learned the proper way to roast meat on a gridiron, Alethea stole between the trees.

The boys neared her end of the field, and she peeked around a tree. Paulus drove the small makeshift chariot pulled by a goat. His thin brown hair clung to his flushed cheeks as he tried to maneuver it. He swatted the goat, and it took off toward the other end of the field. Paulus had eyes like Mpampas, and when Alethea told him so, he'd said that he wished his eyes looked like Grandfather's. This made her mourn Mpampas all the more. His own son didn't even know him.

It wasn't Paulus's fault. Alethea sighed as she made her way deeper into the forest as birds sang and soared above the canopy of trees. He was only three when Mpampas died. It was hard to believe four years had already passed.

When she neared the edge of the woods, she saw a large pine tree that grew close to the wall. She climbed its low branches. Something Vibia would never do. Alethea hoisted herself onto another branch, and then jumped onto the wall's edge.

Still holding the pine branch, she looked around. From here, nobody could see her, not even the guards. She walked farther along the edge of the thick wall until she spotted a high mound of dirt and rocks piled against the other side.

Freedom.

She clapped her hands and did a little dance. Leaning on one hand, she jumped off and slid down the dirt pile. Alethea headed for the other side of Vibian Hill.

After running through the clearing and making her way through more trees, she came to a brook. Holding up her stola, she hopped onto a flat rock and then another until she made her way to the other side. As she climbed the bank, her heart pounded and she breathed hard, but she wouldn't let it slow her down. The desire to be closer to Mpampas drove her. After coming up over the top, she ran into more trees, but even this didn't stop her.

She finally made her way through the woods. And there it was. Her old house, standing on the other side of the field. She stood amazed. It wasn't at all the magnificent, bright-colored house she remembered. It looked much smaller and gray. It resembled an old square rock sitting in the middle of the wide-open land.

Her gaze darted back to the trees and to the opposite side of the field. No one was there. She strode through the clearing and came closer to her old home.

The wind blew, whipping loose curls into her face and sending chills up her spine. She glanced back at the woods. Loneliness swept down on her, and even the woods seemed to be alone and empty. No birds soared in the air, and she felt small, just a speck, surrounded by sky and field.

She fixed her gaze back on the house. Iron grilles barred the windows. Tattered curtains that used to hang in thick masses waved from gusts of wind. She wanted to get closer, but her feet wouldn't move. She imagined herself inside her once beautiful home, and a distant memory came to her.

Visions of Mpampas danced through her mind, his blue eyes, his smile, his laughter. He scooped her up in his arms. Then he sang and danced, spinning her round and round in the air. She lifted her stola's skirt and spun in circles, she was a child again in her father's arms. A breeze carried the scent of pines and grass. It even smelled like the home she remembered.

The sound of her own laughter startled her out of the imaginary world, a world once real, now gone. She faced her old abandoned house again. Dark walls, lonely gardens, and empty rooms now lived there, all a reflection of what lived in her heart.

She edged closer, making it as far as the well.

That last night her parents had fought about Mpampas's God. She'd watched them argue as she hid behind a plant outside her chamber door. Sometime in the night, she awoke to footsteps and whispers and spied her mother sending Portia out with a sealed scroll tucked into her *palla*, her cloak hiding a secret missive. The next morning a slave came running for Mpampas, saying something about a fire in one of the fields. After he left, her mother grabbed all the household goods and anything else she could carry, while Alethea and Paulus were whisked away on a litter and carried to Grandfather's villa.

She stared at the house for a long time, turning the memories over in her mind. She'd always remembered the events that took place just before her father's death, but was too young to comprehend that it had anything to do with her mother's plan to leave her father. Could her mother have planned Mpampas's death? Angry tears blurred her vision and streamed down her cheeks. Portia had also taken part in the plan. Did Portia know what was in that letter? It certainly explained the distrust Alethea had felt all these years. Portia couldn't have known. Her mother had given the scroll to her already sealed. Her sweet, dear Portia. Alethea wanted to believe in her innocence. But how could she when she couldn't even trust her own mother?

She dropped to her knees in the soft dirt and grass and buried her face in her hands. Her nose burned, but she forced back her tears. She wouldn't cry. She was tired of crying. She swallowed hard, fighting the knot that grew in her throat as she gazed at the house.

A strong gust of wind blew at the ragged curtains, chilling her bare arms and the back of her neck. What if someone or something might be in the house? Perhaps an evil spirit was coming to punish her for escaping the confines of her grandfather's villa?

She jumped to her feet, gazing intently at one of the windows. The curtain moved. Was it the wind? Or was somebody in there? She didn't wait to find out. She charged back into the woods, dodging branches overhead and on the ground. She slid down the hill toward the stream, and when she hopped onto a smooth wet rock, her feet slipped out from under her. She landed with a splash, and cold water covered her from head to toe. She yelped and gasped for breath, pushing herself up on the rocks.

As she climbed out of the brook, she shivered uncontrollably. She grabbed the skirt of her stola and ran through the trees, hearing the crackling of branches. Was someone following her? Or were those the branches under her own feet?

She stopped and held her rapid breath. She stood very still and slowly looked behind her. Nothing but trees. She lifted her stola and ran again.

As the woods grew more sparse, she finally came to a meadow. But instead of the wall, she saw a cluster of trees. How could she have missed the wall? She was certain she had gone the same way. Her mouth grew dry from panting. Another desire to run out of sheer panic seized her.

She said a brief prayer to David's God and sang a song to try and calm herself. Instead of going back into the woods, she headed for the trees across the clearing where the wall should have been.

Once she entered the trees, she spotted the meadow on the other side. "Thank you, Fortuna," she cried with relief to the goddess of luck. There was the wall, farther away than she remembered. She ran to it as fast as she could.

When she reached the mound of dirt and rocks, she climbed onto it. She stretched to climb up, but she couldn't reach the top of the wall. She balled up her fist and hit it.

"Fortuna, where are you when I need you?" She put her hands on her now shivering hips. She looked down the mound, searching for rocks she could use to stand on. They were either too big for her to carry or too small to be of any use.

"Now what do I do?" She could walk to one of the gate entrances, but she didn't want anyone to know where she had been. If anyone found out, she would certainly be punished and never have another chance of seeing her house again.

She looked up at the top of the wall and with renewed vigor, jumped. Her fingers barely got over the top and she dropped back down. She breathed deep and jumped again, and then again.

Finally, she got a grip and dangled from the wall. She strained to get a better hold. How would she have the strength to get to the other side?

Desperation took over.

Alethea pulled straight up. She hung from her fingertips, took a deep breath, and pulled again. She scraped her cheek and stola against the wall, and when she got high enough, she used her elbows to pull the rest of her body over the edge. When she made it to the top, she lay on her back to catch her breath. Her arms, as heavy as the rocks she didn't carry, throbbed.

As she finally wobbled to her feet, the wall, the ground, and the trees tilted around her. She tried to focus on her sandals, but black spots and shadows blotted her vision. She knelt down to steady herself, but her body pulled to one side, and she fell to the ground.

Luckily, she landed in a thick bed of pine needles. A painful weight contracted in her chest; she couldn't breathe. She lay paralyzed on the ground. What was happening to her? Would she die here in the woods where no one would find her? She gulped in air, but not nearly enough to survive. Panic streaked through her, and she grasped her immovable chest. Finally, the weight lightened and she gulped in short bursts of air.

She closed her eyes and sighed.

"Thank you, God of David, for making me land on the right side." She froze and looked around for any listeners. It was becoming more comfortable to talk to David's God, but she had to be careful not to do it out loud. As she sat up, pine needles clung to her hair and wet stola. She shook them off as best she could, climbed to her feet, and wiggled her arms and legs. Nothing seemed broken.

Anxious to get back, she ran through the woods. The weighty sensation still throbbed in her chest, and dizziness made her steps falter, but she kept running. When she came to the field, she expected to hear the boys playing, but no one was there. In fact, it was much later than she realized.

As she scurried by the stables, from the corner of her eye, she saw David gawking at her.

"What happened to you?"

She waved her hand casually toward the trees. "I was just walking through the woods."

David threw a rag over his shoulder. "Alethea." He shook his head. "What happened to your clothes?"

She looked down at her stola. The front of her otherwise white dress was now covered in dirt and pine needles, still damp, and even torn in places.

"And your arms. Look at your arms."

Her arms were scraped all the way up to her elbows, where she noticed blood. It was an awful sight, and when she realized her condition, her body throbbed in pain. She had been so desperate to get back, she hadn't even noticed how she looked or felt.

"Fortuna's foot! Now everyone will know."

"Everyone will know what?" He stepped closer.

A glitter of amusement danced in his eyes. David. Her only friend. Of course, she had Vibia, her perfect cousin, but David knew more about her than Vibia ever would. She wasn't going to tell anyone where she'd been, but all of a sudden she realized she didn't mind telling David. Besides, if she got lost next time, he could tell people where to find her.

"I went to my old house."

"You what?" His mouth gaped. "You went over the wall?"

She nodded, grinning.

David looked toward the trees where she had come from. "But, how—?" Then a look of knowledge washed over his face. "You climbed that pine tree. The one that's right up against—"

"How did you know?"

"Then you slid down that mound of dirt and rocks, right?"

"How did you know?" Was he a seer?

"You're lucky you didn't get hurt. Or hurt, more," he said, shaking his head.

"But how did—"

"Don't ever do that again!" David's blue eyes flashed. "Don't you realize—there are barbarians out there!" He paced in front of her, raking his hand through his hair. Then he faced her, his mouth turned down into a furious line. "Suppose you ran into thieves. Do you realize what they could have done? They could have snatched you up and sold you, or much worse." He shook his head as though shaking the thought out of his mind. "Don't ever do that again."

"I had to see it!" Her mind soared, her cheeks flamed, and she wanted to cry. "You don't know how desperately I've been wishing to see it all this time. I never knew I could, I didn't know it was possible. I didn't know that tree was there until today, and when I saw the mound of dirt on the other side, I knew it was my only chance. I had to see it, David." She wiped her nose, making it black, and her hands trembled. "Besides, you're not my master. I can do whatever I please."

He straightened and folded his arms. "I'll tell your grandfather." His light brown hair, falling slightly over his brow, grew darker in the fading sunlight.

"Then I'll tell on you." She stomped her foot for emphasis. "How did you know about the pine tree and mound of dirt anyway?"

He dropped his hands and stared past her.

For the first time, she noticed that the scar on his cheek not only gave him a rugged appearance, but somehow made him more attractive.

"That's what I thought," she said, forcing her mind back to the issue at hand. "You've been going over the wall too." She looked toward the house and stables for any listeners. She should lower her voice. Seeing that no one was around, she put her swollen hands on her sore hips. "So, what have you been doing on the other side?"

He folded his arms again and arched his brow. A half grin formed on his face, revealing his wonderful dimple. "Rescuing someone's doll."

Heat climbed from her neck to her cheeks. How foolish. Of course, he would have gone over the wall to get her doll, it just never occurred to her until now. At the same time, she wondered why he didn't try to escape.

Suppose he'd gotten caught? He could have been sold, beaten, or killed. Or worse, he could have been taken from her.

"I don't want you to get hurt," he said.

She looked up into his concerned eyes. Warmth spilled from her heart to every limb. "I won't do it again."

He nodded as if he'd settled the matter.

"Under one condition," she added.

"What's that?"

"Smile."

"What?"

"Just smile."

"What did you do, hit yourself on the head?" He pursed his lips and smacked her with the rag.

Pain stung her leg. "Hey, that hurts!" She giggled and jumped away.

She wanted to see his dimples and had no intention of promising not to go over the wall. She had to see her house again, and next time, she would have courage enough to go closer, maybe even go inside. But not anytime soon. She scurried away from David.

As she neared the gymnasium, she turned and saw him walking back toward the stables. She called over her shoulder, "You didn't smile!" She stuck out her tongue. For some reason he didn't laugh

at her joke, but just frowned and shook his head. Still, she skipped
to the house. He cared for her and she got to see her house. Life
couldn't be better.

When she had to explain her appearance to Grandmother, Alethea made up a story. She wanted to say she was climbing a tree and
got stuck and nearly fell out of it, but there was no way she could
explain how she had gotten wet. She made it sound like she only
went as far as the stream and after she'd fallen in, came back home.
This, of course, did not calm Grandmother and only increased her
worry. Alethea had to admit, she found her grandmother's concern
somewhat comforting. Her mother didn't seem the least bit worried.

She thought it was interesting that her mother didn't ask how she
had gotten up over the wall, but she wasn't about to offer any new
information. If they didn't ask, then she wasn't going to tell. Besides,
she heard them talking about checking the locks on the small doors.

Mother simply told her not to do it again and called for Portia
to take Alethea to the baths and clean her up for the evening meal.

That night Alethea cried into her pillow. She didn't care if she
woke Vibia. Alethea longed for Mpampas. Why did her mother ignore her? If Mpampas were here, he would have beaten her backside,
but then he would have held her close and told her how worried
she'd made him. She didn't exactly wish to be punished, she just
wanted to know her mother cared—like she used to care. Without
Mpampas, Alethea felt like she was falling into a deep dark pit, out
of control, with no one to keep her safe.

Ω

Several weeks later, Grandmother Renata called Alethea and Vibia
to her side.

"I have a surprise waiting for you in Rome." Grandmother eyes
danced. "You will both be thrilled." She clasped her wrinkled hands
together.

Alethea couldn't imagine what could possibly be waiting for them in Rome, but just the idea that she might be going to the city tingled her with excitement.

"It's very important that you be on your best behavior." Grandmother glanced at Alethea, brushing a curl away from her face.

She knew that comment was only for her. Of course, Vibia never made mistakes.

"And you will make a small gift as a token of appreciation for the gifts you will receive."

"What's the surprise?" Alethea couldn't stand the suspense.

"If I told you, it wouldn't be a surprise, now would it?" Grandmother handed each of them a piece of silk. "I have prepared these squares for you to embroider. They have been soaked in your favorite scents. You are to sleep with them under your head every night."

"Who are these gifts for?" Vibia asked.

"That is part of the surprise." Grandmother grinned. She pulled both girls to her bosom and stroked their hair.

Alethea enjoyed the moment of warmth and comfort. Things like this didn't happen often. Usually, she was standing at the end of her grandmother's accusing finger.

"It will be a splendid time for everyone," Grandmother said.

"When do we leave?" Vibia asked.

"In a few months."

Later, both girls worked diligently on their embroideries.

"I'm sure it will be a kitten," Alethea said. "Won't it be wonderful cuddling a sweet ball of fur?"

"Or perhaps they plan to give us jewels? Or a colorful stola, or golden sandals?" Vibia said.

"Or maybe a new doll?" Alethea wasn't sure she wanted a new one. She preferred the one she already had, even though it was worn and tattered. Besides, why would they travel all the way to Rome for a new doll or a kitten or jewelry?

Both girls, eleven years old, chattered excitedly about the prospects of a surprise. Something splendid awaited them in the wondrous city of Rome.

eleven

Alethea didn't like Rome at all. It was crowded, loud, and filthy. She'd never seen so many buildings and people packed together in one place. Now she was packed into a dressing chamber with Vibia, being poked and prodded by Portia and other maidservants. They were preparing for a banquet; it and the surprise were the only exciting things about the whole trip.

"The girls must look exquisite." Grandmother helped Portia twist flowered vines between Alethea's braids.

Alethea stood before a full-length, bronze polished mirror, staring at her white stola pinned at the shoulders. She pulled at the pink silk, which was too tight around her waist. She wondered why they would want her to look skinnier than she already was. A blue sheer wrap crisscrossed over her chest and the ends hung in a loose knot down her back. Imagining they were wings, she moved from side to side, watching them flutter behind her.

"Be still, Alethea. We can't do your hair when you're moving around like that." Grandmother gave her a stern look as she moved to Vibia.

The thought of a banquet excited Alethea, but Grandmother's anxiousness made her nervous. It was very difficult to be still, and her thoughts were constantly guessing what the surprise would be.

Would it be a pet of some kind? A new toy? A new stola or sandals? Or as Vibia suggested, perhaps jewelry of some kind?

The banquet was to be held at the home of Maximus Demetrius Arnensis. The name meant nothing to her, but Vibia seemed duly impressed.

"Do you have your embroidery ready?" Grandmother yanked a little too hard on Vibia's hair, jerking her head back and making her flinch.

Portia finally finished. Alethea grabbed her embroidery and tucked it into her belt. She had worked hard on her silk square, taking great care to make the dark blue and gold colors swirl just right around its white edges. It would be difficult to part with the silk, and she decided she would make a mantle of the same coloring and design.

She couldn't contain her curiosity any longer. "What's the surprise? Do we get it tonight?"

Grandmother had already made it clear that the banquet was not the surprise but rather what they were celebrating. Alethea skipped toward Grandmother, who now supervised the finishing touches on Vibia.

Her cousin turned, showing off her luscious braids. Alethea wished she could trade hair with her. Vibia's hair was an uncommon color of reddish-brown. The auburn color made Alethea seethe with jealousy. Not only did Vibia have beautiful translucent skin, she had the hair of a goddess. Though Alethea had to admit, her own skin could be just as translucent if she wouldn't spend so much time outdoors.

Grandmother pulled the girls to her. She breathed deeply and smiled.

Alethea clasped her hands together and giggled. Finally, she would discover the surprise.

"Tonight is a very special evening. As you know, one day you will both marry and have children. Vibia, your father has chosen a husband for you."

Vibia gasped and covered her mouth with her hands.

Grandmother turned to Alethea. "Grandfather has, with my help, chosen your future husband. Tonight we celebrate your betrothals."

Vibia jumped up and down, clapping her hands with glee. "Father promised he would find someone young. Is it who I think it is?"

Grandmother smiled and shook her head. "I don't think so. But he is young."

Alethea backed away. "I . . . I don't . . . ." Was this awful news the surprise? What happened to the jewels? The new stola? The golden sandals? "I don't want to get married!"

"You have no reason to be nervous." Grandmother pulled Alethea into a hug. "We have made extensive arrangements with Demetri's family, and I'm sure he's going to like you. You look lovely tonight. Demetri won't be worrying about how thin you are at this stage."

"Demetri?" Vibia shrieked. "She's going to marry Demetri?" She scowled at Alethea. "I wanted Demetri!"

Alethea was about to let her have him when Grandmother slapped Vibia across the face. Alethea stepped back in horror, watching Grandmother scold her.

"You ungrateful child! Have you any idea how much trouble has gone into finding you a suitable young man?"

Alethea put her hand to her own cheek. She had never been slapped the way Grandmother just slapped Vibia, even after all her rebellious acts. But then she'd never been so blunt as Vibia was just now, except for the night she screamed. Good thing she had run away. She watched the scene in a daze. She had better make sure she didn't show any ungratefulness.

The voice of her grandmother ranted and raved, making her ears ring. She was completely and utterly disappointed, helpless and trapped. A prisoner held captive by her own family. And once she was old enough to escape their clutches, she would be thrown into the grips of a man she didn't even know. But what if they expected her to marry him now? Her body shuddered.

"It isn't fair." Vibia stomped her foot, turning toward the mirror, voicing Alethea's own thoughts.

The upcoming nuptials soared through her mind. Tears filled her eyes and her body trembled.

Grandmother pulled Alethea to her bosom. She snuggled into her grandmother's arms. It was nice to be held, even though she felt miserable.

"Forgive me, Grandmother. I am very happy with the surprise," she said, trying to sound grateful even though it was a lie, "but . . . I don't want to get married. I'm too young!" She wanted to say that she had already found a husband but knew her grandmother would disapprove of David.

Grandmother shook with laughter. "Oh child!" She held Alethea in front of her and smiled. "Dear Aucella . . . ." Grandmother wiped a tear from Alethea's face.

"You don't have to marry him *now*." Tears pooled in her grandmother's eyes. "You may wait until you become a woman." Grandmother laughed again and squeezed her close.

With that thought, the future seemed a little brighter, despite her disappointment with the surprise. There was hope, and she would have to find a way to marry David before she had to marry this Demetri person.

Ω

Alethea leaned back against the cushions of the litter. Normally she would have to walk alongside or behind the fancy stretcher, but not today. She smoothed out her stola, trying to appear sophisticated. It was an exciting time, despite her inner misery.

She moved to the veiled curtain to peer outside. The litter tilted, and she gripped the cushions. Thank Fortuna she didn't have to sit on a sedan chair like her grandmother and grandfather did, otherwise she might fall off.

She pulled back the curtain and leaned out. She barely saw

Grandmother and Grandfather ahead. Her grandparents, aunt, and uncle led the procession as they rounded the street corner. The light beige houses, with their green foliage and iron-grilled windows, all looked the same along the street. One thing was different on the Palatine from where she first entered Rome; the streets here were actually clean. She released an exasperated sigh. Where the streets were clean, she wasn't expected to walk, and where they were dirty, she had to wade through the filth.

"Mistress, we can hold the litter steady, if you'd be still," David said with his typical distant air, so as not to give away to the others that they were close. He was one of four slaves carrying her litter.

"Of course," she said, and plopped back onto the cushions, leaving the curtain open to look outside. Too bad she and David couldn't just chat. The slaves knew they were close, but her family didn't, and she dared not risk revealing their secret friendship.

The litter rocked again as she moved, making her stomach churn. The cushions in the litter began to turn and she hoped they would arrive soon. Disappointed that her stomach felt sick, she couldn't make the most of this experience. It shouldn't be long now, since they only had to go to the other side of the Palatine.

After they rounded the corner, she looked on in amazement. Grandmother and Grandfather were escorted from their sedan chairs to a beautiful house. Columns lined large iron grilled windows on each side of the door, while palm trees sprouted on both ends of the house, and colorful flowers spread out like a blanket over the front garden. Her stomach lurched at the thought of who awaited her in this grand place.

Vibia's parents and brother were helped out of their litters, while David and another slave helped Alethea out of hers. A wave of dizziness swept over her as she came to her feet, forcing her to lean on David's strong arm.

"Are you well?" He gripped her elbow.

"I think so," she said. "Just a little dizzy."

He escorted her to the front door of the home of Maximus Demetrius Arnensis.

"How are you feeling, mistress?" David penetrated her with concerned eyes, while at the same time keeping a distant front.

"Better. Now that my feet are on solid ground."

"I have to take care of the litters," he said, his eyes still holding hers. "So I won't be able to escort you inside."

Her disappointment was so great that she couldn't have the support of her best friend during this difficult day that she didn't trust herself to speak, so she simply nodded.

David gave a reassuring squeeze on her elbow then quickly left so as not to raise suspicion.

A slave formally greeted Alethea and the others at the door and escorted them into a vestibule where they were met by a tall gentleman with graying blond hair and sparkling green eyes.

"Welcome! Welcome to my home." He first greeted Vibia's parents, Marcus, and the grandparents.

After greeting the men, he kissed the women.

As he neared the girls, he gave Alethea a wink and kissed her cheek.

"Welcome. I'm Demetrius."

Her stomach knotted. He's so old! How could they make her marry someone so old? She thought he was supposed to be young, yet perhaps this was young? He was old enough to be her father, but she had heard from Vibia that some girls married men old enough to be their grandfathers. Well, it didn't matter anyway because as long as she could help it, she wouldn't marry him. She remembered a lesson from Decimus that women had a legal right to refuse marriage with a man. This she planned to do, despite the punishment that might await her at the hands of Grandfather.

Since she didn't have to marry this man now, it gave her time to form a plan of escape. But how much time did she have? When would she be considered a woman? She'd heard from Grandmother that some girls were considered women at twelve. She hoped that such an early demise wouldn't befall her.

"Please, allow the slaves to escort you into the tablinum. We will begin the ceremony immediately." Demetrius turned to the other guests. Aunt Fabia put her hand on Vibia's shoulder and they followed behind the men.

Just then, a tall, beautiful woman came into the hall. She smiled at the guests and nodded elegantly to Grandfather.

"Welcome," she said.

Grandfather kissed the woman's cheek. "Thank you for having us in your home." He smiled.

"It is my pleasure," she said.

Grandfather turned to follow the slave.

The woman came to stand next to Demetrius and took Grandmother's hands in her own. "How nice it is that you have come." The woman glanced around the guests. "Where is Cornelia?"

"Cornelia said she wasn't feeling well, though I have my doubts, so she stayed home with Paulus and Lucius. Lucius is nothing but a troublemaker, so I thought it best for him to remain at the house."

"Oh, I do understand. Please give Cornelia our wishes of good health," the woman said.

"Come, my love." Demetrius offered his arm to the beautiful woman.

Thanks and praises to the gods, this was not the man Alethea was doomed to marry; it must be her intended's father. She breathed a sigh of relief.

Moving close to Grandmother, she reminded herself that the man for her was somewhere in the vicinity. Grandmother would serve as a nice, solid wall of protection.

They were escorted to the atrium where Alethea spotted an arched doorway leading to an outer garden. She would hide there when opportunity struck. She had to come up with a plan. She wasn't going to marry Demetri, and she had to find a way out of this mess.

"Arnos and his family are waiting in the tablinum," Demetrius said as he walked ahead of the group through the atrium.

"Where is Demetri?" Grandmother touched the arm of the pretty blonde woman.

"He will be joining us soon."

"He is a fine young man." Grandmother clasped her hands together.

"He's looking forward to meeting Alethea."

"I told Cornelia that Alethea simply needs a goal. I said that if Alethea has a marriage to look forward to, knowing her life is secure, perhaps she will become more committed to her lessons and control her behavior."

Alethea hid behind her grandmother, fearing the pretty woman would look at her. Why did Grandmother have to reveal all of her shortcomings?

"Mind you, one day she will make a fine wife, so Demetri has nothing to fear." Grandmother smiled, reassuring the woman, and then widened her eyes pointedly at Alethea.

"She just needs time to grow and learn," the pretty lady said. "Isn't it true she lost her father to that new religious sect? Certainly that's affected her in some way."

Grandmother nodded.

"It's growing quite rapidly here in the city."

"I'm sure it is." Grandmother cleared her throat.

The slaves pulled back heavy scarlet curtains, revealing the tablinum. A shrine held several figurines of gods reflecting the light from nearby candles. Of course, she would be expected to worship the Roman gods in this family too. Thankfully, she had formed a good habit of this.

She dropped behind Grandmother and the woman as they went into the tablinum. They didn't seem to notice she was there.

Before the shrine were four small cushions placed on the floor. To the back of the chamber stood the rest of the guests, chatting happily as Grandmother joined them. It was crowded, and Alethea couldn't see Vibia. She decided it was safer to stay on this end of the chamber, far away from the enemy who could possibly be lurking amongst the guests by now.

While the families continued in conversation, she peeked around the curtain and scanned the atrium. She spotted a few slaves outside, going in and out of a chamber on the far side of the outdoor courtyard. It was still light.

"'But Grandmother,' she'd said, 'I'm too young to marry!'" Grandmother's merry voice sounded in Alethea's ears.

The adults roared with chuckles and snorts.

"I laughed so hard, I cried." Grandmother joined in the laughter.

Heat crept up from Alethea's neck to her cheeks as she listened to everyone make light of her situation. It was bad enough being amongst strangers, one of whom she was expected to marry, but now they were laughing at her.

Tears burned her eyes and nose. The high-pitched laughter rang in her ears, making the room suddenly seem too small. She scurried into the atrium, but where could she go? Where would she hide? How could she face all those strangers when they knew of her foolishness? She turned toward the door of the courtyard.

"Going somewhere?"

She skidded in her tracks. A handsome blond man stood at the open door.

She lost all ability to speak.

His tall figure dominated the doorway, and he grinned. Was he laughing at her too? She hastily swiped away her tears.

The young man strode toward her.

"I'm Demetri, son of Maximus Demetrius Arnensis."

After hearing his name, realization dawned. So *this* was the one Vibia wanted to marry. This was the one *she* would marry . . . oh my. At least he was young, and at his age, could be considered a man. He stood over her and made her feel quite small.

He took her hand in his and gently kissed her cheek.

"And who might you be?"

She stepped back, her face tingled from his touch. Strangers had never kissed her cheek before—such an adult thing to do—and now it had been assaulted by two men in one day.

"I'm Alethea," she whispered.

He straightened and raised a brow, then his lips pulled into a broad grin. "Won't you stay for the banquet?" He held his arm out to her, his eyes dancing.

She hesitated, then dumbly took it.

Demetri escorted her back to the tablinum, her plans of escape temporarily postponed.

Grandmother half smiled as they came to the chamber. She must have been about to come after her. Grandmother always seemed to be on her heels. Her eyes lit up when she saw Demetri at Alethea's side.

Alethea noticed another young man kneeling before the shrine on one of the cushions next to Vibia. He looked younger than Demetri, but definitely older than Vibia. He wasn't ugly, but compared to Demetri, he wasn't handsome either.

Grandmother helped Alethea to her knees on another cushion and draped a mantle over her shoulders, while Demetri knelt on the cushion beside her. Because this was a special occasion, they must be expected to pray and give homage to the gods before the banquet was to begin, so she pulled the mantle over her head.

She longed to be playing in the woods at her grandfather's villa. There she felt wild and free, not stiff, unsure, and foolish, like now. And the thought of marrying the man who knelt right next to her, made her shudder. She didn't know much about marriage, but one thing was certain, this Demetri would never ride a sow.

A priest appeared in long colorful robes. What god he represented, she could only guess; there were too many to keep track of. This was certainly considered a special occasion if priests were invited. He uttered a prayer before them, hands raised upward, while all heads bowed and eyes closed. She peeked over her shoulder to where the adults stood. They prayed too. She turned toward the front. Demetri prayed next to her as the priest continued his long-winded prose.

She bowed her head as though praying and peered over at Demetri. His arms and body were so much larger than her own. This was definitely not the right man for her to marry. He was too big and old to play in the field with her, and he probably wouldn't have rescued her doll either. She doubted he'd ever allow her to stand guard and give him the all-clear as he threw a ball through the roof in the atrium. She also doubted Demetri would ever slosh through the mud with her after a long rain; he was too grown up for all of that. Definitely not what she desired in a husband.

She could feel the floor through the cushion, and her knees began to hurt. The priest stopped praying and began quoting more verses. He seemed to enjoy hearing himself talk, dramatizing certain words like "gifts," "betrothal," and "pleasing to the gods."

She focused on his feet. His stubby toes protruded out of his sandals. It made it difficult to take seriously anything the man said.

After a long period of time, she imagined how comfortable it would be to rest her head on the cushion that supported her knees. She noticed the boy next to Vibia nodding off and fought the urge to do the same.

"And now for the rings," the priest said.

The slight movement and rustle of tunics helped awaken her.

The fathers each handed a ring to Demetri and the other boy. Demetri took her hand in his. It was rough and big around her own.

This was strange, why were they interrupting the prayer with rings? She wanted to pull away, but decided, under Grandmother's watchful gaze, to not be rude.

He placed a ring on her finger. The ring had looked small in his large hand, but it was far too big for her, and slid right off her finger. He caught it and placed it on her finger again. It was then that she realized the significance of the proceedings that were taking place. This was a betrothal ceremony! She wanted to scream, to run, to hide, but there was no way out. She jerked her hand away, and the ring pitched with a resounding clang onto the floor. She crawled after it and snatched it in her fist. Hurrying back to her spot on the cushion, she hoped he wouldn't decide to try again.

He smiled down at her, and she quickly looked away.

The priest closed the ceremony by waving incense over the victims' heads and ended with a prayer. When he was finished, the adults congratulated one another, and Demetrius ordered all the guests into the dining chamber.

It was just the betrothal ceremony, she reassured herself. That still didn't mean she had to marry him.

Massive curtains to the tablinum opened up to the peristyle where the scent of flowers offered comfort and familiarity during this gruesome occasion. As everyone made their way through the courtyard, she spotted another open door that led to the outer gardens where she had earlier seen the slaves. Maybe David was out there somewhere?

Soon they entered the dining chamber, and in its center were tables laden with a colorful variety of food. It was an interesting setup since all the tables were pushed together, giving the appearance of one long table, and having the children dine together with the adults was quite an honorable event. The adults and priest reclined on the couches surrounding the lavish tables at the far end of the chamber, while the young people reclined closest to the door.

"Let me help you." Demetri straightened the cushions on a small couch for her. A slave played the lyre in a distant corner, attempting to create a settling mood for the diners, but it did nothing to soothe her nerves.

She reclined stiffly on the couch, setting her ring on the table, as Demetri reclined opposite her.

The meal began at a slow pace. The appetizers were served and then the main course was set on the tables before them. She plucked the meat from the trencher and choked down the venison spiced with plums, wine, and honey. Under normal circumstances it might have tasted good.

"The indoor plumbing here is simply wonderful." Demetri's mother spoke up. "We had to bring water from a well where we lived just outside of Alexandria. Of course the slaves did the work. That's where we raised our horses you know. This is a thriving city, just as is Alexandria, but I find Rome a bit too crowded." She dabbed her face with a cloth that a nearby slave provided. "Demetri has suffered some minor ailments since we've returned. The doctors can't seem to say what the problem is."

"Oh? And what has been ailing you, Demetri?" Grandmother asked.

"I'm just tired a lot, and sometimes my stomach bothers me."

"Well, perhaps you're just homesick? You haven't been in Rome for very long." Grandmother queried toward his mother. "Just a little more than six months, correct?"

She nodded.

"Give it time. I'm sure it'll pass."

"Demetri has become quite a poet." His mother smiled. "Share one of your poems with us. Share the one about the land; that one is beautiful."

"Not now mother, please." An uncomfortable grin squirmed onto his face.

"Well, he is quite talented."

"Speaking of land," Grandfather spoke up from the other end of the table. "Tell me, Demetri. About the dowry, what do you have planned for the other side of my Vibian Hill?"

Alethea nearly choked. Of course Demetri would receive her father's land. When her father was killed, Grandfather automatically gained back the dowry he'd given for her mother. That meant if she married Demetri, she could live in her old house. The idea of living in her home appealed to her. Yet, the circumstances of whom she would marry—

"I plan to raise horses." Demetri popped a piece of venison into his mouth.

He was handsome indeed, but David held more appeal. After all, this man didn't have any dimples.

He smiled and winked at her.

Her heart skipped, and she gulped a drink from her goblet. She reached out to take some carrots from the platter, and to her dismay, Demetri's hand brushed against hers. She quickly withdrew, slipped the carrot into her mouth, and gulped down another drink.

He chuckled, clearly amused.

Her cheeks warmed. This man was welcome to have the land. She would give it to him, as long as he didn't expect her to go with it. She would tell him tonight that under no circumstances would she be his wife. She was already marrying someone else. Land or not, no matter how much it made her think of Mpampas, it would not be the same living in her old house with some stranger.

"I'm thinking of rebuilding. Maybe tear down the house to build a villa with stables."

She swallowed hard. He planned to destroy her home? Rage pulsed its way into her face. How dare he think of destroying what she held so dear. This made it easier to break off their engagement. She had to bite her lip to keep from announcing her decision that very moment. All he cared about was land and horses; she was just part of the deal. She wanted to marry for love, and if she could, she would marry David.

Thoughts of David filled her mind. He would never sit here and arrogantly talk of horses and land and how rich he would become. David was younger than Demetri, but he was far more handsome, even with his slave earring and scar. He treated her with respect, not because he was her slave, but because he really cared. After dinner, she would go into the courtyard and find him.

"I assume last March you celebrated the Liber?" Grandfather asked.

Demetri nodded. "Dedicated my old tunic and other relics to the gods."

"At seventeen, he is officially a man," his mother said, smiling.

The conversation turned to which part of the land Paulus would inherit, and Alethea shut everyone out. She longed to be with David.

twelve

Thankfully, Demetri never spoke to Alethea, and when she swallowed the last bite of venison, she snatched up her ring. She meant to return it this very night. She stood as the guests were escorted into the peristyle to enjoy the fine entertainment. Fresh air swept over her now that she didn't have to be so near her betrothed. Yet, she still had to find a way to break the news to him privately. How would she accomplish that?

Slaves lifted platters laden with fruity desserts and floated around the room to the mingling guests. Alethea refused, feeling like her stomach might burst. They passed out ostrich feathers and motioned the guests to the *vomitorium*. There they would empty their insides to make room for more food. The thought made Alethea feel like she might lose her meal without the help of an ostrich feather.

She moved close to the door, which led to the outside gardens. Vibia shot her angry looks and didn't come near. Later, Alethea would settle things with her and make it clear that she was welcome to have this Demetri person.

"I'm simply thrilled with the whole evening." Her grandmother's voice rose above the noise of the slaves who moved the couches from the dining chamber into the peristyle and cleared away the plants and statues from the center of the courtyard. "The land promised for Alethea's betrothal is fine land for raising horses."

The adults took their places in the peristyle, including the parents of Vibia's betrothed. They were such quiet people that she hardly noticed them.

Alethea had to admit she was relieved to be engaged to the younger Demetrius, not that it mattered anyway. Tonight she would tell him her true feelings, and she needed to remember to fully express her gratitude. She didn't want to risk getting slapped, nor did she want to waste any time. Who knew when Grandmother might deem her a woman? She was only eleven now. In one more year she would be twelve, and by then David would be fifteen. Certainly, she could try and marry him by that time, and then nobody could force her into a marriage with Demetri.

With all this worry, she hardly noticed the professional musicians and orators appear before the guests. They swirled about in brightly colored costumes and gathered in the center of the room. One gentleman played the lyre with grace and perfection, while another recited lines of poetry to the accompaniment of the music.

When the music stopped and another orator took the stage, she slumped onto a small stool. She only half listened, and nearly fell asleep during the second recital of Marcus Tullius Cicero's works.

When the orators finished, the families mingled. She kept to herself, like a proper young lady, although her true motivation was to avoid Vibia, Demetri, and anyone else for that matter. She wished she could huddle behind Grandmother, but she was too close to the enemy.

Alethea gazed into the outdoor courtyard and spotted David at the far end. She rose to her feet, crept in that direction, and quietly slipped through the doors.

She hurried on tiptoes to the other side of the garden and slipped behind some greenery.

"Like this," David said as he tossed a ball to a small boy who couldn't have been more than two years.

Alethea sank to a stone bench behind some perfectly trimmed bushes. Until now, no one had seen her. Torches and candles lit up the dark garden, and despite being outside, the air didn't smell as fresh and clean as in the country. She wanted to be near David, but she also didn't want to risk being reprimanded for socializing with the slaves. It was one thing to play with them in the field back home at the villa and to talk to David secretly in the woods, but during a formal gathering and as a guest, it would be considered improper. She took comfort in just hearing David's voice as he played with the little boy.

"Catch the ball, like this."

"Mamma, Mamma."

Alethea turned and peered through the bushes.

The little boy ran to a woman. A torch lit up her beautiful face.

Alethea couldn't take her eyes off the slender figure swaying under her fitted stola. The woman's eyes had thick liner on them, much thicker than Grandmother or Mother would wear, and colorful beads of some kind were woven through her black hair. She wore a gold Egyptian bracelet whose bands wove in and around each other from her wrist to her elbow. Titus had shown her something like it before. The woman held the boy in her arms and spoke to him in Greek—Mpampas's language.

The woman looked at David. "I see you meet Alexander, my son." The woman spoke in broken Latin with a thick accent.

Apparently, David and this woman had met earlier this evening. She was not old, perhaps near the same age as Demetri, or maybe a little younger. The woman's olive skin looked smooth under the torch's light as she turned to David.

"I need ask. How find I this community of Christians? If harm come to me, will they care for my Alexander?" The woman nodded toward the little boy in her arms.

Alethea glanced back at the peristyle where music and laughter carried through its doors. Thankfully, no one else had yet come outside. Who knew how Demetri's family felt toward Christians? She wondered if she ought to leave, but if she did, David and the woman would find out she was there and heard their conversation. She didn't want them to think she was spying, so she kept still.

The little boy who had been playing with David squirmed out of his mother's arms and moved closer. She scooted toward the far edge of the bench and continued to watch David and the woman through the bushes.

"Make the sign of a fish, like this." David knelt down.

She spread the branches apart and watched David draw in the sand.

"It's very simple; you don't have to be an artist. It's like a password or a secret symbol that only Christians will understand."

The woman knelt down near David to examine his drawing. Jealousy swept through Alethea. The woman had to be older than David, but she hung on to his every word.

Out of the corner of her eye, Alethea spotted movement.

The little boy picked up his ball and carried it over to her. "Ball," he said in Latin, holding it up for her to see.

She forced a smile, hoping David and the woman hadn't spotted her. She let the branches fall back into place and turned her attention to the boy. A nearby torch lit up his enchanting face. Thick lashes blinked at her over the biggest blue-green eyes she'd ever seen. Raven black hair with small wisps curled near his neck, and his olive-colored skin looked smooth to the touch. The boy flashed a smile and didn't seem to be the least bit frightened or shy.

"Pretty lady," the boy said, smiling. "Pretty lady! Pretty lady!" the boy shouted, running back to his mother.

Alethea cringed and crouched down on her bench. There was no way she could hide now.

David appeared from around the shrubbery and so did the boy's mother. The boy stepped forward and tossed her the ball.

Alethea watched as the ball rolled to her feet.

The little boy hurried to pick it up and held it out to her.

Reluctantly, she took it from him.

"Alethea, what are you doing here?" David whispered. "Why aren't you inside enjoying the party?"

She looked up at David. He wasn't smiling, but he didn't appear angry either, just concerned. She wanted to tell him everything, about the surprise and what a disappointment it had been, and then about this man Demetri whom she was doomed to marry. It would all just have to wait.

"Throw it." Little Alexander pointed his dimpled finger at the ball she held in her hands.

She knelt down. "Here you go." She rolled it past him, and his eyes lit up with joy.

"Your son is beautiful," Alethea said to the woman.

The woman glanced at David with worried eyes.

Tension rose in the air, but Alethea couldn't imagine why. Unless the woman was afraid of being caught speaking with one of the guests? Or perhaps the woman was afraid of what Alethea might have overheard? Despite the fact that she seemed to make the woman uncomfortable, her curiosity about the boy spurred her on.

"Where are you from?" Alethea stood.

The woman's eyes widened, and she almost seemed afraid to speak.

Alethea tried to encourage her with a smile.

"I'm Egyptian. My home was Alexandria."

"Is that why you named your son Alexander?" The name appealed to Alethea, a strong and sturdy name. "The name is Greek, it means 'helper and defender of mankind.' My father was Greek."

The woman smiled and nodded. She seemed to be pleased by Alethea's words.

"I thought I told you to remain in the slaves' chamber and stay away from the guests."

Alethea nearly jumped out of her stola.

Demetri came and stood before the woman, frowning.

Alethea had no idea anyone was near. Thank the gods they hadn't been talking about David's religion.

The woman looked down at her bare feet.

"It was my fault," Alethea said. "She didn't know I was here." The last thing she wished was that anyone should be punished because of her.

"Go back to your chamber, and take the child with you."

David scooped the boy up on his shoulder, carrying him as though he were a barrel of wine. The woman walked ahead of David and ducked inside the slave doors. David followed, leaving Alethea alone with Demetri in the garden.

Her anger flared. How dare he frighten the enchanting woman away when Alethea still had so many questions. She would use her anger to fuel her courage to break off their engagement.

"What did she say to you?" Demetri asked, eyes narrowed.

Alethea stepped back from his harsh gaze. She could see no harm with what the woman had said, so she answered him honestly.

"She said she was from Egypt."

"Did she say anything else?"

"That her home was in Alexandria."

"What else?" He leaned over her as if interrogating her for being disobedient. Grandmother had spoken to her that way so often, she'd recognize it anywhere. How dare he do the same to her.

Alethea straightened to her full height, even though she still had to arch her neck to meet his gaze. "Nothing else," she said, laying emphasis on each word. The woman was just a slave. Why would he be so concerned about what she said?

"Good."

"She was just answering my questions," Alethea said, noticing a flower in his hand. "She has a beautiful child, he—"

"Everyone is looking for you." Demetri shifted his stance. "I was going to give you my gifts before the family and guests, but I couldn't find you. Vibia has already received hers. I thought you would be anxious to receive yours." Demetri stood over her, his green eyes sparkling. "What were you doing out here all by yourself?"

"I needed . . . ." She was about to say she needed to be alone. Really, she needed to be with David, but what business was it of his? She wasn't a slave from whom he needed to demand answers. She didn't belong to him yet, and as far as she could help it, she never would. She avoided his gaze. *Say it. Now was her chance.*

"So, what do you think?"

She looked at him questioningly.

"Of this." He tapped her nose with the flower.

He must be referring to their engagement. Finally, she held the ring out to him. "I might as well tell you now. I'm not going to marry you."

He straightened and appeared shocked, then a look of amusement washed over his face. "Oh really? And who will you marry then?"

Her eyes darted around the courtyard, anything to avoid his green gaze. Her preparation for how she would break the news didn't extend to his response. Flustered, her neck and cheeks went hot.

"David." Trying to appear confident, she needed to convince him that she'd already made plans. She continued to hold the ring out to him, but he wouldn't take it.

He smiled, seeming to enjoy the conversation. "So, I have competition? I'll have to find out who this David is."

Her stomach tied itself into knots. She'd just made a grave mistake. But nobody knew David as "David" except her. To everyone else he was "Damonus." She would have to be very careful not to use his real name around others.

"A Hebrew?" He rubbed his chin, still holding the flower.

She tossed a braid over her shoulder, trying to appear calm.

"Well, he is . . . I mean . . . ." She didn't have to give him more information. It would only make things worse. "It doesn't matter 'who,' it's just not going to be you, that's all." She motioned the ring toward him, hoping he would take it.

He frowned. It was as though her words hurt him. How could he be hurt? He didn't even know her, and for that matter, she was nothing but a child. Still, she held out the ring and kept her chin up. She didn't want him to think that she could be persuaded to change her mind.

He leaned over her and tapped the flower on her nose again. "We shall see about that." Power and determination radiated from his being.

Fear left her feeling cold. She shivered.

Then he grinned, holding the flower before her as he broke off some of its thorns. He took her hand in his and placed the flower in her palm, closing her fingers around its stem and the ring.

"This is a rose. My father grows them in his garden. Be careful not to prick yourself."

It was a handsome flower. It still had thorns protruding from its stem near the attractive bud and near its base; much like Demetri, handsome but full of thorns.

At that moment, Grandmother appeared.

"Oh, there you are, my dear. As usual, we have been looking everywhere for you." She gritted her teeth through her smile. She glanced at Demetri and then back at Alethea. "Have you already given Demetri his gift?"

Alethea cringed. She had expected to feel some sort of joy when she gave away her silk square. Now she felt nothing but sorrow that what she had worked so hard on would go to this barbarian. She unfolded the embroidery from her belt and handed it over to Demetri. She didn't look at his eyes but instead focused on the cloth. She tried to console herself. She would make another one, only next time it would be a beautiful mantle.

Grandmother turned and called for Vibia as she and the rest of the guests, their chatter and laughter, spilled into the courtyard.

Demetri took the silk square. "Thank you." He held it under his nose, taking in its scent. "Jasmine." He took her hand in his and bowed down near her. "The Egyptian rose." He spoke just loud enough for her to hear. "When you, like the rose, are in full bloom, I will break your thorns and make you mine."

She went limp and cold, and the world spun. She wanted to scream with fright. She yanked away and scurried over to Grandmother.

He came up to them with his hands behind his back.

"You have a wild filly on your hands. Let us hope she grows out of it." With that, he turned to watch the other guests.

Alethea's anger flared. The last thing she needed was for Grandmother to think she was out of control. Then she realized she hadn't shown any form of gratitude toward the man.

"I assure you, she will grow out of it." Grandmother gave a painful squeeze on Alethea's arm.

"She simply needs to be broken in and tamed." He looked down at Alethea and smiled. "The spirited ones are most valued."

Her stomach turned. How dare he compare her to a horse.

He gazed at the singers who began to perform. "By the way, does your family happen to know a Hebrew by the name of David?"

Alethea's heart stopped cold.

"Of course not. We don't associate with Jews."

He glanced down at her and her cheeks burned. He looked back at her grandmother and smiled. "I need to gather the gifts for my future bride."

"Yes, of course." Grandmother nodded.

After Demetri left, Grandmother glared down at her. "What have you been saying to that boy? I was hoping you would at least know how to behave yourself at this feast. How many times have I told you—"

"Come, Renata." Aunt Fabia took Grandmother's arm and pulled her to her side. "Vibia is about to present her gift to Arnos." They watched as Vibia gave her silk square to her betrothed.

Alethea ground her teeth to keep from exploding. How could she possibly "behave" herself at a betrothal party that was sprung on her only a few hours ago? She wanted to stomp her feet, to shout and scream, to cry in a heap on the ground. She straightened with pride that she hadn't done any of that.

After Vibia had given her embroidery to Arnos, Grandmother led Alethea to stand before the guests. All eyes were on her, while the slaves sang and played their instruments behind her. As long as she wasn't expected to speak, she could stifle the explosions of sobs that threatened. She felt sick inside and wished she could faint, anything to escape. Of course, there was no such luck.

"The moon and stars, and you," Demetri said, coming to stand near and motioning toward the guests, "are all witnesses to the gifts I shall bestow on my betrothed." He then presented a bejeweled doll from behind his back.

Alethea reluctantly accepted it. Of course, she didn't like it. She already had a doll. The one Mpampas had made with his own hands.

He then pulled a necklace from his belt and held it up for the guests to see. Everyone gasped, and Grandmother's face lit up with a big smile. He placed it around Alethea's stiff neck. A beautiful emerald jewel shone from its pendant.

As the guests admired the stone, Demetri stepped back. It was a pretty necklace, and it made her feel important. The color of the large emerald reminded her of his green eyes. She let it fall against her neck and refused to look at it anymore.

"What a beautiful stone," Aunt Fabia said.

"Of course." Grandfather stood with his hands behind his back and rocked on his feet. "I wouldn't expect anything less from the family Arnensis."

Demetri turned his back and took something from a slave, then faced her, holding a furry bundle in his hands.

A kitten.

A tiny, precious, orange and white kitten mewed in his palms.

She wanted to snatch the ball of fur from his hands, but stood very still and forced back her smile. Oh, how she wanted that kitten. Perhaps Demetri wasn't such a horrible person after all?

He held the animal out to her. With trembling hands, she took it and held it against her chest. It brushed against the necklace he'd just given her. The poor kitten. It wasn't his fault he came from Demetri.

But what about David? David could never give her such lovely gifts, yet what he did give was friendship. She could never have that with Demetri. She wanted the kitten, and the necklace was beautiful, but she tried to make herself not want them, not if they were from Demetri. Still she snuggled the kitten against her cheek, while everyone sighed and smiled.

It was then she realized Demetri had disappeared, but just when she was ready to let out a sigh of relief, he came from around the house with a pony in tow.

A pony? What would she do with a pony? Pull miniature chariots? Perhaps she could use it to cart her belongings when she'd escape her family? The wild thought almost made her laugh, but by his smug grin, she realized her snicker was misunderstood as he came near with the beautiful creature.

"He's for you to ride." Demetri led the pony to stand beside her. "Would you like to ride him now?"

She stepped back and shook her head. "No, thank you." She tried her best to sound sweet. She thought it might be fun to ride the beast and pretend to be a Roman soldier. She'd never seen a woman ride such an animal, but she wouldn't give Demetri the pleasure.

A look of disappointment washed over his face.

She fought the urge to stick her tongue out at him. Let him be disappointed. He deserved it for having scared her with his nasty words.

"So be it." He turned and smiled as he escorted the pony back around the house through the awe-struck crowd.

When the excitement died down, the two girls were made to sit away from the family and the rest of the guests. The men and women reclined on the couches that had been moved into the courtyard. By this time, scantily dressed women appeared and danced in and around the guests, while others played the lyre, panned flutes, and tambourines.

She watched in fascination. The women were beautiful, and they danced with spirit and at the same time, a gentleness she wished to emulate. Their sheer veils and wraps glided in and around the adults.

Arnos's father reached out for one of the dancers and pulled her onto his lap. The woman laughed and together they shared a drink from his goblet. Arnos's mother stood and stormed into the house. Nobody else seemed to care or notice.

Alethea longed to be at home, but she took advantage of the private time with Vibia and leaned close, squeezing her kitten against her chest for comfort.

"You can have Demetri." She held the ring out to her. "I'm not going to marry him."

To her surprise, Vibia scowled. "You think it's that easy? And what will Grandfather say? He promised you to him. Besides, the priest has already blessed your betrothal."

"I don't want him," Alethea said, certain her own will should make a difference. "You should be pleased. I'm giving him to you."

"And I am sure Grandfather will be pleased as well," Vibia said sarcastically. "You will be severely punished, and if they find out how ungrateful you are—" Vibia shook her head, casting a grave look "—maybe even killed."

Cold fear washed over Alethea. Killed? Grandfather had killed her father. What would keep him from killing her? But that was because her father had been a Christian. She wasn't a Christian, but her refusal to marry Demetri might very well ignite his anger. After all, look at how angry Grandmother had become when Vibia was ungrateful. Yet, Vibia was still willing to marry Arnos. Alethea really did need to think this through. According to Decimus, any Roman father had a legal right to put his children to death. Her heart sank. The situation seemed hopeless.

"By the time I'm twelve, I will find someone else to marry." Alethea consoled herself. She had to hold onto her dream, or she might die without the need of a sword.

Vibia let out a snort. "I doubt you'll be ready to marry at twelve. As for me, I will definitely be ready. I am far more mature than you." She patted her braids and smoothed out her stola. "I'm sure Grandmother would beg Grandfather not to allow you to marry so young. She would rather have her curls straightened before she would ever let you marry at that age." Vibia giggled. "You would make a fool of her with your antics."

Alethea shrugged off the statement. She was used to Vibia's insults.

Vibia tossed a braid over her shoulder. "You're so ungrateful.

Demetri gave you some fine gifts." Vibia looked down at her feet. "All I got is this cheap anklet and necklace. I didn't get a pony, a handsome jewel, or a cute kitten like you. If he does wish to marry soon, if I were you, I would happily accept." She sighed. "Still, I'm sure we won't be expected to marry until we're fourteen. Let's hope I won't have to wait until I am sixteen, that's so old." Vibia pinched her face in disgust.

Alethea's dark world brightened and she grabbed hold of this small ray of hope. She had more time.

Ω

That night when the partiers had finally gone to bed, David crawled over sleeping bodies. Each slave rested on his own pallet, and he was careful not to bump anyone and jar them awake.

Tonight was the night he'd been waiting for. The night he would find Sarah. Or find out what happened to her. He'd been so anxious to return to Rome, he could hardly contain himself. His hands trembled and his feet moved anxiously as he crept over his friends.

When they'd passed under Rome's gate, a surge of anticipation had overwhelmed David. Walking through the city streets had been torture. He kept watching for familiar faces, familiar homes. Anything to find a hint of his past.

He scrambled from the bedchamber and tiptoed toward the door. Slowly, he lifted the latch. It creaked and echoed down the narrow hall as if to sound off an alarm. David held his breath. He looked behind him. No movement. No sounds. He lifted the latch higher, until finally, the door opened.

With the door ajar, he slipped into the night air. He knew exactly where to go. He'd find his father's old friend, Manius. David jogged along the dark street, avoiding wheeled carts pulled by men and horses up and down the hills. He'd forgotten that wheeled carts were only allowed through the streets at night for fear they might kill a pedestrian. He'd better be careful. He passed by houses, fountains, and statues and was careful not to trip on the large paving stones.

How this brought back memories. He was ten years old again. Not much had changed. The mud brick apartments loomed above him on both sides. An emptiness wrenched through his gut, the same emptiness he felt the last time he stole through these streets.

A huge cart came toward him, rumbling on its giant wheels. David pressed against the side of a mud-brick building, bringing back memories of that fateful night. The night he lost his parents. He held his breath as the cart barely missed him. After it passed, he took off running.

Finally, he came to Manius's house. At least it used to be his house. Hopefully he still lived there. David pounded on the door.

Silence.

Glancing over his shoulder to see if he'd been followed, he pounded until his knuckles ached. This might be his only chance to find her.

Shuffling sounded on the other side, and the lock clicked. The door opened just a crack. "Who's there?" a voice came from inside.

"I'm David. A friend of Manius."

David caught a glimpse of the person's tunic on the other side and then part of his face.

"We don't know any David."

"David, son of Aaron." Manius clearly still lived there.

"We don't know you."

"Yes, you do!" David stepped closer to the door. "Tell your master I've come. I need to speak to him."

The slave nodded and closed the door.

David stood on the stoop and glanced around into the dark streets. No sign of Titus. Noise and shadows from wheeled carts moved about.

The door flew open. Manius, much smaller than David remembered, stood before him with messy hair and sleepy eyes. "This better not be a jest," he said, his tone weak from sleep. "Who are you?"

"It's me. David. Son of Aaron, the scribe. You and my father were good friends."

"David?" Incredulous surprise came over the man's face. "Our David?" He ran his hand down his face as if trying to wake up.

"What happened to Sarah? I need to find her." David's voice choked as he said the words, afraid of what the truth might reveal. "Is she . . . is she alive?"

"It's you." The man's voice was almost a whisper as he drew out the words. He grabbed David by the arms. "It's really you!" He cupped David's face in his hands.

Manius's familiar touch and smell enveloped him like a warm embrace, bringing him home. Only his mother and father had touched him in such an intimate manner. David's stomach ached, carrying the same homesick sensation he felt when he'd first been enslaved.

"We thought you were dead."

If they thought he was dead, perhaps that was Sarah's fate. "Is she alive?" How he longed to remain here with this man who knew his father so well, with this man who worshipped Elohim, his Creator, the God above all gods. "I can't stay."

A shadow loomed. Titus and armed guards came toward them. Recognition settled in his eyes when he saw David. "I knew I'd better watch you." He started toward him.

"Who are you?" Manius asked.

"I wasn't trying to escape," David said, meeting Titus's gaze. Then to Manius, "I'm looking for Sarah."

Titus grabbed David by the arm and yanked him between the men who stood guard around them.

"What are you doing?" Manius asked, bewildered.

The guards pushed Manius back toward his door, pushing him away from David as Titus dragged him away. His stride faltered, barely keeping up as Titus jerked him by the arm down the street.

"Where's Sarah?" David shouted, his throat closing in on his words as Manius's voice rose in protest toward the guards.

"Silence, boy!" Titus shoved David by his collar against the wall.

"I had a life before this," David said between clenched teeth.

"I told you. That life is over." Titus jerked him away from the wall and shoved him down the street.

David tried to keep up with his pace. "Was it so easy for you to give up your past? Your father? Your mother?"

"I had no choice." Titus yanked him along. "And neither do you."

David knew he'd get a lashing for what he'd done. "I just had to find my sister." Tears burned behind David's eyes, and it took all he had to fight them back. It was all in vain. He still didn't know if she were dead or alive.

"She's alive!" Manius's voice carried down the street.

David glanced over his shoulder as Titus continued to tug him along. Joyous relief sprang through him.

"Why are you doing this?" Manius shouted, struggling to break free of the armed guards. "You're treating him like . . . it can't be! The boy's not a slave!"

"Silence him!" Titus shouted at the guards, his voice a charge that one didn't ignore. But dare they harm a Roman citizen?

Unable to break free from the guards holding him back, Manius shouted, "David, you're—"

The hilt of a sword came down on David's head and blackness consumed him.

Later that night, David lay on his stomach between the other slaves. It didn't matter that his back and legs burned from the scourging. It didn't matter that his flesh twitched in pain with each delicate movement of the air. Nor did it matter that he couldn't roll over and fall asleep. All that mattered was Sarah. And his silent tears of relief.

thirteen

Alethea lay on her back, and David lay on his back opposite her on the wall. The pine tree provided just enough shade to keep them cool. She scooted up towards him so that her head touched his. She'd thought about asking him to pray with her just so he would hold her hands, but she didn't want to be deceitful. Nor did she wish to anger his God. After all, she was still waiting for Him to bring back Mpampas.

"David?" Alethea whispered as the birds called to one another from the trees. "How long does it take your God to answer prayers?"

"It depends." He released a long breath. "Sometimes He answers them right away, and other times He waits."

"Hmm." She would just have to wait then. She rolled over onto her tummy, careful not to fall off the wall. "David." She twisted her hair between her fingers and weaved it into his hair. She liked the way the sun cast light through the shade of the trees and how it made some of his strands light up like gold.

"Yes." His eyes remained closed.

"Are you my friend?"

"Humph. Of course."

Birds twittered above their heads as a long silence between them thickened on the air. She hoped he'd say more about their friendship, but when he didn't, she continued. "They're going to make me marry Demetri, and I don't want to marry him. So, I was thinking . . . ." She waited to see if he was listening.

"Hmm, mm?"

"I was thinking, maybe you and I should get married, then I won't have to marry Demetri."

David smiled, then he chuckled, his eyes still closed.

"What's so funny?" She pushed up on her elbows. "We wouldn't have to get married now. We can do it after I turn fourteen. That would be a decent age to marry, and Vibia doesn't think I'll be ready for marriage until then anyway." She rested her chin on her fists, holding her breath. She knew marrying a slave was impossible, but if he did want to marry her, maybe they could run away?

David rolled onto his side and pushed up on his elbow. He narrowed his gaze and looked at her. "Are you serious?"

"Yes." She twirled her hair around her fingers so she wouldn't have to look him in the eyes.

He sat up and let his hands dangle between his legs. He shook his head, then cast a side-glance at her.

She stared back down at her hair, avoiding his gaze.

"Are you asking me to marry you?"

She nodded, her cheeks hot.

The buzz of flies and the sounds of locusts increased their volume. Alethea could even hear the sun bearing down on them. Despite the noise, David's silence stretched out like a long speech from her schoolmaster that would never end. And like her schoolmaster, this silent "speech" communicated information she didn't wish to know. She twirled her hair some more. Finally, she couldn't endure the quiet any longer. "Don't you want to marry me?"

"Of course . . . I mean—" He ran his hands through his hair. "It just isn't possible."

A long breath of relief escaped her. Thank Fortuna. He did want to marry her. "It's hopeless." She rested her chin on her hands. "I'm doomed to marry Demetri." Sticking out her lip, she hoped he might feel sorry for her, give in, and say yes. "He's so cruel. He's not nice like you at all. He compares me to his horse, and he doesn't even have dimples."

"What do dimples have to do with marriage?" David chuckled and shook his head. "Aucella, oh Aucella. You're so silly." He gazed at the trees. "I'm sure Demetri will treat you well. He probably compares you to his horse because he doesn't understand you. After all, how many girls would dare refuse marriage to someone so rich and handsome, not to mention young? Most girls would be thrilled to marry a man like him."

"Well, I'm not!"

He leaned back on his hands. "He gave you some really nice gifts."

"All he cares about is the land he's going to get."

"You have to give him a chance. Maybe you need to be more friendly and look for the good things in him?" He sighed. "You need to start thinking of the good things about him." He leaned close to her, his face serious. "Promise me you'll do that. I want you to be happy. If you don't start seeing anything good in him now, you'll be miserable."

"But I don't want to marry him." She clenched her fists and her throat hurt from the knot building there. "You just don't want to marry me."

"Alethea, it wouldn't matter. I'm a slave. You can't marry a slave." He frowned and furrowed his brows. "It would be impossible, even if we did wish to marry. You know that."

"But you're my best friend!" Tears spilled down her cheeks and her throat burned. "We can run away together. Marry in secret."

He gave her a disapproving look.

"Then I'll pray to your God. He can do anything. If He can part the Red Sea, as you said He did, then He can find a way for us to marry."

"We better get back." He cleared his throat. "People will start looking for us." He jumped to his feet, keeping his balance steady atop the wall, and reached out for her.

She took his hand. It was bigger than hers and she savored every moment that he touched her. Why would he try to convince her to like Demetri, let alone marry him? He said he wanted her to be happy, but only David could make her happy. And that's when it hit her. She loved David. No one cared for her as much as David, not even her own mother. David was everything. How could she not love him?

She would pray to his God every day if she had to. Desperation took over. She couldn't lose him. She was determined to marry her best friend.

Ω

Several months later, Alethea ran to the gymnasium. "Do you know where Damonus is?" she asked one of the slaves.

"I believe he's in the woods, mistress."

She hiked up her stola and ran to the trees. Ducking under a branch, she searched the woods. "David! Where are you?"

"Here!" His voice echoed through the trees.

When she found him, he was doing the splits on top of the wall and punching the air.

"Doesn't that hurt?" she asked, surprised to see him in such a strange position.

He smiled. "Not anymore." He placed his hands flat on the wall and pushed his whole body up into the air, slowly stretching his legs out above him into a handstand.

She watched the muscles flex in his tanned arms and back. At fourteen he was beginning to look more like a man. His balancing act intrigued her.

He fell backward toward the ground.

"David!" Her heart went to her throat.

At the last moment, he arched his back and landed on his feet.

"I thought you were falling." She crossed her arms in order to control her trembling.

"What are you doing here?" He stretched his sweaty arms. "Shouldn't you be learning something in the kitchen?" He grinned.

She knew he was teasing, and she couldn't take her eyes off his muscles. "I can prepare food quite well, thank you. And I pity anyone who doesn't have the privilege of tasting my cooking," she said, even though there wasn't much she knew how to prepare. Still, she hoped to impress him.

"I pity the one that does," he said.

She picked up a pinecone and threw it at him.

"Hey!" He blocked it. "You've got a good aim. Maybe you should become a Gladiatrix and throw javelins at your competitors?"

"I'll throw one at you if you don't hold your tongue."

"Oh yes, I better hold my tongue, you might decide to poison me."

Shaking her head, she giggled. Taking a deep breath, she crossed her arms, recalling why she came.

"David."

He looked at her. She knew the seriousness of her tone would get his attention.

"I can't remember what he looks like."

David straightened and furrowed his brows.

"Do you remember what they looked like?" She kicked a pinecone.

"Who?"

"Your parents."

He stopped stretching and stared at her. His eyes clouded, no longer teasing.

"Sometimes," he said. "But it's becoming difficult to remember. I'll dream about them, and I'll see my mother and father clearly, but as soon as I wake up, their faces fade."

"That's exactly how it happens to me." She stepped closer. "Do you remember much about them?"

"Yes, but some things I've forgotten."

"I can remember the last night I saw my mpampas. He tucked me in bed. For some reason I can remember that real well." His strong arms and hands moved over the blankets. His dark, curly hair brushed against her cheek when he kissed her. She tried to see his eyes. She had only to look at David to see his eyes. "But his face . . . I can't see his face anymore like I used to."

They walked in silence. A cricket chirped nearby and a squirrel scurried up a tree.

"We have busts of Grandfather, Mother, and of everyone else, so I won't be forgetting what they look like." She wanted to spit. "But because of Mpampas's faith, they threw out any remembrance of him." All because of his faith, she had nothing. "I remember Mpampas telling me about his God, but not very much. You worship the same God as him—" Maybe David could provide the answers to Mpampas's thinking. "Why wouldn't he deny his God in order to keep his family? Wouldn't your God want Mpampas to keep his family?" Wasn't Mpampas's God supposed to be good?

He took a deep breath, but she suddenly wasn't in the mood for answers.

"Why did he love his God more than me and Paulus?" She stopped walking. "Why didn't Mpampas love us? I used to love his God. I used to love his Jesus." A knot formed in her throat. "He used to say that Jesus loved us."

She stomped her foot and pointed a trembling finger at him. "His God doesn't love us and neither did Mpampas." There, she said it, exactly what she felt. She'd raised her voice, but she didn't care.

"But He does love you. And so did your father." David's voice was calm but insistent.

"If Mpampas loved us so much then why isn't he here?" She put her hands on her hips. "We could be together right now, if it weren't for that God of his." She tore the leather band out of her hair, flung it on the ground, and stomped on it. Mpampas had his God, but now he had no family. What a loss.

David watched her, concern in his eyes.

"Mpampas can have his God—*your* God!" She turned to run. The last thing she wanted to hear right now was that Mpampas or anybody loved her. Nobody loved her! They were all lies. If Mpampas had loved her, he would still be here. If David's God loved her, He would bring Mpampas back from the dead. She had been waiting all these years, and Mpampas still hadn't returned. How long must she wait? A loud sob broke between her lips as she made her way to the house.

Ω

The next day Alethea sat against a small pine, weeping with her head on her knees. Even the chipmunk two trees over didn't give her any comfort.

"Alethea!"

It was David's voice in the distance, but she didn't answer. For the time being, she had given up the search, but if she didn't find it, she didn't know what she would do.

Eventually, she heard branches crack beside her, but she didn't bother looking up. She knew it was David.

He cleared his throat and knelt next to her.

"I can't find it anywhere." Her voice broke and she wiped her nose on her knees. "I've looked everywhere, and I can't find it."

Something dangled against her arm.

"Were you looking for this?"

From the corner of her eye, she spotted a small leather rope hanging from his hand. Mpampas's headband. She grabbed it and clasped it to her chest. It hadn't been lost after all; he'd kept it for her. She cried even harder.

He sat down next to her and fiddled with pine needles.

She brushed the headband against her cheek, taking in its scent. Mpampas felt nearby.

"I'm sorry for the things I said about your God. I hope He's not angry with me." She wiped her nose.

"God can handle your anger." He grinned. "No one's anger is too much for Him."

"I don't know what got into me. I just miss him, David." She sniffed, wiped her cheeks, and gazed down at her tear-stained hands.

"He keeps your tears in His bottle."

Her heart skipped a beat. For a moment, she thought she'd heard Mpampas speaking.

"What? What did you say? . . . Who?"

"God," he said. "He keeps our tears in His bottle. My mother used to say that. She also used to sing about it." His voice cracked as he spoke, going from a regular sound to a boyish pitch. His cheeks flushed bright red.

"Really?"

"Of course." He picked a nearby flower and held it in the sun's light. "Elohim says we can know Him by the things He's made." He stared at the lily. "Why did God make flowers?" He turned to her and placed the flower behind her ear.

She liked the feel of his wrist as it brushed against her face.

"Maybe He created them for little girls so they might have something pretty to put in their hair?" David watched the flower as if it might do something.

Her cheeks warmed.

"Do you know how many hairs are on your head?" He studied her, his look serious, as if she would know the answer to such an absurd question.

She frowned and shook her head.

"Why not?"

"Too many to count." She shrugged. "Besides, who cares?"

"He cares." His eyes glimmered. "He cares enough to know."

Cocking her head, she twirled her hair and examined each strand. She flicked the strands in front of her, then drew them along her hand.

"He's gentle enough to make the petals of that flower, and powerful enough to create thunder." David motioned toward the sky.

While he wasn't paying attention, she flicked her hair against his cheek.

Smiling, he brushed it away.

They laughed and their gazes locked.

The only time she remembered David looking at her with such depth in his eyes was when they first met. What would it be like if he kissed her?

His words warmed her inside. Maybe his God loved her after all? As she looked into his familiar blue eyes, her thoughts shifted to Mpampas. If his God really cared about her, he would bring Mpampas back to life.

Mpampas not only lost his family, but also died for his God.

"Why should I worship your God?" she whispered. "If I do, it could mean my life."

David continued gazing at her. "It's important because one day, Aucella, you will die. One day, everyone will die."

Why did he have to talk about dying? She shuddered at the thought.

He picked up a pine needle and tossed it. "Do you want to live forever?"

She laughed. It was as though he read her thoughts. "Of course, but that's impossible. Everyone dies."

"I mean, do you want to live after you die?"

"Yes."

"Then you have to be saved, and the only One that can save you, is Yahshua."

"What does Yahshua have to save me from?"

"Sin."

"Oh, yes. Sin." She put her fists on her hips. "Well, I have no sin, so there's no need for me to be saved."

"Everyone sins, Alethea."

"Not me." She stood to leave, brushing the pine needles from her stola. All this talk about death made her stomach hurt. She thought to ask him how she could possibly live after she'd already died, but decided she didn't want to know. It was all too complicated.

One thing was certain, if she was doomed to die, she wanted to delay the inevitable for as long as possible, and becoming a Christian wouldn't help. But what if he thought she was already a Christian?

After all, she believed in his God, she even prayed to Him. Being called a Christian meant death. She faced David.

"I may believe in your God, David, but I'm not a Christian, nor will I ever become one." Her voice was stern, but she didn't care. All the better to make her meaning more clear.

David sighed. "Just because you believe in Jehovah, doesn't mean you're a Christian."

"Good," she said, relieved. A weight seemed to lift from her shoulders.

"Even the demons believe and tremble."

She stopped to tie Mpampas's headband in her hair. So, even the demons wouldn't live forever. What did it matter? She had never met a demon anyway. Hopefully she wouldn't have to meet any in the next life either. She gave the band a good yank.

"Thank you for finding Mpampas's headband for me."

"You're welcome." He half smiled.

She turned to leave. She might have skipped through the woods, but her feet were anything but merry. Instead, her steps fell heavy on the pine needles as she made her way toward the field. Why did she feel so low? After all, she had her mpampas's headband back safe and sound, and she didn't have the worries of being a Christian. Yet for some reason, the future seemed grim.

fourteen

Alethea wiped her brow as the sun beat overhead. She sat on the couch in the large courtyard while she embroidered the blue and gold borders of her new mantle. It looked just like the silk square she'd given to Demetri, only this was far more beautiful. She'd been sitting there, by grandmother's order, from the time the sun shone on the other side of the garden until it cast a shadow to her couch. Thoughts of Demetri plagued her mind, and she wanted to get away from her grandmother's scrutinizing gaze.

The best place to get away from everything was over the wall. She'd managed to escape several times without incident. Still, she hadn't mustered up courage to get close enough to her old house to peer inside, but the few trips she'd already made were well worth the experience of freedom. She longed to go there now.

She glanced over at Grandmother who busied herself with another sewing project. Vibia looked lovelier than ever perched on her own couch under a palm.

"Grandmother, may I go to the hill and see if they're coming?" Alethea pushed up from the couch.

"If I let you out of my sight, I probably won't see you for the rest of the day." Grandmother pulled a long thread through her fabric.

Alethea's fingers and shoulders were too tense to do any more work on her embroidery, and her legs were falling asleep. "You have my word, when I see them, I'll return immediately."

Grandmother frowned. "Don't get dirty." She shook her head and mumbled, "Not one smudge of dirt when you return."

"I promise." Alethea meant it too. She didn't want to go through any more pains of looking her best for the expected guests.

"Very well then, you may go."

Alethea bounced from her couch. Tingles pricked her feet and up her legs. She tried to shake the sleep out of them as she limped toward the porch.

"If I find one speck of dirt, you'll be confined to the house for a week." Irritation filled Grandmother's voice. All the more reason for Alethea to escape.

"I'll be careful, Grandmother," she called over her shoulder as she swung around one of the pillars of the portico. Her legs felt like their old selves again, and she wished she could run out to the field, but she was a good girl and walked, keeping herself neat and clean.

When she finally rounded the top of the hill, holding her stola high so as not to get it dirty, she spotted Demetri and his caravan of slaves nearing the villa. Why did they have to arrive so soon? She turned back down the hill and shuffled toward the house. She had hoped that he wouldn't actually show up or that his visit would be canceled. Disappointment weighed down her limbs. She couldn't imagine living under the same roof as Demetri for an unlimited time. Now his stay was certain. Demetri and Grandmother would watch her every move. Unbearable.

When she entered the atrium, Grandfather was ranting and raving, which was nothing unusual these last several weeks. He paced the floor and hadn't noticed her.

"He murdered his own brother, I'm sure of it!"

Domitian now reigned in the late emperor's place.

Uncle Servius lounged nearby, sipping from his goblet, seemingly unconcerned about the change of events. He spotted Alethea and winked.

She smiled back and leaned against the impluvium. The fountain wasn't as full this time of year because of the decrease in rains. Uncle Servius's nose and cheeks weren't as pink, and she wondered if he might be sick. He always had something to drink in his hands. Sometimes he acted silly, but she was accustomed to his playfulness.

Grandfather still hadn't spotted her and continued. "What will become of us? Of Rome? Of our homes? A palace. Of all things! He decides to build a palace on the Palatine Hill right atop our homes!" Grandfather's face reddened with rage. One would have thought he'd just heard the news.

"We don't know that he murdered his brother. They say Emperor Titus died of natural causes." Uncle Servius took another drink then set his goblet on a nearby table.

Grandfather paced the atrium, finally spotting her. "Aucella." His voice softened. "Sing for me. Only your voice can soothe my soul in this time of turmoil."

"The guests are arriving." She was not in the mood to sing, and as much as she dreaded Demetri's presence, his arrival was a fine deliverance from a song and dance with Grandfather.

"Take care of these." Grandfather motioned the slave toward the drinks.

The slave took Grandfather's goblet and reached to take the other when Uncle Servius snatched it. He waved for the slave to leave.

"How long will Demetri be staying?" Now that she was sure of his arrival, she couldn't help but wonder how long she would have to endure his presence. She thought there'd been talk of his staying for a few months, but she couldn't be certain. She always tried to avoid the mere thought of his coming.

"I'm not sure." Grandfather pressed his fingers to his temples, likely still fretting over political affairs. "It depends on how much time his family will need to build a new house. It could take several months, or longer."

Longer? What was she to do?

"Where is your grandmother?"

"She's in the courtyard." She followed her grandfather as they prepared to greet the guests.

Alethea and the rest of the family gathered in the atrium. It'd been over a year since she'd last seen Demetri. She wondered if he'd changed much.

Titus escorted Demetri into the atrium.

She stifled a gasp. Demetri stood eye to eye with Titus. She didn't remember him being so tall. He must have grown since they last met. Even his shoulders were as broad as Titus's. She shuddered. Suppose he was as cruel as he was big? All the more reason not to marry him.

Demetri kissed Grandmother's cheek and greeted Grandfather, then he came to Alethea. He bent and kissed her cheek. His touch made her neck tingle, and he smiled.

"You haven't grown much since we last met. In fact, it seems you've shrunk."

So, she was short. He didn't have to remind her of it. Since Grandmother and Grandfather were present, she bit her lip to keep from snapping at him.

"Welcome." Uncle Servius crossed the atrium with Aunt Fabia following behind.

Everyone walked toward her aunt and uncle, so she dropped back from the crowd, seeing her mother walking from the bedchambers toward Demetri and the others.

She then spotted the Egyptian slave woman moving away from Demetri to the other side of the atrium near the other slaves. My, she was beautiful. Little Alexander was by her side. He had grown in the past year, although he couldn't have been more than three years old by now. His mother took his hand. "Shall we go find your friend? You remember David, don't you?"

Alexander shook his head.

"I'm sure you'll remember once you see him," his mother said, her Latin much improved.

"I'll show you where he is," Alethea said, planning her own escape. They made their way down the hall and out the door without being noticed.

David walked into the plaza and stopped when he spotted the woman. "Bahiti." He walked up to her, and Alexander reached out for him.

"You do remember!" Bahiti laughed. Alexander put his arms up and David chuckled. "David," the woman whispered. "I've much to tell."

Alethea glanced around for any listeners. Luckily, no one was there.

David, with Alexander on his arm, turned away toward the gymnasium with Bahiti at his side. "I'm glad you came."

They walked away, leaving Alethea standing alone.

Ω

Later that day, Alethea and Vibia helped as the cook finished up the last bits of preparation for the meals. The cook had gone to call the other slaves to the dining chamber, leaving Alethea and Vibia in the kitchen.

Alethea stood atop the latrina and sang for Vibia; it was a nice way to forget the troubles of life, and it was the only thing that gave her pleasure while stuck in the kitchen.

Vibia buckled over with laughter. "If Grandmother sees us, we'll be punished." She continued to laugh.

"And then, do you remember?" Alethea said, interrupting her song. "Those women moved their hips like this." She continued singing, imitating the scantily dressed dancers they had seen so long ago at their betrothal party. She giggled. "They had so little on." She dared pull her stola to her knee and kicked her leg. "And those stolas, you could practically see right through them. Why did they bother clothing themselves at all?" She breathed deep to continue her song. The notes were low; she had to hit them just right.

In the meantime, she was careful not to step into the latrina; that certainly would have been something to laugh about. She stepped carefully over its hole and made like she was playing a tambourine by smacking and shaking a small platter. She shook her hips and sang as she danced in circles.

She nearly lost her balance and grabbed hold of the wall that separated the latrina from the stove. She bumped into the pot of kitchen wastewater that sat at her feet. She caught it just in time, keeping the water from spilling out.

Vibia laughed, and Alethea forgot her place in the song.

"What do you think you're doing?" Grandmother stood with her hands on her hips in the kitchen's doorway.

Alethea jumped to the ground.

"Both of you bring those platters to the dining chamber right away," Grandmother said, exasperated.

"Yes, Grandmother," both girls said in unison.

Grandmother shook her head and turned to leave.

Alethea glanced sideways at Vibia.

Vibia cast a side-glance at Alethea.

They both exploded with laughter.

"Now!" Grandmother's voice carried from the hall.

Ω

Of course, Alethea was expected to serve Demetri, so she set a platter on a small table before him. He grinned and winked; her cheeks flamed.

Bahiti fanned Demetri. Alethea glanced in the Egyptian woman's direction and she looked away. Perhaps she felt guilty for spending all her free time with David? They'd only just arrived, and several times, she'd seen her and David in deep conversation. All they ever talked about was David's God, and she managed to hear a part of the conversation when he was telling her that Yahshua had to die in order to save everybody from their sins. She'd wanted to ask David more about that, but they would have found out she was spying on them, so she decided to ask later.

She turned her nose up as she walked by the woman to help Vibia serve Uncle Servius, Aunt Fabia, and her mother. David belonged to her and no one else. Bahiti's son, Alexander, wasn't in the dining chamber of course; he was probably with David. They both had taken a liking to each other. She enjoyed little Alexander and would be willing to share David with him, but sharing David with his mother made her cringe.

When the platters had been set out, she hurried through the peristyle toward the atrium.

"You know as well as I do, who and what that woman is. How dare he bring her into our home." Grandmother's angry voice carried from the office chamber.

Alethea stopped to listen.

"Come now, Renata. The guests are waiting as well as the rest of the family." Grandfather sounded impatient.

"It's improper! I will not have that woman in our house."

"By whose standards is it improper, Renata? Most men have a concubine. It just so happens that Demetri has already found his."

"*You* don't have a concubine."

"And for that, you should be grateful. Now let's go eat."

Alethea scampered toward the kitchen. What woman could they be talking about? It mattered nothing to her that Demetri had a concubine. She wasn't going to marry him anyway.

In the kitchen, she poured wine into the goblet she was to serve to Demetri and set it on a small tray.

Vibia came into the kitchen.

"Alethea, you're a fool. Why don't you want to marry Demetri? He's the most handsome man I've ever seen." Vibia giggled, but attempted to calm herself.

Alethea balanced Demetri's goblet on the tray and walked toward the door, being careful not to knock over the hanging pots and pans on the nearby wall.

"I simply don't want him. He's *all* yours," she said with a flourish as though she were an important orator reciting something dramatic. She then made a grand exit from the kitchen.

Vibia followed behind, giggling.

When Alethea came back into the dining chamber, Grandmother and Grandfather reclined at the tables. Grandmother half smiled and was quiet as Alethea set out Demetri's goblet.

Demetri spoke to Grandfather as Alethea helped Vibia unload her tray.

"Now that Domitian is emperor, most everyone on the Palatine is forced to move. It's as though he had his plans drawn up before his brother died."

"I have no doubt he did," Grandfather snapped. "It burns me up. What will become of Rome? Rule under Vespasian and then Titus was peaceful and splendid, not to mention stable. As much as I dislike Domitian, I certainly hope this does not become another year of four emperors. Rome needs stability right now, not chaos." Grandfather raised his goblet and drank.

The conversation continued as Alethea left the room. All she cared about was how the whole change in emperors affected her. Now she was stuck with Demetri until his parents built their new home. If it weren't for these pitiful circumstances, she'd have no interest in politics. She wouldn't mind giving that emperor, Domitian, a good shake; this was all his fault.

Ω

The days and months trudged by since Demetri's arrival. Alethea walked toward the gymnasium where the men had spent most of their time. She hoped to get a glance at David. They hadn't talked in days, and she wondered if he might be playing with little Alexander since he was nowhere else to be found.

Just as she came to the plaza, she spotted a sword leaning against one of the wooden stakes. She looked on either side and found no one there.

She crept up to the weapon. It was different from the short *gladius* she was used to seeing. This one was straight, and from end to end, it came as high as her chest. It looked heavy and she longed to pick it up. Of course, she could already hear Grandmother scolding her for trying such a thing, but she was willing to take that risk. She could use the excuse that she was going to lay it on its side for safety. After all, suppose little Alexander had happened by and knocked the sword over. It could be the death of him.

She again glanced from side to side and found that she was alone. Her hands grasped the sword's cool handle. It was too heavy to pick up with ease, so she dragged it toward her, determined to take a swing at one of the stakes. She tried to hold the sword up before her, but that was far too difficult to make a good swing. She worked her way under the sword, keeping its tip on the ground. If she picked it up over her shoulder, she might gain more leverage. She pulled and with one final surge of strength, she brought the sword up over her head. Her feet planted firmly on the ground and with quivering arms, she faced the great stake.

"What in Jupiter's name are you doing?"

Alethea turned to see Demetri's shocked, horrified expression, but just as she spotted his face, she lost her balance from the weight of the sword. She teetered to one side, too weak to scream. Her cheeks burned from the forced strength it took to hold the weapon.

He lunged toward her and caught her arm and the sword. His strength and power overwhelmed her, and she felt like a rag doll in his hands. His touch made her squeamish, and she tried to pry his fingers off her.

He laid the sword on the ground.

"Let go of me," she said, his hand holding her wrist.

He frowned. "You could have killed yourself." He kept his grip on her. "Do you realize, if that sword had come down, it could have sliced you in two?"

The images in her mind made her palms sweat. She tried not to listen and wished he would let go of her so they wouldn't have to be so close.

"Are you well?" He relaxed his grip and knelt in front of her.

Cheeks still warm, she nodded.

"I won't tell your grandfather. I've heard stories of his beatings." He rested his elbow on his knee. "Just promise me you won't ever do this again. You could have gotten hurt, even killed."

She took a step back. Was that genuine concern on his face?

He stared at her, and she cringed at the thought of his being nice, let alone rescuing her from the sword and from Grandfather. She hated Demetri, and if he continued this friendly behavior, she might scream.

"I don't care if you do tell Grandfather." She turned her nose in the air. "I would rather suffer one of his beatings than marry the likes of you." Having said that, she turned on her heels and left him alone in the plaza. As soon as he was out of sight, she scurried to her chamber.

Guilt throbbed in her chest with the pounding of her heart, and she threw herself on her bed. He had been nice to her! How dare he be nice to her after the way he'd treated her in the garden at his home. Yet, maybe he wasn't being nice to her at all? If she had died under his sword, he wouldn't get his precious land.

Would that sword have literally sliced her in two? It was terribly heavy, and how sharp it'd been, she didn't know. She shook the thought from her mind.

Demetri had barely spoken to her since he'd arrived, and as much as that was a relief, she'd been anticipating the moment he would; she just didn't expect him to be nice. She'd already planned on reminding him of her decision not to be his wife, not caring what the consequences were at this point. He obviously hadn't told Grandfather what she'd said the night of their betrothal. But suppose he would tell Grandfather what she'd said now?

She moaned. When would she learn to keep her mouth shut? She hadn't had to suffer a beating from Grandfather yet, though she heard they were dreadful.

Later that evening in the dining chamber, Alethea set Demetri's platter on his table even though he hadn't yet arrived. Relieved to see his table unoccupied, she hoped she could avoid him the rest of the day. Fortuna's luck was on her side, for she hadn't seen him at all since their confrontation in the plaza, though she dodged him every time she caught sight of his large frame. He'd been looking for her and asking the slaves where she was, but she'd managed to escape each time he came around. She readied his platter as Aunt Fabia and Mother came into the chamber.

She turned to leave, and just as she came to the peristyle she saw the dreaded Demetri making long strides right in her direction. With eyes narrowed, he reminded her of Hercules's grace and strength. She stepped aside, hoping he would pass. His sheer size made her heart climb to her throat. The look on his face made her quiver, and she trembled when he stopped and stood in front of her.

She ducked under one of the plants to leave, but he took hold of her arm and yanked her back to him. Dread poured over her.

He bent down to her level. "I have been searching everywhere for you," he said in a harsh whisper. "You will not disrespect me again. With an attitude like yours, no man would have such a sassy snippet. Consider yourself fortunate that I don't take you over my knee."

The thought of him treating her like a child made her anger boil. Forget the fact that she was a child. If she was to be his wife, she deserved his respect. She bit her lip and gripped the sides of her stola just to keep from striking the overstuffed, muscled giant.

"You will pay for your behavior, though I will not share the news with your grandfather. I show you mercy, for I know what he can and will do if he ever realizes what a sharp tongue you have." His eyes swept over her face.

Trembling, she felt the small hairs rise on her arms and neck. She was tired of him reminding her how merciful he was by saving her from Grandfather's fury. She'd survived this long without Demetri; she didn't need him.

"I will never be yours," she said in the same harsh whisper.

She could hardly believe it was her voice talking. Certainly, she was taking a great risk in speaking to him this way. Perhaps a beating was in order? A woman should show respect to a man, especially her betrothed. It was horrifying, even to herself, that she dared speak in such a manner. Yes, he'd been kind to her in the plaza, and he had seemed hurt by her words in his garden at home. In fact, it seemed to her that perhaps she was the one being unkind. She tossed the thought from her mind and brought herself back to the moment at hand.

Demetri continued to gaze into her face, but to her amazement his lips twitched slowly into a smile, then he laughed. "You have been sent by the gods to torture me."

He wasn't taking her seriously. To keep from screaming, she bit her lip.

Just then, Grandfather appeared.

Demetri turned. "Alethea has just informed me she wishes to sing and dance for us this evening."

She froze.

Grandfather's eyes lit up, and he smiled. "Wonderful." He put his hand on her shoulder and escorted her back into the dining chamber.

She followed, gritting her teeth. She'd hoped to spend the rest of the evening playing out in the field and possibly meeting David in the woods, though he hadn't been there very much since little Alexander was around. When she glanced up at Demetri, his lips turned up in smug satisfaction.

Grandfather wasn't looking so she stuck her tongue out at her betrothed.

He laughed.

Punishment for her disrespectful behavior consisted of dancing and singing for him nearly every mealtime. In the beginning, it proved to be a difficult task, but she finally realized, dancing for him was no different than singing and dancing for Grandfather. She thanked Fortuna that he rarely spoke to her again, and she did all she could to make sure he didn't have the opportunity.

Ω

A number of months had passed since the arrival of Demetri and Bahiti. David was thrilled that Bahiti had found the church in Rome. He'd asked her if she knew Manius. But she hadn't met him yet. David sighed. Surely, she would meet him soon. He would prepare a message for her to give to Manius when she went back to Rome. She was incredibly shy and kept only to the women. At least, that's what David noticed when she spent time with the church here. The only male she spoke to was him. Perhaps that was because he'd approached her first during the betrothal ceremony in Rome. And the fact that he was younger than her probably made him less of a threat. She expressed concern that Demetri became jealous when she spoke to men. David assumed he didn't count as one.

As he made his way to the plaza, he heard men grunting. He approached the corner and saw Aloysius, Servius, and Demetri swinging their swords at the wooden pillars.

A gasp came from a nearby plant. David spotted Alethea crouching behind its thick greenery. Unaware of David, her wide eyes were on Demetri. He wore a tunic from the waist down, and sweat made his chest and back shine as his unusual sword cut into the wood. David cringed. A young girl like her shouldn't be watching such a scene.

"I'd like to see Damonus fight again." Demetri swung.

David froze when he heard his slave name. The men had spent a lot of time in the gymnasium together and enjoyed watching David spar with Marcus and Lucius.

"His movements are fascinating," Demetri said. "Titus taught him?"

"He's quite impressive." Aloysius stopped swinging his sword. "That boy's abilities never cease to amaze me."

David warmed at Aloysius's complimentary words. Perhaps he'd earn his freedom after all.

Aloysius walked to a large basket of wooden swords, picked one up, and smiled at Demetri. "Would you like to experience his skills first hand?"

"Yes!" Demetri straightened. "Have him brought out."

David felt his stomach drop to his knees. Demetri was so much bigger than he was. Would he be able to hold his own against such an opponent?

Despite his anxiety, David stepped out into the plaza where the men could see him.

"Damonus." Aloysius grinned, eyes shining that David so readily appeared.

The men turned to face David. He stood tall before Aloysius, hoping to make a good impression.

"You will duel with Demetri, here and now," Aloysius said.

David nodded, though he wished he could run away and hide. Instead, he moved toward the basket and selected a wooden sword and shield. Demetri grabbed his, and they walked to the center of the plaza.

From the corner of his eye, he spotted Alethea behind the plant, watching with interest.

Titus appeared next to the plant and stood off to the side with his arms folded.

Demetri and David circled one another. Demetri went in for the attack.

David jumped and caught his breath. They were just wooden swords. He couldn't get terribly hurt, he reminded himself. He flinched at the power behind each swing.

Another swing came. Just in time, David ducked and rolled away.

The fierceness of Demetri's thrusts made his heart race. The power behind each forceful arc brought Titus to mind. How often had David fought against Titus? He knew Titus held back. And Demetri's parries weren't very different from those of Titus's.

They clashed swords, wielding them at each other.

Surprisingly, David held his own quite well against the older and much bigger Demetri. In fact, David thought maybe the man was holding back, but when he studied Demetri's reddened face, he knew he gave each swing and thrust his all. That's when David decided to test himself. He allowed Demetri to knock his sword out of his hand. David held his shield up to block Demetri's swings.

Demetri lunged.

David dropped his shield and yanked on Demetri's blade, causing him to spring forward. Demetri stumbled, but he caught his balance and turned. David braced his legs apart as Demetri lunged toward him with his sword.

David dove and rolled away, jumping back to his feet and grabbing his sword on his way up.

Demetri's eyes widened and he smiled, but continued the fight. They parried and David dropped into half splits, ducking from Demetri's blade, then spun on his hands and swept Demetri's legs.

Demetri fell as David jumped to his feet. He stilled his movements, giving Demetri time to stand.

The duel continued and carried on for quite some time. Demetri's movements weren't as quick as David's, and this time when Demetri lunged, David grabbed Demetri's sword, yanking it right out of his grasp. Demetri stumbled forward as David flipped the sword in his hand, taking it by the hilt. That's when David spotted Aloysius's scowl. He had to please his master. Maybe he wasn't meant to win this fight.

Demetri came to his feet, and David tossed him his sword.

He caught it and went in for the attack.

David pretended to trip and fell to the ground, landing on his rump.

Demetri forced him onto his back, brandishing the sword, then held it to David's throat. David's heart slammed against his ribcage. Would Demetri try to hurt him? After all, he was just a slave. He could do whatever he liked.

Stepping back, Demetri allowed David to climb to his feet.

"You're a good fighter." Demetri turned and handed his sword and shield to another slave.

"You put up quite a challenge for your size," Grandfather said, staring wide-eyed at David. "Impressive, indeed."

"The next time I return to the villa, I'd enjoy another duel with this one," Demetri said.

"I'm sure Titus will keep him in good condition for you." Aloysius nodded.

David dropped his sword and shield into the basket and made his way toward Titus. He hoped he'd been pleasing to both Aloysius and Titus.

"Now that the house is finished, I'm not sure how soon I'll be able to return." Demetri wiped the sweat from his brow. "Being in the country does me good. I haven't felt this well since we left Alexandria."

"You're welcome anytime. Come whenever you'd like." Aloysius smiled.

Titus came to David's side, and they stood close to where Alethea was hiding. She kept very still, hoping to remain unnoticed. David forced back a smile.

"You did what the master expected," Titus said. "Well done."

David nodded, surprised that Titus knew he'd let Demetri win. He held onto those words. They gave him hope. He knew he was pleasing to Titus, and with the way the fight ended, Aloysius was very pleased. David took in a deep breath, seeing a glimmer of hope in his future.

Titus walked away, leaving David standing alone by the plant.

"Did you enjoy the show?" He cast Alethea a side-glance.

Alethea gasped. "How'd you know I was here?"

He chuckled, but stopped and pretended to stretch. "I always know where you are."

She beamed with joy. "Then you'll know where to meet me after you get cleaned up. There's something I want to ask you."

He cast her a wary look, but she turned and fled before he could say no.

Ω

Alethea sat on the wall. She swung her feet over the edge and gazed out across the clearing. David sat next to her. His presence made her heart beat faster. It was good to finally be alone with him. She wanted to make this moment last. She sighed and lifted her face to the sun, taking in the sounds of the birds, the breeze against her skin, and the leather and pine scent of David at her side.

"So, what'd you want?" David asked, his voice waking her from her reverie. He gazed off into the clearing, his long legs dangling over the wall's edge. His tanned arms propped him up, and if she moved just a little closer, she might brush against him. He cast a side-glance in her direction.

"Why did He have to die?" she asked.

"Who?"

"Your Yahshua."

David let out a humph. "*My* Yahshua?"

"Yes." She straightened, knowing he was insulted that she didn't call Him her Yahshua. "Why couldn't your God just clap His hands and save everyone? Why'd His Son have to die?"

David sighed. "Good question." He studied the horizon, his mouth closed as if tasting her words. "God wanted the Hebrews to understand how evil mankind is, so He told them they had to sacrifice the best animals for every sin they committed. All that blood . . . ." David shook his head in disgust. "All that carnage was supposed to show us how evil sin is. But the blood of goats and bulls couldn't take away sins. Yahshua is perfect. He is Elohim, so He sacrificed Himself like a lamb."

"But why?" Alethea rolled her eyes and shook her head. "Why didn't God just say, 'Your sins are forgiven' and be done with it?"

David cocked his head. "Because Christ's blood makes us clean. Nothing else can. And without it, we can't be with God."

Alethea crossed her legs. "Well, I'm glad I don't have any sin."

David rested his elbows on his knees and watched her, but Alethea avoided his gaze.

"No one is without sin, Aucella." He leaned toward her. "No one."

She glanced at him from the corner of her eye, but quickly refocused her attention on the horizon. "It doesn't make sense." She shrugged. "Why make someone die when all you'd have to do is clap your hands?"

David stared at her for a while, studying her.

Shifting under his scrutinizing gaze, she leaned forward and watched the birds soar and dance on the air in front of them.

A gentle breeze caressed her cheek as David lifted her chin. He forced her to look at him. His blue eyes fixated on hers.

"Passion," he said.

Alethea took a long shuddering breath.

"What shows greater love?" He continued to hold her chin. "Someone who sacrifices himself to save your life, or just claps his hands?"

His words were powerful and sent a chill down her spine. David released her chin and she felt a tinge of disappointment. She couldn't imagine dying for anyone. Never would she be able to love someone so deeply. The people Yahshua died for owed David's God a great debt. Peering up at David she asked, "Your God loves us, but how do we love Him back? Since we can't see Him, or hear Him, or touch Him." She shrugged. "How do we love Him?" She would have liked to give David's God a hug, but how could she do that when she couldn't even see Him? How could she kiss Him when she had no engraved image of Him?

David stared out over the field and into the trees. "You love Him by obeying Him."

Alethea sighed. For some reason, she didn't like that answer. That was too much work. Obeying Him meant becoming a Christian. Offering a hug and a kiss required less effort. Instead, He wanted everything. She couldn't give everything. Not if it meant her life.

fifteen

Holding a flower to her nose, Alethea sauntered into the atrium. She stopped at the sight of a filthy woman weeping on the floor. A chain dragged from her ankle and a brand mark scarred her upper arm.

One of the slaves from the vineyard. What was she doing here?

The woman lay at Grandfather's feet. Eyes moist, Grandfather motioned for a slave to come.

The woman was helped to her feet, and she leaned heavily on the slave's arm.

"What happened?" Alethea asked Grandmother who stood near-by, dabbing her eyes.

"A wild boar killed her child."

Alethea's heart went to her throat as she watched the grieving woman being led away. "But there are no wild animals in these parts."

"Men were bringing wild boars in for one of the spectacles for Caesar's new amphitheater. Before they reached the city gates, the cage fell and burst open. Several of the boars are running loose not far from here. They were able to recapture a few, but some got away."

Alethea shuddered. Her heart went out to the woman who wept for her lost child.

Ω

Alethea sat with her wooden writing tablet held up to her chin and blew wax fragments off the page.

"Alethea, be careful," Vibia said. "You just blew wax all over me."

"Sorry." She glanced at Vibia who wrote, holding her tablet in her lap. Her paragraph was only half completed, while Alethea was now finished.

Decimus cleared his throat from the other side of the room and threw the girls a stern look. He sat before Marcus, Lucius, and Paulus, instructing them in their work.

Alethea looked at her work with pride. What was that? The wrong word. She flipped her stylus over and smoothed out the mistake with its flat end. She proceeded to write the correct word when Grandmother entered the chamber.

She motioned for Alethea to come.

Alethea wrote the word, blew the wax off its page—only to notice Vibia scowling—and folded the tablet closed. After she set the thin sheets of wood on her chair for Decimus to find, she followed Grandmother into the peristyle.

Grandmother turned. "Demetri is leaving, and I want you to serve drinks. We will be in the outer courtyard."

Alethea nodded and skipped toward the kitchen, stifling a shout of joy that Demetri would soon be gone.

Luckily, she had completed her paragraph for Decimus, otherwise she would be expected to finish it before the day was through. Perhaps this meant she would later be granted free time? And what better way to celebrate her new found freedom than to play in the woods with David.

As soon as the tray was laden down with full goblets, she carried it to the courtyard. Demetri stood with his back to her and spoke to Grandfather, while Grandmother stood nearby. Alethea balanced the tray of drinks and was careful to watch her step as she neared the trio.

"I hope to persuade you. Please, allow me to take her in marriage now," Demetri said.

Alethea froze. She caught Grandmother's eye.

Grandmother turned toward Demetri. "But she is only twelve and not yet in the way of a woman. Surely you can wait?"

"Silence, Renata. I will take care of this," Grandfather said.

Alethea dropped the tray of drinks.

"No!" She ran to her grandfather and fell at his feet. "Please don't make me marry him. Please!"

Grandmother came and pulled Alethea up.

"Please!" She grabbed her grandmother's stola. "Don't make me marry him. I'm too young . . . please." She wailed at the thought of being bound to Demetri for life. She hadn't even had the chance to find a way to marry David yet.

Demetri frowned down at her.

Her anger raged and she faced him. "You are not interested in me, you just want land. You can have the land. Take it! Just let me be!" She ran from the courtyard.

Her cries echoed off the portico as she neared the gymnasium. Everything around her spun. She thought she saw David but didn't bother to be sure. Sobs racked through her as she ran past the stables and into the field.

What was she to do? She would run away. That was the solution. She hated Demetri. He cared nothing for her; he only cared for himself. He was greedy for land. And he'd never care for her unless she was a horse.

She made her way through the trees, snagging her hair on lower branches. She tore herself free, just as she wished to tear herself free from the clutches of that man.

She prayed desperately to David's God as she climbed the big pine, her arms scratched and bruised from her haste. "Please, God of David. Make him go away." She cried as she stepped onto the wall from the tree. She paused long enough to fold her hands and look up to the sky. "Make Mpampas come; make Mpampas come for me. Please save me from Demetri."

She then slid down the mound of dirt and ran through the clearing. Her breath came hard and her heart hammered in her chest, but she didn't slow her pace.

"Alethea!"

She glanced over her shoulder.

David stood atop the wall near the big pine, his dagger poised in his hand. "Come back! There's danger!"

She looked all around. Her vision blurred from her tears. She saw no danger. What was he taking about? A loud squeal came from the other side of the clearing. A pig with large tusks came straight at her.

Screaming, she turned and ran.

"Run this way! Come to the wall!" David shouted, waving his arms.

She ran along the wall toward the mound.

David ran on the wall toward her.

Glancing over her shoulder, she saw the boar and its giant tusks not far behind. She screamed and pumped her arms and legs as fast as she could.

Out of breath, she climbed up the mound, grasping the rocks, pulling herself to the top. Her arms were weak and her legs wouldn't move as fast as she needed. Just as she came to the top, David leaped behind her.

A loud squeal and grunt came from the boar. When she turned, she saw the boar take off down the mound of dirt with David on its back.

Gasping for breath, she thought her heart would beat itself right out of her chest. She couldn't move and lay exhausted in the dirt.

David gripped one of the boar's tusks and stabbed its rump with his dagger, but the boar kept on running. He stabbed the boar again and again, but it did nothing to slow the animal.

The boar tore through the clearing with David on its back. She prayed to David's God that he wouldn't get hurt.

David's face was mean and red as he furiously thrust his dagger in and out of the boar's backside.

The sight brought back memories of them riding the sow in the field.

The boar jumped and turned and sped in circles.

David grabbed both tusks to keep his balance, still holding his dagger. He bobbed back and forth, up and down. When they turned, the rump of the boar looked as though it was David's rump: half man, half boar.

Again, she was brought back to those days in the field with the sow.

She watched the boar kick its stubby hind legs and shake its rump. David's backside disappeared onto the boar's back, while the animal's rounded behind appeared to be a part of David. Her lips tugged into a smile, despite the anger and horror she felt inside. She stifled a giggle.

David bounced all around, but he kept his hold as he jabbed his dagger into the beast. Nothing fazed it. Again, she saw the boar's rump as though it were David's. They zipped by the mound where she lay in the dirt, giggling. Horrified by her own laughter, even as tears flowed down her cheeks, she covered her mouth and hid her face. David was in danger, and she was laughing. What was wrong with her?

Just then, David leaned forward and thrust his dagger into the boar's throat. The boar let out a guttural gag, and blood sprayed in all directions.

She bit her lip, stifling her giggles, wanting to bang her head against the wall. Anger overcame her. Anger at herself for such foolish behavior.

David dug the knife in deeper, and finally the boar came to a stop. It sat on its haunches and teetered as David gave the dagger one last twist. His face was bloody and angry, making her blush from having laughed. Tears still covered her cheeks, and she wondered if she were going mad.

"Go!" he shouted at her, pointing to the wall. "There may be others."

She jumped to her feet and climbed over the wall; she'd never gotten over it so fast.

David followed close behind.

Safe on the other side, she stared at the blood covering David's arm to his elbow. It dripped from the dagger in his hand, and large spatters were on his face and tunic. His blue eyes flared.

"I assume you're not hurt since you found the whole scene amusing."

She wanted to bury her face in her stola. Visions of the boar's behind and David's back flashed through her mind. How shameful! She nearly laughed out loud again. She pursed her lips together to keep from smiling. She forced her attention on the blood, a good reminder of the horrifying situation at hand. Anger coursed through her. How could she do this? Why couldn't she stop laughing?

She couldn't explain her actions when she didn't even understand them herself. "David, I'm sorry." She reached out to touch his arm, the one without the blood.

A scowl etched on his face, and he jerked himself away as if she might bite.

She stepped back, and a sick feeling turned in the pit of her stomach. He had never looked at her that way before. "Are you hurt?"

He shook his head, still frowning. "We should get back to the house."

The look on his face frightened her. It was like looking at a statue, and she couldn't do anything to mold it into something else. Guilt pricked her conscience. "David?"

He ignored her and kept walking.

"David, I'm sorry."

Silence.

They continued walking. The only sounds were the crunching of pinecones beneath their sandals. That unusual frown continued to distort his face.

She could bear the silence no more. Alethea fell on his tunic. "David, please, I'm so sorry. Are you sure you're not hurt?"

"No, I'm not hurt." He stopped. "Let go of me. You'll get blood on yourself."

"I don't care," Alethea cried. "Oh David, please forgive me. I don't know why I was laughing." She hated herself for it. "I'm so sorry."

"Come." He started walking again, shaking her off of him.

She followed. How could she make it up to him? He just saved her life, not to mention, risked his own. And she had laughed. This was awful.

They walked in silence toward the house. With each step they took, her stomach tightened. Tears welled in her eyes and poured down her cheeks as they neared the courtyard.

They came into the plaza, and an astonished look came over her mother's face. Cornelia screamed. She ran up to Alethea and practically shook her.

"You're bleeding! What happened?" Her eyes were wild, examining Alethea from head to toe.

Alethea looked down at her stola. She had gotten blood on herself from David's tunic.

"I'm not bleeding, Mother. I'm fine." She sniffed back the tears and was surprised that her mother showed no concern for David, who was covered in the blood. But didn't Alethea just do the same?

Grandmother and other slaves appeared. Grandmother rushed to Alethea, and some of the slaves hurried to David.

"She's not wounded," Cornelia spat out.

Alethea gasped. Was her mother disappointed that she wasn't hurt? Then she noticed the look Cornelia shot David. Her mother's eyes flashed with anger.

"Mother, Damonus saved me from a boar. He saved my life."

Cornelia stared at Alethea, a look of disbelief on her face. "A boar?"

"Yes, it's true."

"You were on the other side of the wall?" Grandmother's lips pinched together.

Alethea knew she was in trouble.

"You have blood on your stola. How did you get blood on yourself?" Grandmother glared at David. She then took Alethea's arm in a painful grip and pulled her away toward the baths. "Portia, come." She practically dragged Alethea along. "Someone take care of the boy."

Later, Alethea found herself standing in her grandfather's office chamber. He stood before her with his hands behind his back.

"Damonus says he saw you go over the wall, and because of the latest news about the boars being in the area, he followed you."

Grandfather walked toward his couch, sighing. "But I will deal with that later. Of course, we are all grateful to have you returned to us safely." He turned. Anger clouded his dark eyes. "But what weighs heavily on my mind," his voice was a forced calm but soon exploded, "is your horrid behavior before our guest and your betrothed!"

His shout swept over her like a great wind, causing the hairs on her back and arms to stand on end. She held her breath and swallowed hard, standing with her hands at her sides, grasping her stola and focusing on the ground.

"How dare you behave in such a manner!" He stepped toward her. "You will marry Demetri when I say you will. I will not accept any more dramatic outbursts!"

"Yes, Grandfather." Her voice didn't even sound like her own, and she continued to stare at the ground. She now wished for death. She would be forced to marry Demetri whether she liked it or not; that was, if Grandfather didn't kill her first.

"Look at me," he said.

She looked up, staring at his chin in order to avoid his eyes.

"Your Grandmother and I discussed the matter of your marriage to Demetri." His voice became calm. "We, *I*, have decided that you are not yet ready, so he will have to wait." He paced the floor. "In light of your recent behavior, it seems we have made the right decision."

Alethea let out a silent sigh of relief. She could breathe again.

"But," Grandfather continued, "you will be punished for your outrageous behavior."

Her heart sank to her knees.

He turned and picked up a plank leaning against the wall behind the door. Grandfather motioned toward the table. "Brace yourself." He shifted the large board in his hands.

Her knees felt weak as she shuffled toward the marble table. She could hardly believe what was about to take place. Everything happened so fast; she barely had time to think. Tears blurred her vision, her bottom lip quivered, and her hands trembled as she gripped the table.

"Ten lashes, save one," Grandfather said.

He stepped near.

She could hear the swing of the wooden board, and it came down hard on her lower back like a heavy boulder; she cried out and didn't think she could bear another strike.

"One," Grandfather said.

Again, the boulder slammed against her back. She collapsed against the table as painful tingles ran down her spine.

"Two."

This time flames raged across her bottom. She held her grip on the table, and though it felt like fire, it wasn't as bad as when he struck her on the back.

"Three."

Now her legs burned.

"Four."

The hacks continued, hacks like he were chopping down a tree, and her clammy hands lost their grip on the marble table. Her screams and cries echoed off the walls and through her ears. Her face lay against the cold, hard surface of the table, and her tears mingled in with her hair and cheeks.

After the ninth lash, he stopped.

Grandfather, out of breath, set the paddle back against the wall behind the open door.

Still crying, she turned slowly, aching with every move, while Grandfather glared at her.

"You will never behave so foolishly again." Grandfather's voice was grave.

Still sobbing, she nodded. Her entire backside throbbed with pain. She hated him for it, and she hadn't even been punished yet for having gone over the wall. She trembled from the thoughts of what that might entail.

In a rush, Demetri entered the chamber. He stopped when he saw her.

Exposed and on display, she stood with her hands on her backside, trying to rub away the pain, her cheeks flaring with embarrassment. This was not a party or a gathering for a banquet! What was he doing here? She bit her lip to keep from screaming at him to leave. How dare he come in here and act so arrogantly before her. She did everything she could to stifle her sobs, though tears continued spilling down her cheeks.

Demetri cleared his throat and put his hands behind his back. He quickly glanced at Alethea, then away. "Forgive my intrusion. Considering all that has taken place, I will take my leave. If I'm to arrive in Rome before nightfall, I need to go immediately. I bid you farewell."

"Stay one more night." Grandfather walked toward him.

Cornelia came to the doorway of the chamber.

Grandfather motioned toward her. "Take Alethea to her bedchamber. She has yet to be punished for sneaking outside the villa. I want every door along the wall checked and locked, and it's your task to learn how she managed such a feat," Grandfather said.

Cornelia nodded and held a quivering hand out toward Alethea.

Did she see sympathy in her mother's gaze? She limped next to her mother as they made their way to her bedchamber.

"Are you in much pain?" Her mother whispered once they reached the chamber.

Alethea shook her head, ashamed to admit just how horrible she felt.

"Wait here."

Alethea nodded and sat on her bed. Pain shot up her back. She cried out and jumped to her feet. She held her breath until the pain subsided. When she felt she could move again, she turned to the bed. She would have to lie on her stomach. But could she bend over to get on the bed?

Alethea spent the rest of the day in her chamber. After a good scolding from her grandmother, as her mother stood in the doorway with her arms crossed, she finally confessed as to how she made it over the wall. The tree was to be removed immediately, but her punishment was yet to be given. Later, Portia brought food, and she didn't have any news about David.

As the hours went by, Alethea thought about the beating she had received; how could she not, she was constantly reminded of it every time she tried to sit or walk.

She remembered being thrashed by Mpampas, but it was only on her bum, and she didn't recall ever having difficulties sitting and bending afterwards. Well, maybe sitting, but it never lasted this long.

After a thrashing, Mpampas would always hold her and say how much he loved her and that it was his duty to teach her to obey. If she didn't learn to obey him, she wouldn't learn to obey the Lord. Amazing. She actually remembered what he used to say.

At different times during the day, she heard laughter, including Demetri's voice. He must have decided to stay. She cringed. After more hours, she finally concluded she had been forgotten.

Later, Aunt Fabia came with Vibia to the chamber. She took one look at Alethea, gasped, and left the room.

Vibia quietly readied herself for bed. "Demetri wanted me to tell you how sorry he was for walking in earlier, but he was worried," Vibia whispered as she donned her night stola. "He could hear your screaming and was afraid for you."

"Cornelia!" Grandfather shouted from the other side of the house. "I ordered you to take care of your daughter!" The voices neared the atrium.

"I did, Father. I ordered the slaves to remove the tree."

"And what have you done as punishment?"

"I confined her to her bedchamber."

This was news to Alethea. Her mother had simply said for her to wait there.

"You know as well as I do, she deserves another beating. I intend to give it to her myself." Grandfather's voice neared her chamber.

Alethea trembled, and she crawled into bed. She lay on her side to avoid the bruises, pulling the covers up to her neck. She thought she might pass out if she had to endure another one of his beatings.

"I will take care of it, please don't beat her again." Cornelia's voice trembled.

"If you don't punish her this time, I will again." Grandfather's voice came from the atrium.

Her mother's shadow appeared in the doorway. "Sit up."

Alethea sat up. The pain in her back and her legs beat a tremendous rhythm down her spine, but she kept still, holding her breath, hoping it would fade.

Cornelia glanced over her shoulder at the door, then at Vibia who feigned sleep, and back at Alethea.

"How could you be so foolish?" her mother asked in a hard whisper and with a shaky voice. "I told you not to go on the other side of the wall again, and you willfully disobeyed me. You might have been killed." Her mother, still glancing at the door, slumped on the bed. "What were you thinking?"

Alethea pulled at the covers. She wanted to hide, but her mother was sitting on them. "I . . . Damonus was . . . . He saw the boar . . . and . . . ."

"Did Damonus tempt you to go over the wall?" Her mother faced Alethea with a pointed glare.

Alethea looked up with surprise. The solution to her problem just spilled from her mother's lips and landed right on the bed. She wondered if her mother wanted her to say yes.

Alethea's back and legs throbbed. Perhaps another beating would cripple her? She stared at the floor, avoiding her mother's gaze. The lamp from the atrium cast shadows on the tiles.

"Well," Alethea said. "I think he just wanted to show me that he could kill the beast. He wouldn't have allowed me to get hurt." Alethea twisted the corner of her blanket.

"That explains it." Her mother stood, causing Alethea to wince from the pain. She pinched her lips together and hurried from the room, not bothering to say good night.

Alethea's stomach hurt. She crawled back under her covers and stared over at Vibia, who silently stared back.

"Why didn't you tell them sooner what that slave boy did? You wouldn't have had to sit in your chamber all day," Vibia whispered.

Alethea turned on her side and faced the wall.

Later that evening, when Vibia was already asleep, Alethea heard through the window above her bed, the sing of a whip and somebody's cries.

David.

He was being flogged.

Alethea lay in shock. She couldn't believe what was happening.

David cried out again.

Lucius's howls of laughter carried to her ears. "Get him, Titus. Show him who's Master!" Lucius shouted above David's screams.

She buried her head under the covers, but she could still hear the blows and his piercing wails, and Lucius's shrieks of joy. This was all her fault. Each lash of the cat sent stings of pain through Alethea's mind. Torturous waves of guilt exploded within her.

"Stop!" she shouted into her pillow. Remorse and shame brimmed forth into uncontrollable sobs.

Cracks of the whip and David's wails echoed in her ears. Unbearable.

"No pain!" Titus shouted. "You don't feel pain, Damonus!"

The whip sang and David's shrieks tore at Alethea's heart.

"Why don't they stop?" She cried into her pillow.

Every part of her body shook. There was no way out. The deed was done. He was paying the price for her sin.

Finally, the lashing came to an end. Alethea pulled the covers off her head, her hair clinging to her hot, wet cheeks. Footsteps and talking carried from under her window as they probably took David back to the slaves' quarters.

He was silent.

Was he dead? Had he fainted?

Disheveled, Vibia sat up in bed, staring at her.

Alethea turned toward the wall and wept.

sixteen

Weak from the scourging earlier that night, David trembled as he handed his father's scrolls to Ace. "Please, continue to teach the others."

The light from the flames of a torch danced off the walls of the stables in the middle of the night, casting long shadows over Ace's face as he took the scrolls. He stood there, studying David. Probably afraid to speak as he looked at the gashes exposed on David's body, arms, and legs.

Ace simply nodded and walked away, carrying with him David's most valued possessions.

David turned, unable to watch him disappear into the night with his father's manuscripts. He leaned on his hands against the wall. His body ached and twitched with pain. Slaves had rubbed honey on his wounds, though he'd barely been conscious. He didn't think he would survive the scourging. He thanked God he'd finally fainted. It had been more than he could bear, and all he could see in his mind's eye was Alethea's lying tongue acting as the whip.

She was nothing but a spoiled, selfish child. How could she laugh at him while he had risked his life? How could she turn on him and their friendship? He had been there for her in every possible way, protecting her as best as he could. He cared for her like he'd cared for Sarah.

She cared for no one but herself.

He grabbed his bundle and slipped out of the stables. His back and chest continued to twitch with pain as he made his way toward the trees. The night sky shadowed him in a welcome cloak of darkness. He couldn't sleep, the pain was so great. His heavy, exhausted body burned everywhere. Titus had given him the scourging, despite the fact that David said the girl had lied. Titus had believed him, but he had no choice in the matter, and he'd been unable to convince Aloysius that his precious granddaughter could do such a thing.

But why had Titus given the beating with full force, even when he knew he was innocent? Why had Titus been so efficient in meting out his so-called punishment?

Everything David had worked so hard for was now gone. Wiped out with one lie. He slipped between the trees. Aloysius would never trust him again. David had wanted so much to please the man in hopes that one day he might set him free. According to the law, he could have been free. Now his dream would never be realized.

That girl! He had been a friend to her, listening to her cry on and on about her dead Mpampas, while his own parents were lost and gone forever. Not once had he ever cried to her. She probably wouldn't have known what to do if he had. He was finished listening to her sniveling. He wouldn't do it anymore. He wouldn't have to.

Today he would live as a fugitive. He'd wanted his freedom to be according to the law. Now it would be according to him.

"Alethea," he whispered to himself. Her name meant truth. He shook his head. She couldn't even live up to the meaning of her name. That little liar. No, she was no Aucella either. Instead, of Little Bird, she would forever be known to him as Little Liar. He slammed his fist into a tree as the wall came into view.

He should have known better than to become friends with such a child.

He had worked hard to please Aloysius; he was certain the man had even grown to like him, but now it was all ruined. By her! He punched another tree.

"Damonus." Titus's voice came from behind.

David jumped and turned, hastily wiping away his tears. Every gash on his body, arms, and legs cried out in protest at the sight of their creator. He glanced around him. No shadows lurked in the trees. No one to help Titus restrain him. He'd have to outrun him. David stepped back.

Titus didn't make a move for him. He just stood there, watching. The moon's light reflected off his shaved head and bracelets.

David sensed the wall looming behind him, calling out to him. Freedom was just a few feet away. He took another step back.

Titus nodded toward the wall. "Coward," he said, his voice reverberating in the quiet air. He turned and walked away.

Coward?

David watched him go, his white tunic disappearing between the trees.

Speechless, David dropped his bundle on the ground. He side kicked the tree next to him. He slammed his fist into it, then his other. Leaning his forehead against the bark, he punched it again and again. His fists chafed against the tree, but he didn't care. The rage inside him chafed as well. He clutched the trunk, trying to fight back the pain in his knuckles as tears burned their way to the surface. He dug his fingers into the pine, rubbing his face against it, his tears melting against the wood.

The tree. His bridge to freedom.

Ω

Early the next morning, while it was still dark, Alethea got out of bed. She quietly threw on her cloak, wincing from the pain in her back. She had lain awake all night until the first sounds of the slaves walking through the plaza came to her ears.

A dark dread hung on the air. A dread that told her she was alone. That David was gone.

She tried to run through the hall, but the pain in her back forced her to walk. Only the slaves would be up at this time, so she had no worries about running into Grandfather or any other members of the family. Getting to the woods demanded excruciating effort from her injured back. But finally she made it to the tree. It was still there. The slaves hadn't chopped it down yet. Its branches stretched out over the wall.

And over David.

He lay on his stomach, his arm and leg dangling over the side. Dried blood and gashes lined his arms, back, and shoulders. His hands were covered in dirt, and his knuckles were swollen with dried blood and bruises. Guilt ate at her like the wounds ate at his skin.

She crept closer.

"David?"

Slowly, his eyes opened. He squinted, adjusting to the sun peering over the horizon and over his half-naked body. His gaze fell on her, and he dropped his head back down, as if too weary to hold it up.

"David . . . I . . . ." She didn't know where to start. How could she expect his forgiveness for what happened? "I couldn't sleep," she said, feeling like anything she said wouldn't be good enough.

Taking a deep breath, David pushed up, keeping his torso and legs from touching the wall. He braced himself and sprang to the ground in front of her.

Alethea's heart leaped to her throat and she jumped back, pain shooting up her backside.

Unsteady on his feet, he loomed over her, and his blue eyes pierced her through.

She almost didn't recognize him.

His face reddened, and he pointed his finger at her, his large knuckles inches from her nose. "I saved your life from a *pig!* And they whipped me for it!" His voice cracked as he spoke.

He turned his back on her, searching the ground.

She stared at his wounds, his broken flesh. Cuts ran from his back to his stomach and chest. Her body went cold all over. She suddenly felt too weak to stand.

"I'm sor—"

"How could you?" David faced her again, tears in his eyes. He took a few steps back. "Now they despise me!" He paced in front of her, raking his hands through his light brown hair. His gold earring reflected the early morning light. "I have been working so hard to please them. You have undone everything with your lie." David stopped and glared at her, the veins bulging in his neck. "I thought you were my friend?"

A chill came over her, and her stomach contracted. This was the first time he had ever called her his friend without her first having to ask. Now she had ruined everything.

"But I am your friend . . . I—"

David bent over her, silencing her. "You are *not* my friend," he whispered between clenched teeth, and his eyes grew cold. "I wish that boar had ripped you to shreds."

Her heart stopped. She took two steps back, searching his face, his eyes. Surely, he didn't mean it. But his face was set like stone. The face of a stranger. She didn't know him anymore. The sun cast its eerie light over his scarred body.

"Dav—"

"Call me Damonus." He turned, grabbed a bundle from the ground, and marched through the woods, leaving her alone.

Alethea swallowed. Her throat hurt; her back hurt. She choked on her tears and limped back to the house.

Alone.

Ω

Titus would take him to the other side of the Vibian Hill. David would be banished from the villa, but at least he would never have to look at that deceitful, selfish, sniveling face again.

David followed in silence, thankful Titus hadn't reprimanded him for his behavior. His fists throbbed with pain, and he could barely straighten his fingers. His whole body still trembled with rage, and the clotting in his throat was unbearable. He practically wheezed when he breathed as he swallowed his tears. His back and chest continued to burn, and he wanted desperately to lie down, but the pain was too great.

He knew it was time to go. He was grateful he had thought to give Ace his father's scrolls. He knew they would be in good hands if they remained here at the villa. Ace would take care of them and keep them well hidden.

They walked through the plaza and down the hall to the atrium. He would never throw another ball into the fountain. He would never see the inside of the villa again.

So be it.

He would only miss the friends he had made. Of all the people he would miss most, he would miss the church. It had grown greater than he could have possibly imagined behind these protective walls.

After David and Titus passed the beautiful vineyard, they came to a small village at the base of the hill. Men moved about on the gravel road, doing work, carrying *amphora* vessels to be used for the aging of wine. He spotted a wine press inside a stone building. Marble columns shot up on each side of the *sarcophagus* where men stomped grapes with their bare feet. Wine poured into a collection vat next to the decorated sarcophagus that depicted images of cargo ships carrying wine to far-off lands. A potent scent of fruit lingered on the air.

They passed the winepress and soon came to a metalworker's home where the smell of burning metal greeted them. They stopped under the awning where a man hovered close to a hot fire. Titus walked up to him, and without saying a word, the man moved aside. Titus lifted an iron rod off the wall just inside the door. It had a flat iron stamp at its end, and he held it in the fire.

"Damonus come." Titus's face was grim as he stared into the flames.

David came to stand by Titus. He watched in silence as the flames flickered around the stamp. Sparks flew up and died on the stone edge of the fire pit, leaving an ash residue. It reminded him of the open wounds on his body, how the whip left its residue on his skin.

After a long silence passed between them, Titus spoke. "I will continue to train you. I won't be able to come everyday, but I will expect you to buffet your body and be ready when I return. You will still spar with Marcus and Lucius and perform your skills before Aloysius whenever he desires. That means you will return to the villa on occasion, and when you do, I will expect the best possible performance in your technique." Titus turned the rod, and David's stomach turned with it. The stamp glowed crimson in the flames. "You have been pleasing to Aloysius, and he was sorry to see you go, but he could not forgive the immaturity of your behavior toward his granddaughter."

"But I—"

"I know you did no wrong, but Aloysius doesn't want to believe me. I think he knows we told him the truth, but he won't accept it. He loves that little girl too much."

David hated that little girl.

"Remember what I taught you about pain?"

"Yes," David said, fearing where this would lead.

Titus reached his hand out to David.

Tension wafted on the air like the smoke from the fire, burning his nose, and David had a sick feeling he knew what Titus was going to do. As he placed his hand in Titus's, David willed himself to be strong and brought to memory all that Titus had taught.

The man who had been working at the fire gave him a fat stick.

"Bite down," Titus said.

Titus took hold of David's arm.

David bit down, but instinct made him pull away. Titus tightened his grasp on David's arm, holding it in a vise grip. The man grabbed his other arm and twisted it behind his back. David fought to break free. The man shouted toward the street. Several men came running to help.

David struggled to breathe around the stick clenched between his teeth. He kicked and squirmed at the men hovering over him, but the more he thrashed, the more men that came to hold him down. Someone's knee pinned him on the ground, and Titus continued to hold his right arm.

He trembled as he waited for the inevitable, all attention focused on his arm, forgetting his other wounds. Tears welled in his eyes, and he tried to fight back the sobs that burst from his throat.

Titus reached out and pulled the iron stamp out of the flames. The glow of the stamp simmered as he brought it close to David's arm.

David cried out.

"Bite the stick," one man shouted.

"It'll be over soon," another said.

David watched in horror as Titus brought the branding iron down on his upper arm. Pain scorched through his limb and heat from the iron wafted over his shoulder and ear. He cried out, his piercing wails unrecognizable. His skin melted under the scalding heat. His whole being trembled with fiery pain. He felt as though the iron would burn through to the bone.

Titus removed the branding iron and dropped it in a bucket of water.

David's screams broke into wails, and his wails broke into sobs. He barely realized the men had released their grasp. His sweat-soaked body burned the wounds on his back and stomach that had broken open from his struggle. The smell of burnt flesh penetrated his nostrils, and the pain in his arm throbbed through his entire body, every limb and every muscle focused on that one branded piece of flesh.

He glanced down at his wound, trembling. Smoke danced around the black scar. It was in the shape of a "V" for Vibian. Only from David's perspective, it looked like an "A" and it stood for Alethea. As he grasped his arm below the wound, anger seared through his mind for the little girl he would hate forever.

Ω

After David had time to calm down, Titus showed him around the small village. David saw it through blurred vision and barely took in the one main dirt road in its center. It really wasn't a road at all since it came to a dead end at each side. No one was allowed to leave. People were bound with shackles around their ankles, and David had them around his ankles now too. He was tired and weak from the night and morning of torture. He longed to lie down in the field Titus pointed out to him beyond the homes. Farm animals grazed, and crops sprouted from the field where several women bent over working. Children played in a large pond, not far from where the women worked, splashing each other without a care or worry in the world.

Titus led David to a small house set apart from the others where a thin Ethiopian woman came to the door. She looked down at David with large brown eyes.

"This is the boy," Titus said.

The woman smiled. "Oh yes. It's nice to meet you." She nodded toward David.

David forced a smile, only to be kind to the woman. Really, he felt like weeping as he clasped his arm below the fresh wound. It throbbed and burned, burned and throbbed.

"Come in here. I'll show you where you'll sleep."

David followed the woman into the dingy little house. The sun's rays lanced through a window on his left, lighting up dust motes in the air. Another window lit up the back center of the large elongated room. A small bed perched against the left wall in the back, and half the room could be divided by a curtain.

The woman pointed to a mat opposite the bed. "This is where you'll sleep." A folded blanket rested at the base of the mat.

David longed to fall onto the mat and lose himself in sleep, the only way to escape his circumstances. He should have escaped when he had the chance. Then he wouldn't have to depend on sleep to run away and hide.

Coward.

David swallowed, recalling Titus's words. He couldn't deny it now. He was a coward. If he knew he would've had to endure the branding, David would have jumped the wall and never looked back.

The woman pulled the curtain closed to the length of the beds. "I'll close this each night so we'll both have privacy. My name is Taba. From what Titus has told me about you," she smiled at Titus, "I'm sure you'll do well here."

David took a deep breath and sighed. At least he would be treated well by this woman. She was obviously a slave too.

Titus and the woman turned toward the door and whispered to each other. The woman giggled, and Titus chuckled.

How could he carry on with the woman when David had just been tortured? His body burned like fire and he felt sick. He marched past Titus and the woman and went outside. Throbbing with pain, his nose burned as he tried to keep from crying.

"I'll return as soon as I can, Damonus." David was surprised to find Titus next to him. "You'll be well cared for. The men of the village will teach you all that you need to know about the vineyards, as will Taba. She'll prepare your meals and make sure your needs are met." Titus motioned toward David's burnt flesh with his chin. "She'll dress your wound." He grabbed David's shoulders and turned David to face him. "All will be well."

David nodded. He dared not speak for fear he would burst into sobs. He dreaded crying in front of Titus. It had been humiliating when he couldn't withstand the pain of the branding iron.

Titus turned to leave. David watched as his long form disappeared behind the buildings. David went around the house where he could be alone. He sank amongst the weeds and dirt. And wept. Tears streamed down his cheeks, and he wiped his nose with the back of his hand.

" Jehovah-Shammah. Why did you let this happen?" He looked up at the blue sky. "What have I done to deserve this? Haven't I been pleasing to you?"

All the times that David had pleased Aloysius, taught the other slaves about the Lord, and the patience he showed with Alethea

198 ✦ Sandi Rog

turned over in his mind. Sure, he had made some mistakes, but in
everything, David had done his utmost to serve God. He had made
Elohim his Master in all that he did. When something had been
asked of him, he acted as though Elohim Himself had made the
order. The outcome was good. He knew he had been pleasing to
Aloysius and to Titus. He'd been sure of securing his freedom. Now
it was all ruined. All that tiresome effort for nothing.

Why did this happen? He fisted his hands in his hair.

It was time to say good-bye to the hope of freedom. He watched
it fly away with the birds above his head. If only he had wings. He'd
fly away with them. The memory of when he and Alethea met on the
portico his first day at the villa came to his mind. She'd sung that
song.

> Oh, if I had wings like a dove!
> I would fly away and be at rest.
> Yes, I would wander far off
> And remain in the wilderness.
> I would hurry to my escape
> Far away from wind and storms.

Loneliness enveloped him, and his mind turned to the church.
He'd miss his brothers and sisters in the Lord. If only he had their
comforting words now.

A sparrow fluttered to the ground nearby. David watched it peck
the dirt. The bird chirped, making him feel less alone, less afraid.

Just then, a warm shower of realization washed over him. He
wasn't alone, and he didn't have to be afraid. He knew what his purpose was. This was no punishment from God. David had been sent
to teach the people in the village about Elohim.

His hands trembled as he clasped them over his bowed head.
"Father, I now understand. I will serve You here in the same way I
served You at the villa. I just beg You Father . . . . When my work
is done, will You please free me of this place? I want my life back."

He watched the little bird pecking and chirping. Finally, its beak came up with a worm, and he flew away, joining his friends in the sky. David imagined flying away with him, flying high above the clouds, flying away from this place, away from the darkness. His head grew heavy, so he rested his cheek on his knees. Yes. Someday he would fly.

The white clouds billowed above him, turning in the wind, turning and forming shapes. A shadow crept into the white folds and tumbled into a dark cloud. A storm? No. Not a storm. Birds. A flock of birds. They swarmed toward David. Crows perched in the nearby trees, while others settled on the ground next to him. They hopped toward him and pecked at his body. David shooed them away, but more came. He turned over, but the pecking intensified on his skin against the ground. How could there be birds between his body and the ground? He pushed up, and birds were beneath him and on top of him. Crying out, he shoved them away. He tried to get up and run, but his legs were too heavy; they wouldn't move.

The birds lifted from him, but the pecking on his skin continued. The crows formed a black shape of a man standing in front of him. The man swung a whip made of crows. He struck David with it, its lashing intensified the pain on his body. The bird-man became Aulus hovering over him. "You will never be free, whelp!" Aulus's face twisted until it resembled Alethea. Her tongue lashed out at him like a whip. His upper arm stung with pain. He cried out.

"Damonus," Alethea said in a voice he didn't recognize. She reached out to him with bird-hands. The wings were wet and cool on his face. "All is well."

David pulled away from her and his eyes flew open.

"You were dreaming." Taba hovered over him with a wet cloth.

"What happened?" Titus's voice came from the other side of the room.

David lifted his head to see, but the room spun and blurred around him. A bandage bound his upper arm where he had been branded.

"He was having a nightmare again," Taba said, helping David lie back down on the mat. "Do you know anyone named Aulus? He's cried that name out a number of times in his dreams. I think it's someone he fears."

Titus shook his head. "No. I don't know anyone by that name. Has someone here in the village done harm to him?"

"Damonus hasn't spent enough time in the village for anyone to have hurt him . . . except for you when you branded him."

"I had no choice." Titus's voice was a forced calm.

Relief swept over him now that Titus was near. He shivered and pulled at the cover.

Taba helped pull the blanket over him. "All will be well, Damonus. Just get some rest."

Taba moved away and hushed voices filled the room. "It's been two days now, and the fever still hasn't broken," Titus said in a concerned voice.

"Give him one more day, my love, and if the fever still doesn't break, bring the doctor."

David heard shuffling around the room but was too exhausted to open his eyes and see what was going on around him.

"I'm concerned about those dreams," Taba whispered. "He talks in his sleep and calls out names. Alethea is one of them. Isn't she Aloysius's granddaughter?"

"Yes," Titus said. "They were friends."

"Friends? Well, she must have hurt him in some way. When he says her name, he's angry."

David thought of his dreams, and it made his head hurt. He shivered again as he snuggled more under his cover. Alethea . . . she was the last person he wanted to think about right now. He needed to focus on his mission. As soon as he was well, he would teach others about Elohim.

Ω

David stood amongst the waist-high vines. The greenery and fruity scents carried over him in a shower of freshness. The weight of the grape bunches bowed down each small trunk, but the ropes tied to the vine's stakes, stretching from the top of the hill to the bottom, kept each plant upright.

Taba stood next to David. She reached out and plucked a grape from one of the bunches. "To know it's ready to be harvested, test the grape by its ripeness." She turned the grape between her fingers. "It should be fat and juicy." She popped one into her mouth. "And sweet, not bitter." She nodded. "These are ready." She cut the bunch and then placed it in a wicker basket at their feet. They proceeded to the next vine.

David walked carefully, so as not to trip on his shackles. Taba didn't seem to have any trouble and never tripped. He assumed over time he'd become accustomed to the chains. The heavy metal rubbed his ankles raw and rested uncomfortably on the tops of his feet. He'd noticed some slaves wrapped protective rags around the areas where the shackles rubbed. He'd have to do the same.

David reached between the wide leaves and used his small dagger to cut off a bunch. He placed the grapes in another wicker basket. Several baskets were spread out through each row in order to collect each bunch.

"So, what is Elohim?" Taba asked as she cut off another bunch of grapes.

David smiled, surprised by the question. He was wondering how he'd begin to share the gospel with these people. And now, God opened the door. *Thank You, Lord.*

"I'm just wondering because you said that word quite often during your dreams when you had the fever." She popped another grape into her mouth, and David knew it wasn't to test whether or not it was ripe.

"Elohim is our Creator." He motioned toward the vine with his dagger. "He made these grapes here. He made the sky and the clouds, the birds, and everything you see."

Taba pinched her lips together. "Hmm. No other god claims that."

"That's because Elohim is the God above all gods."

Taba studied David as they carried the last basket and emptied it into a larger basket at the bottom of the hill. More slaves filed by them to collect the rest of the grapes and dump them into another large basket at the top of the hill.

David and Taba lifted the collected bunches to carry them to the winepress.

"Tell me more about this God of yours."

And David began to tell her what he knew about Elohim. He thought of how Christ was the vine and David the branch. If he remained with Christ, David would be able to bear fruit. He looked down at the grapes. He was determined that Taba would be their first fruit.

seventeen

"David!" Alethea whispered as loud as she dared as she peered around the corner into the open-air gymnasium.

David sparred with the other boys. He stood so close to her, that she knew he could hear her, but he wouldn't turn around.

How often had he ignored her like this? He'd been gone for six months, and it felt like an eternity. She should march right in there and demand his attention. But her courage failed her. After all, he was banished because of her, and if the boys saw the two of them talking, they might say something to get David into even more trouble. Marcus could probably be trusted, but Lucius . . . she trusted Lucius as far as she could spit, which wasn't very far. The last time she tried, it ran directly down her chin and onto the front of her stola. David had gotten a good laugh out of it.

Oh, David. How she missed him.

"I'm sorry, David," she whispered loud enough for him to hear. "Will you please forgive me?"

"What are you doing here?"

Alethea gasped and turned to face Portia. "Umm, just watching."

Portia's gaze fell on David and then on Alethea. "You know, mistress." Portia looked around them, then back at Alethea. "You don't have to be alone," she said, her voice much lower this time.

204 ★ Sandi Rog

Alethea raised a brow. "What do you mean?" Did Portia know of a way she could sneak off with David?

Portia clasped her hands together and leaned in closer to Alethea. "Jesus would like to be your friend."

Alethea's cheeks warmed. Where was this coming from? Was it a test? A test to see if Alethea believed? And if she claimed to believe in David's God, would Portia run off and tell Grandfather? She may have helped her mother instigate the plan against Mpampas. Alethea's stomach hurt. She didn't want to believe Portia could be so wicked. But she couldn't risk it. Alethea lifted her chin. "I want nothing to do with David's God," she said with a vehemence she didn't feel.

Portia's face turned bright red.

Alethea turned and walked away, only then realizing she'd connected Jesus with David. Oh, no! Her heart sank. Had she now put David's life in jeopardy? Would Portia know David as David, or as Damonus? What could she do? How could she fix it? She stopped to explain her slip of the tongue, but Grandfather walked toward them, grinning. Alethea nodded curtly and kept walking.

Ω

"I should have gone myself," Alethea mumbled. Sure, she would be punished for going over the wall, but at least she could have met with David face to face.

Finally, she saw the boy slave as he neared the wall. She stood at the top of the stairs and leaned against the rail where the slaves' chambers were located. She couldn't quite make out the boy's face. If he was smiling, then she would know it was good news. If he was frowning, then she would know David still wasn't willing to forgive her. Was this not the eighth time that she had sent a message to him, begging his forgiveness? Every time, he had refused.

At last, the boy's face came into view. He was frowning.

Emptiness consumed her. She had no one. The boy stood far enough away from the wall so she could hear him.

"Forgive me, mistress. The message I have is not what you hope to hear," he shouted.

"Then remain silent," she said.

The boy nodded and went on his way.

She trudged down the stairs. It had been a year, nine months and eleven days now since she had seen David. It felt like an eternity. She circled around the house, walked into the large courtyard, and found a stone bench next to a statue of her grandfather. She slumped onto the bench and stretched out onto her stomach. She wanted to cry, but what good would that do? She had already shed rivers of tears over David.

He would never forgive her, and she would likely never see him again. Sometimes he would come to spar with Marcus and Lucius, but she wasn't allowed near the gymnasium anymore during that time, and Grandmother always kept her busy with some boring task.

He no longer cared for her. The realization of her loss finally settled into her mind and into her heart.

She was alone. Completely alone. Fear choked her. She had no one. All because of her lie. She buried her face in her arms. If she'd only told the truth, David would still be at the villa. Still be her friend.

How she ached for him. For his dimpled smile, for his voice.

Everyone sins, Aucella.

Not me.

How those words tormented, haunted her. She wished she could take them back. Take back that haughty air. She needed saving after all.

Sighing, she rested her head on her cheek. "I need a friend," she whispered. If only Mpampas . . . . If only. There were too many if onlys. It was time to move on with life. Perhaps marriage to Demetri wouldn't be so terrible after all? Maybe she could find a friend in him? Clearly, she was losing her mind.

Just then, she heard Paulus's voice in the courtyard. Of course.

Her own brother could be the friend she was longing for. She rolled off the bench and hurried toward him.

"Alethea, look who's here," Paulus's voice carried over to her.

Surprised that Paulus found her first, she turned. Across the courtyard and next to Marcus stood Demetri. His large frame stood higher than Marcus, and her first impulse was to run. Did he plan on forcing her into marriage? Her stomach tightened, but then she reminded herself that this might be her only chance to make things right. If she was doomed to marry him, she just as well make it as pleasant as possible. Hadn't David once begged her to find the good in him?

"Come on." Paulus took her by the arm.

She followed. She needed all the friends she could get, even if they weren't what she wanted. Besides, she knew in her heart she shouldn't have been so hard on Demetri in the past. Though, his behavior wasn't exactly perfect either.

"It's nice to see you again, Demetri," she said, trying to keep her voice from shaking.

Demetri turned. He looked down at her and his eyes narrowed. He didn't seem to recognize her. After all, it had been over a year since they'd seen each other. Surely she hadn't changed that much.

She shifted uncomfortably as his gaze wandered over her. She had grown a lot in the last year. She was finally filling out like Vibia, but nothing mattered to her anymore. She was alone, and her heart ached with emptiness.

Just then, recognition washed over his face. He swallowed visibly.

"Alethea." He cleared his throat. "I didn't realize . . . you are . . . ." He put his hands behind his back and straightened.

Apparently, she had caught him off guard by her kindness. Would he be kind in return?

"Nice to see me?" He cocked his head. "Are you certain of that?"

She nodded. She leaned in close to him, and he planted a kiss on her cheek.

"Perhaps we can spend some time together and become better acquainted. Maybe even . . . friends," she said.

Demetri laughed.

Heat crept from her neck to her cheeks.

The others moved away from them.

"Forgive me. I'm just stunned by . . . your—well, this sudden change of behavior. I suppose we all become mature at some point in our lives. You're not quite the wild filly I once knew."

Anger stirred inside her at his horse comparison, but she kept it at bay. This was her only chance, and really, if she were honest, she deserved every bit of what he said. She was never willing to give him a fair chance, and in the past, she had been rude. Honest, but rude.

"I am still wild in spirit. I've simply found a way to rein it in." She hoped she had anyway. She didn't want to let anyone get too close again. She needed a friend, yes, but she would be careful not to open her heart too much this time.

He straightened and shifted his stance. For the first time in her life, she recognized Demetri's discomfort. He was human after all.

"Do my words shock you?" She stepped back. "I've said far worse things to you in the past."

"You are just so grown up, is all. Forgive me." He cleared his throat. "I'm a bit taken aback."

Fearful that his words might mean it was time to marry, she added, "I still have a lot of growing up to do. My cooking is far from sufficient, just ask Grandmother. Running a household is something I have yet to master."

"I understand, and you don't need to worry. I've promised your grandfather I won't take you until you're fourteen."

Her breath caught in her throat. The very thought, the very idea of him taking her made her stomach churn. Worst of all, she'd be fourteen in two months. She forced a smile and nodded, then turned to leave.

"Good-bye . . . at least until the evening meal." She held her chin high and walked with as much elegance and grace as she could muster. How she missed David. Who would save her now?

Later that day, she found Paulus alone in the plaza, swinging at the stake with a wooden sword.

"Where are the others?" she asked.

"They've gone with Demetri to the other side of the hill," Paulus said, frowning.

"Why didn't you join them?"

"I wasn't allowed."

"Then come with me. We can play in the woods together."

Paulus threw his sword down, and they both ran together across the field.

Something caught her attention when they were climbing to the top of a tree. The big pine hadn't been chopped down. She hadn't played in the woods since David had expressed his hate for her. Being in the woods brought back too many painful memories. And since the big pine had supposedly been chopped down, there was no need to go there. But there it was, standing off in the distance as she swayed in the top of her tree. They must have cut down the wrong one.

Paulus finally caught up to her and they both sat perched on their own branch.

"Do you ever have thoughts about Mpampas?" she asked.

"No, not really."

"You look like him."

"I do not!" he said, obviously insulted by her compliment. "I look like Grandfather."

"It's not a bad thing to look like your father, Paulus. He was a very handsome man."

"He was a Christian." Paulus said the word as if it were poison.

She cleared her throat. His words hurt. "He loved us very much."

"He didn't love us. He was a cannibal."

"A what?" Alethea nearly lost her grip on the tree branch.

"He ate human flesh and drank their blood."

Alethea gasped. She felt like he had just punched her in the gut. "Where did you hear such lies?"

Paulus shrugged. "I don't remember. Everybody knows it."

"Well, it's not true!" Alethea fought back tears. How could people say such horrifying things against Mpampas? Worst of all, Paulus believed them.

"All Christians are cannibals."

Alethea thought of Mpampas and David, accused of being cannibals. She had never heard such horrible slander. "Christians are not cannibals. Who told you such things?"

"I don't remember," Paulus said, now frustrated. He climbed down the branches.

"Paulus wait, come back. Let's play."

"I don't like playing with you." He continued down the tree.

Ω

Alethea's voice carried through the courtyard, and she danced, swinging her silken sash above her head. She hit the last note perfectly and then curtsied to the family. They cheered.

"Sing us a song in Latin," Grandfather said. "I can't remember when you last shared a Latin song with us."

"I can't think of any Latin songs, Grandfather." Really, she could, but Greek songs were her favorite since her father had been Greek. Besides, she secretly defied her grandfather by singing Greeks songs in his presence.

"I realize there are a lot of lovely Greek songs, but I wish to hear something in my own tongue." Grandfather motioned towards Alethea. "Sing something in Latin."

After what Paulus had said about the Christians, she felt extra stubborn at the moment. She knew he must have heard the lies from Grandfather or her cousin Lucius. "I remember nothing in Latin." Alethea held her chin high, perhaps a little too defiantly, because her grandfather frowned. The last time he looked at her that way, she got a beating. Perhaps, she should have held her tongue, but now it was too late.

"She just sings in Greek because our father was a Greek."

Alethea faced her little brother.

Paulus's lips lifted into a smug grin.

A cold chill ran down her spine.

Grandfather turned toward Paulus. "Is that so, son?"

"Yes." Paulus nodded. "She spoke to me of our father this afternoon. She also spoke of the Christians."

Grandfather eyed Alethea.

She swallowed hard. If only she could melt away into the tiles. "I simply asked if he recalled our father. That was all." Alethea's eyes darted to the others.

Demetri frowned, worry clouding his eyes.

"I am not a Christian." She practically choked on the words.

"Most certainly not!" Grandfather stood.

She looked to her mother. Cornelia looked away. She looked to her aunt and uncle. They watched with interest.

"I simply said that the Christians were not cannibals, and neither was Mpampas."

"How do you know so much about the Christians?" Grandfather stepped toward her.

Alethea studied the tiles at her feet. "I just know Mpampas wouldn't do such a thing," she whispered.

"Go to my office chamber."

She shuddered. He would beat her. "But I haven't done anything wrong. Please, Grandfather. I'm not a Christian, nor will I ever be." Even as she said the words, she felt she had betrayed David's God.

"Go!" Grandfather pointed toward the house.

She shivered and went into the house, her heart in her throat.

Ω

"I'm not even a Christian." The pain pinched in Alethea's back as she lay the next day on the wall near the big pine. Her lower back sent sharp shocks of pain through her body. It was an excruciating climb to the wall, but she didn't care. Far from where the big pine was, she saw another tree that grew up close to the wall, chopped down. They had indeed cut down the wrong tree.

She finally climbed to her feet. She didn't care what happened anymore. She hopped down to the mound of dirt and cried out in agony, dropping on all fours from the pain in her back. Tears filled her eyes as she pushed herself up and made her way across the clearing. She hated this world. She had no one anymore.

As she walked toward the trees, even they looked lonely and empty. No birds sang and no wind blew.

When she came to the stream, she followed it until it emptied into a small pool. Loneliness swept over her as she stood staring at the calm waters and listened to the stream trickle into the pond.

No one cared anything for her. Not Demetri, not even Paulus, and certainly not David. She was all alone. Tears streamed down her cheeks. All she had to look forward to in life was marriage to Demetri. She should have been born a horse.

She stepped into the water, its currents uncomfortably cool. Vibia told her once about a woman who drowned herself after her husband discarded her baby. Perhaps that was also her only way out of this wretched life. She eased her way deeper into the water. It came to her waist, and she shivered from its coldness. Would she have the courage to end her life after she'd fought so hard to keep it? At least her death would be on her terms and not Grandfather's. The men were working at her father's home. What they were doing, she didn't want to know. On their way back to the villa, they'd likely pass by this way. She felt a glimmer of satisfaction at the thought of Grandfather finding her lifeless body floating on the water's surface.

A ray of sunlight lanced over the water. She looked up at the blue sky. Suddenly the woods didn't feel quite so empty and alone. She wiped the tears from her eyes and moved into the ray of light. It hugged her in its warmth. *Elohim made the sun.* David's voice swam through her mind.

David's God was all she had. She still prayed to Him and asked

Him to bring back Mpampas. He sure was taking His sweet time in answering that prayer. Perhaps His answer was no. If that were the case, then she really had nothing to live for.

Death.

The one thing she feared most. She wasn't sure she could follow through with what she planned to do now. If she did, would she have to die a second time? Of course she would. She wasn't even a Christian.

The ray of sunlight spread over the deep pond. The cold waters rippled like fingers, caressing her legs and waist, as if whispering to her, waiting to take her life. She gazed into the dark pool, unable to see her feet.

"I don't want to be alone," she said to David's God.

The ray of sun lit up the flowers on the other side of the banks. David's God was gentle enough to form each delicate petal.

God took time to make this flower and its delicate petals. David's words flooded her mind. *How much more do you think He cares about you?*

She looked down at her hair as the ends floated around her. David once said his God knew how many hairs were on her head. If his God found it important enough to know how many hairs were on her head—something she could care less about, and she loved herself quite a lot—then how much more would He care about her heart? Her soul?

A bird swooped down from the sky and back up again. "You care for the birds. Not one of them falls to the ground without Your knowing it." She recalled David telling her that. "What about me then?" Her shoulders shook as she cried.

If she fell to the ground, or drowned herself, would it matter?

No God is worth dying for. Her own words haunted her.

But He died for you.

Yahshua had died. Her thoughts turned to Him. "Yahshua gave his life . . . for me." She lifted her hands. "But why?"

Passion.

She wiped her nose. So, David's God wanted a relationship with her.

A *relationship*.

And He wanted to save her from the agony of this miserable life. If she allowed Him to rescue her, she wouldn't have to fear a second death.

Now she understood. She did have a friend, someone who had always been here for her from the very beginning.

How ironic. To become a Christian would actually take away her fear. If she were a Christian, she could live forever. More importantly, she would live with David's God. He would take care of her and always be there for her. She would finally have a friend she could trust. He would be her mpampas.

But would He want her? She'd been so wrong. So wicked for lying. But wasn't that the whole reason Yahshua died? Because of sin? Her sin?

"Dear God of David, please . . . I want You now as my God, my only God. I'm sorry for what I've done. So sorry." She cried, hearing in her mind the echoes of David's screams from the whip, knowing that Yahshua suffered the same and more. "Please forgive me. How do I come to You? Help me find the way."

"Mistress?"

Alethea turned to the voice, wiping away her tears.

Ace.

"What are you doing here?" he asked, surprised.

Swiping the tears from her eyes, she quickly worked her way to shore, splashing water up the rest of her stola. Had he heard her talking? What was he doing here? She trembled. How much had he heard?

"I was returning from the other side of the hill. The men are working there." Ace offered his hand to help her out of the pond.

"I just needed to be . . . a—alone," Alethea stammered.

"Alone in the water? Outside the villa?" He raised his eyebrows.

Her cheeks warmed.

"Are you well?"

She nodded.

"Portia told me what happened yesterday. I'm sorry Paulus betrayed you."

She looked up at him. His concern and genuine show of sympathy melted her reserve. Tears welled in her eyes.

"I'm not even a Christian." This time she said the words out of despair that she truly wasn't a Christian, rather than out of denial, but he wouldn't know that.

"I see nothing wrong with being a Christian."

Her breath caught in her throat. "You don't?"

Ace shook his head. "I'm a Christian."

The world spun. Where did he find the courage to come right out and admit it like that?

"Do you want to become a Christian?" he asked.

Her heart leaped out of her chest. "More than anything." Her own words surprised her. How long had she really ached to become a Christian and didn't because of fear?

"Do you believe that Yahshua is the Son of God?"

"Yes." Alethea nodded. "I believe!" It felt funny to actually speak the words, especially when she wouldn't have dared confess that just this morning.

"What do you know about Yahshua?"

"I know that He died to save us from our sins. Then He raised up from the dead. I remember that quite well." She smiled. "David taught me."

"And you believe it's true?" Ace asked.

"Yes, of course." She looked down at his sandals. "I've just been afraid."

"Do you believe that you're a sinner?" He crossed his arms and lifted his brows as if he knew of her confessions to David of having no sin.

Heat crept from her neck to her cheeks and she stared at the ground. She thought of David and what she had done to him. "Yes, I am a sinner."

"Are you sorry for your sins?" His voice softened.

"More than ever." Her nose burned as tears flooded her eyes again. She was probably the worst of sinners, especially after what she'd done to her only friend. Paulus's betrayal of her was nothing compared to her betrayal of David.

"And are you willing to sin no more?" Ace bent close to her.

"Yes." But what if . . . her head snapped up. "But what if I make a mistake?"

He half smiled. "You will sin again, mistress. The point is, are you ready to change your heart and do your best not to sin? If you are, then God is willing to forgive you."

"I don't want to sin anymore. I want to do what's right."

"Then you must be immersed to wash away your sins."

She turned toward the pond. "We're here, let's do it."

She went back down into the water. It didn't feel as cool as the first time she went in. Ace followed. When the water came to her chest, she shivered and turned toward him.

"The gospel is all about Yahshua dying for our sins. He died for us and then was buried. But like you said, He rose again." Ace made a fist. "He *defeated* death." A victorious gleam sparkled in his eyes. "In the same way Yahshua died for us and rose again, you too will die and rise again into new life. This is what it means to obey the gospel." Ace motioned to the pond. "This water will be your grave. Here, you will die to your sins."

Alethea couldn't believe the irony of his words. A moment ago, this water might have been her grave, but not so she could gain eternal life.

"Then you will come up out of this watery grave as a new person." He grinned. "I immerse you now for the forgiveness of your sins in the name of the Father, the Son, and the Holy Spirit." Ace placed his hands on her shoulders and dipped her into the water.

She held her breath as the cold enveloped her. Then she came up out of the water. Her hair and stola clung to her body, and she wiped the moisture from her face. Now David's God was hers. She could

216 ★ Sandi Rog

pray to Him, and call Him *her* God rather than David's God. Elo-him would be her one and true friend.

Ace stood smiling. "You are my sister in Christ." He kissed her cheek. "The angels rejoice over your salvation."

A chill of excitement ran through her. She wrapped her arms around Ace and laughed, nearly knocking him off his feet. He chuckled. God had forgiven her of her sins. Now David was sure to forgive her as well. But even better, she had a friend. A Friend for eternity.

Ace hugged her back and they laughed together.

She had never felt so free. Nothing else mattered in the world. She had God. Just then, a realization came over her.

"You were an answer to my prayer," she said. "I just now prayed that God would show me how to become a Christian, and suddenly you were here."

Ace smiled.

She sighed. "I suppose prayers about spiritual matters are a priority," she said, thinking about Mpampas.

"Come, mistress." Ace helped her to shore. "We had better return to the villa."

"Please, call me Alethea. After all, you are my brother now." She had gained a whole new family. What a relief. She was more than happy to replace the family she already had. Could there be more Christians than Ace? The idea seemed impossible. "How many others are there?"

"We will meet together behind the stables before dawn, and you can see for yourself." He winked.

Her heart sang as they made their way back to the villa. She skipped ahead of Ace, and shocks of pain went through her back, but she was too happy now to care. She wanted to shout from the rooftops the new life she had found, but she'd keep it a secret for now. She couldn't afford another beating from Grandfather, and she wasn't exactly ready for a death sentence, even if it meant she would live forever.

Ω

Before dawn, Alethea crept out of bed at the appointed hour. She padded through the house and into the courtyard. The cool night air was still and quiet and she tightened her cloak around her shoulders. The light from the moon helped her to see the way, and she caught glimpses of torches moving toward the stables.

She went through the stables and came out the other side. Some of the horses whinnied as she crept by. She was startled to find a large group of people.

Some came toward her, one of them, Ace. "Come sister, meet the family."

She stepped into the group and recognized several slaves. The stable boys were there, other household slaves greeted her, but then she recognized Portia. Cold fear poured over her. It was a trap, and now Portia was here to turn Alethea in to her grandfather.

"What's troubling you?" Portia's smile faded and she stopped in front of her.

"You!"

Ace stood nearby. "What is it, Alethea?"

"It's a trap. This is all a trap!" She stepped away from the others.

"We are all Christians here," Portia said.

"But . . . ." Could she accuse Portia of taking part in what her mother did to her father? It felt wrong to accuse her. "You . . . you brought the letter to Grandfather. The next day they killed him." Alethea's hands trembled. She had come, expecting joy and love but was met with doubt.

"I feared you had seen me that night, and now I know it's true." Tears welled up in Portia's eyes. "I didn't know what Cornelia had written in that letter." She sniffed back tears. "I knew it was important, since she sent me away by night, but I now know she intended to leave." Portia's desperate expression met Alethea's gaze. "She never meant for him to be killed. She's terrified of Aloysius, and I don't think she'll ever forgive herself for what happened."

Alethea had always loved Portia, and it pained her to place Portia with all the others. It never felt natural. Portia's behavior was always more caring than the others. She was always there when Alethea was hurting. After Grandfather's beatings, she tried to ease her pain, though little helped. So this was not a trap, she had not been betrayed. Relief washed over her.

"Will you forgive me?" Portia said, her eyes pleading.

"Oh, yes," Alethea cried, and she wrapped her arms around Portia. Finally, she found a real family. She was bound to these people in a special way. No one could destroy or take away the sudden friendships God had provided. And their friendships would carry on to the next life.

The others gathered around them, and one by one they greeted Alethea. They were all slaves and greeted her formally.

They settled down on the ground, forming a circle. Some of the men said a few prayers, then everyone sang songs of praises to God. They read from one of the scrolls Ace had in his hands, and shortly thereafter, Ace held out a basket of unleavened bread, and in his other hand was a large goblet of wine.

"We pray to You, Father, and thank You for the body of Christ who suffered and died in our stead. It's in His name we pray, Amen." He broke off a piece of flat bread and passed it around the circle, each one breaking off a piece and eating it. "We do this in memory of His death. The bread is a symbol of His body that was sacrificed for our sins. And the wine represents his blood."

Now she understood why outsiders believed Christians were cannibals. When the bread and wine came to her, she broke off a piece and took a sip, bringing to mind all of what David had told her about Christ's death.

eighteen

In bare feet, Alethea danced for the first time with joy before her family. She danced for God, not for them. She swung her sash around her and sang out in Latin. It didn't matter what language she sang in anymore, she knew in her heart to whom she belonged.

The words were about love, but she sang the words to her God. She even invented some of her own lyrics. Of course, she made them sound like love songs; they could have been sung to a man or a woman. Though the others would be fooled, she knew in her heart, and her God knew, that they were meant for Him.

The things that normally bothered her seemed like petty troubles to her now, except for her marriage to Demetri, but she had time to deal with that later.

She sprang across the room then stopped to hit the low notes good and hard. Funny. She noticed that her voice sounded much better when her heart was in it. She spun around her grandfather, snubbing his smiles, and glided past Demetri's couch. He watched her with an intensity she had never noticed before. He used to ignore her.

She gave the sash one last wave and flung it into the air, watching it plunge to the ground as she held her note. When the sash touched the floor, she ended her song. The family cheered and encouraged her to sing again.

Ω

Alethea waited on the balcony for the boy to return with a message
from David. Apparently, David knew she had become a Christian,
but all these months she had heard nothing from him. She twirled
her hair nervously. She was now fourteen, so Demetri had a right to
marry her.

Finally, the boy returned. "What news do you have?" she asked.
The boy neither smiled nor frowned.

"Mistress. Damonus sends word that if you truly are sorrowful, you
would have made things right by now. He said to live by your name."

The words pierced her heart. He still hadn't forgiven her.

"That will be all," she shouted to the boy, though the knot in her
throat made it sound like a hoarse cry. She turned on her sandals and
headed back down the stairs. What could he mean? At least he had
spoken to her this time. Normally, the boy would have no message
except that she was not forgiven.

How was she to make things right? What did he expect of her?
She shuffled to her bedchamber and threw herself on the bed. Tears
welled in her eyes. Live by her name. What did that mean? She
needed to speak with someone.

She sent for Portia who came immediately by her side.

"What's troubling you?"

Alethea wrapped her arms around Portia and cried onto her stola.
"What must I do to be forgiven?"

"But you have been forgiven, dear. If you're truly sorry and confess
your sins to the Lord, He will forgive you."

"Perhaps the Lord has forgiven me, but Damonus has not. Oh,
Portia. I told that horrible lie. They flogged him because of me." She
went on to tell Portia the entire story, and when she finished, Portia
was able to help Alethea understand what David's words meant. It
was time to undo the lie and tell the truth.

Ω

David walked into the plaza. What a relief it was to be out of those shackles. His legs felt light and he couldn't help but wonder if each step he took was much higher than necessary. Of course, he was allowed to be free of the shackles when he was sparring in the gymnasium, and despite the chains, Titus still expected David to stay in good physical condition. He'd gotten creative with his exercises and stretches, and tramping up and down the Vibian Hill helped.

David stopped and eyed the stakes. He hadn't looked at the wooden pillars since he was last flogged two years ago. They loomed over him like mocking giants, and their wooden scent wafted over him in the slight breeze. He shuddered. When he was at the villa, he'd only been allowed to remain in the gymnasium. Surprisingly, Aloysius never asked for David to come juggle for the family, but that was probably because Titus could do that himself. That meant David never had to step a foot out of the sandy arena.

All was quiet. No one was around. The entire family had gone to the Vibian Hill to worship Mars, and Titus left David alone to become reacquainted with the villa. An animal's paws clicked on the stone tiles. David turned to see a dog wagging his tail and coming toward him with a friendly greeting. He licked David's leg and nuzzled his hand. The only creature there to greet him.

He wondered what happened to Alethea. He half expected her to pounce on him when he arrived. Not that he was anxious to see the little child. Yes, he was grateful she finally told the truth, but it sure took her long enough. Besides, he was happy at the vineyards with no master constantly looking over his shoulder, scrutinizing his every move. Now he hoped Aloysius would do just that. Scrutinize everything. David planned to impress him in every way he could. He'd do whatever it took to earn his life back.

As for Alethea, it'd be best not to go anywhere near her. As soon as he learned he would return, he determined not to get close to her again. The farther away he stayed from his master's granddaughter, the better off he would be. And the greater chance he would have of being set free. Now that Aloysius knew the truth, David hoped to

222 ✴ Sandi Rog

begin where he left off in earning his freedom. He prayed Elohim provided this as his opportunity.

He wandered toward the stables, curious to know how much had changed. Not many slaves were around, and he wondered if he'd meet up with the stable boys or if they were forced to join the family. He was anxious to meet his Christian family again, and he was curious to know how things were going with the master's granddaughter having joined their gatherings. He'd done what he intended while working in the vineyards and planted the church there. David smiled at the irony of it all.

The church was everywhere in this place, and now David hoped Elohim would grant him his request. He would be patient. But in the end, he hoped Elohim's answer for his freedom would be yes.

Ω

Alethea smiled to herself as she prepared the special meal for David. Most of the family was away worshipping Mars outside the villa walls, and she pretended to be unwell so she wouldn't have to join them. This was her opportunity to present a peace offering to David. Butterflies fluttered in her stomach at the thought of his presence. She hadn't even seen him yet.

The wine rolls were ready. Their smell permeated the air. She grabbed a towel and pulled them, one by one, out of the oven. The cook had showed her how to make them, but Alethea would never make them this well for her family. She broke off a small piece and popped it in her mouth. Succulent. The brown crust surrounded a fluffy inside, and the flavor of anise wasn't too much, or too little. Just right.

Grandfather was only too happy to bring David back to the villa. As soon as she told the truth, he jumped at the chance to order David's return, never questioning the reason for her confession. Titus was sent immediately to bring him back. And now he was here.

She danced from one pot to the other in the kitchen as she chewed on another piece from the wine roll. She'd just as well eat the whole thing. Two rolls would be enough for David to be filled. Not to mention everything else she'd prepared. The green beans with pine nuts, the lamb seasoned with honey. Her stomach growled.

Had she known it would be this easy to get David back, she would have told the truth a long time ago. She would make this meal extra special, and nobody would even know about it. The house was empty with everyone gone except for a few minor slaves—and David.

After everything was ready, she summoned a slave to have David wait for the meal in the slaves' dining chambers. She had worked hard on the preparations and would never dare prepare something so scrumptious for Demetri. She tried to appear inept when it came to any type of household preparations in order to delay their marriage. She cringed that she was fourteen. How much time did she have left? Perhaps if she could impress David, he might fall in love with her and they could run away together? Well, it couldn't hurt to try. And pray.

The slave girl came into the kitchen. "Damonus awaits in the dining chamber, mistress."

"Were you careful not to mention that it was me who called for him?"

"Yes, mistress. He doesn't know who sent for him."

"Good. I want you to take this platter up to Dav . . . Damonus, and set it before him. Once he has smelled the food, you may tell him that it's from me. But not until he's thoroughly smelled the food."

"Yes, mistress." The girl took the platter and went up the stairs to the slaves' dining chamber, while Alethea followed close behind.

Anxious to see David's face when the girl presented the platter, Alethea scurried past the girl and motioned for her to follow.

Alethea peered around the corner and froze at the sight. David reclined in front of one of the small tables and petted the dog at his feet. His bronze skin accentuated the golden strands in his light brown hair. Probably from working in the vineyards and staying out in the sun for so long. Then her gaze fell to the muscles in his arms.

They flexed with the slightest of movements. All he did was pet the dog and they bulged. All these things combined with his broad shoulders and large frame made her gasp. She ducked away from the door and pressed her back to the wall of the porch.

Her stomach tied in knots as she tried to catch her breath. He was a man. And so handsome.

"Am I pretty?" she asked the slave girl with a desperateness in her tone she thought she could hide, but failed miserably.

The slave girl stood, holding the tray. She nodded. "You are beautiful, mistress."

Alethea put her fingers to her lips, not wanting David to hear them. "Am I as pretty as Vibia? You must be honest with me. I won't punish you if you say I'm not." She knew she wasn't as beautiful as Vibia. Perhaps it was a foolish question to ask at this moment. She pressed her head hard against the wall and felt the throbbing of her heart. David had grown into a handsome man. Suppose he didn't find her attractive?

"You are more beautiful than Vibia, mistress, and I'm not lying."

Alethea cupped the girl's face in her hands. "Bless you," she said in an excited whisper, then her mind clouded with doubt. She had never been as beautiful as Vibia. How could that be true now? "Are you certain?"

The girl nodded, smiling. "Yes, mistress. You are more beautiful than the Greek goddess Athena."

The girl struggled under the weight of the platter as it wobbled in her hands.

Alethea motioned for her to enter the chamber, while she remained hidden.

She watched as the girl placed the platter on the table. David looked at it with wide eyes. He smiled, taking in its delicious aroma. He reached his hand out to take some food.

Alethea twisted her sash.

"Mistress Alethea has made this for you."

David's hand stopped. He slowly pulled it back and his lips

turned downward into a frown. "Give it to the dog. I want nothing from that spoiled child." With that, he tossed the platter onto the floor. The two wine rolls rolled away and the dog inhaled both in two gulps. He then went for the meat.

The slave girl cried and ran out the door. "I'm so sorry, mistress! So sorry!"

Alethea's hand went to her mouth and tears flooded her eyes. She motioned for the slave girl to leave and leaned back against the wall. Her spirit withered away into the porch. He still hadn't forgiven her, after all this time. She had finally told the truth. What did he want from her? She turned to leave, broken and beaten.

She stepped down the stairs when a sudden wave of anger came over her. He was her slave! How dare he refuse food from the master's table. With that, she spun around and marched into the dining chamber. When she entered, she shuddered with rage as she saw the dog gnawing on the lamb she had worked so hard to prepare.

"How dare you!" She stood with trembling hands on her hips.

David leaped to his feet, his eyes widened. He went to bow, but stopped and met her gaze. "Alethea?"

"How dare you throw my food on the floor and then address me in such a familiar manner." His calling her by her name had come to an end. It wasn't until now that she realized just how proud he was. He should be happy he hadn't been killed for her lie. He should be happy she wanted anything to do with him at all. "How dare you refuse food from the master's table." Her eyes burned with tears. All that hard work. Wasted. He didn't even get to taste the wine rolls. They were perfect.

"Aucella, I . . . ." His gaze swept over her, then met her face.

She marched up to him and slapped him.

He straightened, his broad shoulders towering over her. She swallowed at his massive height. She'd taken on a warrior. But she refused to let that daunt her. He was still her David. His eyes narrowed and the side of his jaw pulsed. Would he strike her back? He wouldn't dare. He was her slave. She reached up to slap him again, but stopped in mid-air, taking a step back. God wouldn't want her to behave this way. She shouldn't abuse a slave, especially when one was her brother in Christ. How dare he tempt her to strike him. She trembled with anger and hurt.

"I told Grandfather the truth! Now it's your duty to forgive me," she said, choking on his lack of forgiveness.

Rage built in his eyes.

She stepped back.

Closing the distance between them, he flexed his arm. "Do you see this?"

She stared at the large, tanned arm he bent near her face. "Your muscle?" she asked, not understanding why he'd wish to show off his body at a time like this.

"No," he said with disgust, dropping his hands at his sides. He bent his arm again and pointed.

Her eyes fell on the V burned into his flesh.

"This is only a part of what they did to me because of your lie." His eyes flashed.

She shook her head. What could she do? She was sorry. He'd never know how sorry. God had forgiven her, hadn't He?

She pointed a trembling finger at the tray on the floor. "I made that food especially for you, in hopes that you might finally forgive me. But you gave it to the dog!" She choked on the tears that formed in her throat.

Feigning dignity, she straightened. "How dare you behave in such an awful manner. Who do you think you are? You are nothing but a slave, and if that is how you wish to be treated, so be it. You can expect no more special treatment from me."

She turned to leave, then stopped and faced him again. "Elohim has forgiven me, why can't you?" To her dismay, a sob escaped her throat. "You put yourself above God. Are you more perfect than Him?"

Her words had a surprising effect, for a stunned reaction reflected in his familiar blue eyes. He may have grown into a man, but he was still the boy she had known so well.

With her final words still hanging in the air, she threw up her chin, turned on her heels, and went for the door, but her foot came down on the dog. He yelped and she tried to regain her balance. She squealed, twisted, and landed with a hard thud on her rump.

She sat facing David. Her gaze fell on his feet, his legs and then his tunic.

He bent down to help her.

"Don't touch me." She slapped his hand away.

He straightened as she tried to climb to her feet, but knifelike pain stabbed her back. She blew out a frustrated sigh.

"You may help me to my feet, but after that, don't ever touch me again," she said.

He pulled her to her feet and continued to aid her.

"No," she said, gasping from the pain.

He released her, and she limped toward the doorway, trying to keep her nose in the air, but the pain was too much.

When she turned the corner and couldn't be seen, she slumped down against the wall, releasing a deep breath. How humiliating. She had put him in his place and immediately made a fool of herself. She had to regain her pride.

"I expect the mess you made to be cleaned up before the rest of the family returns to the house." She called out orders and pointed her finger. "They'll wonder what the master's food is doing sprawled out all over the floor in the slaves' dining chambers, not to mention why the dog is eating it." She clenched her teeth and her blood boiled with renewed vigor. "Since you are so disrespectful, Damonus," she emphasized his slave name, "you can come downstairs when you are finished and entertain the family during the evening meal."

Really, she was hoping to look at him some more. She pushed up to stand but her back pinched. She slumped back down. She'd just have to wait it out. After a bit of time, the pain would subside as it always did.

But while she was recuperating, she decided to continue her speech. "I also expect you to keep your eyes downcast when you look at me." Oh, how she loved the way he looked at her. "We are no longer friends, Dav . . . Damonus. If you ever look me in the eyes again, you will be flogged." Really, she had no intention of ever flogging him. She wouldn't make that mistake again. "Do you hear me?"

"I hear."

Her breath caught in her throat. He stood in the doorway, arms folded. How long had he been there?

Without warning, he scooped her up in his arms and carried her down the stairs.

"Put me down, you . . . you barbarian!" She balled her hands into fists and pounded his chest.

He didn't frown, nor did he smile.

"How dare you." Warmth coursed through her body from the strength in his arms. He carried her down the stairs as though she weighed nothing at all. Again, the pain in her back pinched, and she winced.

"I should have caught you when you fell." He shook his head. "I was afraid to touch you."

She slammed her fist against his chest again, but the zeal was gone. "I hate you!"

"Hate? Are Christians supposed to hate?"

"Don't preach to me, you . . . you . . . *slave*. Aren't Christians supposed to *forgive*?"

He frowned.

"Why were you afraid?" She couldn't imagine that he would be afraid of anything, least of all her.

"It's not good for a man to touch a woman."

"Do you find me attractive then?" An uncontrollable grin spread across her face.

"Yes." His eyes smiled, but not his lips.

"As lovely as Vibia?"

"You are beautiful. I haven't seen Vibia yet, so I don't know who is more attractive." Now he smiled, and that dimple snagged her attention as it always had in the past.

"That slave girl thinks I'm prettier than Vibia." She hoped he would think so too. "She said I was as beautiful as the Greek goddess Athena."

"I've never met Athena. Last I heard she was made of stone. Are you sure that little slave girl wasn't implying something other than beauty?"

Heat crept from her neck to her cheeks. She opened her mouth to give him a piece of her mind, but words wouldn't come.

He set her gently on a sofa in the atrium, and she mourned the loss of his strong arms. Thankfully, no one was around and she remembered her anger. "Don't think this changes anything, Damonus." She stressed his slave name again to make her point.

He turned to leave.

"Stop where you are." She glared at him. "How dare you leave before I've dismissed you."

He turned and faced her. His blue eyes locked with hers and his handsome form filled the room. She forgot what she wanted to say. Really, she hadn't planned on saying anything. She was simply imitating the way the others treated the slaves. It was time David became accustomed to that sort of treatment from her, even though it felt strange.

He had been downright insubordinate. It was her duty to discipline him. Still, something nagged her inside. Would God approve? Certainly, He would. Slaves were supposed to obey their masters, and David was not in subjection. Though, she knew he had a higher status than other slaves, and she had better be careful that she didn't treat him too rudely in front of Grandfather.

He came near and bent down. "Are you hurt, Aucella?" Sincerity reflected in his posture as he touched the sofa.

"My back hurts, but the pain in my heart is far greater."

He frowned and gently touched her cheek with his knuckles.

Pleasant tingles shivered down her neck from his intimate touch. She nearly sighed with pleasure. "Don't touch me." Her words were more of a mumble than a command. "You're a slave, act like one."

He pulled away, staring at her.

She turned her nose in the air, trying to fight the heat in her neck and chest. Surely, he must be happy to be back. Surely, she did the right thing by telling the truth. "You can't tell me . . ." she whispered, shaking her head, unsure. Had she misread him all these years? "You can't tell me there's not a part of you that's glad to see me?"

Again, a light came to his familiar eyes. The boy she remembered. She hadn't misread him.

Confident now, she said, "You are dismissed."

He stood, watching her, searching her face.

"I said, *leave*." She waved her hand to shoo him away, afraid she might leap off the couch and cling to him.

Ω

As David cleaned up the empty platters, his mind reeled with his encounter with Alethea. How right his father had been that it wasn't good for a man to touch a woman. His arms ached for the feel of her again. She was so light in his arms, and so soft. After picking her up, he only wanted to touch her more. If she'd let him, would he have been able to stop?

When she'd burst into the room, her beauty hit him like a splash of cold water on a hot day. In that first moment, he hadn't even recognized her. But then her voice and her words accosted his senses. He'd forgotten the kind of effect she always had on him, but this time it was stronger. He'd been stunned the first time he'd ever laid eyes on her; he was just a boy and she, just a girl. But now, something was different. Very different. He could no longer envision her as his little Sarah.

And her words. She'd rattled off a whole lot, but the ones of his putting himself above God hit him hard. They bit into his conscience. It was so clear and simple to her, all he had to do was forgive.

He glanced at the branded V in his arm as he scrubbed the floor. Could he forgive her for the torture she'd put him through? He'd lived in chains for the past two years. Her teary eyes flashed through his mind. He clenched his jaw. Those huge, brown eyes that always held his heart in a vise grip still had the same effect. They still burned to his soul, desperate to be loved. They made him want to protect her again, like before. And her boldness of speech still captured his heart. Without his ever opening his mouth, she knew his secrets. He was glad to be back, glad to be near her. He shook his head. He was cursed. Again, he'd fallen under her spell. She'd be his undoing.

He recalled her pain when she fell. He wanted to kick himself for not catching her before she hit the ground. But she hadn't landed hard enough to have done that much damage. Something was wrong. Rumors of Aloysius's abuse carried through his mind.

If only he could take her away from this place, far away. She needed him. He understood her in ways no one else did. But who was he to have her? A slave had no rights. Especially not to his master's granddaughter.

One way or another, David would have her.

Yes, she would be his undoing.

nineteen

Every evening since his arrival, David performed for the family. During the day, when Grandfather was in his office chamber and Grandmother wasn't paying Alethea any attention, she took it upon herself to order David around. As long as no one was looking, at least those that mattered, Alethea made the most of every opportunity.

At the moment, Alethea lounged with her mother in the peristyle. The scent of jasmine carried on the air as Alethea, bored to near unconsciousness, admired the colorful foliage. She looked at her mother, a woman she no longer knew or felt any bond with, studying her as she wasted away in her own world. Her mother, who once was beautiful, now lay pale and unattractive, uninterested in the beauty surrounding her. Alethea knew she wouldn't get any conversation out of her, so she looked around for something to entertain her weary thoughts.

David strode from the back gardens into the peristyle.

Alethea's heart beat a little faster and immediately she awakened. She thought she'd become accustomed to seeing him more often, but his handsome form always made her light-headed. It was just David, she told herself. She knew him better than she knew anyone. Still, she couldn't control the fluttering of her heart.

"Dav . . . Damonus."

David stopped and turned to face her. His eyes didn't meet hers.

"Come fluff my pillows." Alethea straightened out her stola and lifted her chin, creating her best pose so she might look as attractive as possible.

David came and stood over her.

She lifted herself to give him access to her pillows.

He grabbed one and punched it, then gingerly set it down on her couch.

She lay back on it as he waited for her to dismiss him.

"Not good enough." Alethea sat up again.

David fluffed the pillow with his large hands, and Alethea admired his knuckles and the masculine shape of his arms below his tunic sleeves. He placed the pillow back down, giving it one last pat.

She lay against it and shook her head. "Nope. Still not right."

This time, David's gaze met hers, his blue orbs piercing her through as she sat up.

Again, David fluffed the cushion and placed it back down.

This time Alethea didn't bother lying on it and shook her head.

David raised a brow. He picked the pillow up, held it in his palm, and gave it one hard punch. Its feathers fluttered to the floor and the fabric flattened.

Alethea gasped.

"Forgive me, mistress." David bowed before her. "I'll fetch you another one." He waited for her to dismiss him.

Speechless, Alethea waved so he could go. David walked away, his large hand making the leftover pillow look like a worn out, limp rag used for scrubbing, the feathers leaving a weeping trail behind him.

She sat up, hugging her knees, since she couldn't lie back on the now uncomfortable chair. Leaning her cheek on her knee, she glanced at her mother, whom she expected to have missed the entire scene, but to her surprise, her mother eyed her suspiciously.

Another servant returned with a pillow for Alethea. She gave it a good whack, sorry David hadn't brought it.

The following day, Alethea ran screaming from the kitchen, sure that David would hear since she just saw him walk toward the atrium. She skidded to a stop in the atrium as David rushed to her.

"What is it?" he asked, hunching over her in a protective manner.

"A spider!" She pointed to the kitchen.

David looked down the hall, then at her as if she'd lost her mind.

"Kill it!" She stomped her foot.

David's stance relaxed, and he sauntered down the hall.

Alethea followed behind, enjoying the view in front of her. His tunic clung to his broad shoulders. Power radiated from his being. How she longed for him to take her into his strong arms.

He walked into the kitchen, his large form making the chamber look small. "Where is it?"

She stood outside the door. "Behind the pots and pans."

David went to the cooking utensils hanging from the ceiling, shoved them out of his way, spotted the spider and mashed it with the side of his fist. He turned and faced her. "Anything else?"

Alethea swallowed and shook her head.

David watched her. She straightened and tossed her hair over her shoulder, trying her best to look pretty for him. When he continued to stare as if he were waiting for something, she realized he was waiting for her to dismiss him.

"You may go." She lifted her chin.

David walked through the door and by her.

His scent lingered on the air, and she took in a long, deep breath of pine and leather. He may have left the room, but a part of him lingered. She sighed.

Days later, Alethea danced and sang for the family. She began next to David as he stood, straight as a column, waiting to juggle. She belted out the first line, in Latin of course, and tried to focus on God. Oh, how she preferred Greek, but she sang for Him and not them. As she sang, she danced between her mother and grandmother, swirling her sash. She always felt the sash made a wonderful dance partner. She twirled by Grandfather and slipped in front of her uncle. The dance movements carried her before Demetri. His eyes raked over her from the top of her head, down to her toes. Uncomfortable with his leering gaze, she flicked her sash at his face. He jerked back.

Alethea laughed.

His lips turned up into a smile, and his green eyes darkened.

Inwardly, Alethea cringed. That didn't have the effect she'd hoped for. That grin told her he thought she was teasing him. Her voice weakened, but she caught herself just in time to belt out another verse. She spun around and glided between her family. She caught David watching her.

David began whistling to the tune of her song. He tossed his rings in the air and began juggling. It made for a nice closure to her routine, and she motioned for everyone to focus on David. He stepped forward and picked up from her act. Relieved, Alethea bowed, but lifted her eyes to see that Demetri still watched her. She hurried from the peristyle.

Later, Alethea wandered the woods, reveling in the beauty beneath the canopy of trees. Hearing a twig snap, she turned.

David.

He ducked under a branch as he made his way in her direction.

How long had it been since they met in the woods together like this? She smiled, welcoming him into her private chambers as the birds also sang their welcome.

He frowned as he stepped deliberately toward her. "You need to stop." He looked at her, his blue gaze severe.

She straightened to her full height and tried to look down her nose at him even though she had to arch her neck to do so. "Stop what?"

"It's not right. It's inappropriate." He studied her, and then he shifted his stance and stared into the forest surrounding them.

"What are you talking about?" She motioned toward the trees as if they might give her an answer.

"I've seen the way Demetri watches you when you're dancing." The words seemed to take his breath away. His jaw pulsed as he waited for her response.

"I've always danced for the family." She stepped closer to him. "Why should I stop now?"

He leaned down over her. "You're a woman now," he said between clenched teeth. "It's different."

Alethea shrugged. "What are you talking about?"

"You should only dance that way for your husband, in the privacy of your chamber, not in public."

"Who are you to tell me what to do?" She put her hands on her hips.

"I'm a man." He thumbed his chest. "I know what he's doing. He's undressing you with his eyes."

Alethea gasped.

David continued to watch her, his eyes blazing with fury. If he knew so well what Demetri was thinking, how often had he thought the same?

Suddenly she felt exposed. As if she were wandering the woods with nothing on at all. His gaze quickly raked over her. Gasping, she slapped him.

He straightened. His flashing eyes narrowed, and he didn't put his hand to his cheek. He simply stood there as a pink handprint appeared on his face.

"If you don't stop," his words were a forced calm, "you might regret it."

She stepped back, studying him. What could he mean by that? Would he harm her? He certainly could if he wanted to, especially the way his broad shoulders loomed over her. Would he reach out and grab her? Harm her with those big hands of his? Or do worse?

Fury and disappointment shook her. How dare he ruin what they had together. She'd never meet him alone again. She ran from him, dodging trees and branches, fearing he might be on her heels. She looked back, but he didn't follow. Never had she felt so vulnerable around David. Her David. The only one she trusted, and for the first time, he frightened her.

The next day, Alethea wandered into the atrium. She'd purposely wandered through the field in her bare feet. Now they were nice and brown with dirt. Earlier, she'd spotted David enter by way of the hall that went past Grandfather's office chamber. Grandfather was on the other side of the hill, showing Demetri the land that belonged to her father, so she knew she was safe to cause more trouble for David. And he deserved it, especially after the way he'd frightened her in the woods. Out of breath from running, she slumped onto the edge of the impluvium just in time for David to come out of the hall and into the atrium.

"David." Alethea made her tone sound as authoritative as possible.

He stopped and looked at her.

"Wash my feet." She lifted her leg and wiggled her filthy toes.

He stood there for a while, his emotions shuttered, as he studied her feet. She kicked them up so he could get a better look. The corner of his mouth lifted.

Alethea straightened in feigned dignity. "The towels and bowls are in the kitchen." She tossed her hair over her shoulder.

He started toward her. "I won't need them."

She puffed up her chest. "What do you mean, you won't need them?" Her tone reminded her of her mother. She lifted her chin.

He stood over her. "Because there's plenty of water here." With an easy lift of her legs, he flipped her back.

Alethea's arms swung, trying to regain her balance, but her body plunged into the fountain. She held her breath as the water enveloped her and her rump landed on the bottom of the pool. She pushed up, her feet finding the bottom. At once, she stood, spewing water from her mouth and turning to find David as he walked away.

"See." He motioned over his shoulder toward her. "Your feet are clean."

Incensed, Alethea looked down at her feet to see that they were indeed clean, only to look right back up at David's retreating form.

Growling, she splashed water at him, but he was too far to be reached. Feeling like a wet rag that needed a good wringing, she crawled out of the pool.

Ω

After roaming through the evening woods, Alethea wandered into the atrium. Music, heat, and jasmine rushed to her senses. David stood near the impluvium, juggling lit torches in the dim light. The dancing flames reflected off the water in the fountain. The lights turned around and around in the air, mesmerizing those watching. Alethea caught Vibia's expression. Her gaze riveted on David's handsome form. Jealously twisted in Alethea's gut.

The music grew in volume. The *sistrum* shook to the beat of David's juggling, and the musician plucked the lyre to the same beat with several notes intermingling. But what made the music come alive around her, flying over her, spinning in her mind were the notes of the whistling pipe.

Eyes fixed on David, Alethea removed the sash binding her stola. She waved it in the air, around her, above her, and at her feet to the beat of the music as she danced in David's direction. All eyes turned to her, and she cast a smug grin at Vibia.

Alethea came around David. She flipped her sash over his shoulder and dragged it down his back as he juggled the fire. She spun away and danced around him. She skipped between the family members reclining on couches, waving and flicking her sash at the onlookers. Grandfather's smile broadened. Too bad Demetri had to be there. His concentrated gaze always made her uncomfortable, but she ignored him this time. And she shoved away David's words about what he might be thinking.

Alethea moved again toward David, gliding, skipping, and turning. She flicked the sash at him. He didn't flinch and kept on juggling, his eyes riveted to one spot, staring off into some unknown place. Why wouldn't he look at her?

She turned around him and ran the ends of the fabric along his strong arms as they moved in time to the music, dragging the sash over his biceps, golden under the reflection of the fire.

Giggling, she turned in front of him and whisked her sash

through the air. The family watched, mesmerized. She recalled the movements the dancers made at her betrothal, and tried to move like those women, hips swaying and arms floating, hoping to capture David's attention. She turned seductively and swirled the sash above her head.

Vibia screamed.

Alethea stopped.

"Look out!" Grandfather stood.

Ash floated from the ceiling. Alethea looked up to see David snatching her flaming sash out of the air, snaking it above her head. He tossed it into the impluvium, and the flames hissed as the water swallowed the delicate fabric.

David turned on her, eyes flashing as he held his torches in one hand.

"That will be all, Damonus." Grandfather motioned with his chin for David to leave.

David nodded, then turned and marched away.

"That was a dangerous stunt, Aucella." Grandfather walked up to her. "What were you thinking?"

"You didn't enjoy it? I saw you smiling." Alethea swallowed hard, hoping he wouldn't beat her.

"He's a slave."

"Of course." She tossed her chin up, trying to hide her fear that he might see right into her heart. "You think I don't know that? I thought it would be more entertaining to distract him, make him fumble."

Grandfather raised an accusing brow. "When your belt caught fire, he did fumble, and he burned himself in the process of saving you from your foolishness."

Alethea's heart stopped. She'd hurt David. Again. "Forgive me, Grandfather. I'll be more careful next time."

"It's not him I'm worried about." He looked down his nose at her.

Movement came from behind Grandfather as the others got up from the couches and sofas.

Uncle Servius yawned and stretched. "Time to retire."

Alethea caught her mother's knowing gaze; she saw right through Alethea's charade, and her eyes pierced right to the truth. Demetri remained on his couch, watching David's retreating form, and then Alethea. Her mouth suddenly went dry. She stood like a statue as the rest of the family filed out of the atrium. Demetri came toward her, his movements deliberate and his long tunic emphasizing his height. Fearing he might also see the truth in her eyes, she looked down at the ground. As he swept past, his strong cologne remained on the air. She watched him disappear down the hall where David had left.

The only one remaining was her mother. She stood, folded her arms, and walked to Alethea. She stopped in front of her.

Alethea lifted her chin in defiance.

"Don't think I'm unaware of your love for the boy."

Cold terror trickled down Alethea's spine. But then, she remembered her mother. She would never have the courage to give away her secret.

"You're my daughter." Her mother sighed. "I know you better than anyone else around here."

Anger caused the room to shudder, and Alethea clenched her fists at her sides. Now, after all these years she chose to confront her, to act as a mother.

"Well," Alethea's voice sounded hollow in the empty atrium, "I don't know you."

Despair clouded her mother's face.

With that, Alethea turned and walked away.

Ω

After the family retired and Vibia's breathing became regular from sleep, Alethea slipped on her wrap and crept from her chamber. Silence drifted through the house as she snuck through the hall that led to the plaza. She rounded the corner and nearly collided with a shadow.

Titus.

Alethea stepped back, gaze focused on the ground, then remembering who she was, she thrust her chin high. "I need to apologize to Dav—Damonus. Do you know where I can find him?"

Titus motioned with his thumb to the stables. "He's there. Shall I send for him?"

"No. I'll go myself."

Titus nodded and stepped aside.

Alethea made her way to the stables, glancing over her shoulder to make sure Titus didn't follow. Seeing that she was alone, she scurried through the empty plaza and through the gate, the evening air cooling her cheeks. A light flickered from inside.

What was he doing in there at this time of night?

As she neared, the scent of manure and hay filled her nostrils. The moon reflected off the mud brick flaking along the doorposts. All was quiet as she crept between the stalls, wooden rafters hovering above her head.

"David?" Alethea whispered into the darkness as she made her way toward the dim light in the back. She turned the corner and there was David hanging from the rafters, pulling his chin above the beam, then down and up again. She stopped at the sight, his muscles flexing and shimmering as the torch cast long shadows about the chamber.

David released the beam and dropped to the dirt floor. Their gazes met and his eyes narrowed. With a severe gait, he walked toward her, jaw tight and hands fisted at his sides.

Instinctively, Alethea stepped back until she came against a wall. His mere presence held her there as though an invisible force pressed against her. Sensing she'd better say something to tame him, she said, "I came to thank—"

"Don't ever do that to me again." His voice was a fierce whisper as he pinned her with his words.

"I . . . I . . . ." Alethea stammered, taken aback by the force of his tone, her apology dissolving on her tongue. In an effort to regain her dignity, she straightened. "Or you'll do what?"

His eyes flashed as he moved closer.

Gasping, she stepped back, but the wall blocked her feet.

David loomed over her, his broad shoulders engulfing her into a cavern and his threatening stance making her aware of how small she was compared to him. The fire from the torch reflected on his face, its softness contrasting with the harsh tension set in his jaw. He placed his palm against the wall over her shoulder, holding her captive. He lifted his other hand, and she held her breath as his closeness whispered a promise of more.

Little by little, he brought his knuckles toward her cheek as if he wished to touch her but didn't dare. His hand trembled, and . . . she waited. His smoky blue eyes drank in her face as they focused on loose tendrils curling against her cheeks and then her mouth. Without touching her, he ran his knuckles down her cheek and then her neck, leaving a trail of heat in their wake.

She shivered from the impact.

He placed both hands against the wall, encasing her in his strong arms, and he leaned in closer. She breathed in his scent. Sweat. Pine. His lips hovered over hers, his breath mingling with her own. He held steady, hovering over her mouth, desire and heat emanating between them.

His nearness sent waves of heat to every limb of her body, from the top of her head to the tips of her toes, and she feared she might melt into the wall before they came together.

"David," she whispered, aching for him to touch her, to kiss her.

A light came to his eyes, and as if awakening from a dream, he pushed away.

Abandoned, she wanted to grab him, to yank him back to her, but she didn't dare touch him, no more than he dared to touch her. Would they even be able to stop if they did embrace? It would be like flint striking stone. One brush of contact would ignite flames between them.

Growling, he raked his hands through his hair, his chest heaving. He paced like a cat wanting to escape the confines of a cage. Suddenly, he turned and punched a wooden beam. She jumped from the fierceness of his thrust, the crack of the wood echoing in the silence, echoing in her heart. Without a word, he stormed away.

Still leaning against the wall, she gulped in a breath. Cold air chilled her, as if a blanket had been ripped off her warm body. She pushed away, her legs wobbly. In a daze, she touched the beam, running her trembling fingertips along the prickly splinters. Shattered by the same fist that dared not caress her cheek.

Breathless, she ran after him.

He marched out of the stables, cloaked by the shadows of the dark night.

Watching him go, she felt as though he were taking a part of her with him, a piece of herself she could never reclaim again, for she'd never shared such an intimate moment with a man. Now, he left her there, empty and unfulfilled. She leaned against the doorframe, pressing her back against it for support. Tears welled in her eyes. "Oh, David." Her hoarse voice carried after him, only to die in the darkness as he left her alone.

twenty

They were being watched.

David kept his hand near the hilt of his sword, scanning the trees. He motioned for the caravan to keep moving as he led the way. The mule behind him swayed with their belongings in the quiet air. A number of slaves followed behind the mule, while Titus followed the newly purchased slaves in the back. David focused on the sounds, trying to pick up on unfamiliar voices in the woods. The sun stood straight up in the sky as they trudged along the gravel road, the crunching of the mule's hooves echoing off the nearby trees.

Beyond the woods, after passing approximately four mile-markers, they would come upon the Vibian Hill. David kept his eyes on the trees. They were a wealthy caravan, so if someone wanted to ambush them, they'd do it while surrounded by forest. And he couldn't shake the feeling that they were being watched.

After taking care of business in Rome, they were heading back to the villa. While in Rome, David never found an opportunity to find Manius again, and he didn't try because he didn't want to ruin the good reputation he'd rebuilt. Besides, he knew all he needed to know. Sarah was alive. But was she well? Was she with Manius?

He'd wanted to locate Bahiti, but never did. He'd sent a letter with her for Manius, but she must not have ever found him. Unfortunately, Demetri never again brought her and Alexander to the villa after that first time.

A flock of birds rocketed to the sky.

"Halt!" David grabbed the hilt of his sword, watching from where the birds had fled. Up ahead along the road, a glimpse of white caught his eye as it moved from one tree to the next. It was one man. One thief. Dare he try to rob such a large caravan alone?

Sword in hand, David sprinted toward the stranger. The man turned to run. David closed in fast, charging into the forest. The man's tunic wasn't that far ahead, and David knew he could catch him. Dodging trees and leaping branches, he neared the intruder. The man's breathing came hard and he glanced over his shoulder. The man tripped and hit the dirt hard, landing on his side. He quickly rolled to his back, but David pinned him on the ground with his sword.

Sweat covered the man's brow and his chest heaved.

David froze with the tip of his blade on the man's chest.

Piercing blue eyes looked up at David, and dark curly hair clung to his frightened face. A leather band wrapped around his head.

David stood over the man in silence. He knew Titus would remain with the caravan just in case this was a distraction for an ambush. The man carried no weapons. So, he must have been the pawn. But there were no signs of other thieves. David felt certain this was the only one. Why would this man take on an entire caravan on his own, and without a weapon? His tunic was clean, so he wasn't needy. And the muscles in the man's chest, arms, and legs told him he was no beggar.

David must have stood there for a long while, analyzing the situation because the man finally opened his mouth to speak.

"Aren't you going to kill me?"

"My God won't allow it." Still, David kept the point of his sword on his chest.

The man studied him. "One God?"

David nodded.

"We must worship the same God."

"My God condemns thievery." David moved his sword to the man's throat.

"I'm not a thief." The man held his gaze. "I come to take back what is mine."

So, he wasn't a thief, and yet he came to take. How did that make any sense?

"Is she there now? With the caravan?"

"Who?"

"Cornelia. My wife. My children are Alethea and Paulus." The man took a deep breath despite David's sword. "My name is Galen Aletheos."

David staggered back, his sword at his side. "You're her father?"

"You know them." Galen's narrowed gaze was confident, despite the fact that he lay helpless on the ground.

David shook his head, unbelieving, then quickly nodded. "Yes," he finally said, barely able to get the words past his constricting throat, nearly dropping his sword at his feet.

"They're alive?" Galen sat up. "They're well?"

David nodded, speechless.

Relief reflected from Galen's face and tears pooled in his blue eyes.

Ω

David looked everywhere for Alethea. After a week of helping Titus appoint the new slaves in the vineyards, David finally had time to talk to Alethea. He hadn't seen much of her since he'd been back, since he'd been in the vineyards. Titus was still busy, so now David took advantage of his free time. He searched for Alethea in the atrium, peristyle, outdoor courtyard, and the woods. He knew all her favorite haunts, but there was no sign of her. The only other place would be the baths, and he couldn't go in there. And if she wasn't in there, he dreaded to think where else she might be. He had hoped her wall-hopping days had come to an end.

David wandered back into the atrium, thinking, hoping Alethea might reappear.

"We looked everywhere." Renata stood before Aloysius, the tension in his stance obvious. "The baths, the gardens, even the stables. She's nowhere to be found."

Aloysius's face turned red. "When I get my hands on that girl—" He clenched his fists and paced. That's when he spotted David. "Damonus."

David straightened. "Yes, master."

"Go find mistress Alethea." He waved him away.

David bowed and left. There was only one place she could be, and if he found her there, he'd throttle her himself. Sword hanging at his side, David ran straight to the woods. Galen's leather headband, wound several times around his wrist, shook from the swing of his arms. Ahead, the large pine loomed up over the wall. He didn't want to take the time to climb the tree, so he raced straight for the wall as he'd done so many times in the past. The sword slapped against his side as he picked up speed. He'd have to watch himself with it. He reached the wall and used all his momentum to jump up. His sandals, damp from the forest ground, gave him traction as he climbed upward. He easily reached the top, surprised he could still do it. Standing on top of the wall, he scanned the clearing and the distant trees. No sign of Alethea. He leaped down onto the mound of dirt and ran for the woods on the other side of the clearing.

He came to the pond and knew that was where Alethea had been baptized, where so many of the slaves had been immersed into Christ. He charged along the stream, crossed over, and ran up the bank. He ran through the forest until he broke through the pines and found himself standing in an open field facing Alethea's former home. Only her old house no longer stood there. In its place was a small unfinished villa with walled-in corrals. Demetri and Aloysius had been spending a lot of time here. Now he knew why. Alethea would be devastated.

That's when he spotted her. She stood in the distance, not far from the edge of the woods, with her hands over her face. He knew she was crying.

He ambled toward her, aching to take her in his arms, aching to take her away from this place.

A large man leaped out of the trees and grabbed her from behind, his beefy arms wrapping around her small torso.

"Stop!" Unsheathing his sword, David charged toward them.

Alethea kicked and screamed. The man put his hand over her mouth, swung her around, and disappeared with her into the trees.

Fear rushed through David's veins. The feeling was all too familiar, and he couldn't shake the images of his mother when Aulus had his hands on her.

He came to the opening in the trees and found a man hovering over Alethea on the ground, pulling on her clothes. Another held her arms above her head. She screamed. Fury pounded David's temples. He side kicked the man on all fours in the ribs, and he rolled off her.

"Run!" David shouted at Alethea. She ran as he swung his sword at another oncoming man. There were three. A fat one on the ground, and two standing—one tall, one bald. David sliced open the tall man coming at him; lines of blood streaked across his chest. The man buckled. The bald one swung his sword. David dodged the blade and fought like he'd never fought before. Blood splattered, only emphasizing the red vision that raged through his mind. He had only one goal. To punish these men for harming Alethea. To punish them like he wanted to punish Aulus for raping his mother. And he'd make them pay for it all.

Using his own blade, David ducked and pushed the bald man's sword in the direction it swung. David side kicked him and ended with a brutal slice to the groin. The man cried out and slumped to the ground.

The fat one came at him from behind. David took the hilt of his sword and plunged it into the man's face. He staggered back, and David raised his sword to finish him off. But the man dropped to the ground. David hovered over him and kicked him below the waist. He'd make sure these men would never rape another woman.

David swung around, ready for the tall one to attack. The man's terrified eyes took in the bloodbath before him, and seeing that his comrades lay motionless on the ground, he turned and fled. David went after him. He launched himself onto the man and they crashed into a tree. David pounded him and slammed his head into the trunk, bashing his skull over and over again. The man passed out, and that's when David stopped. Still gripping the man's hair in his fist, David stood up and let him crumple at his feet. The man lay still on the pine needles. Too still. Had David killed him? Horror shuddered down his spine, and only then did he take in the carnage around him. Three bodies lay lifeless between the trees. He waited for their chests to rise. Two were breathing. He knelt over the man at his feet and felt for his breath. Warm air came from his mouth and nose. Relief gushed forth. Still alive.

David sheathed his sword and ran after Alethea. Just as he reached the stream, he spotted her running along the other side. Crying, she stumbled and dropped to her knees. The thought of what those men could have done to her made him shudder. David caught up to her and lifted her off the ground.

"No!" She swung at him.

"It's me!" he shouted.

She clawed his arms.

"I'm not going to hurt you. It's me! David."

The fight went out of her, and he turned her to face him.

"David!" She clung to him, her arms wrapped tightly around his neck.

He lifted her and carried her away from the stream. As he held her, she wept on his shoulder, her body trembling. He cut between the trees, away from the water, away from the clearing, and settled on the ground with her in his lap. And that's when David noticed his own body shaking. He couldn't make it stop. He'd nearly lost her. She'd looked so small, so helpless beneath that huge man. So much like his mother had looked with Aulus's hands on her. The thought sent renewed tremors of rage through his system.

David grabbed her shoulders, taking in every part of her, her face, her arms. "Are you well?" he asked, his voice choking.

She nodded, then wrapped her trembling arms around him again, sobbing.

He hugged her, holding her close, running his hand down her small back. "I won't let anyone hurt you." The thought of those men touching her made him squeeze her tighter to his chest. He fisted his hand in the ends of her tangled hair. "Ever."

He held her that way until her crying subsided into small sniffles. She loosened her hold on him and curled more into his lap, laying her head on his chest. He held her there, afraid to let her ago, afraid of what could have happened to her. They didn't speak. The only sounds were the birds in the trees and the occasional scurrying of a squirrel or a chipmunk.

"I can't go back to Grandfather's," she whispered against his chest. "I'm not safe there, and I'm not safe at Mpampas's home either." She cried again and moved in closer. "I'm only safe with you." She clung to him, his tunic in her clenched fists. "I don't want to go back, David. Please don't take me back."

"What happened?" What had he missed? He'd only been gone a couple of weeks, but in this household, he never knew what might happen next. Had Demetri touched her? A shudder of rage—and what he would do—ricocheted through his body.

"In two days, I'll be forced to marry Demetri." She wept again into his tunic.

"He didn't hurt you, did he?"

"No. But he will." She squealed. "I can't marry him, David. I just can't."

David felt like his heart was being ripped from his chest. The thought of her belonging to any man other than himself made him want to hit something. Hard. He knew this day would come, sooner than later. He'd hoped to have found a way out of this place before then, a way according to the law. Now he'd have to escape with the master's granddaughter. He shook his head. If he ever got caught, it'd be his death. And even worse, what would become of her? What kind of man would put her in such danger? But he had to get her away from this place. Then a thought struck him. Of course. He could take her to Galen. He squeezed her tight. That's what he'd do. But he couldn't tell her. He didn't want to get her hopes up, just in case he failed. He didn't dare fail. The thought made him want to slam his fist into the tree next to him. He was her only hope. What could he do or say to put her at ease until then?

That's when he remembered the headband wrapped around his wrist. As her trembling subsided, he untied it and then inched away from her. With red eyes, she looked up at him, continuing to cling to his tunic. He let the band dangle between them.

She saw it. "Oh." In an obvious daze, she patted her hair. "It must have fallen out." When her fingers touched the band that was still twisted in her hair, she looked up at David, questions in her eyes.

Suddenly, he wondered if she'd believe him. He could hardly believe it himself. Had he not heard the man say his name, or seen Galen's reaction when he told him Alethea was alive, he might not have believed it himself.

"He's alive." They were the only words he could force past his constricting throat.

He watched her face as she studied the band. She took it between her trembling fingers and brought it to her nose. Her eyes widened and she shook all over.

She pounced against him, clinging to his neck. "Where is he? When's he coming? Where'd you find him? How'd it happen? Does Grandfather know? Is that why he wants to rush the wedding? Oh, David!" She cupped his face in her hands, her eyes lit up with joy, a joy he'd never before this day seen shining in those brown orbs. "He's alive!" She hugged him, squeezing herself against him, and that's when David began to awaken to the close proximity of their bodies.

252 ★ Sandi Rog

He held her away, though she was still in his lap.

"Is he coming, David? How can this be? How?"

"We were returning from Rome and I thought I saw a thief. I went after him, and that's when he said who he was." He took a deep breath, preparing to tell her the whole story, at the same time, fighting off the temptation she'd become in his lap. "Your grandfather meant to kill him, but it didn't work. The horse dragged him away, but it stopped not far from the road. He was nearly dead when someone found him. Whoever it was picked him up and sold him to the highest bidder. After years of being sold and resold, a Christian jeweler purchased him. When the jeweler heard his story, he set him free to reclaim his family." David ran his hand through his hair, needing to set Alethea away from him, but unable to bring himself to hurt her feelings. "That's all I had time to find out."

Trying to avoid her scent, her softness, David glanced away from her as she took in what he'd just said. He looked down and noticed his bloody sword and the blood on his tunic. So different from his encounter with Galen. He hadn't shed any blood on that day.

Alethea clung to his tunic. "Where is he? When's he coming?"

David took a deep breath, knowing she wouldn't like the answer. "He's in Rome." He'd told Galen to go to Rome and find Manius.

Alethea slumped down. "Why? Why isn't he here?"

David couldn't say more. He didn't know what Galen had planned, and if one of them didn't act soon, it would be too late. He had to find a way to appease her, something to give her hope. That's when he changed his mind about his original plan. Why keep it a secret. If he failed, he would disappoint her, but she needed something to cling to. Besides, he wouldn't fail. How many times had he been able to escape? This time, he had no reason to stay. He'd take her away from here and return her to her father. Where she belonged. Whatever happened to David after that, didn't matter. Even if it meant death, he would find a way to get Alethea out of here.

"I'm going to take you away from here. Before the wedding takes place." There. He said it.

The joy in her eyes matched that of learning that her father was alive. It sent a thrill right to his heart. Giggling, she hugged him. He put his arms around her. She kissed his forehead, his nose, his cheeks.

David's control snapped. He clasped her head in his hands. Her hair curled around his fingers, and he pulled her in.

Alethea froze, her lips parting in a small gasp.

David held her there, inches from his face. How long had he loved her? From the moment he first laid eyes on her every fiber in his being cried out to protect her, to shield her, to have her. He brought her closer. Her eyes closed in invitation, and he knew she longed for this as much as he did. Sweet jasmine filled his senses. Their breath mingled and he longed to taste her, to breathe her in. He brought her lips to his and her softness ignited a fire in his blood. He had to stop. But he didn't want to. He kept kissing her, and she kissed him back. He could so easily take this too far. He must stop! Regretfully, he pulled away, breathing heavily.

Alethea gazed up into his face. "God has answered both my prayers today," she whispered. "Ever since you taught me how, I've been praying." She grinned up into his face, her eyes sparkling with unshed tears. "Praying that God would bring Mpampas back to life."

David tried to bring his mind to her words, to pull his thoughts away from the force of his emotions. Did she say she'd prayed for God to bring her father to life? Of course, that shouldn't surprise him, but it did. Where did she get the idea to pray for such a thing?

Then she looked down, a tinge of pink coloring her cheeks. "And I've been praying that God would find a way for us to marry."

David froze. He thought he'd become used to her surprises. Marriage was impossible. He was a slave. There was no way for them to be legally bound. He never should have kissed her. However, for his own selfish reasons he wasn't sorry. He'd never forget their first kiss. And their last.

Let her believe.

Let her learn the ugly truth when she was with her father. That way he could comfort her after David broke her heart.

twenty-one

Even after the joyful news, David could feel Alethea trembling in his arms as he carried her back through the gates of the villa. He walked between the guards who kept a lookout in the watchtowers. They didn't stop him as he continued along the edge of the woods, past the stables, and up to the portico where Renata let out a loud cry when she spotted them coming toward her. She ran up to them, putting her hand on Alethea, but not saying a word, choking them back with her tears. Soon, Aloysius, Demetri, and Cornelia were there to meet them.

David set Alethea down before her mother who stood motionless, not even offering a hand of comfort to her only daughter. David never understood the woman. Renata wrapped a cloak over Alethea's trembling shoulders and began leading her away.

Alethea stopped. She turned and looked right at him. "Thank you, David," she said, her voice choking. She then allowed Renata to lead her away.

David stood frozen, like the marble columns along the portico surrounding them. She'd called him by his name. His real name.

Demetri straightened, his eyes wide with realization.

Aloysius didn't seem to notice as he grabbed Cornelia by the arm and jerked her along. "Why can't you be a mother to the girl?" He shoved her ahead of him as they all turned to follow Renata and Alethea into the house.

By now, Demetri's eyes narrowed into slits, studying David. He motioned with his chin to David's sword. "Why is there blood?" His voice was a forced calm.

David took a deep breath. "She was attacked."

Demetri's face paled.

"There were three of them. Hiding in the trees near your place."

"You took care of them?" Demetri's tone mounted with the fury in his gaze.

"Yes."

Demetri nodded, continuing to study David, seeming to absorb his answer. "Did they touch her?"

David wasn't sure how to answer. Of course, they touched her. That's what he just said. She was attacked.

"How far did they get?" Demetri's voice rose in command.

David clenched his hands into fists, wanting to pound one in Demetri's haughty face. "They didn't," was all David could bring himself to say.

Demetri's shoulders relaxed and he wiped his nose with the pad of his thumb. "I hope you weren't expecting a reply to that letter you sent."

David gave him a questioning look.

"I really didn't think it appropriate that Bahiti act as your courier." Demetri shrugged. "I rarely allow her out of my sight these days."

Now David understood why he'd never heard back from Manius. Apparently, Bahiti wasn't able to find Manius to pass on a verbal message. He almost chuckled at Demetri's comment about never letting her out of his sight, especially considering he was here and she was still in Rome. He knew without a doubt that she'd be meeting with the church.

David turned to leave.

"Yes."

David stopped and looked over his shoulder.

"Yes." Demetri raised a brow. "You may go. *David.*"

Ω

That night, a scream echoed off the walls throughout the villa, jolting David to his feet and charging, sword in hand, to the atrium. He'd been sitting in the courtyard, leaning against the wall, just below Alethea's bedchamber window, and he'd fallen asleep. Another scream ricocheted through the house as he ran toward Alethea's room. Vibia came stumbling out of the chamber, blanket pulled tight over her shoulders.

"She's having a nightmare," Vibia said, scurrying as far away from the door as possible.

David skidded to a stop. Dare he go in? He ached to be by Alethea's side, but he didn't dare go into her private chamber. As he stood by the door, contemplating what he should do, Portia and Cornelia whisked by him. He sighed and leaned against the door.

Aloysius, pulling on a tunic and carrying a lamp, came up to him, Renata following close behind. "What happened?" he asked, voice groggy from sleep.

"She had a nightmare." Vibia, sitting on the edge of the fountain, motioned an irritated hand toward the room as if it was the stupidest thing she'd ever witnessed.

"Because of the attack." Aloysius looked at David, worry clouding his eyes. Then he narrowed them. "She never should have gone past the villa's gates!" He began to pace.

Portia came to the door. "She's just frightened. She's not been harmed."

"Don't leave me alone!" Alethea cried.

"You're no longer needed, Portia," Cornelia called from the chamber.

Portia looked back into the room, then at the others, and then back again, clearly unsure what to do.

"Go check on Paulus."

Portia glanced one last time into the room, pulled her cloak tight, and left them all.

"All is well. I'm here." Cornelia's voice carried to their ears. So foreign, since David, nor any of them for that matter, ever heard her speak in a motherly tone.

"Please! I want Damonus." Alethea's voice broke into sobs. "He'll keep me safe."

"I'll stay with you, dear."

"Why now, mother? You've never been here for me before." Alethea cried.

Cornelia came to the door of the chamber, trembling hands on the doorposts. "I'll sleep here tonight. Vibia, you may sleep in my chamber."

Renata nodded her approval. She took Vibia under her arm and led her away. Aloysius followed, but stopped and swung around. "Damonus. Stand guard at her door tonight. Make her feel safe."

David bowed. "Yes, master."

The night wore on as David stood guard outside Alethea's bedchamber. She'd finally calmed down as her mother shushed her to sleep. He'd never witnessed Cornelia act in a motherly fashion to Alethea until this night. What caused the change? Was it Aloysius's rebuke?

"David?" Alethea whispered from her chamber.

David straightened by the door. "I'm here."

"Please don't go."

He closed his eyes against the pain in his chest. He ought to just carry her away tonight. Take her to Galen right now. But Cornelia was in the chamber. They'd never get far, unless he incapacitated her, but he couldn't bring himself to harm a woman.

"I'm right here," he whispered back, his voice hoarse.

"Sing to me, David."

He cringed every time she said his real name. But they'd be leaving soon. Besides that, Demetri wasn't around to hear it. Not that it mattered, since he now suspected something between David and Alethea. He'd left immediately after David brought Alethea back. David wondered where he was going with the wedding day drawing so near.

Now David wanted to kick himself. He should have taken Alethea to Galen the moment he decided to take her away from here. He never should have reentered the gates of the villa. He should have taken her straight to Rome. However, everyone was already searching for Alethea, so they likely would have caught up to them, and then where would she be? He'd be dead, and she'd be without hope. Perhaps it was good that he brought her back. At least now, she could bid her family farewell. If not literally, at least in her mind, in her heart. Tomorrow, first thing, he'd take her away from here.

"Please, David."

"What?" he whispered into the darkness, knowing Cornelia could hear every exchange.

"Sing to me."

David shook his head. "I can't sing."

Alethea cried, sniffling into her cushions.

"Fine." He clenched his teeth at the thought of singing where her mother could hear. But he knew it'd comfort Alethea. So, quietly . . . he sang.

Ω

David couldn't stand still any longer. It would have to be now or not at all. If only he'd had time to prepare, make a plan he knew would work. After a lot of deliberation, he realized the best time to escape was now. In the middle of the night.

Despite Alethea's shock after what happened, he knew her family would busy her in the morning with wedding preparations, and she'd never be able to leave their sight. If he tried to sneak her away during their ministrations, she'd surely be missed. They'd send out search parties and a hunt would ensue. He could wait the night before the wedding, but he felt uneasy about waiting that long. They might keep a more vigilant watch over her during that last night for fear she might try to run. He couldn't risk that chance.

Taking a deep breath, David crept into Alethea's chamber. Two beds lay against opposite walls. The steady breathing of each woman filled the quiet air. David knelt over Alethea, taking care that his sword didn't scrape against the tiled floor. Alethea rested peacefully in the moonlight. He hated waking her, disturbing the brief calm the night allowed. He'd have to wake her carefully so as not to startle her, or her mother might also awaken.

Alethea's dark hair tumbled over the pillow and onto the bed, free of the thick braid he saw her wearing every morning on the way to the baths. Some black wisps framed her face, and her long lashes rested like motionless butterflies against her cheeks. He longed to touch her, mourning the fact that she'd never be his. He brought his hand up to her face, tenderly brushing his fingertips from her temple to her lips. Perfect lips he longed to kiss.

She smiled and stirred. "David," she whispered.

He glanced over his shoulder, seeing that Cornelia was still breathing evenly, deep in sleep.

Alethea's eyes fluttered open, just like the black butterflies they resembled. She stretched and yawned. "I could smell you, your wonderful scent." She settled back down, but then her eyes shot open, fully awake now. "What are you doing in here?"

David glanced over at Cornelia again. She didn't stir.

"We have to go," he whispered. "I'm taking you to your father."

Alethea gasped, but quickly covered her mouth, glancing over at her mother. "Now?" she said.

"Now is the best time." David stood, fighting the temptation to help her out of bed, but he didn't dare touch her in this state. "I'll meet you in the atrium. Hurry."

They'd need food. He left her chamber to sneak into the kitchen. He found some wine rolls and cheese. He grabbed enough for the two of them and stuffed them into a sackcloth hanging from one of the pegs on the wall. He found a small flask of wine and stuffed that in as well.

When he crept back into the atrium, Alethea stood outside her chamber, leaning her tired body against the wall. She tugged on her cloak, a light fabric that framed her curves. She tightened it around her neck. It would never do. If he took her on the road looking like a little rich girl, they were sure to be robbed or attacked. She'd have to wear one of the servant's cloaks. The simple, brown wool wouldn't attract undue attention. He could get one of the younger boy's cloaks. It'd be much better if she looked like a boy. He rushed away to do that. When he returned with everything in hand, he wrapped the boyish cloak over Alethea and pulled the hood over her head. Her nose crinkled, but she didn't complain. He kept his own cloak over his arm with the sackcloth in his hand and led her to the atrium doors.

David opened the doors, just far enough for them to squeeze through. The cool, night air swept over his skin, like a welcoming blanket easing the tension in his taut body. He led Alethea silently into the woods, grateful for the moon that lit their path between the familiar trees. They reached the wall, and David helped Alethea up into the big pine. He followed right behind her. When they reached the top, he tossed the sackcloth and his cloak on the other side of the wall and helped her down.

After her feet touched the ground, she turned into his arms. "This hardly seems real. You have no idea how often I've dreamt of this."

David held her close, praying that they'd make it safely to Rome. He couldn't fail her. He slipped on his cloak and tied the sackcloth around her waist. He dared not explain to her that he needed her to hold it in case he needed to fight. Thankfully, she didn't protest or remark about it.

He guided them along the wall. When they reached the road, he pulled up both their hoods, and kept her on his left side with his right hand on the hilt of his sword. "It's best not to talk," he whispered to her as they hurried along. He didn't want thieves to hear her feminine voice. "Pretend you're a boy," he whispered again.

"How do I do that?"

"Don't sway your hips."

"What? I didn't know they were swaying."

David cringed as he looked down at her. There was no way anybody in their right mind would think she was a boy. "Just stop sway-ing them," he said.

"Is this better?"

He moved slightly behind her to take a look. Bad idea. He never should have set his eyes on her. "No."

"How's this?" She straightened, but that did nothing to hide her hips.

"No." He shook his head.

She stopped, tossing her chin up. "Then what do you suggest?"

"Hold your cloak open a bit. That might help."

She opened her cloak and began walking.

David sighed. Maybe it was because he knew Alethea hid under that mass of wool that it didn't matter what she did, she'd never resemble a boy in his eyes. He simply nodded, and they started walk-ing again.

Ω

Just as they left the forest behind them, David relaxed his hold on his sword. They'd made it without incident. Now if they could just reach the gates to Rome. The sun's rays lanced over the horizon, casting his and Alethea's shadow over the road in front of them.

"Are you hungry?" David whispered the first words since leaving the forest.

"No." Alethea shook her head.

David wasn't hungry either. Perhaps it was the desperation he felt to reach Rome's gates.

"I can't believe I'm finally going to see him."

David knew she meant her father. "We're not there yet." He still feared failure. He didn't dare get his, let alone, her hopes up.

She frowned up at him.

"Do you have any regrets?" He kept his gaze on hers, fearing he might catch a hint of disappointment.

"Not at all." She shook her head, determination on her face.

David sighed with relief. But they still hadn't made it. If he failed, they'd both feel regret.

As the sun rose, they reached the Via Labicana where green fields lit up like emeralds and blue fields of flax glinted like sapphires along the road. The square gate came into view, and David's heart pounded a little faster. He glanced down at Alethea, a grin on his face. She smiled up at him beneath the hood of her cloak.

"Pull back your hood." He didn't want them to look like they were trying to hide who they were. If they looked confident, the guards at the gate wouldn't think anything of the two of them walking alone. Perhaps they'd think they were just a couple, heading into the city for the day's market.

They both pulled back their hoods, David putting on a confident air, something that came naturally for Alethea. There weren't as many people as David had expected in order to lose themselves in the crowd.

Just as they approached the towering gate, several men came through led by two men, one of them quite large. David's eyes wandered in their direction as he kept a firm hold on Alethea's elbow.

Alethea gasped and she stopped. David tried to tug her along, but she wouldn't move. "Demetri." She'd only whispered his name and began to walk again, but the fact that they'd stopped and taken notice of them made the men look in David and Alethea's direction. At first, Demetri didn't recognize them buried under their cloaks, and he looked away, but he looked back at them, and the recognition registered on his face.

"Alethea?" Demetri stopped. The man next to him walked two paces before he realized Demetri had stopped. The man followed Demetri's gaze.

At that moment, Demetri recognized David. "Where's your grandfather?" Demetri looked around them, seeing that they were alone. He drew his sword and came toward them. "Alethea, stand back."

David drew his sword, pushing Alethea behind him.

"Guards!" Demetri shouted at the gate. "A slave's escaped!" He charged for David. Their swords clashed and David held his own. He knew he could take down Demetri. But dare he in front of the Roman guards who now charged toward them with their own swords drawn? What would become of Alethea if he failed?

The guards came at David. He fought them off, two, then three of them. Demetri dropped back as David fought, swords clanging, each man coming at him. David worked to keep his footing on the thick stones and found it distracting as he tried to keep his focus on each man around him. He dropped into a half split, but the stones made for an awkward descent. Still, he was able to block the swords and even cut one of the guards in the thigh. The man fell. David went after the second, slicing him easily down the length of his arm. Crying out, he dropped back.

David did everything in his power to keep from killing the guards. The temptation to thrust the point of his sword into their flesh was great. The third guard's swings weren't as powerful as the first guard's, and David easily took hold of his opponent's blade by guiding its point down. David lunged in, still holding the man's blade down, and punched him in the face, knocking the man backward. His grip on the sword loosened and David snatched it from him. He flipped the hilt of the man's sword into his own hand, avoiding cutting himself completely. How often he'd done this trick with Titus, he didn't know. David turned in circles, waving the swords around him to avoid any new attack. Several men stood around, watching as if they were at Vespasian's Amphitheater.

"David!" Demetri's voice called. David turned to see Demetri holding Alethea from behind with his own sword at her throat. David froze. "Drop the swords and I won't have to hurt your girl."

Seeing his sword against Alethea's neck and hearing the way he said "your girl" made David shudder. He pointed at Demetri with one of the blades. "She is a Roman citizen! Release her!"

"She's no more a Roman citizen than you are!" Demetri shouted, tightening his hold on Alethea. Her silent, brown eyes pleaded with

David. "She hardly looks like one." He shook her up and down, emphasizing her wool cloak.

The men around them chuckled. David glanced at them, wielding his sword. The men backed off, waving their hands as if to ward off any coming blows.

"David!" Demetri shouted again. "I mean it. I . . . will . . . kill . . . her." He lifted his chin, his gaze fixed on David's. "What is she to me, your woman? She's worthless, just a slave."

Would he? Would he dare harm her amongst all these witnesses? But then it occurred to David that they were all Demetri's slaves who would lie for him.

Demetri moved toward David, still holding Alethea in his grasp, and David noticed a small cut on her neck. Demetri leaned in close. "You'll be blamed for her death, of course. I'll just say I caught you trying to escape with your hostage. When the guards tried to capture you, you threatened to slice her throat, but accidentally did it anyway."

The wicked idea wasn't far from the truth as David watched Demetri's sword again come too close to the wound that was already there. Reluctantly, and in utter defeat, David dropped his swords. Demetri smiled, then motioned with his chin to the guards and other men standing around. Someone grabbed David's arms and bound them behind his back.

"Get your sword off of her," David said. "If you kill her, you won't get your land." David grasped at anything to get Demetri to obey his command. Demetri let his sword fall. David thought Demetri was a better person than that. He always thought he'd seen a bit of good in him, especially in his concern toward Alethea and keeping her out of harm's way from Aloysius. But this moment had changed all of that.

"Do you honestly think I would have done it?" Demetri shook his head, casting David a smug grin. Still holding Alethea in a firm grip by her arm, Demetri motioned to the others around him. "I'll take care of this." The guards dropped back, and Demetri's men came forward, including the tall man who had been walking at Demetri's side.

"David, allow me to introduce Chlothar. He's a local gladiator. Surely, you've heard his name. I hired him." Demetri straightened as if proud of his latest rental. "I thought a gladiator fight would make a nice surprise for my wife-to-be." He shook Alethea at his side. She kept her gaze downcast, tears dripping onto the ground at her feet. David's chest clenched. He had failed her, and now her life with this man would be even worse than what it might have been had he not caught them together and learned of their love for each other.

"Aren't you curious who Chlothar is going to fight?" Demetri leaned in closer to David as the men behind him tightened their grips on his arms. "To the death."

Alethea cried out.

Demetri cast her a fierce look. "Maybe with your lover dead, you'll be able to focus on your marriage to me."

"Don't hurt her." David's fists ached to defend Alethea. "This was my idea, not hers."

Demetri glared at David. "She'd better be untouched." The shock of his words sent involuntary shivers down David's spine when he thought of Demetri's hands on Alethea.

"She's innocent." He spoke between clenched teeth.

Demetri tugged Alethea along. "We'll find out. Won't we?"

"You have no right to do this!" Alethea shouted. "David was my escort. He was taking me to my father!"

Demetri kept walking, shaking his head. "Have you lost your mind, woman?"

"My father is alive!" The fury in Alethea's eyes warmed David. She'd been so quiet, so helpless, he thought for sure his failure had crushed her spirit.

Demetri laughed. "You have lost your mind!"

They kept walking, and the men pushed David forward, away from the gate, away from their portal to freedom.

twenty-two

Knowing her father was alive gave Alethea the will to fight. She'd come so close to having her dreams come true. How dare they take them away.

Grandfather stood before her, face almost purple, as he ranted and raved about her "disappearance." Of course, the entire villa had been searching for her, and everyone, especially Grandmother, was hugely grateful for her safe return. Titus stood behind her with David still in bonds, and Alethea would do whatever it took to defend him.

"I was not his hostage." Alethea shot a glare at Demetri for his lie. "He was escorting me to my father!"

Her mother gasped, a guilty look clouded her eyes, but she erased it as soon as Grandfather turned to her.

"What is she talking about?" Grandfather glared at her mother.

Cornelia shook her head. "I have no idea."

Grandfather faced Alethea again, but something in her mother's eyes betrayed her. She wasn't telling the truth. Did she know Mpampas was alive? But how could she know? And why didn't she say anything?

"Enough of this nonsense!" Grandfather motioned toward Titus. "Fifteen lashings save one."

"No!" Alethea cried, crumpling to her knees.

Demetri grabbed her by the arm, and brought her to her feet.

"I'm telling you! My father is alive, and you will pay for what you're doing!"

Gasps came from all around. Grandfather had been about to leave, but he stopped when she said the words. Slowly, he turned on her and stepped forward. Alethea straightened. He slapped her. She fell from the force, but Demetri held her up. She struggled to free herself from his grasp. She wanted nothing more than to put her hand on her burning cheek, but he wouldn't let go of her arms.

"Don't ever speak to me like that again." Grandfather's voice was a forced calm. His gaze held hers, then his eyes widened. "What happened to your neck?"

"Ask Demetri," was all Alethea could say.

"The slave's blade nearly cut her through." Demetri tightened his grip on her arms.

"That's not true!" Alethea twisted. "Check his blade! There's blood on Demetri's sword."

Grandfather cast a glance at Demetri's sword, a hint of doubt clouding his eyes, but immediately he straightened. "Take her to my office chamber."

Demetri jerked on her arms and yanked her through the atrium. She shook her head. He wasn't even interested in the truth. Once Demetri had her alone in the chamber, he forced her to face him. "Why'd you do that? Why did you talk to him that way?" His eyes were filled with worry. "I never meant to harm you. You've got to believe that." With the back of his knuckles, he reached toward her neck, but she pulled away. "Now he's going to beat you. If you'd just let him believe that the slave had taken you hostage, you'd be safe."

Alethea wanted to slap him. "As long as I'm in this house, I'm not safe." She held his gaze, telling him without words how she wouldn't be in this house had it not been for him.

"Just tell him it was the slave." His eyes pled with her. "He doesn't want to beat you. I'm sure of it."

Grandfather came into the chamber, and fear shuddered down her spine when she saw the wooden board in his hand. It made her think of something that might be used in a game or a sport, but instead it would be used on her. She swallowed, fighting the urge to do as Demetri suggested, tempted to betray David with another lie. She'd never make that same mistake again.

"Umm." Demetri stepped in front of Alethea. "May I speak to you privately?"

Grandfather straightened, letting the board sag at his side. "What is it?"

Demetri inched closer to Grandfather. "It's between us."

"Go." Grandfather motioned to Alethea. "Wait outside the chamber."

Alethea went to the hall and Grandfather closed the door behind her. What could Demetri need to say at a time like this? She waited, leaning against the wall, worrying and wondering about David. When would they start the scourging? She couldn't bear the thought of what he'd suffer. She waited, kicking at the tiles, pushing back and forth against the wall, listening down the hall for Titus and the whip. Her knees nearly buckled when she imagined what the glass woven into the leather would do to David's flesh.

Her mother crept up to Alethea, her hands to her chest, fear in her eyes as they darted to Grandfather's chamber door. She swallowed visibly. "How'd you know?" she whispered, barely audible to Alethea's ears.

"How did *you* know?"

"He sent word, a message." Her voice trembled. "It came shortly after Damonus brought you back from the woods."

"Why didn't you say anything?" Alethea gritted her teeth. "Is that why you're being nice to me all of a sudden? You've never cared in the past, but now that you know he's alive, you care." Alethea shook her head. "Why?"

Her mother clutched her stola, hands white against her chest. "I couldn't accept his new God. He can have his God. I just need him." A smile quivered on her lips. "I now know I am nothing without him."

"But what about me and Paulus?" Alethea took a deep shuddering breath. "Weren't we worth anything to you? Don't you think we needed him too?" She choked back tears. "And what about Paulus? He has no interest in Mpampas."

Her mother looked down at the floor. A woman Alethea barely knew. A stranger.

"Why are you glad he's alive? I thought you wanted him dead." Anger flamed in Alethea's mind. "You instigated the whole thing," she said between clenched teeth, trying to keep her voice down.

Her mother shook her head. "I only hoped he'd deny his God. As soon as he denied his God, we would come back to him." She lifted her hands. "I never expected him . . . to die." Tears formed in her mother's eyes, revealing for the first time, true sorrow and guilt.

The door came open, and her mother spun around and walked away.

Grandfather stopped in front of Alethea. He looked down at her with sympathy, then turned to leave. Demetri came out of the chamber, watching Grandfather disappear into the courtyard.

"What'd you say to him?"

"I convinced him that you'd lost your mind, falsely believing that your father was waiting for you in Rome, so you begged that slave to take you there. When he realized he had a willing hostage, he took you."

"What?" Alethea raised her hands. "But that's not true!" She pointed to the courtyard where the tall, wooden stakes stood, waiting for David's flogging. "He'll be punished!"

Without waiting for a response, Alethea ran to the courtyard. Titus was already tying David to a stake.

"Make that twenty save one!" Grandfather shouted.

"No!" Alethea cried out. She ran to her grandfather. "He didn't kidnap me! He wasn't trying to run away." She clung to Grandfather's tunic. "Please! Listen to me!" Tears burned her eyes as they swarmed down her cheeks. "It's my fault!"

"Master." Alethea stopped at the sound of David's voice. "I did take her hostage. She's not to blame for any of this."

"No! David, how can you say that?" Alethea sobbed and ran to David. "Untie him!" She tugged on the ropes. She looked up at Titus. "Untie him! I command you!" With trembling fingers, she tried to loosen the ropes around David's wrists. The wails and screams from his last whipping echoed in the memories of her mind. Not again. She couldn't bear it again.

"Alethea," David whispered. Her hands froze and she wiped her nose on her arm. "It's going to be fine. All will be well." David's gaze held hers.

"But all will not be well. They're going to flog you!"

"Go back to your grandfather. Go back to Demetri."

Alethea fell to her knees, hugging the pole and David's legs. "David." She wept against the prickly bark. "Don't let them do this to you." Her voice choked back more sobs.

"If I didn't know better, I'd say you love this boy." Grandfather stood over her now, face red.

"I've got her." Suddenly, Demetri was at her side, pulling her to her feet. "She's exhausted, distraught. It's been a difficult two days. I'll take her to Cornelia." Grandfather watched them. A look of relief passed over David's face as Demetri tugged on her and escorted her away. Grandfather turned back toward David, motioning for Titus to begin. Alethea couldn't help but be reminded of that horrible day. The day Grandfather motioned for Titus to tie her father to a horse.

Ω

David felt like the wooden doll Galen had made for Alethea. He hugged the stake as he tried to keep his legs from collapsing. He'd managed not to cry out, fearing Alethea might hear his wails. He didn't want to upset her anymore than she already was. He'd hoped to black out, but Jehovah-Shammah hadn't been so merciful.

Titus unbound his hands. His stomach and chest were covered in splinters. But that was nothing compared to the burning on his back, arms and legs. Had he not stayed up all night, made the long trips to and from Rome, he might have felt stronger, but right now, he feared his legs might give out on him. Titus tugged him to the slave with the bowl of honey, prepared to cover David in the salve.

"We'll have none of that." Aloysius eyed Titus. "Take him to the gymnasium." Aloysius clapped his hands and rubbed them together. "Let the games begin."

Ω

David stood on wobbly legs in the gymnasium. Every part of his body trembled and cried out in pain. He wished he could lie on the ground, but even that wouldn't bring him comfort with all the cuts on his body. Titus stood next to him in silence.

"I'm sorry I disappointed you." David finally brought himself to speak.

"That girl's been nothing but trouble."

"She's not to blame." David glanced at Titus, then back at the door, waiting for everyone to arrive. "It's true what she says. Her father is alive."

Titus's brows furrowed. "How?"

"Remember the day I thought thieves were about to attack the caravan?"

Titus nodded. "There was no blood on your sword."

"It was him. Galen."

Titus sighed, long and hard. "It was me."

David shook his head. "What?"

"I tied him to his horse." Titus shifted his stance. "At Aloysius's command."

David sensed the discomfort in Titus. Something Titus rarely showed, even when whipping him. It could have been easy for David to be angry at him, but he no longer saw him as a powerful man. He saw him as a slave. A slave that did his master's bidding, an animal, an object. David thought how hard he'd worked to earn Aloysius's favor so he might be set free. All for nothing. And that's when a thought struck David. All the times Titus gave in to Aloysius's orders, administering the full force of his whip. "Did Aloysius ever offer you freedom like you said he did?"

"No."

David chuckled without humor. He'd always looked up to Titus, never daring to cross him, even seeing him as a father figure. Titus always ignored David's escapades with Alethea, ignored his teaching other servants about Elohim. Now he realized, maybe Titus was afraid. Curious, but afraid. David no longer needed to fear him. After all, what did he have to lose? He was going to die anyway. He kept his eyes on the door, waiting for the man who would kill him.

"There's a Master you can serve that's greater than Aloysius." David felt like he was talking to Alethea back in the woods, telling her that God was bigger than her grandfather.

"Aloysius is master enough for me." A low chuckle rumbled in Titus's chest.

David sighed. "But in the next life, it won't be enough."

At that moment, Lucius skipped into the arena and hopped into the stands, rubbing his hands together eager for entertainment. Marcus ambled behind and took a seat above his brother. Frowning, he leaned his elbows heavily on his knees.

The rest of the family, including the women—to David's horror—entered the gymnasium. Demetri escorted Alethea, and David's stomach lurched at seeing her slumped form. Why were they bringing the women to witness this deadly combat? It was likely for Alethea's benefit. He clenched his teeth. She watched David as she took her seat, her eyes wide with fear.

Aloysius followed behind, walking with an arrogant stride, his sword hanging from his belt.

Titus turned David, giving him a sword and shield. The sword felt heavy, and so did the shield. It'd be impossible for David to fight this well-trained gladiator.

"Remember all that I've taught you." Titus's voice was calm and sure. He clearly had more confidence in this fight than David. "It's not strength that wins a battle, but the mind, the heart."

David locked eyes with Titus, no longer needing to look up to him to meet his gaze. "Apply that to your life."

Titus lifted his chin. "You can win this fight."

"So can you." David's voice was low, quiet. He turned and walked into the center of the small arena, his body aching and burning. Ready to die.

The large man, Chlothar, entered the gymnasium wearing the armor of a Thracian. David was pleased. The man's leg guards would keep him from moving very fast and would prevent him from being too agile. His heavy helmet and its large crest with the long griffin curving upward toward the sky would also help to slow the man down. The man's small, square shield would do little to protect him, and his parma, with its short curved blade, was a tad smaller than David's gladius; the swords would be equal to do battle. But even if David were faster and better equipped, would he be able to kill him? He shook his head. He already knew the answer to that.

"Let the games begin!" Aloysius shouted.

"No!" Alethea's voice broke through the crowd. She crawled over her aunt and uncle in the stands, making her way toward Aloysius. David gritted his teeth. Why didn't they stop her? Now what was she up to?

The gladiator moved far away from her as she made her way into the arena. Several feet from David, she stepped in front of the stands and stood before her grandfather. She cast a side-glance in David's direction, and then turned her back to him as she faced her worst enemy.

All the weariness left his body as David sensed she was attempting to delay the inevitable. But to what extremes would she go? Instinctively, he readied his hand on the hilt of his sword. He had nothing to lose, concerning his own life, so he'd do whatever it took to save hers.

Alethea straightened to her full height. "I am a Christian!" she shouted for everyone to hear.

Gasps carried up from her family, followed by murmurs and whispers. Aloysius stood as straight and still as one of the stakes in the courtyard. Gradually, all fell silent as Aloysius's face reddened. But he made no move toward her, his hands at his side, motionless. Then, without warning, he slapped Alethea. She stood her ground, covering her cheek. Then he slapped her again. She stumbled to one side. This time, he raised his fist.

"No!" David shouted, Demetri's voice echoing the same cry from the stands.

Aloysius's eyes widened. He grabbed the hilt of his sword.

David sprinted toward him, readying his own gladius.

Screams carried up from the stands.

David met his master's blade with a fierce blow, knocking him backward.

Aloysius lost his grip and his sword flipped to the ground.

David blocked Alethea with his arm, pushing her away from himself and her grandfather. He felt the edge of a blade against his throat. From the dark shadow standing next to him, David knew it was Titus.

Cornelia stumbled toward them as Aloysius bent to retrieve his sword. He came toward Alethea again. David jerked away from Titus's blade, pushing it behind him. He lunged in front of Alethea, ready to take her grandfather down. Fear reflected in the old man's gaze as David towered over him, his eyes darting from Titus to David. Titus moved in.

"No!" David pushed Alethea farther behind him, deflecting Titus's blade, keeping a wary eye out for Aloysius.

"Stop!" Aloysius shouted at Titus. "You'll kill her."

Titus backed off, but David didn't lower his blade, ready for Aloysius to come for him. A slave was worthy of death for disobeying his master, let alone threatening him. What did it matter? He was going to die anyway.

Aloysius straightened to his full height, his sword in his hand. "Throw down your sword." Aloysius spoke in a firm tone, but David could hear the slight tremor in his voice.

"Alethea, come here." Cornelia moved in closer. "Come away from that slave."

Alethea moved, but David held her behind him. "Not yet." He didn't trust Aloysius, despite his reaction to Titus. David sensed Aloysius would find pleasure in harming Alethea himself.

Aloysius's face went bright red with rage. "How dare you!" Spittle flew from his mouth as he spoke. "This behavior is deserving of death. First you will be scourged, and then you will die by my sword."

"What more can you do to me?" David had already been scourged, and he was already sentenced to die by the hand of the gladiator—a much more interesting death than dying by Aloysius's sword.

Aloysius stepped toward David, his blade poised.

David crouched, gladius ready.

Aloysius hesitated, fear and uncertainty on his face. He started toward David again, but stopped when David tensed. He then glanced around, as if unsure what to do. His gaze fell on Cornelia, and his jaw tensed. "If you had been a better mother!" He lunged forward and plunged his sword into his daughter.

Renata screamed and rushed from the stands.

Alethea screamed from behind David.

Cornelia dropped to her knees, holding her bleeding stomach, as Renata raced to her side.

Crying, Alethea tried to get to her mother, but David wouldn't let her pass. "No!" She cried and clung to David's back, weeping onto his burning wounds.

Aloysius turned to David and Alethea, his face white, a stark contrast with the blood dripping from the tip of his sword. Eyes wide and bulging, he pointed his trembling blade at Alethea as she cowered behind David. "Her blood is on your hands!"

David clenched his teeth and hissed. He glared at Aloysius, as if reaching through the distance between them, yanking on his chin to force him to meet his gaze. "You coward." He knew Aloysius went after Cornelia because he didn't have the courage to go through him to get to Alethea.

Aloysius snarled at David. "Today, you will die!" He straightened, took a deep breath and raised his sword above his head. "Let the games begin!"

David pushed Alethea behind him, walking backward away from Titus and Aloysius.

Chlothar, the gladiator, stepped farther into the arena, moving toward them. David continued to push Alethea behind him. Surely, he wouldn't attack while Alethea stood nearby. Renata hovered over Cornelia, her face in her hands and crying. Demetri stood near them, motioning for Alethea to come as Aloysius and Titus walked to the far side of the arena away from the stands.

"Go to your mother," David said.

Alethea clung more fiercely to David's burning back, trembling against him. "I just wanted to protect you. I didn't mean for this to happen." She sniffed behind him, her voice small and terrified.

"You're not to blame."

The gladiator moved in closer.

"Go," he said, urgency in his tone.

Alethea ran to her mother just as the gladiator ran at David like an elephant charging for war.

twenty-three

David crouched, ready for the gladiator. Just as Chlothar closed in, David dove away, curling into a roll. The fire on his back and shoulders made him cry out. Shuddering, he barely made it to his feet. After all the excitement, David had forgotten about his exposed wounds. Unsteady, he turned to face the back of the gladiator. Chlothar glanced from side to side. It would have been a great opportunity to go in for the kill, but of course, because of Elohim, he couldn't do it. And he was too weary to do anything else.

Chlothar turned and spotted David standing several feet behind him. Again, he charged. And again, David dove away, clenching his teeth against the burning on his back and arms, swallowing a cry. In agony, he rebounded to a standing position.

Chlothar straightened and faced David. The massive gladiator made David think of a bear chasing a squirrel. It was almost humorous. Chlothar walked toward him this time. David stepped back, partially relieved. He didn't think he could roll away again, but to fight this giant would require strength, and David had little left. He hadn't even tried using his sword yet, but there would be plenty of time for that, assuming David would last that long. Perhaps he could try to sweep the gladiator's legs; although, that would make more sense if the man was running. He walked so slowly that he'd likely be able to catch himself before hitting the ground, or avoid David tripping him altogether.

The man's slow gait gave David time to think. And he didn't like to think. Not at this point. Was he really ready to die? If only he hadn't failed in his attempt to save Alethea. He glanced up at the stands to find her. She wasn't there. Nor was she by her mother. Where was she? Demetri was still there, watching with his arms crossed and a smug grin on his face. At least she wasn't anywhere near him. He cringed. She'd be forced to be near him for the rest of her life. It made David ache with jealousy and despair.

Where could she be? Where else would she go but over the wall. Over the wall to escape the insanity of her family. If anything happened to her, he'd . . . what? What could he do? He'd already failed her once. There was nothing more he could do. If Demetri had any sense, he'd go after her. He wouldn't be standing here right now, impatient to watch David die.

The gladiator came at him. David backed away from his thrusts and blocked them with his shield. Chlothar's powerful hacking pushed David's arm back. He kept a vise grip on the leather thong, fearing he might lose his hold. The gladiator kept pounding as David ground his teeth, holding his position. If Chlothar kept hacking, he might penetrate the metal. And if he broke through the metal, it wouldn't take much to crack the wood. And if he got through the wood, one of those hacks could sever David's hand.

The weight and awkwardness of the man's curved blade crashed into him as Lucius, Demetri, and Aloysius cheered. Their cheers sent shudders of anger down the length of David's weakening arm with each forceful hack. He'd given of himself and served this family with the hopes of one day being set free, and only now did the emptiness of that dream hit him. It struck him with each thrust and strike of the gladiator's blade. Struck him with the meaninglessness of his attempted escape. An escape that would only serve to make Alethea's life more miserable. And now, who knew where she was. How could her family be so blind, so foolish? But seeing Cornelia's lifeless body out of the corner of his eye answered that question. The gladiator's hacking thrusts penetrated David's shield and his blade stuck there. The women in the stands gasped and cried out. Chlothar tried to pull his blade free, but David held on with both hands, careful not to lose his hold on his own sword. Chlothar jerked again and again, finally twisting the blade free and yanking David forward off his feet.

The gladiator's shield came up and struck David in the head. A blinding light seared through his vision. He jumped to the side, but not in time to avoid the man's blade. A deep, burning slice set his arm on fire. The gladiator came for him again. The women in the stands gasped, and Lucius shouted with joy, while Demetri and Aloysius cheered. David stumbled away, avoiding another lethal swing. With all his might, he threw his shield. It spun through the air like a saucer and hit Chlothar in the torso, causing him to buckle. It gave David time to regain his balance and run. Too quickly, the gladiator straightened and charged at him.

David charged also. Two strides short of colliding, David dropped into a half split and swept Chlothar's legs out from under him. The giant man fell like a tree, landing with a heavy thud and a grunt. Air escaped his mouth as dust carried up from his fall, his foul stench invading David's nostrils.

David leaped onto the gladiator to hold him down, every ounce of rage focused on the monster who was trying to kill him. And for what? A game. David pounded Chlothar's helmet with the hilt of his sword, pounded as the ground and air shuddered around him in waves of murderous fury. Chlothar tried to roll, but David leaped up and shoved him back down with the heel of his foot, putting all his weight behind it. He thought of Aulus and how badly he wanted to do this to him. He kicked the man in the torso, and just as he flipped the blade of his sword and raised it to plunge it down, someone caught David's arms from behind.

Voices shouted around him, voices he didn't recognize, and one voice he did recognize. The voice connected to the hands on his arms.

A voice he knew but hadn't heard in years. David let his arms fall, releasing his fierce grip on the sword. He spun around.

Wide, horrified eyes met David's. A familiar face from his past. Manius. And then his voice, his words became clear in David's mind.

"Stop," Manius whispered, now that David faced him.

David glanced down at the gladiator. Dare he let his guard down? The man didn't move. The threat was over. Trembling, David let his sword fall. He sensed a change in the atmosphere. He looked around. Chaos and Roman guards.

And Galen. Alethea's father crouched over Cornelia, weeping.

What were they doing here?

Guards grabbed Aloysius. Taking him by his arms, they put shackles on his ankles.

"How dare you!" Aloysius shouted. "What is the meaning of this?"

An Imperial Magistrate unrolled a scroll and read it so everyone could hear. "Vibian Cornelius Aloysius! You are under arrest for attempting to murder Galen Aletheos, your son-in-law, and for enslaving a Roman citizen, David, son of Manius Sergia."

The words didn't make any sense. Was he dreaming? Was Manius really standing before him, or was he just a figment of his imagination? Perhaps Chlothar had succeeded in killing him after all. Perhaps he was in heaven. But wouldn't his wounds be healed? His limbs trembled and every part of him hurt. Wouldn't heaven be a better place than this?

Manius's eyes fell on the gash in his arm. "We need to get that bandaged." He motioned for a slave holding a bowl and cloth wraps.

The slave smeared honey on David's wound. The pain burned like fire, but quickly, the honey soothed. He clenched his teeth. It was real. This was really happening. Manius was here. Galen came. And Aloysius would finally pay for his crimes.

Chlothar.

David turned to look at the gladiator lying on the ground. "Did I kill him?" A shudder rose from within. Had he committed the one act that was an abomination to Elohim?

Two guards pulled Chlothar to his feet. He leaned heavily on each one, and David sighed with relief. Had it not been for Manius, his brother in Christ, he would have killed him. In his hopeless rage, David would have killed a man.

"I've never seen anyone fight like that boy." Chlothar's voice came from within his helmet that the men were trying to remove without success.

"You are free, David." Manius helped bandage his arm, the pain keeping David's senses on high alert.

David barely registered Manius's words. Surely, he didn't understand correctly. Perhaps Chlothar's blow to his head had damaged his mind in some way.

"Free." Manius grabbed David's arms, trying to get the words to penetrate his mind, but the pain from his grasp made David wince. "Sorry." Manius released his grip.

Now David knew he was hearing right. "How can that be?"

"You are my son."

David shook his head. He knew that wasn't true.

"Just before your parents were taken, your father and I made arrangements for me to adopt you. We made it official so that you could become a Roman citizen and not suffer persecution." Manius's gaze held David's. "He never had a chance to tell you. It all happened so fast. Too fast. Sooner than we expected."

David shook his head. "They knew, you knew, they'd be executed?"

"No." Manius shifted his stance. "We hoped we were being overly cautious, but your father's father was a devout Jew. He did not like the fact that your parents had become Christians. He was especially angry with your mother, since she was the first to leave the Hebrew faith. I don't believe he meant for anything to happen to you and Sarah."

"Sarah." A cold tremor shook David to the core. "Where is Sarah?"

"With me." Manius smiled. "I found her the morning after your parents were taken. She's been with me ever since. I went back later to collect the scrolls, but they were gone. I'm sure they were there when I found Sarah, but they were gone."

Sarah was safe. That's all David heard. She was with Manius all this time. He'd worried and prayed so much for her. A sob of relief escaped his throat. She was alive and well. Then his thoughts shifted to Alethea. Where was she? He looked around. Guards swarmed the place, and the family wandered around aimlessly, bumping into each other, distraught. Marcus remained in the stands, still sitting with his elbows on his knees, watching everything unfold around him. Demetri walked away, shoulders slumped in defeat.

"The villa is being confiscated by Caesar. He's demanded control of all local vineyards," Manius said.

David turned to him, ignoring the ministrations to his wounds. "I'm free."

Manius nodded. "Better. You're a citizen."

David looked past Manius, over his shoulder, and across the chaos. Titus stood erect, no emotion on his serene face. Without lowering his gaze, Titus bowed to David. How odd that the roles were reversed. Titus respected David as a Christian, as a Roman citizen. Suddenly, David realized, Titus had always respected him.

David met his tormentor's gaze. The person who purchased him, beat him, taught him, and gave him his father's scrolls. He straightened his bloodied back, and in one quick nod, David forgave his friend.

"I have to go." David turned to leave. He had to find Alethea. He made his way through the gymnasium doors and sprinted toward the woods.

If she went over that wall, he'd—he felt for his sword. Gone. Of course. What if he needed to fight? He sighed. He was so weary of fighting. He'd have to make due. She was likely heading back to Rome, and she'd have to go through the forest by herself. He'd better find her soon before barbarians did. For all he knew, he'd arrive too late. That thought made his feet pick up their pace. He swerved between the trees and leaped over branches and dodged protruding limbs. He knew this forest like he knew Alethea. The big pine came into view. And there she was. Lying face down on top of the wall with her face buried on her folded arms. Relief washed over him. He raced for the wall and ran up the side, then leaned on the edge just above her head.

"Are you well?" he asked, breathless.

She lifted her cheek on her arms, sniffling. "David?" she whispered, not looking at him.

"Yes?"

Her head jerked up, her brown eyes wide with surprise. It was as if she didn't believe he was really there. "You're alive?"

"Why'd you leave?" He reached out and twirled his fingers around a curled lock of her hair, relieved to find her well and not lost or in the clutches of barbarians.

She wiped her nose. "I couldn't watch you die."

David frowned. Of course. What a stupid question. She'd already witnessed the death of her own parents, and then to have to witness his death was too much. He tried to lighten the mood and forced a half smile. "Well, thanks for the confidence."

Her face brightened as if waking from her nightmare. "It's you! It's really you!" She threw herself around his neck, hugging him so tightly he barely needed to hold himself up on the wall.

After she loosened her grip, he jumped down and motioned for her to come, reaching his hands up to catch her. She scooted halfway off the wall and dangled from its edge. He caught her around the waist and settled her in front of him. And at that moment it was as if he were seeing her for the first time. She could actually be his. He was a citizen. They could marry. He could see the little girl he wanted to protect, the little girl he watched grow into this beautiful woman. He took in the shape of her face, her deep brown eyes, her pink lips, and dark hair reflecting the sun. He allowed himself to look at her as he'd never dared look at her before. As his. He backed her against the wall. She sucked in air as she studied him, hopefulness in her red-rimmed eyes. This time he would allow himself to kiss her. To kiss her with the knowledge that he could have her.

He leaned over her, one hand on the wall. He combed through

her hair, moving the soft curls between his fingers. He brushed his knuckles along her cheek. She leaned in toward him, moving her cheek against his palm like a cat begging to be petted.

"Will you—" Suddenly, David was worried that she might refuse. He took a deep, shuddering breath. "Will you be my wife?"

Desperation reflected in her gaze, as if she were afraid she might lose him, afraid this entire experience was a dream. "Of course!"

Smiling with the greatest joy, a joy he hadn't felt since he was a child, he cupped her face in his hands and kissed her. Intoxicating. She wrapped her arms around his neck, clutching her fingers in his hair. They slid down the wall together, kissing the whole way as if they were starved for each other. As if they'd been walking through a dry desert all these years without water, wandering the wilderness without food. But David knew if he didn't stop now, he'd never stop. He pulled away, unwinding her hands from his neck, chuckling.

He scooped her up into his arms. Her soft, light form always amazed him, and now he'd allow himself to loosen some of the reins on his control. He felt her against him, every curve of her, and it was then that he was reminded why it wasn't good for a man to touch a woman. But now she was his woman, or would be. And the sooner, the better.

David didn't dare carry Alethea back into the gymnasium where she would have to again face her mother's lifeless form, so he set her down in the plaza where he'd taken his last beating. Roman soldiers came in and out, escorting a weeping Renata and other dazed adult members of Aloysius's family to the atrium. Alethea watched in shock. "What happened here?"

"Aloysius is under arrest for attempting to murder your father."

Just behind the soldiers came Galen, eyes red from crying. His gaze fell on David and then on Alethea. He stopped as he studied her from head to toe. "Alethea?" His voice choked.

"Mpampas?" Her voice was barely audible, but loud enough for Galen to hear.

"You're well?"

Crying out, Alethea threw herself into Galen's arms, weeping on him. "Thank You, God. Thank You, God. Thank You!"

Galen squeezed her to him, turning with her in his arms. "You look so much like your mother." He burst into sobs.

They hugged for a long while, holding each other. Finally, Alethea cupped his face in her hands and kissed him. "You shrunk."

A roar of laughter ripped out of Galen and David joined in. That's when Paulus, who was standing behind Galen, came into view. Galen put his arm around Paulus and Alethea and squeezed. "My family."

Paulus's face looked unsure and David wondered if it might be too late to win the boy over.

At that moment, the guards carried Cornelia's covered, lifeless body by them on a litter.

Galen closed his eyes.

"She loved you, Mpampas," Alethea whispered. "She told me she never meant for any of this to happen."

Galen nodded, still unable to speak.

Manius then came into the plaza and put his hand on David's shoulder. "Let's go home." He walked toward the atrium.

Now that was a new concept. David had no idea where home was.

As if reading his mind, Manius turned to him. "My house."

Ω

Was it just this morning he walked on this same road? It felt like a lifetime ago. It couldn't have been the same day. Surely, weeks, months, even years had passed.

David trudged over the gravel as they neared the woods. He felt like he was climbing a mountain instead of walking on a flat road. He reached for the hilt of his sword to protect against thieves, but his hand fell on air. He forced himself to relax; plenty of guards surrounded them. Two followed behind him and Manius, while one led the way in front of Alethea, Galen, and Paulus.

Alethea clung to Galen's arm while Paulus avoided his outstretched hand.

David kept his eyes on Alethea as she bounced and giggled, apparently very excited about what she was telling her father.

"David—"

He started at the mention of his name and strained to hear. David stumbled, but righted himself before anyone noticed. The mountain grew steeper the farther they got into the woods. Out of habit, he glanced from side to side, watching for thieves.

Again, David stumbled, and Manius caught his arm.

"Are you well, son?"

David nodded. "Fine."

Alethea and Galen kept walking along, and only then did David notice Galen's slight limp. His stiff back made David uneasy. Did he not like what Alethea was telling him? Suppose she told him about their kiss? David wouldn't blame Galen if that infuriated him. But he didn't think Alethea would go that far. He cringed. He never should have taken such liberties. Yet, perhaps if Galen knew they had kissed, he'd give Alethea to him? But that wouldn't be the right motivation for Galen to give up his daughter. And David would want his father-in-law's respect.

David's body suddenly felt heavy and the trees became like water, moving toward them. Thieves? Black shadows filled David's vision. He grabbed for his sword. Nothing.

"David!" Alethea's hands were on his face, in his hair.

He opened his eyes. Alethea's dark curls brushed softly against his bare chest, a stark contrast with the fire on his back and arms. Why was there so much pain?

Manius crouched over him. "The boy's exhausted."

Galen hovered next to Alethea. "I can't imagine what he's been through."

Nearby branches snapped. Paulus tossed stones into the trees. Soldiers stood around, their backs to them as they watched the woods.

"He's been through so much, Mpampas." Alethea sniffed and

wiped her face, her warm tears landing on David's chest, burning his exposed wounds. "He saved my life so many times. Today, he tried to return me to you. We made it as far as the gate, but Demetri caught us. David could have been killed." She cupped his face in her hands. "He could have escaped years ago. But he never did. Today, he tried to save me."

Alethea's words surprised David. He didn't know she was aware of his sacrifice.

Manius put his hand on David's forehead. "Can you hear me?"

"Yes," he said, his voice raspy. He wanted desperately to take a nap, a nice long nap right there in the middle of the road. He no longer cared about thieves. He had nothing to lose.

Except . . . "Alethea." He tried to sit up. Manius put his weight under David's elbow, and Galen lifted David's arm over his neck. They heaved him to his feet. Dizziness overwhelmed him. He lost his balance, but the two men steadied him.

"It won't be long." Manius's reassuring voice comforted him as he urged him to take a step closer to Rome.

"We're going home, son." Galen urged him to take another step. "We're all going home."

twenty-four

David had heard Alethea sing plenty of times, but this was different. Her tone floated on soothing notes, as though she were relaxed and calm, no longer afraid.

Each note emphasized the purity of her voice. If he could see the song, he felt certain it would soar like a bird's wings, flying through the mosaic halls, turning the corners until it floated into the chamber where he lay.

Aucella. Now he understood why her father called her little bird.

The realization that she was there in the same house made him come fully awake. The bedchamber looked vaguely familiar with its iron-grilled windows, long flowing tapestries, and fat cushions on the bed.

How long had he been lying in this room, dead to the world? He remembered a slave bathing him, cleaning his wounds. He remembered that because it was so painful. The crusted honey had locked the sand into his cuts. They still throbbed, but the burning was gone.

He recalled a woman checking on him, tending to his wounds. He'd hardly looked at her, he'd been so overwhelmed with exhaustion. He wasn't convinced she was a slave. She seemed too elegant to be a slave. And she smelled like his mother. She must have been a dream.

He knew one thing wasn't a dream. Alethea's voice. And she was here. That gave him the strength to crawl out of bed and slip into the nearby tunic hanging on the wall. When his head was in the tunic, he heard a small gasp coming from the door. When his head was free, no one was there.

David followed the song as it floated through the halls. The tiled floors felt cool on his bare feet, bringing his body to life. How long had he been asleep? As he made his way through the house, David remembered it now from his youth. Not much had changed, other than the fact that it seemed much smaller. The marble columns were the same, only not quite as tall, and the mosaic, which had been new the last time he saw Manius, was still the flowered pattern David remembered. It brought to mind the night David snuck out to find Manius, to find Sarah. Only, he'd never made it this far.

"Master David is awake."

Alethea's song came to an abrupt halt.

The voice announcing him as Master David—strange—must have belonged to the gasp.

He came into a large hall where a curtain fluttered open to reveal Alethea hurrying toward him. A slave woman stood nearby, smiling. Alethea threw herself into David's arms and he nearly lost his balance. She hugged him so tightly, her arms pressed into the wounds on his back, but it didn't hurt terribly. Not enough to pry her arms away. He loved the feel of her against him. Then he remembered Galen. If Alethea was there, so was her father.

Alethea looked up at David with tears in her eyes. "You've been asleep for two days. I thought you'd never wake up."

David cupped her face in one of his hands. "I'm awake now." He smiled down into her dark, concerned eyes. He longed to kiss her, but he didn't dare. Not when he knew her father was likely on the other side of that curtain.

"Your sister's here." Alethea grinned up at him.

David's heart stopped at her words.

"We've been praying for you. She's anxious to meet you."

He'd actually meet her? Here, now? What would she look like after all these years? How old would she be? She was just a year younger than Alethea. Would she be as tall as Alethea? The strongest memory he had of her was when she was crouched in her nook, hiding under her blankets. The night he abandoned her. Would she despise him for what he did? She spent a terrifying night alone without anyone to comfort and protect her. All because of him.

"They're coming." Alethea faced the curtain.

David stood frozen like a statue. They? Who was "they?" Her father, certainly. Maybe Manius. Anyone else?

Sarah.

He would actually meet his sister. After all these years of wondering, of hoping, of praying. He waited for her to come through the curtain. He'd been waiting for this moment since he was ten.

Shadows moved. He could make out Manius and a slender form following behind. David's palms grew clammy. It would be her. His Sarah. Manius pulled the curtain aside, revealing a woman—a lighter version of David's mother. He held his breath. She even moved like their mother. She was in his dream. Only she wasn't a dream.

David's eyes burned and he swallowed back the knot forming in his throat. Her gaze held no malice. A little taller than Alethea, she moved gracefully toward him, keeping her chin down with a shy smile on her lips. A flush came to her cheeks. Her face was the same as he remembered, only not as round. A memory of Sarah's lithe form peering around their mother's skirts came to his mind. She hadn't changed much. She was still just as shy as ever. She came to stand in front of him, a smile filling her face.

"Brother." She stood on her toes and kissed his cheeks.

David took in a shuddering breath. Her scent wafted over him. The same scent as their mother. His eyes burned with unshed tears. He stifled a sob. He wanted to grab her, to pull her to himself and never let her go. His baby sister was a woman now. All those years of childhood lost.

"You took care of me." David was referring to the last two days he'd been asleep. A woman had tended his wounds. It had been his sister. His little Sarah.

She nodded, smiling at the ground.

Manius came up to them. "Good to see you awake, boy." He patted David's shoulder, relief in his gaze.

David winced, the wounds still sensitive on his back.

Galen joined them, smiling.

David looked down at Sarah. He knew he had an audience, but that didn't matter. He'd failed her, and there was no secret about that. "I'm sorry," he said, barely able to force the words past the knot in his throat.

The small brows above her eyes furrowed.

He realized he'd have to explain himself. He took a deep shuddering breath, hoping his voice wouldn't crack under the weight of his grief. "For leaving you that night."

Her eyes rounded with concern. She put a trembling hand to her mouth. "Oh, David." She shook her head as though she didn't believe his words. "No." Swallowing visibly, she continued shaking her head. "You don't have to apologize." Tears filled her blue eyes, and she motioned toward herself. "I'm fine. I was just worried about you. When you came to Manius that night, we were so relieved. You were alive! But we didn't know where to find you." She motioned to Galen. "Not until Galen came. He said you sent him." She touched David's hand. "It was an answered prayer."

She actually forgave him. It was as if he'd been carrying boulders on his back, and now their weight was lifted.

"Manius has been a good father to me, David."

His sister. She was alive and well. The relief he felt was tremendous, so much so, that the burden of his guilt and grief nearly came barreling out in wails. He took a deep, shuddering breath and reached out to her. He took her face in his hands. "You look so much like our mother."

Tears welled in her eyes. She stepped toward him, and they embraced. David choked back the sobs that threatened. He was free. At last he was truly free. Free of slavery, and free of guilt.

"Are you hungry?" Sarah asked.

Only then did David realize how ravenous he felt. "Yes."

"Alethea prepared a feast for us. She's a wonderful cook."

David glanced down at Alethea, a half smile forming on his lips. "Really?"

"Yes. She's been taking good care of us."

"And no one's been poisoned?" David asked with a smirk.

Alethea straightened, her haughty air returning with a flourish. "You just better eat it this time."

Tears still in his eyes, David laughed.

Ω

David walked through the garden, allowing his fingers to brush against the flower petals along the neatly trimmed bushes. He took in the scent of jasmine and thought of only one person. Alethea. She turned out to be a good cook after all. He chuckled. If only she knew how to make more than one dish. They'd all eaten wine rolls, green beans spiced with pine nuts, and lamb everyday for the past two weeks. Thankfully, Sarah offered to "help" and added some variety.

Now it was time for David to claim Alethea for his own. As soon as David had gotten back on his feet, Galen had treated him like a leper, slipping out every time David entered a room, avoiding him when he tried talking to him. David decided to give the man time. After giving Galen these weeks to enjoy his daughter, David couldn't bear the wait any longer. He knew Galen was hiding in the courtyard, and the path he'd taken would lead to a dead-end. The man wouldn't be able to escape.

For the first time in a long time, life was good. David had managed to find a way to make a living. He never dreamed he'd become an entertainer, but juggling was highly valued amongst the rich, and David had already secured a number of clients. Thankfully, no one he solicited had slaves that could juggle.

As he wound his way along the path of Manius's courtyard, David found Galen waiting for him. He stood with his back to him, and David stopped a few feet away.

"Now that I finally have my daughter, I've lost her."

David swallowed. He knew he should feel guilty, but he didn't. If anything, he felt Alethea was more his than Galen's, and by his comment, Galen too, seemed to realize that fact. Still, David didn't dare voice it.

Galen turned to face him, a stern look on his face. "How will you provide for my girl?"

"Juggling." David cleared his throat. "All I need is your blessing."

Galen sniffed, chin still raised. "She told me everything. All that you did for her all these years. How you took care of her, protected her."

David nodded.

Tears welled in Galen's eyes. "I was so worried. I thought for sure Aloysius would distort everything I had taught her, contaminate her mind the way he did Paulus." He shook his head. "Little did I know, the Lord had provided a guardian over my little Aucella." Galen lifted a black, leather rope from around his neck. "I couldn't be happier than to give her to a Christian, a man who has been her protector all these years." He held out an amethyst stone hanging from the leather rope. "To you."

David took the stone in his hand, studying its unusual shape. Dark purple, almost black in color, infused its center and gradually became a lighter lilac color at the tips of what reminded him of icicles. The icicles shot out in all directions, forming a star. A three-pronged, gold bail clamped around three of its arms and clasped it to the rope. A stark contrast against the purple.

"This is all I have of material value. My last master gave it to me. It's never been cut, and its shape is one of a kind. It's all I can offer for her dowry."

"But you don't have—"

"Allow me this. She's my only daughter." Galen lifted the leather rope over David's head, letting the heavy stone fall against his chest.

David had never worn jewelry before, so it felt unusual to have the weight of the stone hanging from his neck.

"Amethyst is a Greek word. It means not drunken. Greeks believe that if a man wears an amethyst he won't become intoxicated." Galen smiled.

David raised a brow, half-smiling.

"But I believe it won't help you any. Alethea is already in your blood, and you'll never be sober again."

They both chuckled, but David couldn't help but think of the truth in his words. After all these years, to think he could have escaped and learned he was a citizen. Had it not been for Alethea he would have done just that. He wouldn't have remained enslaved. Now he understood. His life was not his own. It belonged to Elohim. And He had His own plans.

Was it worth it?

Yes.

Like the heavy stone hanging on his neck, the weight of a new revelation came down on him. He shook his head at the enormity of it. Freedom. He wasn't free. He would never be free. For the rest of his life he would serve one Master.

Elohim.

epilogue

David leaned over Alethea. Her dark hair cascaded over the cushions and over his arm in jasmine-scented waves. Contentment wrapped around him like a warm blanket. Was there ever a time he didn't want for anything? Alethea finally belonged to him, and only him. This had to be a taste of heaven.

He dangled the amethyst stone over her. It swung from the leather rope, back and forth, back and forth, capturing the rays of sunlight through the window. The purple reflections danced over her hair, her nose, her lips.

"It all worked out for good, didn't it?" she whispered, her brown eyes blinking up at him.

He wanted to touch her, to kiss her, but he forced himself to listen.

"What others meant for evil, God meant for good."

David thought about her words. He wouldn't be lying here with his wife in marital bliss had it not been for all that had happened. She was right.

Alethea pushed up on her elbow, her hair falling over her shoulder, and she studied him.

He wanted to push her back down, but he didn't, exercising the restraint he'd had to use most of their lives together.

"Don't misunderstand, but . . . ." She trailed her fingers over his chin, sadness reflecting in her gaze. "In a way, I'm glad I betrayed you, David." She took a deep shuddering breath, staring at the scar.

"Had I not lied, I never would have realized how sinful I am. How much I need Yahshua." Shaking her head, tears welled in her eyes. "I'm just sorry my sin had to cost you so much." Her breath hot against his skin, she brushed her lips along the branding mark on his arm.

David closed his eyes and remembered the pain, the agony. Could he be thankful for what she put him through, thankful since it meant she'd found salvation? Was the whipping, the branding, worth it? He'd already come to terms with his slavery, knowing that God meant it for good, knowing that it meant Alethea's salvation. The branding and the scourging were all just a part of being a slave. That could have happened to him without her lie. So, if going through those painful circumstances wasn't in vain and was actually a blessing for her, then yes, he too was happy.

"Yahshua paid a much higher price than I ever had to pay," David finally said. "For us both. For everyone."

Lips parted and eyes wide, she looked up at him. "Yes."

"Elohim can take our sins and find a way to use them for good." He ran a silky lock of her hair between his fingers, thanking God for the good that came of this.

"He can change us if we let Him." Smiling with delight, she bounced closer to him, her softness and her scent filling his senses. "Change us for the better."

David nodded, a sly grin pulling on his lips.

"What?" Her brows furrowed in playful apprehension.

"If we want Him to *change* us, we need to be moldable, flexible."

She shrugged. "Of course."

"For example, if He wanted you to lie down right now, you'd have to be willing to bend to his will." David pushed her back against the pillows.

She giggled. "I think we're talking about your will now, David, not Jehovah's."

David grinned, hovering over her. "We've learned to be happy with Elohim's will." He kissed her. "Can you learn to be happy with mine?"

Breathless, she smiled, her brown gaze drinking him in. "It's fascinating how you've managed to *change* the direction of this conversation."

THE END

Soli Deo Gloria

Acknowledgements

First and foremost, I want to thank my Heavenly Father. You knew about this story before it was a glimmer in my mind. Thank You for letting me bug You about nearly every line, every scene, and every chapter. And for all those times I got stuck, thank You for showing me how to get unstuck. Throughout the writing of this story, You led me to all the right people who would help me become a better writer, which leads me to...

My closest friend and editor, Wendy Chorot, who saw this story from its infancy and watched it grow into the work it is today. You've ridden the rollercoaster ride with me from the thrilling highs to the desperate lows and never asked to jump off the tracks. You've been a shoulder and my cheerleader, and more importantly, you never let me give up on David and Alethea—and especially your favorite, Titus.

A huge thank you to Karsten, Whitney, Kirsten, Aaron and Chelsea. Thank you for your sacrifice and support while I've had to spend time behind my computer.

I'd also like to thank my agent, Joyce Hart, for believing in my work and for loving this story.

Thank you to American Christian Fiction Writers and all the on-line groups associated with ACFW. You've taught me a lot and helped me to grow tremendously as a professional. And last but not least, to all the folks at HEWN, both HIS/HisWriters' groups, RWA, and *all* my wonderful critique partners.

Look for

Yahshua's Bridge

book two of

Iron and the Stone

Fall 2011

---

*For a full listing of DeWard Publishing
Company books, visit our website:*

www.deward.com

DEWARD
PUBLISHING COMPANY

CPSIA information can be obtained at www.ICGtesting.com
Printed in the USA
BVOW041450220213

313983BV00001B/26/P

9 781936 341023